THE SAME RIVER

Jaan Kaplinski

THE SAME RIVER

Translated from the Estonian
by Susan Wilson

PETER OWEN
London and Chester Springs, PA, USA

PETER OWEN PUBLISHERS
73 Kenway Road, London SW5 0RE

Peter Owen books are distributed in the USA by
Dufour Editions Inc., Chester Springs, PA 19425-0007

Translated from the Estonian *Seesama jõgi*

894.545

This translation first published by
Peter Owen Publishers 2009

ISBN 978-0-7206-1340-7

Printed in the UK by CPI Bookmarque Ltd, Croydon, CR0 4TD

The translation of this novel has been supported by
the Estonian Ministry of Culture, the Estonian Literature Centre
and Traducta. The publisher gratefully acknowledges this support.

The publisher acknowledges the support of Arts Council England.

He had never been to the funeral of a clergyman before. The Teacher's coffin stood in the church; about twenty ministers acted as pall-bearers. After the address they filed towards the deceased in succession, made the sign of the cross and recited a few words from the Bible. Then the others said their farewells. He was taken along by the crowd, looked for the last time at the man resting there, his face both beautiful and proud, not as it had been in life. He did not see a great deal, however; his eyes welled up, full of tears. He was heavy and light at once, grieving and comforting. Irina picked up the flowers, and they left without looking in the direction of the coffin once more where they were starting to fasten the lid. The flow of people took them outside the church; he was still fighting back tears but was beginning to feel better. He remembered how once – it was when he was already back from Leningrad, when Ester was away and they had made it up with the Teacher – he had said to the Teacher that a good person was necessarily amusing, a bad person was not. And that he thought the Teacher was amusing. The Teacher had become more serious and had not replied. Perhaps being amusing was not to his liking. Now, there in the coffin, he was not amusing. Perhaps the dead are not amusing. The dead are not good or bad. The dead are just dead, and only good must ever be spoken of them.

Outside it was sunny and windy. The coffin was carried to the hearse waiting by the gate; the sides of the open lorry were lowered. Behind the car stood the column of ministers, then family, students and other people. He now felt like a student. He had helped to organize the funeral, had spent two days travelling by car to the town, organized the burial plot through friends, found the place to hold the funeral meal. When he heard of the Teacher's death he had been at a meeting in Tallinn. He had immediately gone to the station and travelled back to Tartu on the first bus and made himself useful until ministers who were admirers of the deceased came forward, took charge of the organizing, doing so magnificently. In the Soviet time the ministers had been good PR-men; they knew where to get hymn sheets printed in a hurry, where tableware could be borrowed, how to make a funeral meal and other things.

He walked in the funeral train. The wind tousled his hair and occasionally whirled dust into his eyes and mouth. The road was only surfaced with asphalt in the middle, and the funeral party sometimes walked on the cobblestones alongside the pavement. He thought how amusing the phrase 'funeral train' really was; the word now belonged to another context, with an express train, a goods train and an armoured train, not funeral rituals.

9

The cemetery was not far. At the gate six of the younger ministers raised the coffin on to their shoulders. At first they went along the main path which was already almost dry, then turned off on to a narrower, muddier path where the movement of the funeral train was slower; there was barely room here for four people to walk abreast. On one side of the grave stood a great arbor vitae, on the other a maple. He looked at the grave and the reddish-brown pile of earth beside it and thought how graveyard trees survive their roots being cut through all the time. Perhaps it helps that each occasion when the roots are cut means an abundance of nutrients on which the trees can feast. The maple blossom was almost in bloom. It reminded him of a few of the Teacher's verses which went something like:

> ... through the falling maple blossoms
> flies a soul-butterfly,
> bearing the last word to the sunset ...

But there were no soul-butterflies, although the weather was so warm that day that a red admiral or brimstone butterfly doubtless fluttered about in some sunny spot sheltered from the wind. Flowering snowdrops were visible on several graves. The burial service was taken by one of the ministers who had been at university with the Teacher. He did not remember what the man said, but he did remember his wonderful smile, a warm, open smile he had rarely seen on the faces of Lutheran ministers although he had seen them on the faces of Buddhist and Orthodox monks. The Teacher had never smiled like that; he had been melancholy, although sometimes he laughed so much that he cried. He liked laughing. The dead do not laugh; the dead can merely smile. Although there in the coffin he was not smiling; he was downright serious.

The coffin was not opened at the grave; that is not the Lutheran custom. When he picked up his three handfuls of earth he felt that it was moist and cold. And rust-red. From iron you were formed and to iron you shall return, he thought, heretically. The Teacher had not really been formed from the red earth here of South Estonia, he was from the western limestone area, where great snowdrop windflowers and lady's slippers grow.

A grave had been found for the Teacher in an old German cemetery which had been left to grow wild after the war, where gravestones, crosses and small chapels had crumbled and been ransacked. Some of the graves were still there, some had been repaired by university people; new stones had even been erected to replace some of the broken ones. Here in the old German cemetery he now rested among the German bones he had written about in an angry poem of his youth.

He had hated the Germans; he had said so directly once when they were sitting by the hot stove at his house. But just as the dead do not laugh, neither do they hate.

There were a number of speakers: a writer, an archivist, a church representative and several other people from places he had worked or where he had been respected. Also among the speakers was Jüri Targama, who always seemed to be going to a funeral or returning from one whenever he met him. He also sat next to Jüri on the bus which took them to the funeral meal. Jüri's nose was red and he smelt of brandy. They talked about the Teacher, obviously, and obviously Jüri could not help but say how he had always taken a bottle of brandy with him to the Teacher's as the Teacher was a connoisseur. He thought somewhat sadly that it had never occurred to him to drink brandy with the Teacher. He would not have dared go there with a bottle, and he had never been offered vodka there either. Not even coffee most of the time, just cigarettes. All his life the Teacher had been a heavy smoker.

Speeches were given at the funeral meal. He also had to speak, but the words did not come out well: he was unable to suppress his as yet raw feelings or express them in a way more fitting for a funeral address. Two of the Teacher's young followers sang a couple of songs which they had composed using his poems as lyrics. One of them, a poem he had known for a long time, was about how butterfly orchids spread their white prayer carpet before him for his last steps. His last unspoken words will be written by the blue flight of a swallow into the blue sky among the same white clouds of his childhood.

He went to the toilet once and saw Jüri Targama sitting in the corner room with a few companions drinking brandy. Jüri beckoned to him, filled an empty glass and he could hardly refuse, even though he never had any wish to drink brandy except perhaps in the winter when he had got very chilled or when he had a sore throat. As he went back he clearly remembered an evening at the Teacher's in the depths of winter. The Teacher had again been deep in depression; somebody had doubtless wearied or exasperated him. He swore at his followers, said that the Estonian people did not really need him, and when, Ellen tried to argue back, he said to her, 'Well, once I'm dead, dissolve my body in strong acid, and every time anyone praises me you can ladle some of it out on to them.' In a way it was true, and yet it was not, for the Teacher was being buried in accordance with the practices of the Evangelical Lutheran faith in a German cemetery, his followers and friends were speaking about him at his funeral meal in the manner befitting the dead, and no one remembered his most desperate words and thoughts. He had died, and after death people change more quickly than during their lifetime. They become myths, heroes of folklore, the person people want to see because they can no longer prevent the change themselves, they cannot say anything cruel to their supporters and critics.

The funeral meal ended early. Ellen said goodbye to everyone; she embraced him and Irina and said a few kind words of thanks to both of them. He had been moved; he had almost become one of the Teacher's close friends, accepted into his inner circle. Yet he also felt a small alarm bell ringing inside him. Just as the Teacher had never, even less so in death, been accepted as he was with all his quirks, moods and imagination, he himself had not, in fact, been accepted into the Teacher's inner circle just as *he* was. For him the road was akin to that of Paul who became his Teacher's follower after his death. He knew, though, that he did not want and could not bear to be a follower. That road was uphill to him. He had always been at a distance from the living Teacher; now he could get close to the deceased man's image: he could accompany the followers lighting candles before his icon. But he had no desire to do so any more. Perhaps it was now much easier for him to get closer to the Teacher as he had been in life, to that lean, short-sighted man who did not know where to put his hands, who sat in company, abashed, shoulders hunched only to straighten up and burst into life on those occasions when he could talk about something he truly regarded as important, be it the American-Indian myths, Bhakti mystic chants or Thomas Müntzer.

When they left the funeral meal a light drizzle was falling. The earth smelt heavy, the blossoms on the maple growing in the garden next to the house were budding like the ones on the maple in the cemetery earlier. Give it a week, he thought, and the first withered blossom will fall on the Teacher's grave which bears nothing other than a cross, a year of birth and a year of death.

Irina was driving. When they got home it was time to start putting the children to bed. Elo had made them something to eat: there was a smell of fried onion in the apartment. Art and Riina ran up to them shouting, 'Mum, Dad, what have you brought us?'

They had even managed to bring something – some currant bread left over from the funeral meal which had been put aside for their children.

Before going to bed he went out on to the veranda. The rain had stopped. The earth here smelt, too, although differently: the neighbours had put manure on the garden. Further off, among the willow bushes, something was glinting: the freshet which flooded the meadow every spring. Duck quacks rang out in the darkness. Above the neighbours' poplars shone a crescent moon. He wondered whether the water level was still rising, whether it would reach the lower edges of the vegetable garden, or whether it was starting its gradual fall. Each year he expected a really powerful flood like the ones in his childhood after the war, but they no longer happened. No longer did people travel in boats between the houses at the lower end of Marja Street; no longer was the ice next to the bridge destroyed by explosives. His home town had become narrower, tidier and more irksome. And now that the Teacher had died as well, his home town was even less than it had ever been; it was even more foreign and distant.

There were no nightingales yet; there were still a couple of weeks to go before their arrival.

2

The person who had told him about the Teacher was the same Jüri Targama. Jüri and he had met at a young writers' evening when he gave readings of Rimbaud translations. Jüri was pleased that someone was actually translating Rimbaud and had invited him and a couple of others over. He was divorced and was living with his mother, who had cancer, in a little old house in a rundown area on the edge of town. They drank wine and talked into the early hours about French poetry, the German Army and hetaerae. Occasionally his mother would begin to groan in the next room; Jüri went to give her a morphine injection; his mother stopped groaning after a while and they continued talking. On another occasion they went to a restaurant after the literary evening, ate a potato, beetroot and herring salad, drank vodka and danced. Jüri was with his attractive younger sister, who was asked to dance by the air force officer from the next table twice. Aleks Luuberg, who was with them, had soon had a skinful and began to bait the officer. The others tried to rein him in but to no avail: Aleks threatened to smash the officer's face in. He was a show-off and, being on the skinny side, would undoubtedly have been given a good hiding by the pilot if he had really gone to hit him. The only thing they could do was pay the bill and leave, taking Aleks with them. They went uphill; for some reason Jüri and Aleks talked at length about horse-riding, Jüri's sister walked arm in arm with him; they talked about opera and ballet. He felt sick but did not dare say so, bravely waiting for when they reached Jüri's. But no sooner had the men stopped talking about horses than they remembered the Teacher, whom they both knew. They asked him whether he knew the Teacher, and when they heard that he had only read some poems and articles from the period when Estonia was independent, Jüri promised to take him to the Teacher's the next day. The Teacher was reputed to know dozens of languages, including exotic Asian and African languages. Aleks's path took another direction. He now managed to find his way through the park by himself to go home; he went behind a bush, put his fingers down his throat and tried to vomit. He did not succeed, but the retching made him feel better. On the way home he no longer felt quite as sick as he had before, and perhaps only the smell of vodka betrayed the fact that he had been to the restaurant to his mother and aunt. When he shut his eyes in bed it felt as if the bed and the room were swaying and spinning like a carousel. He thought the restaurant, the salad and the vodka genuinely vile, as he did many things he had tried at the invitation of others. Even Jüri and Aleks's cultural narrative was repulsive. Only Jüri's sister was not repulsive; he liked her, but she was a lot older than him, and anyway he did not know how to approach her. Only in his dreams did they meet, in an old log cabin somewhere; Jüri's sister was in a black slip, she smiled and lifted it up for him to see that there was nothing underneath it. He stood next to her and pressed himself against her, wanting to be naked as well, when suddenly he ejaculated and woke up. He had to take a handkerchief quietly out of his trouser pocket and wipe himself. Fortunately, he had woken up at just the right moment and been able to clutch himself so that the sperm wouldn't spill on to the sheets. He would be able to wash the handkerchief himself during the day; sheets were more tricky. At night it was difficult to move about without his aunt, who slept in her own bed in another corner of the room, hearing. If he turned over more noisily, coughed or went to the toilet, his aunt was sure to ask him whether he was ill. He had trained himself to move soundlessly in the dark, suppress his coughing and turn over as little as possible because he could not bear these kinds of questions.

Since Grandfather had become paralysed things had become easier at night – his own movements and coughing were covered up by the invalid's moanings and groanings. During the day Grandfather was in fine fettle – he even went out, listened to the radio and talked politics with the visitors – but at night he would become ill, his paralysed arm would itch and ache. He was probably frightened, too, and he called for Grandmother every night. She was sometimes so tired that Mother or Aunt took a turn at nursing. On a couple of occasions Grandfather had soiled the bed, and the women had been very angry; Grandfather had cried and apologized. He understood that this was also a power game. The women seemed to enjoy the fact that Grandfather, who had once been a wealthy or important man on whom they had thoroughly depended, had now become a small, stooping shell who clung on to life, his wife and children and was unable to do anything at all without them.

This did not irk him directly. He had always lived more in a world of women, heard more of women's stories, trotted behind his mother and grandmother. Grandfather was in a world beyond them, a world of his own friends, books and Voice of America; a world where women regarded with gentle scorn almost everything that was so important in the men's world. In actual fact, the men's world had crumbled along with the old Estonian Republic, and in its ruins women lived, went to work, stood in queues, sewed new clothes for the children from the old ones and sold what there was left to sell of their old effects.

Grandfather's illness did not bring him closer to his grandson. The grandson distanced himself gradually from the women's world, although it was difficult for him – he didn't know how to behave in men's company. Grandfather, by contrast, fell even further under their care. They swapped roles: the child was becoming a man, the man a child. The child becoming a man heard the groaning in the room next door, the eighty-year-old man's weepy declarations of love for a woman with whom he had lived for nearly sixty years; through the door he smelt the scent of eau-de-Cologne which was supposed to mask the stench. He was aghast, pitying and embarrassed all at once. He would have liked to help his grandfather, to say a few soothing words to him, but he didn't know how. That sort of thing was not part of their family lore. They never talked about how they felt about each other. Everyone in the family lived and died alone, separately, like snails in their shells. If someone inadvertently or in desperation stretched their soft body a little way out of the shell, they scared themselves as well as the others.

He had gone to the university in the morning, as usual, then had sat in the library and, after lunch, had gone to the café. He found Aleks Luuberg there, who was already delivering a lecture to his admirers on the sexual culture of the South Sea Islands, with particular focus on the customs surrounding male circumcision and on all the types of little wooden sticks and rings with which they decorated their penises. Aleks had a wonderful memory and an even more wonderful fantasy which embellished his memory. When he felt thirsty after talking for an hour, an admirer would bring him a cup of coffee (Aleks never had any money); another summarized the best bits for his girlfriend who hadn't caught the opening. He managed to exchange a few words with Aleks, reminding him of the previous evening at the restaurant and the promise to go to the Teacher's.

It was definitely not Aleks's style to leave the café in broad daylight, but this time he made an exception; he was ready to take him to the Teacher. Perhaps he wanted to go there himself, and the young, keen university student was an appropriate excuse to do so.

3

They crossed a small park and went up the hill. The maples had flowered; the blossoms lay thickly on the pavement under the trees. The chaffinches were singing in the park – prrp-poo-leet, prrp-poo-leet. Aleks took inspiration from them and their call, which, in his childhood, he had imagined as 'parp alight, purple light', giving him and his childhood friends the idea of finding out whether farts would indeed burn with a purple light. One of them had bared his behind and farted, while someone else had struck a match. The fart did indeed burn – with a beautiful blue flame – but one of the boys managed to burn his bottom, and the story came out. Mother warned them that some shepherd boys had once been messing about doing the same sort of thing, and the flame from the fart had spread inside, through the boy's bottom, and burnt his guts so badly that he had died. They argued with Aleks whether this was really possible, but as neither of them was expert in physiology or physics, they changed the subject slightly. He asked Aleks whether the name of the ancient Russian god of thunder meant 'farter' in Estonian. Aleks could not give a definite reply, even though he had majored in Russian at university. However, he liked the underlying idea and developed it, moving on to the ancient flatu-lighting rituals of the Slavic and Finno-Ugric peoples. The flatus had to symbolize thunder and the flame lightning. These rituals could be used, for example, to ensure sufficient rainfall. They created a fantastical picture of drought-ridden farmland encircled by squatting men, and perhaps women, too, bottoms aloft, and the thunder shaman walking around with fire stick and flint in hand. If the road to the Teacher's had been longer, they might have managed to work out the main features of the theology and liturgy of farting, but time was against them. They turned from the main road into a small side street. In the gardens the cherry trees were already in bloom and the garden-warblers were singing.

A large pear tree grew in front of the Teacher's house, its buds a blush of pink. On the step sat a black-and-white cat washing its face. They stepped on to the porch. Here hung the occupiers' slate for the names of residents which bore, in chalk, the faded word Adam. It could have been what was left of the name Adamson or Adams. There were four flats on the slate. They went up the steps and stood in front of the door, which did not have a nameplate. The colour of the door was probably from the days of the Estonian Republic of the 1920s or 1930s; he was unable to guess whether it had been creamy white or whether it had faded to that colour over the years. There were also a number of marks in the door from drawing-pins or nails – various small labels had probably been pinned to it. Aleks rang the rattly doorbell. He thought vaguely that the lobby had something of an oddly old-fashioned Estonian air about it, even in its smell. That house had its own individual smell; it had remained itself, and in defiance of the Soviet presence it had still retained a little part of its real essence.

Behind the door came the sound of footsteps, and the door opened. There stood a brunette aged about forty, who, at first glance, had something of the baroness about her. Perhaps it was her long, narrow face, perhaps her peaked nose, or maybe something less definable. Like the house in which she lived, she, too, had retained something from the 1930s, the time of the independent republic. That era had to have something Baltic-German about it, something of Dorpat, the German name of Tartu.

They greeted each other. Aleks asked whether the man of the house was at home and whether he had a spare moment; he had a couple of questions and had brought along a gifted young poet and philologist who was very interested in oriental languages. He was not pleased by the compliment, but the open door was not the right place to make an issue of it.

The man of the house was indeed at home, working. The lady invited them to step inside and went to enquire whether he was free to receive visitors. The hall smelt strongly of cigarette smoke; a couple of landscapes hung on the wall: exotic places with palm trees and volcanoes. The other wall had shelves from floor to ceiling, housing most of the Russian classics – the works of Turgenev, Dostoyevsky and Tolstoy in the original language.

The woman came back and said to come on through, Alo would continue working for a couple of minutes then would stop. She led them to the living-room and asked them to take a seat. Most of the room was occupied by bookshelves and a large Chinese birch tree. Under the window, in pots, were other flowers that he didn't recognize. Only at one point was the wall not entirely covered by shelves; here there hung another painting of an exotic landscape, but this one had a person in it – an exotic, naked girl with blossom in her hair, entering the water.

The woman took a seat as well, lit a cigarette and said a few words to Aleks. As far as he could make out, Aleks's wife had done some typing for her and the Teacher and had some more to do. This was nothing to do with him. He looked around the room, mostly scrutinizing the books on the shelves. Here, too, the exotic seemed to prevail: he noticed the full edition of Frazer's *The Golden Bough*, books in the Arabic and Hebrew languages and travel books about America and India. On another wall were academic publications about American Indians, a Russian-language collection of writings about the world's peoples and a series of books headed 'Atlantis'. He would have liked to see what was hiding behind the title, but he did not dare. The woman finished talking to Aleks, said that Alo would be with them directly and left.

They sat quietly for a moment. Then came the sound of rustling in the doorway. He glanced towards it. A small, red-breasted bird had appeared on the doorstep. It stood there, cocked its head, spied them for a moment with its black eyes and hopped on both legs like a sparrow into the next room.

'That's their garden-warbler,' said Aleks. 'They always have injured birds in the house; the lady of the house treats them, and they become completely tame.'

Now there came the sound of footsteps from the hall. The man of the house came through the doorway wearing tracksuit trousers and felt slippers, welcomed them and bowed deeply, in full ceremony.

'We thought that this time you'd taken the shape of a garden-warbler,' said Aleks. 'Or did you send a soulbird to herald your arrival?'

The man of the house gave a rattling laugh and shook his head. 'Aleks, you're hopeless. We have talked about the robin any number of times, but to you it's still a warbler.'

'*Mea culpa*,' replied Aleks. 'My soulbird just must be different . . . Ellen must have told you I've got a couple of questions? Those "Persian Motifs" of Yesenin's. And I've also brought a great admirer of your poetry with me. He's a poet himself. Allow me to introduce you.'

They bowed to each other and shook hands. The Teacher's hand was warm and soft but not flabby. He was wearing glasses so thick that it was difficult to say whether he was looking his interlocutor in the eye or not. His bearing was strangely loose and tired. At first sight the Teacher might have appeared old and shabby, but anyone with a sharper eye had to admit that there was also something about him that was completely the opposite – he was an ill, tired person from whom, nevertheless, a strange force emanated. Like the shamans, he thought; they were often ill people, yet they had more power than the fit and strong.

They sat down; appropriately there were three smaller armchairs in the room. The Teacher took a packet of cigarettes out of his breast pocket and said, 'Aleks, I know you smoke, but how about my other visitor?'

He replied that he occasionally indulged in the odd cigarette.

'The occasional cigarette is more effective,' said the Teacher. 'I believe that our problem is that we don't know how to use the poisons that the Native American enchanters and Chinese alchemists invented. We get too used to the poisons, and they cease to have any effect. The right thing to do would be to abstain for a while. There should be something of a ritual, even about smoking.'

He offered his visitors the packet of cigarettes with the ritual motion. They did not decline. They drew on them in silence for a while, then the Teacher asked Aleks what his questions were. Aleks fished a crumpled scrap of paper out of his pocket which bore a number of Russian phrases and Persian names that he wanted to know how to write correctly. The Teacher told him how he thought they should be written in Estonian and explained his understanding of the Russian phrases. It took a few minutes to resolve the matter. Then the Teacher turned to him, 'But you can't really be —'s son?'

He had no option but to say that he was, although he had never even seen his father, who had been deported to Siberia in June 1941. He had to explain to the Teacher what he knew about his father's fate. There was not much to tell: his father had died of hunger and exhaustion in the war somewhere in Viatka Gulag, closer to his birthplace of St Petersburg than to Estonia, which had become his second homeland. The Teacher nodded sadly, and his jowls drooped sadly even more. The colour of hopelessness and death spread over his face.

They were silent for a moment, then the Teacher continued, 'Aleks said that you also write poetry.'

He said he'd written some, yes. The Teacher was interested in whose poems he had read and whose he had liked the most. He named some of the Estonian Sooth-sayers group as well as Pushkin and Lermontov, Shelley and the classics of French modernism, Rimbaud and Baudelaire.

The Teacher nodded in appreciation. 'Very good choices. Do you read them in the originals?'

He said, self-consciously, that yes, he had tried to, and that he could generally manage it.

'Then you must read the poems aloud and learn them by heart. It's one of the oldest and most effective ways of learning languages,' the Teacher went on. He talked about the ancient Celts' legal texts, which were in verse to make it easier for lawyers to remember them, versified philosophy, Parmenides and Lucretius and even a learned poem by an Italian Renaissance doctor about syphilis.

On Lucretius, the Teacher could not help adding that reading it had made him understand how stupid *De Rerum Natura* was on several fronts. Yet it seemed absolutely the best thing for contemporary materialists. He sensed the Teacher's interest and compassion, and his initial self-consciousness eased. He said that he knew a lot of Lermontov's poems by heart as well as Estonian poetry by Sang and Talvik but that he didn't know much in English or French because he wasn't really sure how the English and the French read poetry.

The Teacher and Aleks laughed, and the Teacher suggested going into the forest to read out loud there in private. That was how he, in his youth, had read Rimbaud's 'Le Bateau ivre', which, to his mind, was Europe's supreme example of poetry.

He remembered an extract from 'The Waste Land' by Eliot, which he had recently read in an anthology, and he asked the Teacher for his opinion of him. The Teacher thought that he was a very good poet but was trying too hard to be pope and judge. He was also quite a character and, in his own mind, a prophet like Ezra Pound but in a different way. Had he read any Pound? He had not. The Teacher thought that he should. Pound had understood what poetry was. Europeans have generally had such an understanding only rarely. The Celts alone had never lost the feeling for poetry, and Germanic and Roman Europe had relearnt it from them a couple of times.

'But what about ancient poetry?' He could not leave the question unasked.

The Teacher did not like most Latin poetry; in his view the Romans had lost their original forms under the influence of Greek and squeezed their language into a form which was, in fact, unsuited to it. But the Teacher was more or less content with Catullus, as he was with Tibullus and Propertius. The fact, however, that the boom time for Latin poetry was so brief was evidence to him that there was something rotten at its foundations. The spirit of poetry had faded, and they had tried to replace it with all sorts of formalistic jiggery-pokery that had apparently been used most in the court of the Vandals in fifth-century Carthage.

'So the Vandals weren't such fearsome destroyers?' he had to ask.

The Teacher again laughed his rattling laugh and said that compared to the Romans the Vandals were gentle and cultured creatures. The Romans destroyed an incredible number of peoples and cultures and established a state that began to break down and decay soon after it had attained its maximum extent.

Aleks, who had had to be quiet and listen for a while, could be quiet no longer and chimed in with a question as to whether it was true that, even though the Romans were not great poets or philosophers, their genius lay instead in statehood and law-making. The Teacher said that in his view the genius of Rome was perhaps indeed apparent in military organization, in conquering and occupation. Even Rome's engineering achievements – roads and bridges – were bound up most directly with strategy. In matters of state administration, however, the Romans were, in his view, fairly inept. Roman law had been produced by jurists originally from Phoenicia, such as Paulus and Ulpian, who, as far as he understood it, knew a thing or two about the laws of the Semitic peoples. The cult of law and law-making indeed appeared to be furthest developed by the Semites, who were genuine law-making nations. The holiest thing the Jews had, even today, was the book of law, the Torah, and the relationship between God and men was also conceived as a legal contract. It was therefore only natural that the Semites tidied up Roman law for the Romans.

'Meaning that in conventional understanding there are lots of myths about the Roman state?' he asked when the Teacher paused.

This time the Teacher did not laugh but merely gave a wry chuckle. 'They aren't really myths; they're more like the accounts you find in almanacs or children's stories, like the ones written at the beginning of the last century to educate the Estonian people. Most people, after all, are mentally at primary school or nursery level and incapable of taking anything more sophisticated on board. In our civilization most people do not want to do anything but read and reread children's stories, read things which keep them in their childhood and do not allow them to grow into adulthood.'

'So perhaps we could say that in Western civilization culture is more like curtains than a window; it tends to obscure rather than show us what is outside,' said Aleks.

'Yes, we could put it like that,' said the Teacher. 'An English writer once wrote that in Western man great intellectual curiosity merges in strange combination with equally great intellectual fear.'

He said that the Teacher was probably above intellectual dread. The Teacher shook his head sadly and said that he would like to hope as much but could not be confident of it. Fear had many faces, and because people are afraid of fear itself they disguise the fact from themselves, putting on a complex act and creating a myth or, more precisely, a fairy-tale, of themselves for themselves.

He had to ask whether there was an important distinction in the degree of mythologizing between Soviet and Western society.

The Teacher shook his head sadly again. 'It is such a fascinating temptation for us to go along with the story told to us by the Voice of America or any number of other radio stations from over there. But it is not, in fact, that much better than our press. The press is a tool of ideological power on both sides, as you are undoubtedly taught at university, and ideological power utilises mythology. I have thought that we should create the same sort of folklore motif register for the press that Stith Thompson created for folklore texts. I started to, but I don't really have time for it. The new mythological motifs should be compared with the old, then the whole thing would make sense. Already Aleks is aware of the lament of mine that people should live for at least three hundred years, then we would manage to finish something off properly. The seventy or eighty years we have are spent on the tomfooleries of youth, learning and making plans. Here I am, cursing others for writing and creating fairy-tales, but what have I written apart from that? The same old fairy-tales. I've had plans, of course, to write my own summa, a single great book containing everything I think about the affairs of the world. But I would have to study so many important branches of learning. The most philosophical science of our time is physics – as a matter of fact, it is the only philosophy still left in the Western world. I have not been able to read Einstein, Schrödinger or von Neumann as thoroughly as required. And I do not have a thorough knowledge of botany either. Botany would be able to tackle the gibberish of Darwinism, to show that the point lies not in the struggle to survive but in the number of certain forms in which life can exist at all and from what and into what it transforms . . . But what's the point of saying all this? I believe that it is entirely possible to live for a couple of hundred years, but the faith of one man here cannot make any difference. The belief would have to live in the culture, be part of the culture. Yet our world is becoming increasingly childish. Here people live for children and the young people, here people fear and shun becoming adults . . .'

'I remember that once you wrote that there were probably only a couple of adults in the world – Buddha, Krishna and Lao-tzu,' said Aleks, getting an opportunity to slip in a few words.

'Perhaps a few others. Who knows what sort of people the Mayans or the Incas had or what the Siberian shamans thought? But in our seventy or eighty years it takes a genius to reach adulthood, and the majority of people don't get anywhere.'

'But isn't it true that if there were more time people would still stop developing at an early stage, they would still remain children and be afraid of becoming adults?' he asked.

The Teacher nodded. 'Yes, I believe that the underlying factor is fear. Perhaps it's what the Christians call *amarthia*, sin, and the Buddhists *duhkha*, suffering. A number of intelligent psychologists have said something on the subject, but I am poorly acquainted with psychology.'

'So do some cultures have less of this fear and the cult of childhood?' asked Aleks.

'Yes. Sometimes, when I am in a very dark mood, I think that just as there have only been a couple of mature adults in the world there have only been a couple of genuine cultures, the forest-people cultures and the Chinese – before the Europeans and Japanese set about destroying them.'

'But what about the Mayans and Incas you mentioned just now?' he asked.

'I don't know much about the Incas, but I dabbled with the Mayan language at one time. I read *Popol Vuh*. Er, do you know what *Popol Vuh* is?'

Only very vaguely, he had to admit.

'Well, *Popol Vuh* is the epic of the Quitché people. It was written down in the sixteenth century but is mainly pre-Christian, and it is also a simply beautiful text; if you read it you will understand what a sacred text is. It is not the waffle of the Baptists or the Mormons' book but a genuine scripture. I got hold of an original Quitché version, began to read it with the help of a German translation and compiled a small vocabulary and a grammar. I thought that I could not endure being a lecturer in Estonia or Germany for long; I simply could not bear to spend years writing the same thing on the blackboard again and again and explaining what the glottal stops in the Semitic languages are. I thought I'd stay in the job a couple of years then go off somewhere, perhaps to Polynesia, the Marquesas Islands or the Mayan region. I thought I'd compile an accurate written language for the Polynesians or the Mayans – their problem is that there are so many different dialects, and they are barely mutually intelligible. They need a written language to be worked out and their own state founded. But then the war came, and I couldn't go anywhere any more. But perhaps it was better that way, even. Otherwise I would most likely have been an Arbenz supporter in Guatemala, and the Yanks would have hanged me.'

The story had touched on one of his secret dreams. Unable to disguise his excitement, he said, 'When I was a schoolboy I dreamt of driving the whites out of America. Now I think I'd like to go to Peru and help the Quechua Indians free themselves from the white man. Perhaps we could agree that you should go to the Yucatán Mayans and I'll go to the Quechuans in the Andes.'

'Reminds me of the Molotov–Ribbentrop Pact,' threw in Aleks. 'I'm ready to stand as witness and record your secret agreement to divide America into spheres of influence.'

The Teacher took the view that it was perhaps best to leave it as an oral agreement, as no secret agreement can remain secret once it is written down.

That was how it was left. In the meantime it had begun to grow dark outside and they all felt it was time to bring the discussion to an end.

He was the instigator. They got up, the Teacher saw them into the hall, bowed ceremonially to Aleks, then to him and said, 'I would be very pleased to look at your poems some time.'

That was what he had secretly been hoping for, without daring to articulate the hope in words. To get closer to the Teacher, into his inner circle of students and friends, to sit at his feet and listen to his wisdom, which had put his head in a spin even at their first meeting. He did not know how to do it, but now the Teacher himself had made the first step, had offered another meeting. That was the main thing; the poems were perhaps only an excuse. He didn't know it, and it wasn't important. The important thing was that he was able to come back here soon.

'Could I come some time the week after next?' he managed to ask in a whirl.

Yes, he could.

Then Ellen appeared in the hallway and said goodbye, too.

Outside, the first stars were shining in the sky. The sky itself was mysteriously, deeply blue. They walked towards the town centre.

Aleks was strangely quiet for a while, then he said, 'Today he was in a very good mood. That really doesn't happen very often.'

He hardly listened to Aleks's words and simply stored it mechanically in his memory. He felt no interest now either in Aleks's brilliant, surreal cultivation of thought or in women. The contact with the Teacher had freed him for the evening from even his hunger for the erotic.

'I imagine you don't know why he lost his place and vocation for the priesthood,' Aleks went on.

He did not, of course. What did he know about the Teacher at all? According to Aleks, the story was that when the Russians invaded in the 1940s and closed the theology faculty the Teacher had lost his professorship. He had managed to continue to give his language lectures, and his friends had found a part-time pastoral position for him as well. His sermons had been strange but of interest to the intellectuals. He had held the post at the beginning of the German occupation, too, but later another theologian with whom he shared the job found a sheaf of pornographic photos and drawings among his papers – the good man of the cloth thought them pornographic anyway. It turned out that he had photographed and drawn pictures of naked female students of his. He was in some of the photos with them, also starkers. That was enough. The young theologian was defrocked and was allowed thereafter only to service the Church as a teacher of languages and history. Aleks said that he had never seen the scandalous nude photographs for himself and didn't know what, precisely, was actually in them or what the Teacher was accused of. The Teacher had apparently defended himself, though, by saying that he was researching absolute pornography. Aleks didn't know what this absolute pornography was, but the idea amused him. Before they said their good-byes they stood at the corner of the street for a while, and Aleks took the idea to the absurd as usual.

When he arrived home, Grandfather and Grandmother had already gone to bed. Mother was sitting at the table correcting children's exercise books and his aunt was reading.

'Have you had anything to eat? Shall I put the kettle on? Would you like some milk and bread pudding?'

Fussing of this sort had always annoyed him. He never knew what to tell his aunt or grandmother what he did, in fact, want. Indeed, what he would have liked most would be to choose something to eat from the cupboard himself when he was hungry without making a big deal of it. He didn't want to be the only child in the family, the one whom all the women felt the need to fuss over, but without knowing how except in the most trivial of ways, like asking whether he was hungry, whether he had got cold, whether he had clean socks and a clean hand-kerchief.

This time he really did want something to eat. At the Teacher's they had only smoked; cigarettes and enthusiasm had carried the feeling of hunger away, but now it had returned. There was no need to boil the kettle; he would make some cheese sandwiches himself and have some bread pudding with milk.

Mother finished her marking and put the kettle on for herself. She asked guardedly whether he had been to the library or at a friend's. Usually these kinds of questions irritated him, but this time he was euphoric from the recent meeting. No, neither, someone had taken him to Professor Alo K's. His aunt knew the Teacher. Before she retired she had worked in the German section of the book-shop, and the Teacher had been there at least once or twice a week. His aunt liked him; he had greeted her with a bow and would sometimes chat about the books he chose or found. Mother only knew of the Teacher – his wife must be Mrs N's friend, and Mrs N had introduced them once at a concert. The Teacher was reputed to attend lots of concerts.

What had been his impression of the Teacher?

He didn't know how to answer that question. He couldn't say that he was in awe, in ecstasy. He remembered that Jüri Targama had said that the Teacher knew about sixty languages. That was something he could tell Mother. Languages were an objective, neutral thing that they could talk about in their family. So they talked about the languages the Teacher had been involved with and what he might know.

Languages were something that united mother and son. When he was a tiny child his mother had studied philology by correspondence course. When she read about linguistics and history in bed the child snuggled up to her and read alongside her. That was when he had learnt about language families; he knew who the Semites, Indo-Europeans and Dravidians were and could even tell visitors how many speakers there were of, say, Tamil or Amharic and where they lived.

The Teacher presumably knew a number of Dravidian languages, and he himself had said he had written a grammar of Mayan. Mother did not have the same enthusiasm for that area; she was certain in her European leanings, her youth in Paris and Milan where she had studied singing. Her world was the Italian opera, Michelangelo and Anatole France. Her son had started out with them as well, had read Anatole France, been to concerts when operatic soloists from the Theatre Estonia in Tallinn had visited Tartu, had learnt French and Italian from his mother, but they no longer held any magic for him. Magic lay with the Mayans, the Dravidians, the Borobudur and Angkor Wat, the places never reached by Roman soldiers' feet, where missionaries' work was not yet done. In Europe, the places that held magic for him were Ireland, Wales and Iceland.

He had rummaged through the library's Celtica catalogue and had tried to teach himself a bit of Welsh. He didn't dare learn Irish – it looked too complex and perhaps also too majestic and noble. Like Chinese. He had learnt to think of many things in the Estonian fashion: they were too great, proud or sacred for him. So instead of trying to learn Irish he tried to learn Welsh and, instead of Chinese, Arabic.

He thought he would be unable to sleep, but that turned out not to be the case: he didn't even notice the point when a thought became a dream. Anyway, he met the Teacher again in his dream. The Teacher said that he had been waiting for him for a long time, that he had to ordain him as a member of the Order of the Eastern Garter. He took him into the back room and from there through dark rooms full of old books and sculptures until they reached a stable-like area with shelves around. There were no books on the shelves, only nests where hens, ducks and turkeys were hatching. On another wall there was a manger upon which a large bird was lying. They went closer, and he saw that it wasn't a bird but Jüri's beautiful sister under a blanket that looked like it was made of down. 'Say "Borobudur",' ordered the Teacher. 'It's Amharic.' He tried to say it, but his tongue was rigid and no words came. The Teacher began to laugh cruelly, picked up the cow chain next to the manger and put it around his neck. Then he took his trousers off. Under his trousers he was wearing a suspender belt like the ones women wear. He lifted the blanket and clambered into the manger next to Jüri's sister.

4

The following days carried on as normal. He went to lectures, sat in the library and café and listened to Aleks's and Peeter Härmsoo's poems. They were quite good. Peeter read one on the evening before his next visit to the Teacher's when all three of them were together. The parts that stuck in his mind were:

> Archbishop Suryamuryaptatnam of Rajputana, Miles Davis and
> half a sack of early spring potatoes roll around in my head but
> the only way out is through poetry

> on the day they are turned out to pasture the cows are given saxo-
> phones despite concerns about food the cowshed door is open

> the sounds of rumination and the harsh but honest grass domi-
> nate the scene

> triumphantly the animal technician plunges into the depths of
> Tõravere.

Peeter was his first acquaintance from university. He could almost call him a friend, if he had dared to use the term. The word 'friend' felt too pompous and grand for him. Perhaps it was also because it was one of the basic words in the Soviet lexicon: 'Friendship' was the label applied to the shop, the bridge, the cultural centre and biscuit brand. In his latter years at secondary school he had had no friends, at least since he had started to read poetry and write it himself. He no longer had anything to talk about with his classmates; they had other, earthier and more tangible interests. He did go to the dance at the former girls' school, but he didn't get on very well, even with the girls: he tried desperately to think of something to talk to them about while dancing, and as he was unable to come up with anything he was for the most part embarrassingly quiet. The fact that it does not pay to talk about modern poetry and faith was something he had already learnt from experience. He had no one to read his own poems to or with whom to talk about poetry. He had met Peeter in the first autumn, when all students were sent to help out at collective farms. He discovered that Peeter knew something about modern poetry, could recognize constellations and knew by heart the names of all the bishops of Ösel-Wiek. He kept company mostly with Peeter, especially after it came out that they both wrote poetry. They hung out together a lot, sometimes with a couple of girls, and discussed poetry, telepathy, Yugoslav Communism, four-dimensional space and the Orient. Peeter didn't like drinking spirits, and under his influence he began to drink sour Georgian wine which had to be swallowed with cheese. They had a few bottles of wine with them and acquired more from the village shop. They sat together on many evenings in the attic room of the farmhouse, which was the place allocated as the boys' living area, and held club nights to which a few girls were also invited.

Peeter's father had a fairly senior post in a ministry, so his son was able to rent a room in Tartu and continue his club evenings there. This did not, of course, stop him from sitting in the café every day, where he soon joined the circle of Aleks Luuberg's followers. Peeter was really the only person who was capable of keeping pace with Aleks. Their favourite pursuit was free exploration of thought, sometimes in the form of a poem. They both always had scraps of poems in their pockets and folders that they were ready to read aloud. That's how it was this time, too. When Peeter allowed his animal technician to plunge into the depths of Tõravere, Aleks found himself unable to resist the temptation to talk about how one of his fellow female students, who had studied history in Estonia, started working in Siberia as an animal technician. The job had gone so well for her that she obtained certificates of honour, attended gatherings organized for the best workers and earned loads of money, so much that when she came back to her homeland she was able to build a decent house in Merivälja. He asked Aleks whether the woman worked in Merivälja as an animal technician or a historian. Neither, she started working for the Estonian Consumer Cooperatives Society. He remembered that one of his own male relatives was awarded best-worker status in Siberia. The man was an ordinary farmer in Võrumaa, but in Siberia he became a beekeeper; he was also sent certificates of honour, roubles galore and also built a house, but in Saue not Merivälja, another nice area near Tallinn. His wife, who was apparently a distant relative of the poet Henrik Visnapuu, wrote poetry during her exile and sent it to her homeland in letters. His grandmother had kept them and sometimes read them to her women friends.

Aleks had also been to Siberia and written poems. They were written partly in Russian. He was in a prison camp for a couple of years, in exile in a small town in the area around Kirov where there were only three local intellectuals – the doctor (a Jew, of course), the pharmacist and the retired accountant of a river port. They had played bridge semi-secretly and had taken the young Estonian into their midst to make a fourth hand. This proved very useful to him; he was fed well, and before they sat down at the bridge table they talked about literature and read poems, including poems that had been officially forgotten in the Soviet Union and were unavailable to ordinary people. As material evidence Aleks read out one of Sasha Chernyi's poems and one of his own works in Russian, a fragment of which he still remembered:

My hobby is to want to laugh out loud even if the quack is only
living off a heap of hemp.

It reminded him that two volumes of Radhakrishnan's history of Indian philosophy in Russian, which he was obstinately trying to read, were waiting for him in the library. At university, philosophy was taught only after young brains had been sufficiently washed in the history of the Communist Party of the Soviet Union. He could not bear to wait that long, though, and instead began sooner with whatever came to hand. There wasn't much in Estonian: Koort's papers in the old editions of *Looming*, Nietzsche's *Zarathustra* and Will Durant's stories about the history of philosophy in the series 'Living Science'. Fortunately, he had begun reading Russian literature at school – at home they had more Russian great literature than Estonian, some of it with the old Tsarist-era 'yats' and 'fitas', and effectively supplemented the knowledge of Russian he had acquired at home. He could not actually say why he began to read Indian philosophy in particular rather than Plato, for example. This interest in the Orient must have been innate or in the air around him. He and Peeter both studied oriental languages as options; he studied Sanskrit and Arabic, and Peeter Hindi. For a month after they had begun their oriental studies Peeter would talk only of Indology, yoga and reincarnation, which he was familiar with from a Russian book with a hint of theosophy published at the turn of the twentieth century. He learnt Devanagari script, and they sometimes used it between themselves as a secret alphabet during lectures on Communist Party history to write obscene messages on what they heard. When the old Estonian duffer Martson, who had come from Russia, posed the rhetorical question 'What did the Party ask its best representatives to do at this difficult time?' Peeter wrote 'To fuck off' in Devanagari on the edge of his notes, and he replied with 'To fuck right off'.

He listened to Aleks's latest poem and got up. Karmen and Liia were just coming up to their table. He would have stayed with pleasure. He liked Karmen, who was studying medicine, although he felt he didn't know how to approach her. He desired and feared women and the combination of desire and fear had become a huge wall between him and the fulfilment of his desires. And, apart from that, Malle might be in the library, too.

Malle was indeed in the library. She was reading Kolozsvári Grandpierre's Hungarian fairy-tales. They winked at one another conspiratorially. He took up his Radhakrishnan and tried to immerse himself in the ideas of the Mimamsa school. Unsuccessfully. He heroically kept at it for half an hour but could not stop stealing glances at Malle. Nearly every time Malle glanced towards him in the same way and smiled. Malle's smile was something that rid him of his nervousness of women. It was at once sisterly and motherly. Malle was pretty, although not especially sexy. She was studying Finno-Ugric languages and sang in a women's choir. They had met at concerts and had attended several together. Malle had also seen some of his poems, but if they had anything in common it was more music and linguistics.

He then remembered that the cinema was showing a French film that he would like to go and see. He would like it even more with Malle. He took a thick copy-book out of the drawer, tore out a sheet of paper and wrote on it: 'A visit to the last screening at the Saluut Cinema is proposed. I will provide a ticket and company if this is agreeable.'

He folded the paper over, making it into a dart, wrote 'Malle' on it and tossed it to the neighbouring table.

The dart came back by the same method and landed right in the middle of Indian philosophy. The reply was simple and brief. Her note slanted across the upper left-hand corner: 'Suggestion received. Agreed. [Signature]'.

Malle's father had been the manager of a state farm.

The film was fairly sad. The action took place in a Parisian slum, the characters an Apache on the run from the police, his tramplike friend and his sister, whom the Apache seduces. In the end the tramp kills the Apache and justice prevails.

When the lights dimmed in the auditorium, he took Malle's hand; Malle did not object. She had cold fingers which warmed gradually when he stroked them. They sat like that until the end of the film, hand in hand. He glanced at Malle once or twice. The light reflected from the cinema screen played on her face; she had a peaked nose and high forehead on to which her dark ringlets fell, giving her something of a classical air. For a second she reminded him more of the ancient goddesses of antiquity than a student of nineteen in her second year.

When the film ended and they were on their way to the exit with the rest of the crowd, Malle was Malle once more. The idea that he would escort her home was a matter of course. As if in concert, they turned into the longer road which went up Toome Hill. When they had walked beyond the university he slipped his arm under Malle's, and they climbed the hill arm in arm, suddenly in silence. He squeezed her arm closer, and she reciprocated. They paused under the first street lamp as if by agreement and looked at each other, still in silence, and smiled. When they moved on he asked Malle whether she had had a garden and yard to play in when she was a child. Malle said that when she was a really young child she had, but when her mother and father divorced they had moved into a big house with their mother that didn't. There was a park near by, though, and her grandma would take her and her little brother there for walks.

So during their childhoods they had been for walks with their grandmothers, one of them in one part of Estonia, the other in another, without knowing anything of each other. He thought that Malle's grandma might know something of his grandma or at least something about his grandfather because his grandfather had sold all kinds of teaching materials to schools: globes, textbooks, skeletons, pencils, set squares and protractors. Malle's grandma hadn't been a teacher, however, so there was no reason for her to know anything of pencils, skeletons or set squares. Or of the salesman of many years past who could get no sleep now because of the tingling in his paralysed arm and his fear of being left alone in the dark.

He asked Malle if she had been afraid of being in the dark by herself. Malle had not. But then again, she had never been in the dark that much. She had slept in a room with her little brother; her grandma had slept in the room next door, and the door was always open.

Was Malle's grandma still alive? Yes, she was. She didn't go out much any more but was always busy at home, watching television and knitting socks.

Malle was six months older than him. They had both grown up without their fathers, he since babyhood, she since primary school. They had both grown up among women; neither of them really knew much of the world of men, that world of war, hunting, the smell of tobacco and beer, cards and bawdiness.

He squeezed the girl's arm, thinking that they had so much in common. He felt something which could be tenderness and empathy but equally a desire to be closer to the girl's body, to be allowed closer. Nascent lust was vague at first – he could not imagine how it was kindled – yet his body knew something without the aid of fantasies. He felt her warmth, the scent of her flesh and hair that blended with the fragrance of the park in spring.

They reached the large lilac tree where the buds were already opening and stopped by it. The lamppost was far away.

'We could seek our fortunes, except it's dark,' said Malle. 'Do you like looking for good luck among the lilac blossoms?'

Once, as a child, in a garden in Tartu he had found a lilac blossom with twelve petals. Malle thought that this meant he must be a lucky person. She had only ever found the plain old blossoms with five petals.

They turned to face each other. He looked at Malle. Her eyes were completely black in the dusk, the distant lantern-light glittering in them like little stars. He held her close and they kissed. It happened easily and naturally, almost without any fuss. Malle had very soft, warm lips. He had read that women close their eyes when they kiss, but men keep theirs open; but he couldn't. His eyes shut almost by themselves, and behind his closed eyelids he saw thousands of burning sparks scattering in every direction as if he had his own internal little firework that had been waiting within him for a long time and was now being set off.

They walked on in silence. He felt that now there was something between them that tied them together; they walked and breathed to the same beat. Did they also think the same things?

'You lit the sparks,' he said when they had left the park and turned on to the road on the edge of the student dormitory.

'You lit them yourself,' replied Malle. 'I saw them even with my eyes closed.'

It was sunny the next morning, but in the afternoon it clouded over and the first shower of rain fell. He knew that he had fallen in love a little, although, surprisingly, it did not make him giddy. Quite the opposite: everything was clear and tidy, his senses sharper than usual. The most surprising thing, though, was a kind of miraculous hitherto unknown calm. He wondered whether this was tranquillity, contentment. Such contentment did not have much to do with sex. The touch of Malle's warm lips and cool hand seemed to have extinguished his lust and restlessness.

When he was thirteen, single-sex schools were abolished and girls arrived in their class. This changed his life completely. He sat sideways more, endlessly swapped messages with girls and had fallen in love with several of them at once. At around the same time he discovered poetry and began to read the Soothsayers, Lermontov, Pushkin and Eino Leino. He thought of little but poetry and girls. It was thrilling at first, but he soon began to realize that girls thought not about poetry but about boys, pop stars and clothes. He began to realize that he did not know how to talk to them about anything. He lived in a different world from the people with whom he happened to share a classroom. His world, his books, Mozart and Handel were strangers to them. Nor did he understand how they could write silly lyrics in one another's notebooks when there was Heiti Talvik and Lermontov, when there was poetry. This stirred him to protest. He even tried to talk about it, to read Talvik and Lermontov to the girls. Only one, however, showed any interest. Her name was Olga, and her parents were Russian Estonians and Communists. He wrote his own fighting poem in Olga's notebook:

> Pegasus, when do you tire
> Of taking your dung out of your byre?
> When will you finally see the light
> and realize that your poetry's shite?

He was a young, committed moralist and gradually lost contact with girls. Nor could he be found among the boys after he discovered poetry and classical music. It was a crossroads. Behind him lay fishing, cars and the model aeroplanes he had carved out of wood in the countryside and painted the colour of aluminium.

His few friends and classmates took a different path: women and vodka appeared in their conversation alongside cars. Vodka held no particular attraction for him, and the talk of women simultaneously sickened and irritated him. The stories were vulgar and squalid, a woman featuring only in so far as she let the man have his way. But the fact that she let him earned her no thanks, only scorn. The flow of scorn and animosity in the boys' stories startled him. He had grown up among women, was accustomed to the women's world; he could not take exception to women; he did not feel like a man when he did so, as his classmates did.

He wondered whether, in scorning and hating women so much, the men were in fact scorning and hating their own burning desire that made them play at courtship which sometimes felt meaningless and humiliating to them; the desire that made them run after women to whom their attachment was nothing more than overwhelming lust. This was how yesterday's carefree slum-boys fought and protested against the enslaving, ignominious lust for the women that the annoying teenage girls had suddenly become, upon whose moods, yeses and noes their lives would increasingly depend.

They could not admit that they were running after women, that they were slaves to their lust. They had to demonstrate to themselves – and more so to everyone else – that they were in complete control, that, in fact, the girls were the ones doing the chasing and the boys picked the one they wanted. Girls meant nothing to them. There was no talk of male lust, only of female lust, which was dangerous in its insatiability – a lecherous woman was like a vampire who would suck the life force out of a man. There was both thrill and comfort in the thought of a woman, dangerous as she may be, lusting after a man; in the thought that a woman might humiliate herself over a man.

He didn't know how to play this male game. There was something in it that he rebelled against. He did not know how to treat women as inferiors let alone as dangerous creatures. He could not unlearn the rules and values he had learnt in the women's world. To him a government of women was a natural thing that was absolutely normal. If anything dismayed him, it was the fact that the very women who held this power none the less put up with the men who both lusted after and scorned them in this way. The fact that they adopted the rules of a game in which they were to be conquered and seduced, as if they were indeed weak, as if it were in their nature to submit to men and do their will.

He remembered what a shock it had been for him when he realized that girls preferred not him but the boys who knew how to play this very same vulgar male game well – boys who smoked in the school toilets and went to parties smelling of alcohol.

Why were things like that? He slowly began to realize that both boys and girls were frightened of all the changes that they had undergone. They were afraid of themselves, their changed bodies, and they were afraid of the people to whom that body strangely, irresistibly drew them. In all that fear and confusion a game was something definite, something clear and simple in its banality. Perhaps that was why the game was played, dances attended, girls seen home, kisses cadged, invitations to the cinema extended ... The game helped young people get together.

Perhaps his mistake was that he was too serious, that he didn't know how to play. He didn't know how to chat to girls at dances. And there were no girls in his circle with whom he could have talked only about Mozart, Lermontov and Talvik.

If he had had slightly more earthly interests he could have been accepted as one of the girls. Such boys did exist; he met one at university. He was a small, flaxen-haired guy who moved only in the company of girls, sat in their rooms in halls, flicked through the fashion magazines and discussed the new cut of a dress or hairdos. Unlike that boy, new cuts of dress and hairdos were of no interest to him. Since childhood they had been for him a ritual part of the women's world into which men were definitely not admitted. He was taken along to the seamstress and the cosmetics lady, but, once there, he was forgotten; the women spoke their own secret language among themselves with its own weird Germanic vocabulary: 'kurte', 'porte', 'krous', 'talje', 'antsuhh' and 'antproobe'. He felt left out and humiliated.

The same thing happened in the men's world. It, too, had its own secret language and its own rituals. Here it was hunting, the beer hall, sauna and female conquest. Hunting, the killing of animals, was something he had been averse to since childhood, beer was something he did not desire and sitting in the sauna was something he could not tolerate. If he had felt at home anywhere else in the world he would not have cared about the men's world. But now the one option open to him was to attempt to live on its fringes. He was unable to be completely on his own. He might have learnt to be if there had been no women. No blind, scorching desire that occasionally spilt over so violently and maddeningly that it was frightening. Even at school there were a couple of girls whom he had desired in this way. He even tried to dance with one of them but did not get any further with her. He understood that he and his desire – did they perceive it and how much? – were of no interest to them. He could perhaps gain access to them through the men's world, through smooth talk, through uninhibited, bold behaviour and the faint smell of beer. Talvik and Dostoevsky were no help here.

During his time at university his approaches had, on a couple of occasions, been rejected with some amazement: so did he, an intellectual, poetry-minded young man want the same as the others? It meant that access to women via the men's world was also closed to him.

Yes, this intellectual, poetic boy did indeed want the same thing as the others, maybe wanted it even more than the playboys who had already wheedled their ways into the beds of several teenage girls after parties at Kalev Cultural Centre.

He could not remember how it started. There was something in his very early childhood, something that strangely tempted him and gave him no peace.

Certain pictures in books, certain stories he'd heard, certain books. When there was no one in the house he would clamber on to the sofa, take down the *Encyclopaedia Estonia* and explore the entry under 'genitalia' and the pictures under 'copulation'. But this was not yet true lust; it was more of an odd curiosity in something that was a family taboo.

True lust came later. He remembered that better. At his great-aunt's house in the country there were lots of old magazines; he read them over hours and days each summer in the attic. And somewhere in those journals he began to seek out and find the things that aroused and fed his lust. *Estonian Woman* and *Farmer's Wife* contained advice for women on pregnancy, contraception and gynaecological problems. He learnt what was meant by menstruation, menstrual disorders, vaginal discharge and the known sexually transmitted diseases of the time. This was one side of the matter, the hard gynaecological reality. He could find the other side in literature, even in old editions of *Looming* literary magazine, annual volumes of which had been bundled into chests in the attic. His great-aunt's husband had been a headmaster and a teetotaller. Instead of vodka he bought books and subscribed to journals. He could no longer remember the title of Karl Asti's story in *Looming*, the story with the naked and brusque lust. On the one hand, the brusqueness excited and attracted him; on the other, it frightened him even more. But by reading how the hero made the pretty Jewess his lover he felt a purely physical sensation that required physical satisfaction. He was taught to masturbate by his own young and restless body. It was constantly in his mind: the warm summer afternoon in the hayloft where he had slipped away with a few copies of *Looming*, where he had left his first semen. For a short time this gave him contentment, but it was mingled with shame and torment. Fortunately the journals from the old Estonian Republic were enlightened: they contained no horror stories about masturbation causing softening of the brain and other gruesome side-effects. But there was none the less a shameful quality about it, something which only the bad boys talked about, and even they only did so in the abstract. Even then wanking was a thing of anecdotes alone: no one admitted to doing it.

Self-pleasuring did nothing to help bring him closer to women though; quite the opposite. With his sexual interests he receded further into the shadows. Sex became something even more secretive, something he could not talk about honestly to anyone. At home, things like that were not discussed at all as such, and it was inconceivable for him to talk to the girls he danced with at parties about what he felt, wanted and did secretly in the hayloft or in the toilet of the communal apartment. With girls he had to play some kind of courtship game that never worked out for him. Why did girls still have to be surrounded like a fortress in the Middle Ages – in armour, complete with fluttering colours and a drum tattoo?

There was supposed to be a different kind of erotica these days. Boys and books talked about it. There were man-eating women, there were prostitutes, there were women of easy virtue. They didn't have to be seduced and conquered; they were always ready. They waited for and searched men out themselves, especially attractive young men.

Why had he never met a woman like that? Did they really exist, or were they just a myth in the imagination of men and boys? Or was there nothing in him that women liked? Perhaps he was an ordinary, awkward adolescent boy distressed by his nascent sexual hunger and an equal hunger for human intimacy? He could not stop dreaming about a particular type of woman, a beautiful, slightly older woman who invited him over on various pretexts – perhaps she needed him to carry something, change a fuse or hang a picture. The woman offers him coffee and a glass of wine, they sit on the sofa; the woman's skirt rises above her knees. She looks deeply into his face then strokes his head. The woman knows everything, she undresses him fully and . . . It was good to dream about it. How to enter a woman was a problem for him; he didn't properly understand how it went. The pictures of the open vulva that he had happened to see did not fully explain where to get in. Why did something which came so naturally to cats, dogs, flies and dragonflies, without their having to learn anything about it, have to be so complicated for human beings? He was already worried about how he would perform once he was in bed with a woman. What awaited him was like an initiation, a celebration of his becoming a man. He felt that he would not be a man, would not be an adult, until he had known a woman, in the biblical sense of the word. Virginity was becoming an ever greater burden. He would have liked to catch up with the others. The boys from the capital city Tallinn, especially, had had their first experiences as men while at school and talked about it in the way fishermen talk about a catch. He had nothing to say. Once when they had come back to the dorm from the inn – he had occasionally spent the night there with people on his course – the conversation had strayed to some girls who were always up for it, and they had even gone around to knock on the door of one room. The door was not opened. Later he thought that perhaps he had escaped yet another humiliating experience. The fact that the girls refused his artless approaches was less of a problem. The thing he was really afraid of was that he would not perform.

But now there was Malle. Malle had something motherly, soft and warm about her. He was in love, and his love liberated him, at least for a while, from his secret burden of sexual desire and fear.

And there was the Teacher who was expecting him and his secret poems. That was an initiation, too, an initiation that he also feared. Just as much as if Brigitte Bardot or Gina Lollobrigida had asked him to spend the night.

8

The flowering period for the pear tree in front of the Teacher's block was already coming to an end, and white blossom was falling from it. From somewhere near the garden came the song of the pied flycatcher.

He had his poems in a briefcase, re-created on the new typewriter sent by his uncle, titles and page numbers in red – it had a two-colour ribbon. He had thought through his questions, too; they were on a slip of paper in his pocket.

The door was opened by Ellen, who smiled in recognition. Yes, Alo was expecting him. Would he be so good as to come in? Warmth cascaded over his back and head. His ears must have turned red – that's what always happened to him. He was mortified and overjoyed all at once. He had been expecting him; the Teacher had been *expecting* him!

The Teacher bowed as theatrically as he had the first time and smiled. His handshake was warm and soft, although no longer as weak and distant as before. They sat down. A pack of Tallinn cigarettes was on the table.

The Teacher took his first puff and then asked whether he had brought his poems with him. The question was superfluous. He took out a slender file bearing the Russian word for 'folder' and handed it to the Teacher. He felt that this was more than just a handshake. It was his offering, his gift of longing for and devotion to the guru. The guru took the file and flicked through it. He could hear the rustling of the papers and the rapid, sonorous throbbing of his heart. Then footsteps could be heard. Ellen came in carrying a tray and three coffee cups, sat down with them and lit a cigarette. The Teacher closed the file. Were they the poems, Ellen was interested to know. Could she see them, too? Of course. What did he have to give the Teacher and his wife? Almost nothing. He was a beggar; he came only for what he could get. So it was good that this small trifle that he had was of interest.

Would he be able to keep the poems for a while, for a week, asked the Teacher, then he would be able to read them at his leisure in the evenings? His prayer had been heard somewhere up above and far away. The Teacher had sprung a trap that the student would not have dared to set. He was given the scope to come back here for a third visit. Perhaps he would then find other opportunities and might even begin to come and sit at the Teacher's feet one or twice a month and listen to his magical voice.

The robin appeared in the doorway again, hopped around the room, stopped once, cocked its head and looked him in the face and went out through the other door.

The Teacher flicked through the file, his gaze lingered somewhere for a while, and on one occasion his mouth broke into a smile, and he pointed something out to Ellen, who also smiled and nodded. He supposed it could be one of the poems bordering on the surreal, some of whose characters were originally from Russian history:

> Varangians wielding tridents
> emerged from Ilmen's foam
> for in Pushkin's sinful flesh
> there dwelt a memory of living water.
>
> It fermented in an oaken tub
> where the workers' hopes were stored
> until at last one October day
> they raised their yellowed heads.

He knew that it would have been wiser not to write poems like this at all or that at least he should not show them to anyone. But the Teacher was not just anyone. Not for even a moment did he have any doubt that he could be the channel by which the poems would find their way to places they should not go.

Then the Teacher put the file to one side and said, 'You must come back some time and have your manuscript back. I see your typewriter has a very attractive typeface. Is it your own?'

Yes, it was his own or, rather, their own; they'd got it from his uncle in New York. An Olympia model.

The Teacher picked up the file again and inspected the typeface. 'Very nice,' he said. 'One of the most pleasing typefaces to read. I see that the Germans haven't changed anything about theirs; it's exactly the same as before the war. You remember, Ellen, it was the same on our first machine.'

'The one you gave to Juhan when he fled to Sweden, you mean?'

'Yes. Don't you remember?

'Have you been taught the Latin *Habent sua fata libelli* yet? I thought that type-writers might also have their own fate. I bought my typewriter in Germany from a Jewish university student who was emigrating; he had got it from the editor of a left-wing newspaper that closed down before the SS cleared it out. Juhan never made it to Sweden, though; the boat must have sunk. The typewriter's probably lying somewhere at the bottom of the Baltic now.'

He said that he had already studied some Latin at secondary school.

The Teacher said he was happy to hear it. He admitted that he couldn't read Latin as fast as he could read Greek, but one would have to be utterly idealistic to hope that anyone still learnt Greek these days.

He confessed that he had thought about learning it.

The Teacher was interested in what he intended to do with it.

He replied that he would read poetry and understand exactly what Plato and Aristotle thought and said. But he could not refrain from confessing that his interest in languages had come about when he had happened to read a book on the riddle of Atlantis as a schoolboy. That was when he had resolved to study languages that were spoken in the region where Atlantis was reputed to have been located. He was unable to pursue Atlantis quite so seriously any more, but the interest in languages had remained with him.

The Teacher laughed. He had started to learn Latin and Greek when he found a heap of old papers that had presumably started life with a pharmacist. There were German or Russian letters among them, but several of the letters and prescriptions were in Latin. It bothered him that he did not understand them and he decided to learn the language. But yes, he acknowledged that his was a much narrower, more personal interest compared to the student's. Which languages was he now learning? the Teacher asked.

There weren't that many. He could read English. He had a good knowledge of French, German, Spanish and Latin and some Sanskrit and Arabic, although he hadn't made very good progress with them, as sometimes the lecturer cancelled lectures and sometimes he was unable to attend. He enquired whether the Teacher also knew those languages.

Sanskrit, of course, although the Dravidian languages were of greater interest to him. No Japanese or Chinese. His involvement with Egyptian had killed any interest in hieroglyphics. He had translated Chinese texts, some Mencius and Xun Zi, via German and English. The reward for learning Chinese was the infinite variety of things to read. As for the Egyptians, although he had read the more interesting texts there was nothing more to be done with them. He could become an Egyptologist and study, for example, the phrases used to address the gods Thoth and Ammon or attempt to reconstruct the vowel system of ancient Egyptian, but he had no vocation for it and the university would not have paid him to do it.

He asked the Teacher what he would have liked to do if he hadn't had to do a paid job at the university.

The Teacher smiled and said that he didn't think anyone had really asked him that before, so he would have to think about it for a while.

Ellen made use of the pause in conversation. 'Do you remember you once said that you would like to study the gnostics and rehabilitate them, Valentinus and . . . ?'

'I can't do that, a whole new little library of gnostics has emerged from the desert sand in Egypt now. I've only seen particles of it. Thomas's Gospel and the story of the Thunder Spirit.

'I think I mentioned last time that I thought about going to Guatemala or Polynesia. But later on I thought that I should take a broader view of things. That I should create a worldwide opposition to Europeans' sprawl and terror, a kind of union of ancient peoples, natural peoples.'

'Didn't the Japanese try to do something like that during the war?'

'The Japanese were my greatest disappointment,' the Teacher replied. 'I have read their poetry, but the way they devastated China and the things they did in Melanesia and Micronesia were not much better than the devastation wrought by the Germans in Eastern Europe. Warriors, samurai, have always been so terribly important to the Japanese. I should have known; I had read about them. Just like the cult of the knight in Europe. Anyhow, the cult of the knight, it should be said, is a small step towards the things personified by the SS and in existentialist philosophy – death is more genuine than life, only a murderer is a real person, only killing and dying take us to the heart of humanity . . .

'What interests me about the Chinese is that they have never made a cult of warfare. Oh, the Chinese emperors made war all right, but it was with very clear national aims. The Chinese would view war for war's sake as complete madness. But if you read the so-called heroic epics of the European Middle Ages, there is nothing in them but fighting – and killing, of course – just for the sake of fighting and killing. Valour for valour's sake, war for war's sake. And the Europeans have never been able to extract themselves from this culture of making war. It would appear that the Japanese haven't been able to either.'

'So it's a bit like schoolboys who enjoy a good fight, the ones who retaliate if someone attacks them,' he said after a while.

The Teacher smiled. 'Yes, you could perhaps look at it like that. And if a child grows up in a society where scrapping has its own worth and the strongest fighter is held in the highest regard . . . Where do you start in a culture whose list of great men is made up mainly of brawlers. Ask schoolchildren or teachers for the names of ten great people in history – who will they nominate? Obviously Alexander the Great, Caesar, Genghis Khan, Napoleon . . . the French would add Charlemagne, the Russians Peter the Great, the Germans Frederick the Great. Maybe Shakespeare or Goethe or Mozart. But the war leaders are at the top of what you probably call a leader board. I have often asked people, the answers are fairly similar. And there's no big difference between Russians, Estonians and Germans.'

'So do the Chinese and the Indians have a different kind of leader board then?'

'The Chinese begin with the greatest rulers of the ancient world who built dams and canals and taught people to cultivate the land. Then come Confucius, Meng-tse, Lao-tzu, perhaps Buddha and several other teachers and perhaps some poets. Not a single war leader. In India the board includes semi-mythological figures such as Krishna and Rama. And a raft of all kinds of gods that have been incarnated in human form. Goes to show that, in contrast to the Chinese, who view the past realistically, Indians have a somewhat mythological view of themselves where the earthly and the divine were mixed. But among the genuine, more realist heroes of today Gandhi, who preached non-violent resistance, occupies the top spot.'

'Have you asked Chinese and Indians then?'

'Yes, in my time, I did, in Germany. There was a young Chinese man there. His leader board was more or less as I have described. And he said that others thought the same way. Of course, I don't know what the Communists there nowadays think, but I don't believe they are capable of completely changing anything in China. The floods pass and the rivers flow back into their beds.'

'So what's your own leader board of great men like?'

The Teacher gurgled a laugh. 'Why is it so important for you to know? As it happens, I haven't really compiled a serious table for myself. But on a couple of occasions when I've been thoroughly fed up with Caesar's admirers I've given rankings to some of the people I most admire. But I do not even believe it possible to draw up a list of the world's greatest men. World culture does not yet exist, although it is talked about. There are a number of cultures and some links between them, some peaks that stand out high above the landscape around them and are visible from afar. Like Buddha or Lao-tzu or Christ. For me, though, the great men are the ones who tried to rescue culture from bullies. Like, for example, the trans-lators who translated Greek philosophy and literature into Middle Persian, the ones who then translated them into Arabic, and the third group who translated from Arabic into Latin. They brought Western culture back to the West. The Jews of Toledo and Sicily. I could tell you their names, but they would mean very little to you. At the moment. One name I will mention, so remember it: Cassiodorus. A man who did not write much but who founded the Vivarium Monastery in Calabria in the sixth century and housed a collection there of all the manuscripts, all the ancient literature he could get his hands on, and rescued them from those who would destroy them or burn them. He was probably one of the first people to act in this way. Later there were others like him. Cassiodorus, a learned man who did not have the time to ponder his own greatness, a man who simply did what he had to do. Sometimes that is the most difficult thing.

'Put to one side the great men referred to in your school books, the Alexanders and Caesars. Alexander who burnt down the Persian royal palace in Persepolis, burnt down the huge library of a nation. The Romans who burnt down the library at Alexandria. An entire culture built on the ruins of the others, which contains something worthwhile only because there were people whose actions were the opposite of those of great men, the opposite of the people who admire the great deeds of great men.'

'The Jewish library is what Alo's thinking of,' commented Ellen in the pause following her husband's impassioned sermon. 'With the help of Professor M he managed to rescue most of the Jewish books whose removal from the university library and destruction would have been ordered by the Germans. They muddled up the numbers, moved some of the card indexes somewhere else and only gave the Germans a few hundred almanacs, magazines, trivial storybooks and other items that were not difficult to replace. But all the best literature survived.'

'So is Cassiodorus your patron saint?' he asked.

'Oh, I would be quite prepared to light a candle to him and ask him to intercede with God on my behalf. Perhaps he would understand me better than most others. Only, as far as I know, he's not a saint, the Church has not canonized him.'

Meanwhile the questions he had thought up in the library seemed so trivial and empty that he didn't dare even think about them, so fascinating was the world that the Teacher had introduced to him in his narrative. But now the Teacher himself had approached the issue that was on his mind, although he was not sure even now how to articulate it properly.

'There's one thing I would like to ask, but I'm not sure how. It concerns Cassiodorus himself, on the one hand, but, on the other, the people who did not regard him as an important man . . . And the others, the people who brought Christianity here with sword and fire. The people who burnt the heretics . . . Are Christianity and the Church more on the side of Caesar and Napoleon or of Cassiodorus?'

The Teacher shook his head, smiling. 'Oh, I really must ask the rector, Klement, to pay me for all the lectures I give young people here, all because the university does not provide an education worthy of the name. Not now and not during the Estonian Republic. The difference was, I was able to deliver the lectures in a lecture hall then. Now I have to do it in my own living-room.'

'Now don't exaggerate, Alo,' Ellen interrupted. 'During the republic the university was different from today's Soviet university.'

'Oh, don't let's argue over which is better.' The Teacher didn't want to get embroiled in the issue. There was a feeling that this was not the first time that he had had a different view from his wife on the Estonian Republic. He focused on his visitor's question again. 'Christianity. Has there ever been any such thing as Christianity? What do Christ, Peter, Augustine, the Inquisitor Torquemada, Luther, Erasmus and Schweitzer have in common? Nothing I can find, apart from a few words and names. But are words so important? Do words make someone a Christian? Did Christ say to do as he said but not to do as he did?

'At university you are taught Lenin's view that each culture embodies two distinct cultures – one for the gentry and another for the proletariat. One could also say that Christianity contains two different Christianities – one for the oppressors and the powerful, and one for the tortured, the martyrs and the oppressed.

'Have you ever thought *who* Christ was speaking *to* and what he said? Was he asking the poor and the sinners to repent? Did he teach them that it is not all right to slurp their food at the table or pick their noses? Did he convert the Greeks and the Romans to Judaism, did he ask them to dress like the Jews and pray to Yahweh?

Did he think that stealing, fornication, drinking and prostrating oneself before wooden gods the worst things one could do? No. Jesus said practically nothing on those subjects. The evil is entirely in the heads of the superior people of our time – priests, scholars, businessmen and government officials. In the heads of the people who thought themselves better and more righteous than everyone else, who thought they had the right to live in greater comfort than everyone else, to dictate to and oppress others, to judge them and live off their labour. That's how it is.'

'Alo, you should have become a real pastor. Your sermons are always so good,' Ellen couldn't help but say.

'You know very well that that was none of my doing. If I had given sermons like that in church I wouldn't have been in the priesthood long. Patronage was everywhere in the Estonian Republic . . . Anyway, at the university they let me be and allowed me to hold lectures. Until they found someone else who knew Hebrew and Greek.

'But let's consider this more closely. Let's think about the world of Jesus today. Who do you think he would teach here, whom would he rebuke, in whose defence would he speak? Who in the world today regard themselves as better than others and force others to follow their traditions and even grow wealthy on the back of their work and property? Who are these people? They're certainly not the Papuans, the forest Indians or the Polynesians. They are respectable Christians – the warmongers, businessmen, missionaries, the people more concerned with the natives not having more than one wife, with their wearing clothes, singing in choirs and their children bowing and curtsying, holding their forks correctly in their left hands and knives in the right and not picking their noses at the table than about whether the people living on their plantations are dropping dead from hunger. These respectable people attend church as expected and donate money for missionary work so that pagans can be converted to Christianity and be turned into respectable people just like themselves.'

'Alo, Alo, you always say yourself that it makes no sense to fight ghosts, but that's precisely what you're doing now. Where are these respectable people of yours in Estonia who are demanding that their children bow and curtsy and give money to missionaries? They're either living in communal flats with one kitchen or they're six feet under in Siberia . . .'

'Don't worry, they haven't gone anywhere. Europe and America are full of them, and there are more missionaries than ever. I read somewhere that there are about ten thousand of them in New Guinea. That's a whole division, several regiments of Christian soldiers.'

'So do you think that missionaries are the most un-Christian Christians of all then?' he asked as the Teacher lit a cigarette.

'The devil knows who the most un-Christian person is. But missionaries are the clearest example of the absurdity, the contradiction of it all. The people who should be converting and repenting are the very ones gaining converts and penitents from among people who are in fact more righteous than they are.'

'So do you think that the Papuans and Bushmen should send missionaries out among the white men to convert Christians to their own faiths?'

'No, I would not want any converting in the sense of conversion to any kind of religious faith. Christ said very clearly that he studied not religion but humanity. The Samaritan – the Samaritans were viewed by Orthodox Jews as dreadful heretics, pariahs – was in fact the more righteous man, and he pleased God more than the respectable Jews because he helped a man in distress. From the Christian point of view, the conversion of the Samaritan to Judaism or the conversion of a Jew to the Samaritan faith is simply nonsense, just a change of labels. The thought process behind it is more or less the same as persuading basketball players to become footballers or vice versa. Christianity is goodness, goodness without distinction between "us" and "them". Therefore many peoples are more Christian than Christians are themselves.'

'Like who, for example?'

'Well, to give an example from near by, then take the Mari people. To them, everything was like them, everything lived and had to behave respectfully and considerately towards everything else. The Mari greeted the forest when they walked through it, they greeted the stream as they crossed it, they asked forgiveness from the tree when they cut it. The same is true of lots of Indian and African peoples. But there's a lovely story about the Mari that you probably don't know.

'Most of them are not baptized, and even the ones that are haven't abandoned their ancient nature-based religion. But at the end of the last century a sect called the Great Candle was formed, and its members, influenced somehow by Buddhism, were vegetarian pacifists; they did not make animal sacrifices, they wore only white clothes and were very devout. And when war broke out in Europe in July 1914 the men of the Great Candle gathered together and performed a ritual which I believe should be included in all books on the history of that war. They put on their cleanest, whitest clothes, collected up all the old weapons from the village – rifles, swords, firelocks and pistols – and dug a large grave and buried the instruments of war according to ritual. This means that they were symbolically burying war; they denounced war. And at the same time Europe's top brains were making bellicose patriotic declarations. The great German theologian Harnack condemned the French; the French Catholic writer Claude poured fire and brimstone on the devil's henchmen, Luther and Kant, and believed that the Virgin Mary would help the French Army . . . Now, you tell me who should be sending missionaries out, who should be teaching whom about the most basic aspects of humanity, respect for life, as Albert Schweitzer put it, one of the few true Christians among the Christians?'

'Hang on. Schweitzer was a missionary,' Ellen interjected. It was clear from her face that she didn't entirely agree with what her husband was saying.

'A missionary ... Perhaps he had to take on the title to get the money to establish his hospital. He was a theologian, too. A very learned theologian. What he wrote about the history of research into the life of Jesus is still one of the best books in the field today. But the book irritated plenty of powerful and respectable clergymen, so much so that at first Schweitzer wasn't even given permission to perform his real missionary work: he was able only to treat the sick; he wasn't even allowed to preach in church – he was regarded as too much of a heretic for that.'

'Wouldn't it be all right for Christians to post their preachers with, let's say, the Mari and the Maris to post theirs with Christians? So that there's like an exchange of preachers or missionaries or something.'

'You're not the first one to think that. Presumably you don't know that Leibniz had the self-same idea in his time. He thought that as Europeans had missionaries in China the Chinese should send missionaries to Europe to teach Europeans Confucian thought.'

'Did anything come of it?'

'Only in as much as Leibniz was nearly thrown out of the Lutheran Church.'

'So you must be like one of the missionaries who preaches the type of Christianity to Christians that they should learn from non-Christians?'

'You could say so, yes. That's a very good way of putting it.'

The room, which was full of blue smoke, fell silent for a few moments.

He felt it was time for him to go. For the moment everything had been said, although he could have spent hours and days talking about the same things. But he mustn't ask the Teacher everything at once, wasting his time on private lectures and private homilies. It would be better for him to read something recommended by the Teacher and ask him to comment. He knew that the Teacher had poems and articles, that he had been published in Estonian journals and newspapers. And he might ask for something by Schweitzer as well.

The Teacher did not have anything by Schweitzer, only a book about him. He could have it to read some time. The Teacher refused to show him his poems. Some other time. Yes, he had to have some offprints from the Republic days still. He got up and went to another room to look for them.

Ellen asked, 'Have you seen Under's latest collection, the one that's been published in Sweden?'

No, he hadn't. Ellen said that she could lend him *Sparks in the Cinders* for a short while. It would certainly be useful and worth while for a young poet to read Under.

And that's how he left the Teacher's, a couple of offprints in his briefcase, one about China, one about the spiritual imagery of the Siberian peoples and a poetry collection by Under.

Outside it was beginning to grow dark. The blossoms on the pear tree shimmered in the dying light. A flycatcher was still singing.

He looked around and felt how wonderful it was that the world was the same as before, the same as when he had arrived at the Teacher's. The potholed street full of puddles, the Pobeda car outside the building next door and the dog patrolling behind the fence on the other side of the road. And yet something had changed. Just as in Yeats's poem 'Easter 1916':

> All changed, changed utterly:
> A terrible beauty is born.

He knew Ants Oras's Estonian translation of the poem, and that's how it felt. Everything was changed. Everything was beautiful.

At home Grandfather was a bit better. He was sitting in the big room and listening to the BBC Russian service. This had previously been a source of irritation. Grandfather was hard of hearing and so would have the radio on very loud. That would disturb his mother's preparations for her lessons. Now and again he would have liked to listen to some music. Once, when he was still at school, his grandfather had come to listen to the radio when a Mozart violin concerto was about to come on. He lost his temper, struck the radio with his fist, breaking the glass on the dial, and ran out of the apartment. He spent several hours alone walking along the streets that evening, smoking. When he came home the shards of glass had been cleared up. No one said a word to him about it, not even Grandfather. They never spoke of it again. Each time he looked at the radio he felt something knotting deep inside. It was like hatred, yet it was not hate. It was probably shame. Fortunately Grandfather was still in good health at the time.

But now he took the Under out of his briefcase and showed Mother and Grandfather. Grandfather began to leaf through the book, and even Grandma came in from the other room. They remembered Under's previous collection from before the war, *With Sorrowful Mouth*, and Grandma still knew some of the poems from it by heart. Grandfather and Mother remembered Under as a person, so they had plenty to talk about. He thought he would copy the poems out for himself before he took the book back. He told the others he would. That's good, said Mother, then she would be able to look at them at her leisure once the pressure of school was over.

That night he fell asleep wonderfully easily, as if sinking into the soft colours of a feather pillow. When he opened his eyes it seemed to him that he had only just dozed off when, in fact, it was already morning. He was surprised that he had not had a single dream. If he had he would certainly have dreamt of the Teacher.

9

The university had a feeling of spring fatigue about it. He wondered whether his ever increasing dislike of lectures and his reluctance to attend at all could be attributed to it or to the fact that after his meetings with the Teacher the things the lecturers said seemed boring and sometimes downright absurd. To say nothing of the history of the Party and the military. But even the language lessons and lectures on general linguistics were dull. As a child he had sat at his mother's side, read her linguistics notes and had gained a very clear picture of the world's languages and language groups. Virtually the same notes were now being read in a dull, schoolmasterly manner by a man who had been at university with his mother. He read well, he paused in the right places, he spelt out which parts should be underlined and repeated the more important points. He listened, wondering what it was that was really bothering him most. It had to be the fact that the lecturer did not discuss things with them but, instead, read his notes out, avoiding any kind of human contact, steering away from jokes and interesting illustrations or from addressing any member of the audience personally. He had his own term for this kind of lecturer: he called them 'pedagogues'. A pedagogue was different from a teacher. A pedagogue was part of the great machine that trained them; it fed them information, turned them into young specialists. The first step was obviously dehumanization. That was what he thought and what he wrote in his notebook, the one which said proudly on the first page 'Diary of Thoughts'. He wrote in the diary mostly when something made him angry. He'd started with it at school, soon after the crushing of the Hungarian uprising in 1956. Then he read a malicious article in the Russian journal *Foreign Literature* about how the revisionist Imre Nágy had said that good capitalism was better than bad socialism. The article held this up as an example of the utter moral bankruptcy of Nágy and those like him, a cautionary example of where revisionism, or deviation from the basic truths of Marxism-Leninism, could lead.

> I feel as if my mind is like an ant in an ant-lion trap. I want to climb out, but I always slide back down to the bottom where perhaps someone's jaws are waiting, ready to seize me and chew me into something more palatable, eat me, make me a new person. I'm reading all this and I don't understand. First, I don't understand how this can be believed and be taken seriously. Is there something wrong with me, or is there something wrong with all of them? There are so many of them: the whole propaganda machine of a

great country, tens of thousands, hundreds of thousands of journalists, writers, 'political advisers', Party members. They all say that revisionism, the process of criticizing and re-evaluating basic truths, is bad. But I don't understand why. Everything in the world has developed through the process of basic truths being criticized and re-evaluated. Why is it all right for physics or linguistics but not for philosophy and history? Why was Einstein acting correctly when he altered Newtonian physics, yet Nágy is a criminal when he questions whether socialism is always as good and sacrosanct as has been thought. Isn't the heart of the matter faith, religiousness? Faith is when something other than the truth is accepted as true instead of the real truth. Is faith born of fear of the truth? Or of a desire to go along with everyone else? Why can't I, then, have faith in either the Bible or Lenin? Why is it so distasteful and difficult for me to talk to believers, Communists and lunatics? They all seem the same to me. Perhaps they are?

Religiousness was genuinely something that disturbed him. The same diary included his first lengthier piece, entitled 'Europe and religions'. The thought behind it was very simple. Europe meant freedom of thought, a free mind; the religions were the enemies of Europe and the free mind. Yet Europe had coped with religions so far: Charles Martel pushed Islam back south of Poitiers; the Reformation overpowered the Inquisition; the Allies defeated Fascism. The latest and most dangerous religion, though, was Communism. Europe, with America's help, had built a protective wall against Communism, just as the Romans did against the German Goths. But the tragedy in Hungary showed that they were not prepared to come to the aid of those people behind the wall who were fighting their own war there behind enemy lines against religion, or Communism. What was this? Egoism or wisdom on the part of the West: Communism had to be allowed to fry in its own fat, to die a natural death.

He didn't write much about Christianity in his schoolboy piece on religion. Now, reading pieces from that time, he thought that he probably didn't regard standard Christianity as a religion; religion to him was something fanatical, intrusive and malign. He hadn't noticed anything of that nature in the Lutheran Church – as a matter of fact he hadn't noticed the Church itself at all. Those relatives and friends of his who went to church did not talk about it or their faith much. Had he simply grown up among Christianity, however thin and weak its atmosphere?

As a young man Grandfather had been a socialist and an atheist. He didn't go to church. To the end of his days he did not believe in God, but he had a high regard for Christ: Christ was, in his view, a good and noble person and a moral teacher. He had a broad group of friends, and they included a number of ministers. But there was nothing in them that he could associate with religiousness. They perhaps reminded him more of actors: they spoke vividly, clearly and sternly. And a lot. He couldn't remember whether they had ever argued with anyone; life had probably taught them to nod sagely at the things people said.

There was one pastor whom he had probably seen in their apartment only once. Mother could not stand him; she said that K had started to visit Grandfather more frequently, probably in a bid for his soul. He knew K's daughter, of course – he danced with her at school parties. He liked her, but she had a steady boyfriend and soon after she finished school they married.

As a schoolboy he sometimes went to church at Christmas, but the feeling he came away with was definitely something other than a religious one. The dull talk and slow hymns in the cold church full of people – it was not nourishment for his soul. It had no soul, no poetry and no music. He discovered poetry and music during adolescence. Suddenly, overnight, reading Lermontov's poem 'The Ship of Air'. He could no longer remember how he happened to read it – perhaps Lermontov was taught in literature lessons at school; perhaps he wanted to see whether he was able to read poetry in Russian. He could. Including the ballad about the emperor who in the dead of night sailed a phantom ship to the shores of France and called to his old grenadiers, his wife and son. But no one came: the grenadiers and his son were dead, his wife was married to another. Dejectedly the emperor approaches the ship, tears in his eyes, and it takes him back to his distant island. And suddenly he felt that tears were welling up in his eyes, too, the great sorrow of the long-dead emperor, his grenadiers and son took hold of him. But there was something more behind the sorrow, something greater than it. That something was alive, it had come from somewhere, it had entered his being and was now living in his young breast, pulsating and breathing alongside him. It was poetry. From that moment on he could not live without poetry. He read Lermontov, Pushkin, Nekrasov and later on Estonian poets as well. The Estonian poets seemed bizarre and ungenuine at first. They did not have the beautiful freedom and naturalness of the great Russians; they were too heavily influenced by everything poetic. The poetic took on for him the same type of disparaging connotations as the word 'pedagogue'. Pushkin and Lermontov were so simple and clear, their poems were almost like prose, but there was a wonderful feeling none the less in their perfect rhythm and rhyme. They had the magic, the enchantment, the harmony, that he had long thirsted for. Harmony that contained sadness and joy, sorrow and fun, alongside each other with a comic feel, sometimes in true combination, sometimes truly as one entity. That was probably the place also occupied by God, Christ and the Bible.

The poetry he discovered could not have been poetry without them, without turning to God, without prayer, without anguish, trespass and forgiveness. As a fifteen-year-old he wrote these lines of poetry entirely naturally:

At the onset of full autumn
you suddenly see and recognize
upon a bloody chopping block
the bloody head of a man

you, too, are called Johannes
before Someone you come
and, laying your head upon the block,
you think: he's already on the way.

The aching storm and urging in his young breast had to be articulated, needed great words. He found the great words in the poetry of Christianity. Christianity was poetry to him, a poem of great, beautiful words, prayers and curses:

Whosoever believeth in me shall not perish. I am the resurrection and the life. The darkness comprehendeth not the light. Woe unto you, scribes and Pharisees. You shall be cast into darkness, there shall be weeping and gnashing of teeth.

He read John's Gospel sitting under the window at home and he felt as if some kind of great, wonderful bird had descended from high above and was looking directly at him. Perhaps it was the phoenix, the Ancient Egyptian bird whose timeless breast bore many markings, including a cross.

He was now also reading Estonian poetry, and his favourite poets could not survive without such great words either. August Sang said that when a star appeared to a traveller the traveller was as a fisherman in Galilee. Heiti Talvik said that only if we gave the last morsel of our last loaf to a hungry person would our prayer be pure in Jehovah's eyes.

And he had his own great words, which he read as if they were mantras and put into his own poems. He could not say that he believed them. He was unable to be religious; his understanding was sceptical as before, his soul unbelieving. But scepticism and unbelief do not give a young man the great words he needs. So he lived as a believer and a non-believer at the same time, although he did not identify it as a contradiction. Poetry simply had to have contradictions. A poem could amalgamate anything with everything: St John with Leole Lembitu, Lucifer with the apostle Paul.

The weather was warming up. He and Malle went for a walk together, a long circuit beyond the town limits and alongside the river. Malle was no longer wearing a coat, just a thin, flower-patterned calico dress and a light jacket. In the evening light he took Malle's hand. He talked to her about the Teacher, poetry and faith; she talked about the grandma who had brought her up, sung to her and told her fairy-tales. Her grandma was a Russian Estonian; she had seen the horrors of the Revolution and the Civil War but had later escaped to Estonia. Grandma's sister had been religious. She lived in Pärnu but sometimes visited for a day. She was extremely friendly and helpful but was always trying to bring her relatives to religion and Jesus. Sometimes women from church would visit her, and they would read and sing. Once she had sung just 'hallelujah' and 'hallelujah' all by herself. Malle asked what 'hallelujah' meant, and her great-aunt had said that it was 'praise the Lord'. Malle asked why the Lord had to be praised. The woman replied that God had given man everything: life and bread and children and a home; God loved us. Malle thought of the boy next door who had drowned in the pond in the garden and his mother wailing horribly and crying and asked whether she had to praise the Lord because her son had died. The old lady said that the Lord had taken the boy to be with Him in heaven, and that it was much nicer to be there than at home in the garden. Malle asked whether there was a pond and a flowerbed in heaven, but the old lady didn't want to talk any more; she said that there was much more to heaven than that but that Malle was still too small to understand it all.

Before going to bed that night Malle asked her mother whether she could go and be with God now, like their neighbour Andres. This frightened her mother, and she said that she definitely didn't want Malle to go and be with God. Malle said that she didn't want to go there for ever, only once to visit God. Mother didn't think you could just visit God. God never let anyone who was with Him come back. Malle then decided that God had to be evil if he wouldn't let her go back to her mum, and she didn't want that kind of God. Mother said that she didn't either, but that they shouldn't tell the old lady because she didn't have any children or any close family and that meant that she needed God a lot. So Malle didn't talk about God to her great-aunt any more.

Malle's body was warmer and softer than before. He felt its pull more and more strongly. The initial desexualizing rapture was on the wane, and it was increasingly clear that his body wanted something and did not agree that a kiss and a caress should be followed by each of them having to go to their own homes. He didn't want to go home. Not only because of Malle's warm body, he just wanted to be away from the apartment, to go somewhere where he could be by himself without his mother, aunt, grandmother and grandfather. He wondered whether he could live alone like a lot of the other students from other places. But he could not imagine life like that. His imaginings were always pierced by Malle, by how they would be in bed together – it was a passionate and thrilling fantasy, all the more so because he wasn't really sure how to visualize it and tried over and over again. Also, how they would wake up in the morning, how Malle walked in her dressing-gown, combed her hair, how they would get dressed together, have breakfast and go out, say hello to the neighbour, and the neighbour would respond to their hello by asking where the young couple were off to so early in the morning. He thought he wanted to get married, that he wanted to have his own home, his own room that he could share with someone he had chosen himself, someone he *wanted* to live with.

He had not chosen his home, of course. He had been born there; he just happened to be there because of other people's desires, by chance. Their home was not really home even to the others. They had been left without a real home when the Germans confiscated Grandfather's house and gave them an apartment in the town. He had a vague memory of the apartment. He had had his third birthday there. He'd been ill, though, and had sadly watched guests, his cousins who now lived in Sweden, and a couple of friends' children, running around shrieking. He remembered that the apartment was full of furniture and that there were lots of crates and trunks in the hall. Grandfather's house had had twelve rooms; the apartment had only (funny to think 'only') six. They had had some of the furniture, pictures and books taken to relatives' in the country, and those had survived. Tableware and two dinner sets that had been in the cellar had also made it, but everything else had been destroyed when the house was hit by a bomb. That was when Grandfather had found somewhere to stay with friends whose large apartment had been abandoned in a hurry by its tenants when the Germans had fled – the man was probably in their employ, perhaps even in the Gestapo's. There were insinuations to that effect, but it was not spoken of. He and his mother had been war refugees in the west of the country, with relatives on his grandfather's brother's side where belongings were also stored. When he and his mother managed to get back they had already settled into a new life as well as they could. There were trunks and crates in the hall once more. His aunt slept on a folding bed; Grandmother and Grandfather had their own bed in the back room; he and his mother slept in his parents' marital bed.

He got his own bed when he reached adolescence, before the changes taking place in his body began to be noticeable to himself and others. It occurred to him that he might have got so used to sleeping alongside his mother that he would not be able to sleep well alone. He could not and nor did he want to. He wanted to sleep with a woman. With a girl. With Malle. But the road to that goal was long and complex.

On the road to the dormitory they turned off into a small park where, under the maples and among the lilac trees, there was a bench that couples and drunks would move further into the bushes; the park warden (he wasn't quite sure whether such a post existed) would pull it back out into the open again.

He saw that the bench was unoccupied and said, 'I don't want to go home yet. Let's sit down for a bit.'

'Just for a bit then,' Malle agreed. 'I still have some homework to look at for tomorrow.'

In one respect it was better on the bench; in another it was worse for kissing than standing up. Because they couldn't do it properly any other way, Malle had to sit on his lap. She was no featherweight; she was built like a proper farm girl. But at first he barely felt the weight – it hid in the shadow of her closeness, her warmth and her passion.

They kissed – it was more like an extended existence within a kiss than kissing. It was as if time was passing more slowly – heat and cold, heavy and light became confused. A meteor shower played behind their closed eyes, the dance of thousands of burning sparks.

The kiss quenched the thirst but sparked a new, deeper, darker hunger. Their noses touched, and they looked into each other's eyes. The girl's face was a dark sky with tiny twinkling stars. He wondered whether it was the reflection from lamps in the distance, but that wasn't important just now.

'I think I've fallen in love with you,' he said, surprising himself a little.

'I know I've fallen in love with you,' came the reply.

One of Malle's hands was on his shoulder. He put one of his hands under her jacket and slid it along her back. He could feel her shoulder-blades, her spine, the flesh on her back; he reached her hips and as far as her buttocks. His hand moved itself along her thigh, to the edge of her dress, caressed her thigh and then slid where it had only ever previously been in his dreams. Her inner thigh was warm and smooth. The girl squeezed her legs together hard. He left his hand there between them for a while and felt the blood pulsating in his fingers. He was happy, so happy that even desire was somewhere far away. He realized that he should not move his hand, and so he did not. They kissed again. When their lips drew apart he could no longer leave his hand where it had been, he moved it forward and nearly reached the place where her thighs ended, but then Malle took his hand, pulled it out from under her dress and on to her lap.

'Can't go there,' she said.

'My hand doesn't know it can't.'

'Tell it then.'

'I don't know if it will listen to me.'

'Dear, good hand,' said the girl, stroking his hand, 'just you sit here nicely in my hand. Don't you leave me, OK?' They stayed like that for a few moments, then the girl said, 'I have to go now.'

He would have liked to protest, although he felt that the spell was breaking. His desire was fading, he could feel that his legs had begun to go to sleep under the girl's weight, and his stomach was rumbling. They kissed again, stood up and set off.

'*Hasta la mañana*,' he said to Malle at the dormitory entrance.

'*Hasta la mañana*,' came the reply.

They were both going to Spanish classes.

He stood on the other side of the road for a few moments and watched as Malle reached her door, turned, waved to him and disappeared inside. Then he set off towards home, in the exact direction of the half moon that had risen over the rooftops and the park trees. There was the smell of smoke and earth in the air. Somewhere, someone was having a bonfire.

Mother was still up. Grandfather had been poorly. He had taken a sleeping pill and was asleep. Mother asked if he wanted any supper. He ate a few pancakes and drank some milk. He would have liked to say something to her, but she didn't ask and he didn't know how to broach the subject. He thought he would invite Malle over some time.

When he went to bed it was already nearly one o'clock. A party was leaving the inn singing, 'Far away, far away over the bank, in the free tides of the Volga . . .'

10

Time passed quickly. He had written all of the Under out in his grey notebook, illustrated the title page and written in block capitals SPARKS IN THE CINDERS. He was also mentally preparing an outline of the things he would ask the Teacher about – Dravidian languages and their relationship to the Finno-Ugric languages was one and another was the Tasmanians. He had read that they had been the most archaic of the world's peoples and had lagged furthest behind in terms of development. He had also decided to try once more to persuade the Teacher to read him some of his own poems. Or let him read them.

Not a single blossom was left on the pear tree, and there was no trace of them left behind on the ground. The expression 'flower froth' encapsulated it perfectly, he thought: the flowers evaporate, melt into one, like a froth. Where does the white of the froth disappear to? What about the whiteness of the flowers? Are they both just an illusion?

The black-and-white cat was sitting on the steps again, washing its face. The cat was evidently not an illusion and was obviously not thinking about what was an illusion and what wasn't.

The Teacher himself came to open the door. He looked more cheery than the other times. His voice was more like that of a young man's when he said, 'Have you come for the poems? Come on in. I have a visitor, but perhaps fate has decreed that the two of you should meet here today.'

A blond, bespectacled young man was sitting in the room, smoking.

'Allow me to introduce you,' said the Teacher.

The young man's handshake was warm and firm. There was something about him that he liked at once, something that was both delicate and strong, intelligent and athletic.

'Rein is reading theology,' said the Teacher. 'I was at university with his father. His father subsequently received further training in Novosibirsk *oblast*.'

Ellen appeared in the doorway with a tray and some coffee cups. 'Rein is like a son to us. He has two sisters, and his mother had no work at the time and no apartment. So she used to do some typing for Alo and the children stayed with us, too.'

He gave the Under back to Ellen. The Teacher got up and went into another room; he returned some moments later carrying his exercise book and extended it towards him with a bow.

'There are some very good poems in here,' he said. 'I couldn't help myself; I've put little plus signs next to them in pencil. I've done a couple of underlinings, too, in places where I think something could be expressed better, I mean more succinctly, more accurately or more vividly. But otherwise . . . perhaps I should also say that you must continue to write. Some people need gentle reassurance. It's probably not such a big issue with you. I get the impression that you're somewhat uneasy and tense in the company of others but free and confident when writing. That's no bad thing to be.'

'Would it be worse the other way around?' enquired Ellen.

'Yes, at least where the poetry is concerned. No doubt about it,' said the Teacher. 'Someone who is self-confident does not generally start writing poetry. He has no issues with himself or, at any rate, fails to recognize them; he shoves them aside and lives fully, with both feet on the ground. He becomes a leader and steers both traffic and people. Someone who writes poetry neither leads nor allows himself to be led. Poetry is an island that stands alone. Poetry is autonomy.'

'So what about if poetry is written in accordance with strict rules, in the classical style? There's no *auto-nome* in that, no following your own rules, so how can the poetry be an island that stands alone?' Rein interrupted.

'Can classical poetry ever be poetry?' the Teacher asked. 'It's more of a social game. That's the type of poetry, the type of understanding of art, that has always prevailed in Europe. Europe has always worn a suit of armour, and its understanding of freedom has always been that the old suit of armour must be swapped for a new one. Adopt new rules, learn to play the new social game.'

'Is the same true of modern art?' he asked.

'Well, what is it you call modern art?' the Teacher went on. 'There's the type of modern art which, like the romantics, tries to find expression in something that regulated art could not and would not allow. Art that tries to penetrate more deeply looks more boldly into the dimness within and around us. And then there is another kind of modern art created by cunning businessmen who have discovered that the word "modern" is a good brand. Modern art carries the "fashion" brand. The art isn't as important as the brand; the artist has to be able mentally to supply the brand for his own work and will serve customers with that brand. Modern art like this is, in fact, even more classical than the art that once came into being at the whim of kings and emperors. Here art comes into being at the whim of businessmen. And it has to bear that alien whim, that alien armour with its alien coat of arms.'

'Like our art here,' he said.

'Like our art here,' the Teacher repeated. 'Here and everywhere. Everywhere where there are brand names and men's memories are brief enough for it to be little trouble to proffer something old and recently forgotten as something new.'

Silence grew. Rein blew a beautiful smoke ring followed by another, smaller one.

'Were you taught that at school?' Ellen teased.

'Yes, at school, but not by the teachers, only the big boys.'

'Well, naturally it's always a greater pleasure to learn from the foolish than it is from the wise.' Ellen would not let it drop.

'So what do you want,' demanded the Teacher, 'when an entire culture is constructed on the basis that the new and the young are better than the old? One must rid oneself of the old, the old must be cast out, whether wise or foolish. Consider first and foremost the fact that it is old. Similarly the new. It's as if we're living in a fashion house. In a fashion house no one ever asks whether the new dress is *better* than the old one. It's just *new* and *modern*. That's why I also resist the expression "modern art". As if it were really of any importance whether it is *modern* or not.'

'So what is this cult of fashion based on then?' he asked.

'That's an easy thing to ask, but the answer is not at all easy to give. And in all seriousness I for one don't have any simple answer I can give you. The one I like best is that of a Chinese ethnologue. He regards family relationships as one of the most significant factors in culture – a charmingly Confucian point of view, isn't it? – the primary relationships such as father–son, mother–son, brother–brother, mother–daughter and so on. In each culture one of those relationships is dominant and dictates many of that culture's main features. In places where the father–son relationship is dominant, such as China, there is no desire for rapid change; the important thing is continuity, gradual transition. The old is not replaced by the new, it does not have to disappear, to perish, to make way for the new, instead the old gradually becomes new but is retained in the new just as the father lives on in the son. The son in his turn becomes a father and so on. A society of that kind is traditional, conservative, but not rigidly so; the old does not have to *battle* against the new. In the West the man–woman relationship is dominant. And according to Doctor Hsu this means rapid jumps, uncertainty, the unexpected. The Bible says that a man leaves his father and mother and cleaves unto his wife. In his view this shows that this was already the custom among the ancient Jews, that this Western-type innovation began with them. Here a man leaves the relationships he has always had and creates a new one from scratch. The old is cast aside. And in Western literature there is a very important struggle for the right to marry for love. The battle between the old and new relationships. Parents would like their children to stay with them, or at least decide who their spouse will be, but the children want that right for themselves.'

'But didn't it used to be the same in the West? Parents would choose a spouse for their child never mind what the young people involved had to say about it,' threw in Rein.

'That may well be the impression one gets from reading the pitiful love stories about the lives of kings and counts. For them marriage was an act of politics and economics – as it was later on for the rich and powerful. Marriage was a union of property, nations and concerns. But among the ordinary people things were simpler and more humane. The ethnography of Estonia proves as much. The idea that your daughter could be forcibly married off or a wife taken for your son against her will was more likely to become a reality in areas where that was the practice among rich "Mogri Märt" farmer types. Why was this or that partner unsuitable? It was always because of money, because they were poor. But once upon a time the choice of marriage partner and bedfellow was clearly more of a matter for the young men and women themselves.'

'Oh, please don't say that young people choose better and more wisely than their parents would on their behalf,' said Ellen.

'Well, if parents really did want the best for their children, as they all say they do, they would be able to choose a life partner for them more wisely than the young people themselves could,' the Teacher agreed. 'I could give some good advice to certain people here if anyone wanted to hear it.'

'Matchmaker service open here as well,' Ellen commented. 'Perhaps you should start with these two young men here?'

It was alarming, amusing and fascinating all at once. Allowing the Teacher to find a wife for him. A wife he would choose for him. Yes, how about Malle? Could it be Malle?

For a moment he didn't register what the others were saying. Then he felt compelled to ask, 'What should my wife be like?'

The Teacher laughed. 'I should give it some thought. I feel I know you quite well. After reading the poems and so on. So I perhaps know the types of young lady that would suit you very nicely. I also know, though, that I am not in the business of matchmaking. Read some psychology. That should sort it out. There are a few very simple rules that people should know. Especially if they want to commit their life to someone else.'

'Such as?' asked Rein.

'Such as the fact that the man and the woman both subconsciously look for a parent and a child in the other person. And if there is no match of ideas there will be misunderstandings. And then there's the old question of whether similar people are a better match than dissimilar people. There's no simple answer to that. For example, most of us are takers or givers. Givers like looking after others; takers want to be looked after. Two givers can live together splendidly, two takers cannot make a good job of it. A taker and a giver make a good match.'

'How do you identify who is a giver and who is a taker?' he asked.

'It requires extensive observation, especially of more significant situations such as on journeys, travelling or, let's say, before pay day when the money's run out. In many families one partner will forego his or her favourite dish without perhaps even registering the fact; the other partner, of course, feels compelled to have it.'

'The second partner is, of course, the man and the first, the one doing the foregoing, the woman,' said Ellen.

'That's how things have been in our culture: men have been trained more to be takers, and women givers. However, psychologists have shown that things go deeper than that, that there's perhaps even something hereditary to it. Occasionally women become bigger takers than men, possibly as some form of payback, overcompensation. Just as the biggest drunkards often grow up in teetotal families.

'This can all be identified using various tests, but they're not in fashion with us. If you come across them anywhere, try them. I dabbled in them a little as a young man. For my own amusement. Some people collect stamps; I collected psychological types. There wasn't much literature about it at the time, but there's a lot more nowadays. In America, for example, the armed forces are involved with a lot of practical psychology – all air force and submarine personnel are selected on the results of a thorough testing process. They have to get on with each other; otherwise the military machine would not operate smoothly.'

'But love,' he couldn't help asking, 'do people usually fall in love with someone who would be a good match, or is there no connection?'

'As little or as much as the connection between summer weather and winter weather,' came the Teacher's reply. 'Falling in love, love, getting along in later life are very different things, as the divorce statistics show.'

There was silence for a while.

'Could I see your poems?' asked Rein.

He had no objection, only he didn't want to hand over the notebook until he had studied the Teacher's annotations and underlinings.

Would Rein be coming back here soon? Perhaps, although he wasn't sure. Maybe they could meet up over the summer if they didn't do so before. He could come over to their house. He'd have to think about it.

He felt now was the best time to ask the questions he'd prepared about Dravidian languages. 'You said you'd had some dealings with Dravidian languages. Is the closeness to the Finno-Ugric languages that some people have discussed just a coincidence, or is there something to it?'

The Teacher lit a cigarette and inhaled deeply. 'I assume I don't need to explain the difference between typological similarity and language families?'

No, there was absolutely no need. He had read about it himself, and it had been discussed in lectures.

'The typological similarity is in many respects high, even astoundingly so. For example, negation in several Dravidian languages is expressed by means of a verb as in modern Finnish and old Estonian: *minä en ole, sinä et ole* . . . There's also a lot of onomatopoeia in Dravidian languages, and it is similar in structure and has a plethora of word pairs like our "*lihma-lohma*" – "rickety-rackety" – or "*sinka-vonka*" – "zig-zag". There is even a word of this type that describes the darkness of the night.'

'A bit like *"pilkane pimedus"* – "impenetrable darkness",' he said.

'Yes, a bit. But the instances of such words as *"pilkane pimedus"*, *"uhiuus"* – "brand new" – or *"risti-rästi"* – "criss-cross" – are much greater in their languages. They're called "echo words". And there are other things that coincide, but things are more of a puzzle when it comes to the question of whether languages are related. When I looked into it in Germany there were no etymologies, and grammars of the individual languages were few and far between, too. There are more of them now, but they are no longer obtainable. I don't know whether there's any point in studying the matter. Investigating a language family is rather like researching an aristocrat's family tree – it's mostly an eccentric hobby, nothing more.

'Look, you can go back several thousand years into a language family if you're dealing with the languages of major communities. But in the Mesolithic or Palaeolithic eras, when human communities were small, there was the potential, I think, for languages to get mixed up in so many different ways that it makes it difficult to talk about a family. Imagine that there was a community of twenty people where the women were from a different tribe or clan and they initially spoke a different language from the men. Something had happened to the men; they were killed while hunting or in a war. The women were left with the children and new people joined them who spoke a different language. It's my view that a community of that kind may construct a hybrid language that is a descendant of several different languages but related to all of them, even though their individual languages bear no relation to one another. Until now, linguists have believed that languages cannot combine on an equal basis; one of them will always retain its grammar and basic vocabulary while the other loses its. I believe that it is by no means impossible that this has happened in the past.'

'So the potential link between Dravidian and Finno-Ugric languages may be the result of some kind of a blending process dating back to the Stone Age?'

'I don't know. I'm more inclined to think that there is more to it. We all come from the south, at least from the area out of the reach of the glaciers. And the ancestors of the Dravidian and Finno-Ugric peoples may well have lived in close proximity somewhere in the south for a long time – perhaps they in their turn had the same ancestors. But later some of them went north, some perhaps, went south and some west. They migrated where there was empty land, following the retreat of the glaciers maybe. Later, in the Neolithic era, when agriculture emerged and both food and other things were in storage, movement from poorer areas to more prosperous ones began: from the wildernesses to the cultivated lands, from the country to the town. Like in the Old Testament story of the Jews who wandered in the wilderness until they reached Canaan. The Jews were neither the first nor the last to wander there. Wave after wave of people came, as beggars or soldiers, conquerors or refugees.'

'So then the towns began to grow, like Babylon, and . . . ?' he asked.

'Yes, but not as much as you might think. The towns were alluring but ruinous. It was good to be among people in the towns, but one was also among rats, fleas, lice and flies. And that meant that the towns became breeding-grounds for disease. The number of deaths in towns exceeded the number of births; new people were always coming in, but for the most part they kept the number of citizens constant. Now and again there would be an epidemic and the towns would be left completely empty. Until new people came to take the places of the dead . . . This is perhaps one explanation for the disappearance of several peoples. Why did Acadian replace Sumerian as the language of Mesopotamia? You should keep in mind that the Sumerians were town-dwellers, they had no hinterland, no rural population. So when a plague virtually wiped out a Sumerian town – plague is mentioned in their literature; they cast spells to appease the plague god – the Semites wandered in from the wilderness. Nomads are better protected against plagues than town-dwellers. In the end there were so few Sumerians left that their language was not preserved.'

'Didn't the Semites just wipe the Sumerians out?'

'No, I don't believe so,' the Teacher went on. 'The Sumerian language was sacred to the Acadians; it was taught for over a thousand years as a dead language, just as Latin would be in Europe later. It couldn't have been the language of an enemy or of a despised, inferior people. Estonians would not adopt Russian for use as a ritual language in the way the Acadians did Sumerian, and neither would the Greeks adopt Turkish.'

It seemed that neither of the young men knew or was capable of asking anything else. Rein looked at his watch and said that he would definitely have to go in half an hour. He thought he would leave, too. But then he remembered one more thing. 'Last time we talked about your poetry. You said perhaps I might see it some time. Would it be possible?'

A wry smile spread across the Teacher's face. It was difficult to make out whether the request pleased or annoyed him. Perhaps even he didn't know.

'Alo, you can't back down now,' said Ellen. 'You've been able to read his poems, why don't you show him something of yours, too.'

'The stuff I've got isn't neatly copied out,' pleaded the Teacher, persisting in what was by now hopeless resistance.

'Perhaps you could read something from the newer poems you wrote last spring and summer,' volunteered Rein.

The Teacher sighed heavily – or pretended to – got up and went into another room. They could hear him opening cupboard doors, rustling papers, before he reappeared in the doorway, holding a thick file stuffed full of sheets of paper. Wordlessly, he sat back down in the armchair and began to rummage through them. The others waited in silence. Then he took out a sheet of paper which had once clearly been a page of an almanac, raised it to his eyes and contemplated it for a few moments. Then, softly, he began to read:

> Already there's sorrow in the thrush's song,
> and the bracken has buried the path on the slope
> you followed to the river, little onlooker,
> and pausing amid the fragrant hay
> you see the sunpatch straying in the pine trunk.
> Like a finger, it motions you hither, yon
> or from time itself the glimmer of darkness,
> a spark to resin slumbering many years past
> now, suddenly, quickened in your childish glance.
> And the first shy step taken
> under a sun which once shone here long ago
> under the amber pines which once rose up here.

'What's an amber pine?' he asked.

'It's what you call the pines that used to grow around here but more on the hills of Scandinavia – amber is made from their resin.

'This poem is about one of my childhood experiences or insights. I had read a Chinese fairy-tale book in German that included a story similar to the ones the Celts abound in – about a young man who chances upon a fairies' home and stays there. I felt a huge, profound sorrow, the sort of sorrow that comes from the fact that the age-old fairy story was not true. I left the house secretly and went up the field to the forest. I walked around, the sun was already going down and was shining on the bark of an old pine tree next to the path. I stood and saw how the patch of sunlight moved gradually like the hand on a watch, and suddenly I saw a completely different scene, a different forest. The sunpatch was in the same place, but the pine was completely different, much, much bigger and taller. There were lots of them; I was in the middle of a great primeval forest; it was thicker and darker than our forest. I realized that I was somewhere else, in a different time and place, yet strangely I felt no fear at all. There was a good, happy feeling, as if I felt that this time the ancient tale had come true, only I wasn't sure what sort of ancient tale it was.

'I stood there under the immense tree, and I remember thinking that I probably shouldn't move or I would break the spell. But then a big blue dragonfly flew straight towards me – it might have flown into my face if I hadn't jumped to one side – and then I don't remember what happened, although I do remember I sat there in the same place. The sun was already setting, it was cold, the midges were biting my face and hands. I realized that I had probably been there like that for a couple of hours ... When I got back home my mother and grandmother had been worrying about what had happened to me. I said something about watching the birds – I was a would-be ornithologist at school – and that was how it was left. Later I visited the place often, but nothing of the kind ever happened again. Although, I must confess, I would have liked it to.'

Again he felt his head spinning. Most likely because of the smoke rather than the Teacher's story. He wanted to say something, ask something, but he didn't quite know how. 'Did . . . did you find any explanation for the experience? Did you really find another place in space and time or was it just an illusion?'

The Teacher laughed. 'I think the experience taught me to understand that the word "illusion" should be used with caution. Later on I studied books on botany, and, from what I remember of that forest, it fits: I was in an Oligocene or Pliocene forest, I don't know where, perhaps in what is Estonia now. Clearly I can't be here now and there then at the same time, although I can't even be sure on that point. Either the Tertiary period is here now and there are some kind of rifts or tunnels in time that one can travel through to get there, or one of my experiences is false: either here now or there then.'

'But there were no people in the Tertiary period!' exclaimed Rein. 'How could you really be there?'

'No human remains have been found in northern Europe in strata from the Tertiary period,' corrected the Teacher. 'That does not mean that there were no people there. And besides, I didn't see myself, I saw this ancient forest. I don't know who I was – perhaps I was a creature that was part-man, part-ape.'

He suddenly had a thought that he had to share with the others. 'But might it not just be that the pines and ferns, the forest, weren't bigger, but that you, in fact, were smaller? You didn't chance upon the earth but yourself in the past?'

The Teacher looked straight at him. 'I hadn't thought of it like that. It may well be worth considering. Next time I will tell you whether it could have been like that. But, in fact, I should go there and see; it would be a kind of *experimentum crucis*. Ontogenesis or phylogenesis.'

'We could have a little trip out there in the summer,' said Ellen. Perhaps seeing the puzzled look in his eyes, she added, 'All of us, of course. Alo and I occasionally go on a little trip across Estonia. "Wilt thou the poet understand? / Then get thee to the poet's land," as Goethe wrote.'

'Stop, or they'll think we've got busts of Goethe and Schiller on top of the cupboard in the back room,' laughed the Teacher.

'Honestly, what is it you've got against Goethe that means you always have to make some comment when I quote him?' grumbled Ellen. 'But Rein will probably have to go soon. Are you going to read any more poems or not? To my mind, if I'm allowed to say three words in German, *einmal ist keinmal*. Read a bit more.'

'Thy will be done,' said the Teacher and thumbed through his pile of papers again. The next sheet he found bore the word INVOICE on the back. He read:

Still powdery snow falls on the field track
as the whirlwind swept over the void.
Is he, too, homeward bound? Soon only
your pulse and the ticking of the clock
will disturb your dream and the slumberings of your old house.
The pendulum still works, but not the cuckoo:
can I still remember his voice and face?

Two axes strike, space is a chopping block,
into the darkness tumble heads and splinters . . .
If everything there is dark, cold and mute,
and the thought for the day gives up its final spell –
who is protecting me and the birds in the heavens?

They spent a few moments in silence, then Rein said, 'I really must go now.'

He said he had to leave, too. His questions on the Tasmanians were unasked, but he had the feeling that he couldn't cope with any more. It had been a lot to take in, perhaps even too much. He wanted to go outside into the fresh air.

'Please visit us again,' said the Teacher when they said their farewells in the hall and gave his good wishes for more beautiful poems.

'I don't want to be a nuisance, but if I have something to ask you then I will come,' he said. 'Or perhaps if I can borrow an important book.'

'Just a moment,' said the Teacher. 'I'd like to give you a book – I think you'll like it.'

He went into the back room and returned with a book. The cover bore a picture of hills and the title *My Encounter with India*.

'I liked this book much more than all the others written on the subject. The author writes very beautifully and has managed to consider serious issues with a good sense of humour.'

He thanked the Teacher and wondered whether the book was also a sign that the Teacher really did want him to visit again. It would have been too fantastic to believe, nevertheless.

He would bring the book back in about a month; he couldn't read English any faster.

Certainly, that was fine. There was no hurry for the book.

Outside they were met by the warm, fresh spring air. Somewhere close by in the garden a chaffinch was singing loudly.

He had recently heard from someone at university that the Lutheran Church had some kind of distance-learning courses whereby you could train for the ministry. Is that where Rein was studying?

Yes. What other choice did he have?

'Couldn't you go abroad, perhaps to the GDR or Finland?'

'The Germans and the Finns would be more than willing to take our people, but the Central Committee won't allow it. Well, it would, but we can't agree to their conditions.'

'What do they want you to do?'

'To send their own people to the West using us as cover. More or less one real theologian and one fake.'

'And you won't agree?'

'Not so far – at least, not while the present bishop is in office.'

'Can't they just get rid of him?'

'Their powers are limited here. The bishop must have a proper theological training and be acceptable both to the local ministers and the Churches abroad with which we have the closest links. And they don't have any of their own people among the clergy.'

'Haven't they tried to infiltrate you?'

'Oh yes, but it didn't come off. A couple of lads were smuggled in as students with us, but one didn't even start at the school and the other failed for spiritual reasons. There are certain characteristics that are required even for a post as an ordinary provincial pastor that the spy couldn't fulfil. He'd had no contact with his congregation; the people sensed immediately that he couldn't be trusted, and in the end he was found out. He'd made a porn film in Pärnu with some Muscovites. They wanted to use it in some anti-Church thing, but our bishop went to the Central Committee, said something and the matter was hushed up.'

'So the Church is the only democratic institution in Estonia?'

'I suppose you could say that.'

'And this distance-learning college of yours is the only place where you can get the proper training?'

'Only for training for the ministry.'

'What lectures do you have apart from theology?'

'Languages – German, Latin, Greek and Hebrew. History of the Church and philosophy.'

'And there's no historical materialism, dialectical materialism or Marxism?'

'There's no need to study them to become ordained. But we are required to invite lecturers to talk about Marxist philosophy and political economy.'

'Militant atheism, too?'

'No, nothing on those lines. Nothing would come of it.'

They turned into an unpaved side street.

'I'm almost there,' said Rein. 'One of my relatives lives here – my sister, too, as a lodger. Some friends have to drive to our home village today and promised to give me a lift.'

It occurred to him to ask where Rein actually lived. Rein gave the name of a small village that he knew very well.

'It's not very far from the place where I used to spend every summer with relatives when I was a child. Surely you must know it?'

Rein thought he did, although he'd never been there.

He stood in front of a gate that led into a small yard where, away from the street, there stood an old wooden building that had sunk slightly into the ground. A dog began to bark in the yard, and Rein shouted 'Quiet, quiet' to it. The dog whined and gave another yelp but of a different kind; the rage was gone.

'You can come and see us in the summer, if you've got the time and the inclination. We're definitely there for the whole of July and August. There's a bus. But phone the pastor just in case, then you can be sure your journey won't be wasted.'

He said he'd definitely take him up on it. He cycled a lot, sometimes even from the town to his aunt's, a good eighty kilometres away.

Oh yes, Rein would be pleased to see his poems and perhaps show them to his sister. He promised to bring them with him.

They said their goodbyes. Rein rang the doorbell. He turned to leave.

When he reached the city centre it began to rain. He quickened his step, although the rain was quicker still. He had to hang his clothes up to dry at home. His aunt hurried to find a dry shirt and handkerchief and make him some hot tea: spring colds could strike you unawares.

The door to the back room was closed. Grandfather had got worse again.

He would have liked to read the India book for a while, but there was nowhere to read. He thought he would get up early in the morning and go to the library. It was peaceful and quiet there.

11

He and Malle studied together, mostly in the library but sometimes, when the weather was warm and fine and they didn't need to carry a pile of books with them, somewhere on a park bench. In the evening they sometimes went to the cinema. They lingered longer and longer over their walks home afterwards, and their caresses became ever more passionate. His hand knew her body almost completely and now virtually had permission to touch the places that had previously been off-limits to him. Desire was not dimmed, however, by these furtive visits; instead it grew, became keener and sharper. He knew he wanted Malle. He wanted to take her naked and enter her, enter the warm, gently moist cleft between her thighs that his hand sought more and more often to break into and not move away from.

He wanted to talk about his desire to Malle, but it was difficult. Much more difficult with words than it was with kisses and caresses. But little by little he learnt how to express his desire more clearly in words. He wanted to be with her completely, really completely. He wanted them to spend days and nights together, just the two of them. He wanted them to be like the first people, without clothes, without shame in a garden somewhere where there were lots of trees, where they had time to learn about each other's body. He wanted to know her body like he knew his own, all over, inside and out.

When he whispered as much to Malle between kisses, he felt her stiffen; her body, which had clung to him in abandonment, became tense; even his hand had to move away from where it most wanted to be.

He didn't understand what it meant. When he was caressing her, touching her, her body was molten and open to everything, so why should words have completely the opposite effect on her? He tried to ask her about it, but asking was even more difficult than talking about his swelling lust. And the questions that he did ask were more distasteful to her than his expressions of desire – at least, he received no clear answer to them. Malle would either close his mouth with a kiss or say, 'Please don't say such things' or 'I don't know' or, 'Please stop if you can.'

He sensed that something was wrong, that there was something, some obstacle on her part that was interfering in their relationship, but he didn't understand what it was. Malle was the first woman in his life apart from his mother to whom he had felt so close. And he had not been close to his mother for a long time, but with Malle he really was, but now she had put up an incomprehensible barrier. He soon realized that he couldn't talk about it to Malle herself. He had to understand what had happened, what was wrong, if anything. Perhaps there was nothing wrong with her, perhaps the guilty party was the impetuous haste born of his desire. Perhaps he just had to give her time, perhaps the road to bodily intimacy, to sex, was one to be travelled one step at a time. Perhaps it was more important to talk less and to allow their bodies to talk their own primitive language and make the breakthrough that was not so easily achieved by words. That was what he thought, but his thoughts led to so many questions and doubts and ultimately gave rise to the fear that in the end something was really wrong, that ultimately he would never get to have sex with Malle.

He understood that this relationship with Malle was not easy, and the realization wounded him like a knife. He wanted to be true to her, but he didn't know if he would always be able to. If only she had been that someone, an experienced woman slightly older than himself who would help him.

He and Malle were both afraid of the First Time. The difference lay in the fact that he wanted it faster – he didn't want to wait any more, to worry whether he would manage it or not – but Malle clearly wanted to put the whole thing off to some unspecified future time.

A heatwave was upon them. Everything flourished, grew and blossomed; the lilacs were finishing. Even over in the library, where it was normally cool, it became stuffy and torrid. He had the idea of going to Peedu with Malle to study somewhere by the edge of the forest and the river. Afterwards they could walk to Elva maybe, and then go back to Tartu. He suggested it, although with a hidden agenda, hoping that perhaps when surrounded by nature he would be able to get closer to Malle – maybe in midsummer, amid the blossoms and the birdsong, her fear would be less than her desire. He didn't know whether she sensed his purpose, but she gave no impression of doing so and agreed immediately.

The weather forecast did not disappoint; the heatwave continued. When he reached the station with a quarter of an hour to spare before the train, Malle was already there in her light-green calico dress with the small floral print. On her forehead a tiny bead of sweat sparkled at her hairline.

Malle had seldom travelled the Elva–Tartu line – in fact, only a couple of times. He, though, had known the route since childhood when he and his mother and aunt had spent a couple of summers in Elva and Peedu. Later on, too, he had often had things going on there. He was able to tell Malle all of this as the train moved through early summer's plump greenery, stopping every ten minutes and allowing passengers, mostly young couples, to alight. He suddenly thought of Stravinsky's *The Rite of Spring*. The arrival of spring and summer was signalled by sexual rites, although not publicly any more. He thought that the First Time had become a rite of initiation in his imagination. He wasn't sure if he wanted to become a man, although he definitely wanted to leave childhood and adolescence behind.

They alighted at Vapramäe. He showed Malle the remains of the ancient sacred linden and the tomb of the Chinese Red Soldier. Relations with China were no longer warm, and neither delegations nor schoolchildren visited the tomb any more, but it was still there. They stopped in front of it for a while and kissed. The beads of sweat on Malle's forehead had grown bigger; it seemed to him that her lips also had a salty flavour.

'Haven't you ever thought about learning Chinese?' asked Malle, as they walked on.

'Yes, but I never seem to have had the energy; it feels too difficult. I think I'd like to learn English properly first so that I don't have to keep looking things up in a dictionary all the time when I'm reading.'

While on the path he held Malle's hand, but then they turned off and he had to go in front. Somewhere here among the bushes and firs there should be some small clearings that couldn't be seen from a distance: safe and sheltered places to be.

They spread Malle's old checked blanket on the ground and arranged themselves on it as comfortably as they could. The next exam was one they both had to do – Party history. It wasn't difficult, but it was repulsive. Old Martson clearly heartily believed what he taught, although he was too old and usually too bleary-eyed to start picking faults in anyone. He didn't particularly like giving fives, but neither did he like failing anyone. As they both wanted scholarships they had to try harder and do enough to get a four. This meant remembering all the Party congresses and conferences and what was done at them. That was a difficult task because according to the official history they were all exactly the same, took only the correct decisions and dismissed the incorrect opinions of revisionists, renegades and others who had been led astray. Unfortunately, the correct and incorrect opinions were so declarative and vague that they tended to become a blur. And woe betide any student who in Martson's presence muddled Party Congress XII with Party Congress XIII and didn't know which was the one that considered – that is, determined – the nationality question.

They had read a couple of pages when he was unable to resist making a comment of his own. 'Have you noticed that the Party is like some kind of superman, an *Übermensch*, that leads, decides, predicts and does other things that people do, except it doesn't consider, believe or think. Does the Party know that it doesn't need to think?'

'One of my schoolfriends is studying veterinary science at the Agricultural Academy. She says that when they carry out a rectal examination on a cow – which means you have to stick your gloved hand into its anus and try to work out what's in its rectum – they all focus on the fact that the Party is guiding their hand . . .'

The country girl in Malle was coming out a bit, the girl who took many things at face value as she would have at home. But unfortunately not everything.

He stroked her buttocks; they were temptingly taut under her red sunbathing knickers.

The sky was almost cloudless; high above a pair of swifts was wheeling, and in the forest towards Vapramäe a chiffchaff was singing tirelessly 'plish-plosh, plish-plosh'. From the river a garden-warbler answered. On his right-hand side there was a higher tussock, perhaps with a stone underneath. There seemed to be an anthill in the tussock; the ants scurried about carrying tiny grains of sand.

He thought that he would like to be an ant for a while and clamber along Malle's body, slip inside under her knickers and watch her from there. Would that vast female body – her mound of Venus like a real wooded hill – have an exciting effect?

He felt that desire had relented in the heat and space; he was even able, despite everything, to read the Party history. But the other desire, the desire for initiation, did not leave him; it reminded him that the day was passing and the shadows would soon be sliding on to the blanket, on to Malle's back and buttocks; it reminded him that they had only half a day. No, first they had to study. He didn't want study to be just a pretext; he didn't just want to seduce her. That may have been his design, but there was also a genuine motive; there had to be. They had to have a break from the grind.

He reminded Malle of this after the first hour had gone by. A human being shouldn't sit down and read for over an hour without moving, one of his medical student friends had said. They put their books aside, sat up and opened the lemonade bottle. It was warm, but it still helped quench their thirst.

Then they kissed. Malle did not resist at all; she was warm and close like in the beginning. They lay down after a few moments, holding each other close. Now his lust returned. He pressed his hand under the girl's knickers, stroked her, groped her more passionately and more determinedly than before; the resistance came belatedly and more half-heartedly, and next minute he found himself pulling her knickers off. Going further was not so easy.

'Please don't, please be sensible,' she tried to cover herself, but it was not easy to do what she wanted.

'I can't ... I just can't bear it any more ... I've never even seen what you look like without them on ...'

He realized that his voice and behaviour were foreign even to himself, and even unpleasant, like the whole situation, like Malle's resistance. Yet he couldn't stop; that would have been even more unpleasant.

Her knickers came off; he felt her finally kick them off herself, almost lifting her foot out of them. A moment later his black swimming trunks were lying next to Malle's red knickers and they were almost naked; they would almost have been ready. Unfortunately, Malle's spirit was not willing and her flesh was weak, as he clearly saw. The thought flashed through his mind that the stories of female conquests were actually true. He had got past the first line of defence, but the real stronghold remained unconquered, the gates closed.

He knelt before the girl like a believer of yore before a goddess and almost prayed to her, begged her to open her thighs and let him receive her blessing. The prayer was little use. Malle also begged him for something, the exact opposite. The boy's prayer was 'Now', the girl's was 'Not Now', and they could not be reconciled. He had to push her thighs apart himself, although he knew that no blessing would be forthcoming this time. His body, exhausted from the excitement, could not feel much, at least it could not find any opening there in this place that he had reached for the first time in his life. In the shade of the hair all was moist but closed, and his body could be patient no longer. The inevitable flow gushed on to the closed moistness.

It was a relief all the same. He sank down, spent, beside the girl and buried his head between her head and shoulder. Something had happened none the less. He wanted to hold her firmly in his embrace; he wanted to rest, gradually sink into nothingness, melt into the summer sultriness through the body that had for a while been so close, almost his own.

He felt something wet trickling down his face. Malle was crying silently.

They said nothing. Then he raised his head and asked, 'Malle, darling, why, why now? I don't wish you any harm, but . . . I just can't, I just want so much to be with you, be with you completely, like this?'

'Darling, I know, I know you want to . . . I want to love you, but I can't . . . do you understand? I'm scared, I'm so horribly scared. I can't explain it. I can't do anything about it. I don't know why I'm like this. I'm really sorry, but I don't want – I really don't want – us to start sleeping together now, right now and . . . I think . . . I hope that it will pass, that I'll get used to you and then . . . I love you, you know . . . Can you wait for me? Can you bear it any longer?'

He couldn't say he understood, but could he bear it . . . yes, perhaps he could. If he really had to. He didn't like it that his desire was so strong, but he couldn't do anything about it. He didn't know how. Desire would be appeased once they were really together completely, sleeping together and waking up with one another . . . Was Malle afraid of getting pregnant? They could do something about that; he would do everything, *they* could do everything, to prevent it.

No. Malle knew enough, she had two friends who were studying medicine whom she'd talked to at length. But the fear was something else, something that intellect could not overcome. It just happened. Like desire just happened for him.

'I knew this might happen. I was afraid to come here with you. But I was also afraid that if I didn't come you'd be very upset . . . And now you're upset anyway. What shall I do with you?'

He felt tears welling up in his eyes, too, now. They lay in each other's embrace, naked, and cried. In the forest the chiffchaff was still making the same 'plish-plosh' sound as before, and a skylark's song was rippling out over the field.

They went to catch the train from Peedu. The shadows were already long, the food bag empty and twenty or so pages of Marxism-Leninism had been read.

He stopped on the bridge, pulled his watch from his wrist and threw it into the river.

'What did you do that for?' asked Malle, startled.

'Let it be a sacrifice. To us, flourishing, to both of us always loving each other.'

'That makes me think that you don't love me . . .'

'I do, darling, but . . . it could be better.'

It was a truly diplomatic reply, although unpremeditated. Did he now have to be diplomatic with his own girlfriend, always thinking how to put things so that she wouldn't be hurt or offended? He knew that he was too direct, and that this often annoyed people. But none the less there had to be someone close, some person with whom he could be absolutely frank and blunt. He thought these things, but he didn't share them with Malle.

As they said their goodbyes at the door of the dormitory the sun was already setting; only from the window on the upper floors could a glitter of reddishness still be seen. Suddenly he felt that the evening shadows had descended, drawing a veil between the two of them. He didn't tell Malle this either.

On his way home through the park the fragrance of the last lilacs found its way into his nose. In a garden somewhere a garden-warbler was singing.

12

Over the following days he felt worse. He didn't even know if it would be more difficult to resign himself to Malle's unwillingness or to his own powerlessness; he simply did not know where things were going or what he should do now. It wasn't exactly the best frame of mind for studying, but he nevertheless managed to memorize the congresses and conferences in the correct order and get a four from Martson. Now he could breathe more easily. He only had the history of language exam and the military test to go. Language exams weren't usually difficult – the subject had always interested him – but the military stuff was ghastly, as bad as Party history although easier. The old colonels, war veterans, were pleasant men with no illusions about university students being trained officers, and so they didn't take their work especially seriously. Nor did they have any objection to going to the inn with the students on the evening of examination day and having a proper party. But there was some time to go before then. He was able to immerse himself in the India book he had acquired from the Teacher and read Wells's *The First Men in the Moon* and *The Time Machine* in English.

Outside it was suddenly summertime, a thing vast and free. His thoughts were already in the country at his great-aunt's where he had spent many a summer week each year since his childhood. He was now making his plans to travel there when the exams were over. And call in on Rein.

He and Malle were seeing each other less. Sometimes he felt an enormous yearning for her, and then he would seek her out at the library or the dormitory and they would go for a walk. But there were things they did not talk about, and Malle seemed to like it that way. They caressed and kissed, but there was something different in their caresses and kisses. He wondered whether it was wariness or even a slight estrangement. Sometimes he felt they both needed a bit of time to be on their own and make sense of their own feelings. If that was at all possible.

When he left for the Teacher's with the fully read India book the heatwave had passed. The weather was cool, the clouds low and occasionally there was a cold fog.

'Please forgive us, Alo has a visitor at the moment. They are discussing work matters. Could you come back later or tomorrow at about the same time?' Ellen asked him at the door.

Of course he could come back either later or tomorrow, for now he would merely return the India book. But he asked Ellen to decide which of the two times would be better.

He hoped it would be 'later', but Ellen said she couldn't say how long Alo would be with his colleague so tomorrow would be better. She apologized; perhaps his hope for today had been all too visible in his face. All there was left to do was say goodbye and go. Where? Home? To the café where presumably Aleks would be ensconced with his little group, perhaps Peeter, too? To Malle's? In fact he didn't want to go anywhere. He had geared himself up for meeting the Teacher, talking to him. Talking to someone else, listening to someone other than him just wouldn't do; it wasn't what he wanted. He would much prefer to be alone, but there was no right place for it. Not in the town. There was only the attic or the barn with the books in the country, but there was still a while to wait before he could go there.

His legs took him automatically in the direction of the railway to the edge of town. That was where his ski trips had started in winter; the atmosphere of the railway in summer was no draw to anyone except for the birds, drunkards, stray cats and dogs who found shady patches among the mugwort and willows. He went along the path which led to the dam and then over it. No train was visible. He bent down and put his ear to the rail: someone had told him that this was a way of hearing a train that was still far away. This time there was no sound. The train was evidently further than far away.

He remembered how as a child in Peedu they had put kopeks on the railway tracks. When a train went over them it left the kopeks splayed out like enormous pancakes. He still had a couple of them even now somewhere in a drawer. If he was sure that the train was coming soon, he thought, he would still put some kopeks down for it even now. It would have been an absurd thing to do, although he couldn't and wouldn't have wanted to do anything more sensible. Best of all would be just to switch himself off until tomorrow. To be non-existent, to be someone else, even a child – well, all right, the child who once lived alongside the railway in Peedu, counted the coaches on the trains and put kopeks on the tracks.

He didn't want to stay and wait for the train, though – and the weather wasn't exactly the best for sitting and waiting either – so he carried on along the path. On the other side of the railway there were fields and spinneys. The path became what you could call a country road. He went off to the left; this way the road should double-back towards the town.

The rain had held off for a good hour. Occasionally, to the south a small patch of blue sky peeped through. In defiance of the wretched weather a skylark was singing overhead.

He reached some kind of warehouse surrounded by a high, board fence – parts of which had fallen down – topped with a nailing of barbed wire. It made him smile – anyone who really wanted to get inside could easily climb over. Someone had once explained that if you spread your padded jacket over the barbed wire there was no need to worry about ruining your trousers.

Behind the warehouse there was a small glade where two huts stood and a red cow was feeding; most likely one of the huts was its barn. Perhaps it was the one to which the German shepherd was chained. He wondered whether it was possible to keep a cow here just outside the town. Whose land was it? Did it belong to the town or a collective farm?

Behind the glade was the start of the first line of houses, constructed in the 1950s, for which the owners had had to sacrifice so much. The house of one of his great-aunts should be here somewhere, too. They were peculiar people and didn't get on with their neighbours in the flats so had decided to bring their own home here, to dismantle his great-uncle's farmhouse log by log and rebuild it in the town. That wasn't difficult to do; the most onerous job was then to make a real town house out of a log cabin. They had no money to pay for materials and labour so tried to do as much of it as possible themselves. His aunt burst a blood vessel in her head carrying a bucket of mortar up the stairs. She died a couple of days later, and her husband and daughter were left alone in the unfinished house. They were a bit odd, and not many people associated with them: the widower had some faith of his own (he was probably an anthroposophist), made all his own meals and was always arguing with everyone.

The street he'd chanced into led to the stadium, a place of which he had childhood memories. As a tiny child his godmother, who had lived near by, had brought him for walks here. His godmother was the wife of a pastor from Petseri; her husband was in a gulag and she lived with their son Sergei in a courtyard of a large house in the housekeeper's room. They were desperately poor. Mother always said that he should never eat at their house because they never had anything to put on the table for themselves. His godmother was a real Russian who would have wanted the earth to swallow her up if she had been unable to offer her godson tea and buns. When he went to their house there was always a white lace cloth on the table, a samovar on the cloth and a platter of currant buns. She had given her godson probably everything she had to give – a small silver cross, an icon of the Madonna and a Slavonic-language New Testament. On holy days she always brought them a wax candle. He knew that his godmother always had candles in church for him and his father by the Vladimir Madonna icon. And they cost money. This caused his mother some embarrassment. She wanted to help her son's godmother, but she couldn't really afford to – like his godmother, she had no real job or income either. She finally managed to come up with a clever scheme. Sergei would visit them once or twice a week at home or meet up with her son in the town, and the two of them would speak Russian. It was her view that her son should master his father's language fully and, as her own command of Russian was not extensive enough for that, a private tutor was required. Sergei's mother liked the idea, and she had no objection to her son giving conversation classes for roubles. But on each occasion she would give her son something to take, whether it be a cake, a bottle of juice or a jar of jam, and his mother soon realized that the effort to help had come to nothing. The person who benefited from the desire to help was the person doing the helping. He remembered that the Teacher had divided people into two groups, givers and takers. His godmother was definitely one of the clearest examples of the first group, a person whose meaning in life was to give, to serve others.

That had all been long ago in his childhood. His godmother was now dead, and Sergei had gone to Leningrad to study radio engineering. He wrote sometimes and received Christmas and New Year cards; they had always written entirely in Estonian, a language Sergei had not forgotten in Leningrad. He'd visited a couple of times and talked about his life. In fact he would have liked to study something else, perhaps philosophy, but his father's shadow still hung over him, and ridding himself of it would have required grovelling to an extent that he was not prepared to do. The field of exact science was easier. Sergei said that there was one boy on his course whose father had been a clergyman and a girl from a well-known family of aristocrats whose family sent her books from Paris. In philosophy seminars they held very liberal discussions, something which the philosophy faculty students, under the watchful eye of the loyal Marxists, would not dare to do.

Sergei's father, whom his son barely remembered, died in Siberia without reaching home. But at least he had been able to send letters back. Some of them were more in the style of memoirs and religious reflections – his godmother had given them to his mother to read. He wondered whether the letters were still around; they were very interesting. Perhaps it would be possible to send them abroad for editing and publication.

He reached the stadium just as it began to drizzle; there was a new grey cloud overhead. He stood in the grandstand, sheltering, and smoked a cigarette. There was a good view from here of the running track and the football pitch. He didn't even understand why he liked the stadium. He had had bad experiences of sport as a child. He had coped with gym drills but was very wary of ball games. Each lesson he hoped that there wouldn't be enough time for the games that the other boys looked forward to, but usually there was. He could not catch a ball, and, whether it be shooting-ball or basketball, he was a hindrance to the others, something they made only too clear to him. He would have preferred to do something else although it would have been difficult to convince the teacher why he couldn't play ball games and why he didn't want to. So he kept his silence and waited for the end of the gym lesson, for the weekend and most of all for summer, when there were no gym lessons and he could run, swim and ride his bike.

His retrospective was interrupted by a drunken party who, like him, hurried under the shelter of the grandstand. Two girls and two boys, one of them carrying a half-full bottle of vodka.

When they saw him, one of the girls shouted, 'Hey, there's a holy monk here. Looks like he's smoking frankincense and saying his prayers.'

'Don't talk rubbish, he's just pissed off. Some girl prob'ly wouldn't give him one. Am I right?' added the other girl and gave a loud, drunken laugh.

The four of them had turned up out of the blue like a ball in his schooldays; he didn't know how to catch it or throw it back. He tried to stay calm, although he knew it wouldn't end well.

'You bloody bitch,' one of the boys' voices rang out. 'It's you who wants to give him one, isn't it! Go on, lift your skirt up then. P'raps your fanny'll be good enough for him.'

'Bollocks,' corrected the other one. 'You've got such a huge arse. No way's it good enough for the college boy. His type has to have a classier kind of fat arse . . .'

He got up and left. The rain was preferable to the foul language. He would have liked to believe that it didn't really get to him, but he wasn't sure that that was the case. The girls were rough and fat, but there was something about one of them that affected him, perhaps would even have aroused him if he had bumped into her somewhere else. He would have liked to look back, run his eye over her better, but he couldn't. They were making obscene comments about his departure but then found more interesting company and topics of discussion in the bottle.

Would they make love here later, perhaps even have group sex? he wondered as he walked to the stadium gate. A student had said that one of the lads on his course had screwed his girlfriends here on the stadium benches. He would have liked to erase from his mind the picture that the memory brought along with the encounter, but he realized that he wouldn't be able to. The uneasiness from which his visit to the Teacher would have liberated him for a while had been sown anew in his mind. Now he had to wait until tomorrow. It occurred to him that he was like a bird whose desire is to fly high into the sky but finds itself drawn back towards the earth by a fine thread and forced to live in a shitty dove cage watching the doves cooing and mating; the bird never finds a companion to fly high into the air with, to coo and mate with somewhere in the clouds or on some exalted perch beyond them. That was something doves don't do but swallows might.

At home they had a visitor, a distant relative of Grandfather's from the countryside where their family was from originally, a place which was home to several families with their surname; they were probably all related to each other somehow, although he didn't know exactly how. Grandfather probably didn't know either; at least he'd never talked about it in any detail.

The relative was sitting somewhat shyly at the coffee table, clearly unaccustomed to drinking coffee and eating Viennese pastries, and giving them the news from the country. Collective farms had been merged, their wages increased; his grandson was back from military service, and they wanted to build a house in town. In old age it was better to be in town and it was easier for the children to find work. Several people from their village already had a house in town. Grandfather said that if things carried on like this the countryside would soon be empty of people. The relative agreed. During the times of the Forest Brotherhood and the deportations half their farms had been left empty; some of them were being lived in by people who were there by chance, people who burnt the outbuildings down in winter and couldn't be bothered to repair the roofs. Some had come back to their home villages from Siberia, but many had not; they had gone straight to the town. The houses were left to rot, and some of them were already completely dilapidated. The cowsheds rotted and crumbled quickest. Grandfather thought that perhaps it was because the timber in the sheds was always slightly damp and eaten by moths and decayed more quickly than house timber.

Grandfather was in good form – even his hearing seemed sharper. Perhaps it was something to do with the fact that the visitor had a loud voice, as country people always have. He listened to them talking and thought how sad and unfair it was that Grandfather, who spent all his time thinking about the countryside, fields, crops and his orchard that had been taken away from him with his land and his house, was now spending his own miserable last days here in a cramped, communal apartment. He would most likely be a completely different person if he were able to potter about in a garden in the morning, inspecting the apple trees and the bees or watching the tomtits carrying food for their chicks into a nest-box.

The relative spent the night with them as he had to see the notary in the morning. They made a space for him on a mattress on the floor, and they all went to bed that night earlier than they would have otherwise because their guest's eyes were beginning to close against their owner's will.

13

The weather was the same the next day, cool with showers, as if in retaliation for the spring's early warmth. In the morning he sat in the library and read a history of language in a somewhat absent-minded fashion. He wasn't taking this exam seriously; the subject was inherently interesting but had been so pared down in the syllabus that only a superficial, trivial element had been left behind. The history of language was a mass of rules that allowed French and Spanish words to be made out of Latin ones. It was simple, as simple as secondary-school maths, where he often couldn't be bothered to memorize formulae and instead derived them himself when he needed to. So he skimmed his eyes over what had been written about vulgar Latin and Latin dialects. As an example of the latter all textbooks use the lines of a Latin poet who reproaches the Spaniards for not drawing a distinction between the words *vivere* and *bibere*. Since in modern Spanish, too, the letters 'v' and 'b' sound the same at the beginning of a word, it may be surmised that this peculiarity in pronunciation is very ancient. As is the understanding that living and drinking are almost the same thing.

What really interested him were languages about which not much is known, not even the language group they belonged to – Iberian, Ligurian, Etruscan languages. Had he ever asked the Teacher about them? He thought not. As a rule he needed to make a record of what to ask the Teacher in a notebook somewhere so that the important things would not slip his mind. He didn't have a notebook, all he could do was take a scrap of paper on which he wrote 'Etruscans, Iberians'.

The rain had probably stopped; the sun was shining through the window right on to his table. A couple of hours more, then he would go to the Teacher's; it probably wasn't polite to go at midday, this was probably his best time for work. What to do in the meantime? He had had enough of the history of language. Perhaps have a look at what the library had on the Iberians and the Etruscans. He went over to the card-index catalogue, selected 'Linguistics' and flicked through. It was really thrilling. He liked dealing with rare, strange things, with the Irish people's own language rather than English; instead of French, the languages spoken in Southern Europe in days long ago. He had the soul of an archaeologist or perhaps simply a collector. Or perhaps the soul of a scholar who is interested not in the known but in the unknown.

There were two books on the Etruscans: a newer one in Russian and a study in German from the beginning of the century. He went up to the assistant, Salme, who knew him well, and asked for the keys to the linguistics cupboard. It was a sensible move; he knew that he would spend at least a good hour rummaging through the cupboard. One more hour after that and he could go.

When he left the library, the Russian book on the Etruscans in his bag, a shower had just passed overhead and the sun was shining again. The wet asphalt was steaming.

This time the Teacher opened the door himself. He was sad and thin and seemed a lot older than he really was; his eyes did not have the same spark as they had on previous occasions: they were grey and empty. Only his bow was as it had been before. It gave him the courage to think that his visit was not just an inconvenience.

The ceremony of being seated and offering and lighting up cigarettes also happened as it had the first few times. But something was different, and he suddenly felt unable to initiate the conversation. The scrap of paper with the questions on was still in his shirt pocket, although it would embarrass him to take it out. They sat like this for a while in silence, smoking.

Then the Teacher, as if continuing with a ceremony under way, asked, 'How are the exams going then?'

That was easy to answer, as were the questions that followed about his family and what he was planning to do in the summer. Here he took the opportunity to talk about his plan to go to Rein's and ask about Rein's family.

The Teacher and Rein's father had studied together at secondary school and had gone on to university together to study theology. Rein's father had become a proper theologian and clergyman, but the Teacher, in his own words, had made nothing of himself. Apart from a nuisance to others.

'The Chinese have a lot of beautiful sayings. One is about me: "Frogs laugh at the dragon floundering in a puddle."'

He couldn't stop himself from saying that not everybody who watches the dragon is a frog and not all of them laugh at it. Some admire him and are ready to learn from him.

'What, young man, what?' the Teacher replied, with unexpected sarcasm. 'It is not worth learning from dragons how to flounder in the mud or how to wail, but it is worth learning to fly from them. I, however, cannot fly; I have clearly failed as a dragon. It would be wiser to abandon me and learn something more sensible and more important. Like book-keeping or how to drive a car. And instead of thinking and harrying your brain you could learn the dictionary of common sense by heart. It has a phrase for every situation in life; with a bit of practice you will still earn a reputation as a witty man. What more could one wish for?'

What more, indeed? He felt that it was difficult for him to respond to this question which, obviously, was not meant to be answered. Nevertheless, he felt as though he was in a predicament. 'Maybe, I don't yet know what else . . . but what I do know is that driving and learning the dictionary of common sense and the stuff you said won't bring me satisfaction. Perhaps I need something else?'

'Are you sure?'

Yes, he was sure. No qualms whatever.

'I believe you are right. But do you know why that's so? Why you wouldn't settle for what 90 or even 95 per cent of people would settle for? Do you like being different, better than others? Were you damaged as a child, made a fool of, or are these things of no importance? Or is what interests you is simply the subject itself, the real Truth, if I can use that word?'

'Ristikivi said in one of his poems: "I don't say Truth, it's too vast a word."' He felt unable not to quote from the poem, which had been among his favourites for a number of years.

'Beautifully said. Have you got the text?' enquired the Teacher.

He felt relief; suddenly the thought flitted through his head that his companion's sombre mood was a pretence or slightly overdramatized. The depressed Teacher had in any event shown that he had an interest in something (he clearly had not feigned it) and, moreover, that he would be able to do something for the Teacher, do him a service and wrangle a pretext for visiting him.

Yes, he had the text and others, too. He could bring them over and show him.

The Teacher nodded. 'I would like that. I remember Ristikivi well. I once talked with him at length. I expressed my surprise that he wrote just prose. To my mind a small people like the Estonians cannot have decent lengthy prose. He disagreed. He said that he had written some poetry but that writing prose was simply of greater interest to him . . . So it would be good to know which poems he had now published.

He remembered by heart a couple of lines from 'Land and People' and recited them:

> 'Bluish lines
> in the light of fields;
> burgeoning veins
> in early March.
>
> 'Break defiantly
> winter's barrier.
> Straying, seeking
> they reach the river.'

The Teacher nodded thoughtfully. 'Beautiful fragments, but only fragments. I am reminded of Rimbaud. You must know it:

'It has been found again.
What? – Eternity.
It is the sea departed
to the sun.

'Don't you think there's some similarity in the rhythm and mood?'

Yes, there was some similarity. Although Rimbaud's used bigger words, as the French always do. Eternity found again. The sea fled away with the sun . . . He wanted to agree with the Teacher. But the Teacher seemed to have sunk back into his earlier depression. He, too, remained silent, not knowing how to continue the conversation. Then he remembered what had led them to Ristikivi and Rimbaud. Truth, a word which to one of them was too vast. Yet eternity was clearly not too vast for the other.

'Going back to the truth . . . I think I'm not all that interested in being different from others. As a child I was always bullied at school for being different. I had a Russian name, a Russian father, I was afraid of ball games and knew some French words. Sometimes I wanted so much to be like the others, to feel an interest in sport, technology, buying, selling and swapping stamps, catching fish and telling dirty jokes.'

'Did you try?' responded the Teacher. He wasn't sure whether there was irony or genuine interest in his voice.

'Of course I tried. And managed it until I hit puberty. Except for sport. I built a two-tube radio, I read books on cars and electric motors, I went fishing, collected stamps and fought back when provoked. I was almost accepted, I almost belonged, although I was a bit of an oddball. But then everything changed. I discovered poetry when I read Lermontov. It made this life and this world so grey and empty all at once that I was no longer able to conform . . . I began to go about alone, be alone, to write poetry and read it, too. That's probably when I began to think as well. I remember one occasion that was definitely significant for me. We had a half year of optional Latin at school. I wanted to learn it, of course, and the guy I shared a desk with came, too, at the start but didn't keep it up. He said it was because Latin was of no use. I didn't like that idea. I tried to defend my choice and suddenly a thought came into my head which I find hard to put into words right now. It was something like, fine, Latin is of no use for the things you want. But would what you want – say it was studying technology – be of any use in anything else? Is it not the case that the use can simply be pleasure? You've got your own goals, and the things that are useful to you are the ones which help you achieve them. I've got my own goals and uses. Your goals and mine are our own choices, and neither of us can say that they are any use.

'It also occurred to me to wonder what use it was to argue over usefulness? I did a mental somersault and realized that somehow I had thought myself free.'

The Teacher nodded. 'That's a really good story. I can truly say that that is how someone begins to think. But it is also thinking in self-defence, searching for truth that is strong enough to stand up to rational truth – truth that is a sword or a shield. But is there such a thing as truth that is neither sword nor shield but simply truth?'

He had to confess that he hadn't entirely understood what the Teacher had said. The Teacher explained. 'There's a Sufi story about a holy man who was walking around, carrying a burning lantern and a pitcher. When asked what they mean, he says that the water is for dousing the flames of hell and the fire is for burning down paradise. Then people would love God for Himself, not because of any promised punishment or state of blessedness.'

'Yes, but hell keeps on burning in the minds of most of the faithful, and St Peter is standing at the gates of paradise.'

'The mystic wasn't talking to everyone, only to those people who understood.'

'Yes, but there's a paradox . . . It reminds me of something that happened when I was a child. Hell and paradise in miniature. I had a great-aunt whom I was afraid of. Sometimes she was spiteful and made me stand in the corner when I'd done something she thought naughty. But she often had chocolate or sweets for me. Once, when she was on her way over, my mother told me I had to be a good boy – likely as not she was a bit afraid of Aunt Ella as well. I said I would be a good boy because then Aunt Ella would give me sweets. Mother said that I wasn't to think like that; a good boy had to be good without thinking of sweets or of the punishment which being naughty would bring. I thought about it and didn't understand how I could be a good boy at all. I *knew* that I would be rewarded for being good and punished for being naughty. I couldn't not think about it –'

'Do you really talk like that: "couldn't not think"?' the Teacher interrupted.

'How should I have said it?' he asked in a panic.

'Well, one possibility would be to say "couldn't help thinking", that's a more correct Estonian way of talking. Or "leave unthought" or even "remain unthought". It really pains me how a disciplined Balto-Finnic language is going to pot, becoming Indo-Europeanized and more primitive. When the Russians came I hoped that at least we had escaped the German influence. But not a bit of it; exactly the opposite happened.'

'Could you give me some more examples of Germanization in the Soviet era?'

'There are so many of them in the language. Some of them came in through Russian. Like "*kujutab endast*" – "represents" – "*predstavlyayet soboy*". What sort of Russian is that? When I read Russian newspapers or newer books it crosses my mind that the last person who had a decent grasp of Russian was Count Tolstoy.'

'But *War and Peace* is half in French!' He was unable to suppress his surprise.

'*War and Peace* is nothing special in terms of language. But just read his fairy-tales, textbooks, things he wrote for children. Compare them with today's

Russian-language schoolbooks that we translate into Estonian, then you'll see.'

Ellen came in, sat in the empty chair and lit a cigarette. The Teacher remained silent and his head sank a bit further.

'So, in your view, during Estonian independence and the Soviet era, Estonian language and culture have continued to become Germanicized?' he pursued the issue which had stirred his interest.

'But of course. Germanized habits and attitudes have not gone anywhere. The Germans' cast-offs are always the best and newest. What the Germans have, we must have, too. Take the verb *haben*, brass bands or comic plays. All our energy has been spent on imitating and admiring the Germans. Old Veski added words to the Estonian language by going through Pavlovski's German–Russian dictionary and identifying the words which didn't exist in Estonian, then taking equivalents from dialect words. Several people worked on this to ensure that the Estonian language would become Germanicized and Russified semantically and lexically.'

'But German and Russian are completely different,' put in Ellen.

'They were, yes,' the Teacher continued. 'Russian used to be a proper Eurasian language with a Finno-Ugric substratum, but it's becoming an increasingly Europeanized, second-rate, impoverished European tongue.'

'Can't you ever stop berating the Germans and Europeans, Alo?' sighed Ellen. 'Our guest has got the impression that you hate the Europeans and the Germans.'

'What do you mean, "impression"?' said the Teacher hotly. 'I do hate them. I've hated them half my life, and I'll hate them till I die. Germany is Europe's heart and soul, and Europe is a phantom, a zombie, a delusion, which we all reverentially believe in. In fact, Europe does not exist. Eurasia does – or, more accurately, Eurasia together with Africa and Oceania, the great supercontinent of the Old World where there are several different kinds of geographical and cultural areas. But Europe is not one of them. Europe is divided into separate areas, and the more important ones extend over its boundaries. Take the Mediterranean, for example, the Taiga region, the steppes and semi-desert. The southern Italians and the Greeks are closer to the Palestinians and Algerians than they are to the Finns or Dutch.'

'So how did this vision of Europe come about then? Who founded this thing that you call the phantom of Europe?' he asked.

'The lust for the power of the popes and the German people's Holy Roman Empire. In their language it was: "*esse – subjacere*". Existence was limited to who and what was under their power. Everything had to be standardized. One holy Catholic Church, one set of laws, one language, one opinion. Even the names became more and more similar – there are Jaans, Johns, Janises and Giovannis from the Atlantic to the Urals. From the outset the European ideal has been totalitarianism, a concentration camp. And the greatest Europeans, the Germans, have now gloriously made it a reality. And their students are now trying to do the exact same thing the world over.'

'But nowadays power in the world lies with the Americans and the Russians!' he argued.

The Teacher replied, 'I've already talked about the Russians. The Anglo-Saxons are fairly similar to the German Saxons who invaded here in the thirteenth century. The Celts in Ireland and Wales call the English "Saxons" – "*sassenach*" in Irish. And in the Near East (and Greece is effectively part of the Near East) Western Europeans are called "Franks", which is almost the same.'

'Do you think that European civilization today is worse than other civilizations? People live here better than ever, slavery, poverty and want have disappeared from Europe, literacy and the right to vote are universal. Wherever people have tried to find alternative systems to Western democracy things have gone mad like in Nazi Germany and red Russia!'

He could not sway the Teacher, who replied calmly and confidently as if he had had to do so many times, 'My dear boy, in their day Roman slave-owners and Baltic barons could have said the same, and South African slavers can do so now. They also lived or live splendidly, they have no wants or poverty; they are educated and know how to have their say in running the state. The aristocrats, the better people, the more prosperous citizens have always had democracy. It's rubbish that the Greeks invented democracy. The Greeks invented the division of people into people and creatures – slaves, who were merely tools who could talk. There's nothing like that in China or India, the home of true civilization.'

'Oh, Alo, now you really are overegging it,' interrupted Ellen. 'Do you really think that things were so wonderful in China and India and the Europeans only brought distress and unhappiness to the world?'

'That's exactly what I think.'

'Would you have been pleased if the Mongols had conquered Western Europe in their day as well? Or if today's Russians had halted at the shores of the Atlantic instead of the Elbe and had begun implementing the Soviet system from China to Spain?'

'I would have been pleased if the Americans had designed their atomic bomb for Berlin and Nuremberg instead of Hiroshima and Nagasaki. If Germany had been carved up between the victors as Poland was.'

'I simply will never understand your hatred at all!' Ellen said and got up. 'I don't think you wanted to see the Estonian Republic destroyed. Or do you think Russian domination is better than us having our own country?'

'Just listen to yourself – "our own country"! And what a country "our" Estonian Republic was! A country of social climbers who imitated everything German, where the national language was German with Estonian words, where trade was under the control of the Scheel Bank and the rulers, with some exceptions, wanted the Germans to come and take power before the people became too disaffected or the Reds arrived.'

Ellen said nothing more and left.

He got the feeling that he should leave, too, although what he had heard was so surprising and in such stark contrast to everything he had grown accustomed to hearing at home and among his circle of friends that he couldn't help but take up the topic again.

'Don't you think the situation was pretty much the same in Israel during the Assyrian and Babylonian conquests. Would you be on Nebuchadnezzar's side if you lived in those times?'

The Teacher raised his head and looked at him. 'No, why should I be on Nebuchadnezzar's, I mean Nebuchadrezzar's, side, albeit he was an intelligent, tolerant, humane person? I would, though, try to explain to the men with power what many prophets tried to explain at the time. Namely that unless they improve their ways, unless they have concepts of justice and reason, then disaster will strike, a king of Babylon or someone else will come and will spare precious little of their kingdom and power. I would not be in the least bit sorry if a storm were to blow them away, although I would be sorry for the innocent people who succumbed to the wheels of history's chariot along with their arrogant, foolish masters – like the tens of thousands of Estonians who found themselves in Siberia or in exile because the leaders of Estonia and Western Eurasia were incapable of conducting a wise policy.'

'What should the leaders of Estonia and Europe – sorry, Western Eurasia – have done differently between the two wars?'

'Estonia should not have followed the trend for dictatorship and aped Mussolini and the others but should instead have remained true to its democratic constitution. And a lot of small steps should have been taken, perhaps establishing a government in exile, in any case not banning people from emigrating as Päts did after the pact on the military bases. That was merely the final act of the tragedy, however. The first acts were staged largely without any involvement on our part. What the *entente* did was complete madness. First Germany was subjugated and humiliated as much as possible; the German people were made beggars by the reparations. Lenin said that the Treaty of Versailles held the seed of another war. That much should have been plain to any sensible politician. It wasn't. And then, when Germany had fallen into depression, desperation, it was no surprise that a party like the NSDAP emerged and took power. That was the moment when someone should have intervened. In the beginning there was the time for it as well as the opportunities, and Hitler even provided a good pretext by taking armies to the Rhineland. The last opportunity was just at the beginning of the war when the Germans flung their entire army at Poland in a Blitzkrieg leaving practically no units in the west. The French could then have launched an offensive and made enough ground. This would, it's now clear, in all probability have produced mutiny among the senior military and the removal of the Nazis from power. With very little difficulty and few casualties Hitler could have been ousted and the world war would not have happened.'

'And Estonia would have remained independent?'

'If that's what you call independent, then yes, clearly. And likely enough the Germanized administration here would have changed, too.'

He felt he should go. The Teacher was clearly in a bad mood; perhaps he felt ill. But he was reluctant to leave. For the first time he saw a person who was talking about Estonian affairs and the former republic completely differently from the way others did when such matters were discussed at home or among his friends and acquaintances at university. What the Teacher had said was something that squared with the newspapers and official history books. It astonished him, although it did not distress him. He would have had no difficulties in replacing his own views with the Teacher's – but he would have to understand them better first.

14

The lilacs had blossomed, seeds were already falling from the maples and the jasmine in the parks had opened. The exams were over, including the military exam, which he had celebrated with the colonel and several bottles of cheap wine in a waterside inn on the banks of the Emajõgi. All but one of the boys had got through: the odd one out was the pale-faced historian Viljar who had started at the Naval Academy and then, when it came out that his father was abroad and that he would consequently never be allowed to visit capitalist countries, he gave up on his dream of being a sailor and came to university. But his nerves were shot, and he was occasionally prone to losing control of himself completely. Like now: the colonel had started to scold him, and he had leapt on to the table and left the room by jumping from one table to the next. Peeter Härmsoo had not had the best time either. His first exam question was 'A soldier's duties in the event of an attack'. As he knew nothing specific about any duties of this kind he talked in a loud, agitated and shrill tone about a soldier having to know the decisions of the Party and government and having to be guided by the teachings of Marxism and Leninism. The second task was the Kalashnikov. Peeter managed to strip it down, but when he was trying to reassemble it a spring slipped through his fingers, went flying over the tables and pinged into the blackboard. He got three, a satisfactory mark, and went out through the door; the colonel looked at his retreating back, shook his head, smiled and said, in Russian, 'Interesting fellow you've got there.'

In so doing, without really knowing it or wanting to, Peeter had established a good atmosphere in the exam room that made the ordeal easier for those who followed. And the colonel did not want to fail anyone: had he done so he would have merited only reproach from on high. As a man who had seen action he was only too well aware of the value of the officer education nominally given at university to philologists, historians and lawyers. So a measure of understanding sprang up between him and the students: he made out that he would teach them and they made out that they would study. It was a game they did not want to spoil and, as a general rule, did not do so.

He had been in the examination room with Peeter and could not help but chuckle with the colonel at his performance. The colonel sat with an apparently faraway expression, looking out of the window. Was he thinking about going fishing – what other entertainment was there ever in Tartu in summer? – or was he already awaiting an invitation to the waterside inn?

They had fraternized with the colonel in the inn. He was touched and told them how he held the Estonian people in high regard and loved them and how sad he sometimes was that the Estonians had no respect or love for him or others who had shed their blood for their freedom. The boys tried to console him, but this made him even more sentimental and he began talking of his memories of his home village somewhere in the Smolenski countryside and about how all his good friends had been killed in action, some in the Winter War, some in Moscow, some in Poland. Yes, the old man had actually fought since '39 and been wounded twice. He explained that when he went back to his home village he found not a single house standing, only the chimneys were left and the apple trees were in blossom in the gardens. It had been springtime, the swallows whirled over the burnt ruins looking for nesting-places but could not find any. Neither could he; the army was the best place for the homeless, and so he joined up again.

Some more wine was ordered, and when he left with a German philologist there were already tears in the colonel's eyes, and he and a lad who had been in the army were trying to sing a melancholy song about the apple trees under whose branches dear mother awaits in vain her son's return from the war.

University and Tartu in the flush of July were reminiscent of a theatre after a performance when the spell has suddenly broken, the audience is moving towards the cloakroom and the actors are removing the makeup from their faces. The university had its own spell, its own rhythm and soul, which suddenly vanished. Lots of people had already gone home, the students living in dormitories were packing their things and looking for somewhere to take the stuff they didn't dare leave and didn't feel like lugging home. Peeter Härmsoo brought them a trunk full of books and a radio and borrowed the poems by Under he had copied out. A young man from Pärnu left two small paintings inherited from a deceased aunt. Malle's exams were also over, and she was setting off for home. They had an agreement – unspoken – that Malle would stay for a couple of days more. Her roommates had left and her room was free. One evening they strolled along the Emajõgi river, walked up around the edge of the forest, picked a bunch of daisies from the roadside and went to the dormitories through Tammelinn.

The dormitory was like a bird's nest from which most of the chicks have already flown. Down at the concierge desk a stranger was sitting and yawning; in the corridor they passed a couple of young men with Caucasian faces; a radio was playing on the floor upstairs. Even the smells had changed: instead of the stench of toilets and fried eggs there was the stench of paint and chlorine – clearly major cleaning and repairs were already under way somewhere.

Malle's room was chilly and empty, the only reminder of its winter cosiness was the picture of a cat on the wall by her bed and the round clay vase where they now placed the daisies they had picked on the way, which had already faded a little. They were thirsty, hungry and sweaty. Malle had a cold shower in the bathroom; he merely washed his neck and face. The water was tepid at first; the demand for water was so low that it had time to warm up in the pipes.

Malle put the kettle on the gas in the kitchen and made sandwiches from some left-over bread, cheese and onions. They ate in her room, exchanging meaningless sentences. They did not talk about the thing they were thinking about most. Malle's fears had given him courage which had surprised even himself: the previous day he had been to the chemist's and bought a packet of two condoms, which were now in the back pocket of his trousers. This fact gave him a hollow feeling inside, and he no longer even knew whether what he felt most was lust, unease or the wish that everything would work out this time.

When they had drunk their tea and eaten their sandwiches they sat on the edge of the bed. The kiss was long and passionate, and by the time it was over they were lying on the bed in an embrace. His hand was already under her trousers on her buttocks. Malle let it stay there for a moment and then said, 'Let me.'

No one had ever said anything more wonderful to him – at least that's what it felt like to him at that moment. The girl took the bedspread off the bed and said to him, 'Please don't look,' took off her clothes and crawled into the bed. In a moment he was there, too. He lifted the cover higher than he needed to so that he could for once see Malle from her toes up to her closed eyes. Now indecision suddenly disappeared, leaving a thirsting lust behind; he would have liked to really take Malle, to eat and drink her. Lust had pushed fear aside, and his body was obeying him. He felt ready; the part that needed to be hard was hard. Everything had to go well and beautifully, and it soon would, when underneath him Malle suddenly became stiff as if with cramp and said she was in pain, she couldn't, she was afraid . . .

There's no need to be afraid, he said, comforting her; it's always like that at the start – and, besides, he had this thing with him, so there was no need to be afraid of falling pregnant. He had to get up and find the thing in his pocket, tear the wrapper off and put it where it needed to go. But it was all too much for his organ, its hard willingness fading along with his self-confidence. Malle had turned over, so that she was face down on the pillow. He wasn't sure whether she was crying or not. She was ready to turn back over and take him between her legs, but he couldn't manage it any more. With or without a rubber. All that was left of his great expectations and willingness was something slippery and wet on Malle's mound of Venus and his own hair.

Silently they lay next to each other under the blanket for a while. It had already become darker in the room. Then the girl turned towards him, hugged him tight and covered his face with kisses. 'Darling,' she whispered, 'I really want to make it good for you. But I just can't right now, not yet. I will be able to; we'll just have to wait a bit, that's all. I love you, we'll manage it, don't be afraid, everything's fine, everything's going well. And you love me, too, don't you? You can wait a bit, can't you?'

He felt that everything he said was somewhat strained and insincere, although he had to say it for all that, had to say that, yes, of course he loved her, of course he'd wait, of course everything was fine. But something told him he didn't want to wait any longer. Suddenly he didn't even really love Malle particularly, he just needed to get this overdue initiation done with. Perhaps it would be better if he didn't go with innocent girls like Malle but found someone more experienced with whom it would all be easier. Perhaps it would be wiser first to find just a woman, sex and then, afterwards, love. He didn't say all this to Malle, but instead tried to be affectionate – after this failure she was probably feeling worse than he was.

But, as if reading his thoughts, Malle said, 'I'm probably just not right for you. You should have a different kind of partner. An older, more experienced girl who wouldn't be nervous like I am.'

'I haven't got a girl like that, I've only got you. And I don't want anyone else. Why don't we wait a bit more? And spend some time together now and again, if we can, summer's coming and . . .' As he said it, he knew half of what he was saying was true, half was not.

Summer was here and it was time to separate, to meet summer individually.

He knew he could have spent the night with Malle and maybe have tried again. His people were used to him sometimes not coming home for the night. But he didn't want to. Malle made no attempt to stop him from leaving. It was so wonderful, though, to lie together like that in an embrace. He thought he wanted to be married for that reason alone, because then he would be able to be together in an embrace like that every night. Perhaps that togetherness would be more important and more beautiful than sex. But sex first. With someone who was ready, who wanted it and who wanted him.

As he kissed Malle at the door for the last time and left it was already 1.30 a.m. It was perhaps the darkest time in the light night. A bat whirled in the street and a motorbike droned somewhere far off. It could be someone visiting a girl late at night, like him. Had he done any better?

The next day he had to help Malle with her luggage on to the train to Tallinn, and then he intended to go to the Teacher's house.

He dreamt that the Teacher said he had decided: he would marry the pear tree in his garden. He asked if it was possible to sleep with a pear tree and have children. The Teacher said it was very simple, when the clouds shrouded the houses the pear tree became a woman and they could sexually matriculate – those were the exact words he used in the dream. Grandfather slept relatively peacefully. He was apparently not in any particular pain and he was hard of hearing. Other people's dreams were, however, disturbed by final-year university students (it had probably been the medics' last day) who were continuing their party in the street. The last song he heard as he was dozing off was 'On the Banks of the Emajõgi River'.

15

When he woke up the next morning he suddenly felt, physically, the presence of summer. Even the air in the room was oddly light and the sunshine was radiating. It reminded him of many summers in his schooldays spent at his great-aunt's in the country. On mornings like this it was easier to get up than usual. The light air blew away the antipathy he so often felt in the morning: usually the day had something unpleasant in store for him, whether it be Martson with Marx, the military or something else. He could consider himself an optimist only when it was a delightful summer morning like this or on the occasional evening when he chanced upon a new, interesting thought.

He jumped out of bed and went to the window. There were still only a few people in the street and the asphalt was dotted with confetti and a couple of roses. He suddenly felt an unpleasant thought rising from the bottom of his memory, tarnishing his bright mood. Sometimes it happened that the thought was not yet there, only the anxiety that heralded it. Yes, yesterday evening with Malle. Yet another failure on the road to becoming a man. And he suddenly felt that the anxiety he hadn't felt the previous day was upon him. It began again: the thought went around and around that he had to prepare himself for the next time, to think what to do, in what order and how to go about it. He should have stayed with Malle, they would perhaps have been able to try again a few hours later. For a moment he thought he would go straight there but abandoned the idea. It would be better to collect himself, to do something else; quite simply, he would not survive another failure.

Yet there was something comforting and encouraging, too. For in the evening he planned to go to the Teacher's. He had several questions in his notebook that he intended to ask, although he was aware that in the Teacher's presence the questions sometimes became so trifling and irrelevant that he did not ask them out of embarrassment. In the Teacher's presence he was something of another person, and here at home he could not imagine entirely what kind.

The railway station wasn't far either from Malle's dormitory or the Teacher's house. He hesitated between going to Malle's with some time to spare and staying there for a while or arriving just in time to go and get the train. He reached the dormitory with an hour in hand. They drank tea and talked, but he sensed that something was missing between them this time. Most obvious was the absence of words: that had to mean something. For a moment when he saw Malle in profile she looked suddenly a stranger to him. The strangeness lasted only a moment, but he became even more tongue-tied. When he had carried Malle's heavy luggage into the coach and said his goodbyes – which consisted of only a handshake (they had exchanged kisses in the dormitory) – he felt both sadness and relief.

This time there was no cat on the steps of the Teacher's house, but the pear tree was still there, and it already had tiny pears growing. Far away in the garden he could see two peony shrubs in bloom, one dark lilac and one white. Alongside the garden the white dog rose had finished flowering: there were a couple of blossoms on the tips of the bush, and on the ground underneath it a carpet of white petals.

The Teacher opened the door himself. He was wearing shorts and gave a faintly comic impression with his skinny, pallid legs and their sparse light hair. Somewhere a bird was singing, evidently in the room not the garden.

He said he'd brought the Ristikivi poems he'd promised. This time it seemed that the Teacher was in a better mood: his interest in the poems was not a front. When he sat down in the armchair and lit the cigarette he'd been offered he thought that communication with the Teacher was already developing into a ritual in itself. Clearly the Teacher liked rituals – evidence of this was apparent in his ceremonial bows, the depth of which probably also illustrated his mood (this time he'd bowed very deeply), and the standard questions he asked with a smile. For a moment he had the impression that there was an element of parody in it all; conventionality was at once mocking conventions and surrendering to them.

'So what have you been up to in the last few weeks?' asked the Teacher, now through a puff of smoke. He was unable to get very far with his answer when Ellen appeared at the door, dressed for sunbathing in an unbuttoned, light-blue blouse.

'I do apologize, I'm not exactly dressed for receiving visitors, but Alo and I are not very formal people. I've just been in the garden; we have some flowerbeds. Alo's no great farmer so the flowers are more my baby.'

He asked what flowers they grew.

'We're not real gardeners either. Alo's been interested in botany since he was a child and has taught me to recognize and collect forest plants. We even have some of Estonia's rarer flowers, the ones that you mustn't dig up. But we took them from places where they would have perished in roadworks or land development. Every summer we do the rounds and note the places where something's growing.'

'We've also propagated several plants,' interrupted the Teacher, 'and taken them back to the wilderness. For example the Siberian flag.'

He asked whether it was some kind of iris or gladioli. The Teacher smiled sadly.

Ellen said, 'You see how things are with these city kids. They don't know anything about plants any more.'

He had to acknowledge that this was true. 'I'm not a city child in my heart, though. I've spent every summer with relatives in the country, but it's just that no one's ever taught me to recognize plants. My grandfather told me a bit about birds, but he had no special interest in plants. Anyway, what special plants are there in Tartu on Toome Hill or in Maarja Cemetery where we would go for walks.'

'In that case you should do the rounds with a plant guide in the summer when you're at your relatives',' said the Teacher. 'Start with the prettier ones, the flowers that you more or less know and are generally easier to identify, and then, when you've got them more or less clear in your mind, move on to the more difficult species, like sedges, knotweeds and others. Doubtless you weren't taught at school how to use a plant or bird guide?'

Regrettably, that was not so.

'Hmm, another example of the idiocy in our education system. Biologists and pharmacologists now study at university what everyone should know. What hope is there that people will recognize and care for nature when they don't learn to understand it? In my time children didn't have proper plant guides, but the natural-history teacher always went out with us and we had to collect a small herbarium, identify about twenty species, the ones we managed to identify ourselves. This made it easier to learn the names of the parts of the plants, and anyone who was interested could take it further.'

'There was a different thinking and background to things,' interrupted Ellen. 'Estonians were peasant farmers and peasants have a much deeper interest in the plants growing in their field or meadow. They also had a use for the knowledge: you can tell by recognizing a weed whether the soil is acidic, humus, clay or something else. But for townspeople identifying plants is no different from collecting stamps or pictures of film stars.'

'We're moving further and further away from nature, God's creation,' added the Teacher. 'Our environment is increasingly made by man, comprised of more and more signs. Some people can keep others in their power, including the dead, using signs. We are locked into a world of signs from which we can no longer escape.'

'But isn't it a peculiarity of man? Is it not in his nature to live in a world of signs, to communicate with others using signs?' he asked.

'That's the fashionable way to see it, but in my view such claims are badly one-sided. People need both – an environment with signs and an environment free of signs, which is chiefly found in nature. It's as well to know that when a human child grows up outside a signed environment he won't be able to communicate with others, his development will be arrested. Such things have happened even here in Estonia. For example, a girl near us brought up her child in a cowshed like an animal, and by the time the situation was discovered it was already too late; the child can no longer become a true human being. But the experiment under way should show what will become of someone from our times who has been plucked out of a sign-free environment, plucked out of nature. I do not believe that anything good will become of the child. In order to grow into a human being a person needs certain things that an artificial environment cannot provide. The child must be in contact with nature's voices, smells, animals and plants.'

'But, Alo, how many of the Jews in old Europe in their ghettoes were in contact with nature? They grew into normal people – indeed, on average they were more talented than the rest of the population. Did they have any contact with all the animals and plants?'

'Ellen, Ellen, you know full well that a half-truth is more malicious than a down-right lie! Reflect on how small the cities in the Middle Ages were and how many town-dwellers had agricultural plots and kept livestock. Karja Street – Herd Street – in Tallinn really was where they herded cattle, and even in the Elizabethan age there were fields of crops in London, not to mention vineyards. There were gardens in the ghettoes, and they kept animals there. The Jews were forced to become part of the townsfolk: the *Codex Theodosianus* contained several anti-Jewish laws – for instance, that Jews must not keep slaves. Without slaves farming was impossible at that time. It was nearly the same as the Soviets outlawing collective farmers from keeping a horse and a tractor: they could only be microfarmers. That's precisely what happened to Jews in a certain part of Western Europe as well. In southern France, for example, they had a considerable number of vineyards. But then, what always happens to the Jews happened: they are too successful at what they do – recently even at warfare – and success gives rise to envy. In any case, the Jews' golden age came to an end. Even at the height of the Middle Ages it was difficult for Jews to own land. The land belonged to the feudal overlord; his vassal was able to use it and had to swear allegiance to the feudal lord. The oath of allegiance was taken according to Christian practice. Even here in Estonia in the days of the Tsar it was taken with one hand on the Bible; a real Jew, however, could not make an oath on a Christian Bible. And so the Jews did not become farmers in Western Europe either. Contact with nature was restricted. Only in Eastern Europe, Poland and Ukraine did Jewish smallholders chance upon nature in the raw, near Belovežje. Martin Buber has written beautifully about how the Jews unexpectedly discovered the forests and harvesting and how all this had an echo in the mystical Jewish texts. In the Hassidic Jews we find something we could term poetic pantheism; for them everything – trees, grass, birds and water – was full of God's might and was invested with a soul in the true sense of the word. They believed that scintillas of the world spirit are spread all around, including in nature.'

'Alo, you weren't a professor for long, but I can see that the habit of giving lectures is close to your heart,' said Ellen. 'Perhaps our visitor is not very interested in land ownership by Jews in the Middle Ages or Hassidic mysticism.'

'I know nothing about either, but the latter subject at least is of great interest,' he had to point out.

'Then you must read Buber. Incidentally, weren't your ancestors Jews? Your surname is mainly found among baptized Jews in Russia.'

He confessed that he had never heard anything about it and promised to ask his mother. But it was likely that she didn't know much about her ancestors, not even where they were from originally, only that before the Revolution they had lived in St Petersburg and their ancestors had been minor squires.

'If they were squires then they probably weren't Jewish. Only baptized Jews were allowed to live in St Petersburg, others had to seek special permission from the Tsar. As far as I know some of them even did so successfully. There used to be a goldsmith in Tartu; his father had also been a goldsmith and had lived in St Petersburg with the Tsar's permission, so fine a craftsman was he in his day.'

There was a silence for a moment, which Ellen broke. 'Oh, this habit professors have of giving lectures. Alo, you knew old Professor F better. The thing with him was once he started talking about something he always carried on talking for exactly forty-five minutes straight.'

A smirk appeared on Alo's face. 'Yes, he did. But just think, the old man had been giving lectures day in and day out for nigh on forty years. It's intellectual suicide; things weren't so insane in the days of Yuryev University under the empire, but there was no mercy for lecturers at Tartu University under the Estonian Republic. They were bled dry. It would have been bliss being a private lecturer somewhere in Heidelberg or the holder of a designated chair in the United States.'

A thought came to him. He turned to Ellen. 'I'm not sure if I'm being too nosy, but I'd really like to see your wild flowers. Otherwise I have the feeling that the things we were saying about man's closeness to or estrangement from nature would remain a bit too abstract.'

'Be my guest. I was thinking about asking you to see the garden but didn't dare. We don't have a proper gazebo where we can receive visitors, have coffee and discuss art.'

'You have a very idealistic picture of the people who sit in gazebos, Ellen. I dare to venture that the majority of them don't talk about art, unless cushion embroidery can be described as art, but, rather, about what Mrs X was wearing yesterday when she visited the mayor's wife and who Miss Y was seen talking to during the latest play at the theatre.'

'All right, this is too abstract a subject for us, as our guest said. He wanted to see the flowers, if I understood correctly.'

The garden was bigger than one would have thought from the street and pleasantly shaded like many of the old gardens in this part of Tartu. A quarter of it was the Teacher's or, rather, Ellen's. They had two old apple trees, which were planted at about the same time as the house was built, a strawberry patch and several flowerbeds. In one you could see hepatica and hazelwort leaves, which he recognized from his schooldays. Ellen and the Teacher had to tell him about the others. One bed contained the Siberian flags, still wearing their last blue blossoms, and wild gladioli, which had not yet come into flower. Snowdrop windflowers grew in the same bed as the hepatica, along with the pride of the family, lady's slipper, whose last two flowers were also open. It had been transplanted from somewhere where it had been under threat from logging, before the wildlife protection era. There was a globeflower bush in one border; its flowering period was long since over and it looked a bit weak. Ellen explained that in the height of summer the globeflower leaves usually withered a bit, and mildew and other fungi attacked them. Alo said that in late summer there was nothing to be found in nature that was in full health: the leaves on the trees have been eaten by insects and stained by fungus. Berries were also full of all kinds of parasites. The only plant that was not host to pests and fungal infection seemed to be the yew. But they didn't have one of those in their garden.

He wondered whether he should say his goodbyes now. It might not be polite to go back inside with the Teacher and Ellen, but he felt that he hadn't really managed to talk to the Teacher, and he seemed to be in such a summery good mood.

Ellen solved his dilemma. 'You go on inside for a while. I've still got a bit of weeding to do. I'm pretty sure, Alo, that our visitor has something to ask you.'

'If only I can answer his questions,' said the Teacher, but it was plain from his voice that he said it more for form's sake. They went indoors; he was genuinely grateful to Ellen.

Again he felt that he didn't dare immediately ask the questions that were on the piece of paper in his shirt pocket. For a moment he felt a slight panic: now he was here at the Teacher's, a man who was kind to him and was ready to answer his questions, yet he was unable or not brave enough to ask what he wanted. Perhaps he should learn first to ask the best questions? It was almost an idea . . .

'I don't think I am able to ask you what would be most necessary, useful . . . So I was thinking that first I should learn how to ask questions, as I have this wonderful opportunity to come here and . . . You have been involved in so many things; you know languages that I don't know the names of. But I don't know whether I have the intellect to delve into those things – perhaps I haven't got the talent, perhaps it's something more substantive. And now I think that, when it comes to asking, I should probably first ask about what I should be asking.'

The Teacher said nothing. He could see from his face that the question was really making him think. He blew a large smoke-ring before he said, 'The fact that you approach things in this manner shows that you are the type of thoughtful person who will not feel any contentment until he has explained world events to himself, until he has established some kind of system. But I don't know whether establishing a system is the best response to the questions you are asking. Perhaps there are other possibilities. I am not entirely sure what sort of person you really are, although I do know a fair amount. Perhaps – no, definitely – you are a completely different psychological type from me. That means that my answers – my system such as it is – is not right for you, you necessarily see the world in a different way. You are setting out on building your own system. And if I were now to begin to tell you what the outline of that plan should be like I would be taking on too much responsibility for it. I cannot lay the cornerstone of your philosophy. You must do that yourself. I can, however, help you a bit, answer your questions and lend you books, but, as for the things you should be asking me, that's something I cannot and should not say.'

'But by saying what you've said just now you actually have, a bit.'

The Teacher laughed. 'You are quick to see paradoxes, that's what's making it difficult for you to build your own system. But not impossible. A system cannot incorporate a paradox, as was clear to the scholastics.'

'But must there be a system at all? There are so many of them, all proclaiming themselves the only correct one. All the philosophies and religions. Isn't it possible to make a single, overarching one out of all of them?'

'People have tried to do just that,' said the Teacher, 'but the sum was no better than the original parts. The history of religion includes discussion of syncretism, syncretized beliefs, I don't know whether you are familiar with the concept . . .'

He'd read something about it but that was all.

'Syncretism can be found in late Rome where the people bowed to the gods of Rome, Greece, Egypt and Syria and allowed themselves to be initiated into all kinds of mysteries. This also constituted establishing a kind of system, only the system was an extraordinary mixture of elements from many kinds of religions. Polytheism was behind it, of course, faith in many gods and the idea that they had to be served.'

'Isn't it true that polytheism is more tolerant than monotheism; monotheists are convinced that their god is the only true one, is that right?'

'Not completely. Monotheism occurs generally very rarely as a clean sheet; one could say that philosophical thought verges on monotheism – that's how it's been in India, which is regarded as the classic polytheistic country. However, popular religion verges on polytheism as it does in Catholic countries, and between monotheism and polytheism there are variants of many kinds.'

He felt that this was not exactly what he wanted to ask the Teacher. Then he had a good idea. 'I always wonder how to know how to ask the most important things. If I were to ask you now that if you were my age . . . if you were in the presence of someone who was so wise, with such a wide knowledge as you have now, what would you have asked and what do you now think you should have asked?'

The Teacher chuckled and shook his head. 'Your persistence is to be applauded. Where I am concerned, I had no one whose follower I could be, no one to whom I could put questions about the meaning of life. I was a country boy; my father was a farmer. He was a great reader but also a fervent member of the Moravian Brethren. He wanted me to be a missionary – the fact that I studied foreign languages and was interested in exotic peoples pleased him. However, my views on theology would not have done so if he had lived longer. In fact, I did become a missionary but not in the way my father and the other godly members of the house conceived the job. I don't want to convert Africans and Indians to European religion; instead I would like to convert the converters.'

'You mean Europeans to the religions of Africa or India?'

'No, not that. I don't believe in conversion generally or, one could say, in religions. I believe in the human being – still – and in God and in the tie, the bridge, the ladder between God and man – there are so many metaphors for it in the different religions.'

'So you do believe in God then?'

'Well, young man, I could answer that question either with a "yes" or a "no". In these days of idiotic atheism I prefer, however, to answer with a "yes". But if power ever fell into sectarian hands, the hands of people who asked you that question in the street or on the train, then I would prefer to answer with a "no". Anyhow, I don't believe I shall see that day, although I fear that it is coming, and I am almost certain that it will be more insane than the current sunset era of Communism and atheism.

'You will now, of course, want to know what I mean by the "yes" and "no". "Yes" means that what there is, man's own faith and lack of it, and his doubt and uncertainty is down to something else. Or, as perhaps the Chinese Lao-tzu puts it most beautifully, being dwells in non-being. Or does he say "void" there? I don't know Chinese, and I wouldn't venture to say.'

'But does this all fit together? If being dwells in non-being, then God is part of the non-being, and that means that he doesn't exist!'

'You're strong on logic, and that's good. But I should explain it again. "Non-being" is a word and has a mixture of meanings as all our words do. But you could say that it generally refers to the lack of something. In short, it isn't what could be, what's possible, conceivable, even in fantasy or dreams all combined. This kind of non-being comes from being; it relies on being. There's no sense in talking about the existence of something that lies completely outside our imagination, outside our understanding of what is generally possible. But my argument, or we could say my faith, is none the less a faith in something that is absolutely different from being. But, nevertheless, being relies on it. It does not depend on existence; instead existence depends on it. Does that make sense?'

'I almost believe that it does.'

'Good. If you can follow the outline of my train of thought you can take it further and explain it to yourself more. Another way of putting the idea that existence depends on something else is to say that existence depends on non-being, as Lao-tzu says, if I understood him correctly. This line of thinking also appears in Indian philosophy. They were metaphysicians who loved abstract expressions of this sort. The same ideas have been expressed by other peoples as well in their own myths. Through their creation myths, of which the best known is probably the one in the Old Testament, God created the heavens and the earth and light and all living things, the last among which was man. In the Jewish myth it's a bit confused: it's clearly all compiled from several different texts, but that's not important. The important thing is the contrast. There are two states: before the creation and after the creation. We can say that one is non-being, the other is being. And there is God, power or might, which unites them. We could argue which one the latter is closer to, but that's not the important thing either. The important thing is that some kind of radical change has occurred, something that usually does not happen. Here things become one another. Inside the existence there is a changing carousel, but in the creation that carousel came into being from something that was completely different, something we could call nothing. As theologians say: God created the world from nothing. That event is something which cannot be explained by the laws of being; it is outside existence. Viewed from the inside of existence we can call this a miracle, and the worker of that miracle, if we should care to talk about Him, is God.'

'So the existence of God therefore depends on whether we want to talk about him or not?'

'Not quite. When we talk, we talk in a certain language, using certain conventions, and in our normal use of language it is natural to talk about the causes of things, their purposes and so on. The mythological use of language adopts these as its own and attempts to explain the wondrousness of the world in that language. To be sure, it won't be able to do this without using gods and other beings whose powers and motives do not fit in with our use of language, our logic of existence. Philosophical use of language attempts to explain things differently, to construct a language that would be free of mythological streaks, a language in which it is not necessary to search for a cause, an actor, objectives and so on in everything.'

'Which use of language is better, do you think?'

'I don't know. I think they both have their good and bad points. The mythological use of language keeps us attached to archaic language and thereby to archaic images; it's a locked room, a prison of the imagination. The philosophical use of language breaks out of that prison, although it cannot fully take advantage of the freedom it has achieved; it stands in terror at the prison door. No one has been successful in creating a fully new language free of the weaknesses of mythological language, and perhaps no one ever will. Or maybe someone will manage it in a thousand or ten thousand years. So we will more than likely have to manage with a kind of hybrid language, a combination of mythological and philosophical use of language. That's how the Christian tradition has done things. The philosophical structure was constructed on the old mythological foundation – please excuse my Marxist-Leninist phraseology. And it seems to me that this is one of the better compromises there are.'

'But, by way of example, the Indian religions that you know so well, aren't their foundations and superstructure similar in terms of outlook? Don't mythology and philosophy have a very important role there, too?'

'Yes, they do. But India is a world apart, and it's not so easy to gain access to it as it might first appear. I think the Chinese are, in fact, much closer to us, even though they are almond-eyed and write in strange characters. My hypothesis is that India is the centre of Greater Eurasia. It's the point of origin of all the greatest cultural phenomena of all kinds and the point from which they, and types of religion, have spread. That's why the religions of India are the most complex; everything there is so intertwined in so many ways that it is difficult to separate things out and even more difficult to change anything, whether it be the caste system or religious practice. Therefore the religions of India – and they can be viewed, in fact, as a single super-religion with several branches and movements – are something that cannot be planted in foreign soil. The exception is Buddhism, but to me it's the exception that proves the rule. In India Buddhism has become a small religion of a minority, scattered, lost in the old thicket of religion. In contrast with the so-called Hinduism it has spread successfully elsewhere, especially eastwards from India, and it has maintained its position, despite everything, in some places. It's just about the same with Christianity. It grew out of the soil of Judaism as Buddhism did from Hinduism, but it has not made much headway among the Jews, yet it has among non-Jews, other peoples. Both Christianity and Buddhism are religions of peoples who have been wrested away from their own roots and traditions and were therefore more receptive to a new religion. They think less in a mythological way and more in a philosophical way. And as a result the mythological background can change. At first it becomes simpler and then a new mythology grows up on top of it.'

'And then there's another reformation, or whatever it's called?' he rushed in, offering the Teacher his own wording. It was accepted.

'Then there's often a reformation. A turning back to the original – let us for now call it philosophical – way of thinking. If, of course, circumstances are conducive to it. Different circumstances may produce quite the opposite reaction, such as the reaction in India of Hinduism to Buddhism or the rise of orthodox Islam in Arabia. We could perhaps compare it to the Counter-Reformation in Europe. Yet religion can freeze into its old forms, lose its vitality.'

'Like Judaism you mean?' he tried once more to prompt the Teacher.

This time it didn't go well. The Teacher shook his head. 'No, I wouldn't say that about Judaism. It has always been in a process of renewal, sometimes even radical renewals such as cabbala and Hassidism. My examples would be more on the lines of the old Christian Churches, like those of Ethiopia or Syria. And there are some examples in India. But they probably won't mean anything to you, and I don't feel inclined to go into it now. They are not important except as an illustration.'

'So in your mind religions are a bit like apple trees and need regular pruning?'

'You could put it like that, yes. Religion is like culture or language. If it becomes something to be preserved at all costs, defended, conserved, then it stagnates and moulders. Religion is not static, it's a dynamic thing, not a lake but a river. Or even better, like fire or the wind, always moving. Fire is burning, wind is movement of air. Motionless wind or fire, like a motionless freshwater spring, cannot exist. It is a *contradictio in adiecto* – I hope they've explained that idea to you at the university.'

He knew what *contradictio in adiecto* meant, although he'd come across it in an old encyclopaedia not at university.

This pleased the Teacher. 'Sometimes I almost believe that humanitarian education is as good as dead, but it would appear that I may have to, let's say, reform my view. Ah! If I remember correctly you don't know Greek.'

That was correct.

'Chapter three of St John's Gospel says "the wind blows wherever it pleases", and further on "so it is with everyone who is born of the spirit". The Greek says "*pneuma pnei*" – the "*pneuma*" is the wind, although in our language it's translated as "spirit". The same word occurs in both sentences in the original. It could have been translated as "soul" or "breath", for "*pneuma*" comes from an ancient image that in breath there is power, vitality or, as we usually call it these days, energy. God blew soul, the life force, into the clay form; man carries within him God's power or breath. The Hebrew word for "*pneuma*" is "*ruach*", and there are equivalent terms in many languages – the word "*prana*" in Sanskrit means more or less the same. Sometimes I think that the main difference between people in ancient times and today is that we collect money and objects; they collected this very vitality, life force, *pneuma* or *prana*. It was sometimes understood in very materialistic terms with the result that several peoples hunted their neighbours, ate their livers and hearts and carried their severed heads with them so as to obtain other people's life force for themselves. The Chinese Taoists didn't try to steal the life force from others; they tried to produce and magnify it using a number of methods. They had breathing exercises and sexual techniques to achieve this, chief among which was controlled ejaculation, along with alchemic procedures. Breathing, of course, is especially important in the yoga of India. Many people believe that using breathing techniques it is possible to draw the *prana*-force or energy into oneself from outer space and thereby become a superman.'

'But what's it like in Christian sects?' he asked hurriedly.

'It's there, too, in many different forms,' came the Teacher's reply. 'But I'm no expert in that area. If you want to look for some extreme examples you'll be able to find some in Russia among their dissenters, of whom Rasputin was one. There they believed what the Tantrics in India and the Taoists in China believed, namely that sexual energy can be transformed into the life force, *prana*, divine energy which gives a man special powers, eternal life or certain other miraculous things.'

'Is there anything in it or is it pure fantasy or charlatanism?' he asked, feeling how the talk of sex affected him in a different way from the other topics.

'I don't know,' replied the Teacher; he felt he wasn't in the best mood to talk about the matter. 'In India there are plenty of kinds of sexual derangement that I've never understood. In my opinion there must be some kind of dislocation in people when they see everything as a sex symbol, when fire drilling is discussed in terms of the sexual act, and a huge phallic lingam is honoured as a symbol of the god Shiva.'

'But is sex so central only in religion or in their lives as well?'

'That I really couldn't say. I have never been to India. I am only familiar with some of the religious and, to some extent, philosophical texts in Sanskrit, and a few others in Tamil and a couple of other Dravidian languages. Their traditional literature is very conventional, and if you don't know the conventions you may overlook the fact that what you are reading is not a treatise about flowers and birds but a very erotic text. On the other hand, religious texts have occasionally been written using very erotic imagery. Like many of the texts of the Sufi and even the Catholic mystics.'

'So is there some kind of a link between the mystical and the erotic?' He was searching for confirmation of something that was troubling him.

'So it's often said. Freudians in particular, of course, are certain that they see this link everywhere, but my opinion is that it's like ghosts and apparitions: people primarily see what they believe in, what they want to see or what they fear seeing. Two hundred years ago apparitions, ghosts and the devil himself were sighted in Estonia, now there are reports of flying saucers. There may occasionally be sexual derangement in India, but in the West people's attitude to sex is quite simply completely unbalanced; it seesaws from the Victorian taboos when even piano legs were regarded as indecent to today's apostles of free sex, people who think that all the world's problems will be resolved or will disappear if complete promiscuity can be developed, if everyone can go to bed with everyone else. To them, sex is God and no restraints of any kind must be put on God. To others sex was still an evil that had to be fought using any means. Even by self-castration, as practised by Origen, a father of the Church, or the Skoptsy of Russia. Or by introducing dreadful punishments for sexual infringements as in the Law of Moses or Sharia in Islam.'

He didn't know what Sharia was.

'Have you seen the word Sharia?'

He had indeed come across it somewhere.

'Well, it's the same thing only it's been oddly and incorrectly transcribed from Russian,' said the Teacher, and with irritation in his voice. 'The code of laws of Islam by which a true Muslim must live; it also still forms the basis of jurisprudence even today in a few countries.' It seemed that he was sensitive on points of language. But perhaps his irritation was at something else.

A stillness grew in the room. He inhaled on what was probably his fifth cigarette already and felt that he shouldn't smoke any more. The Teacher was staring in front of him and thinking about something. It looked as though he had forgotten his visitor all of a sudden.

He was already wondering whether it was time to make a move when the Teacher, as if waking up, announced, 'I don't know whether I've answered your questions, our chat went off on such a wide tangent . . .'

'Perhaps so, but in many ways you answered more fully than I could have hoped. At least about how I can ask more intelligent questions in future, if I have the chance.'

'Well then, I hope I can answer more intelligently. But please don't think that I have the ultimate truth. I don't know, maybe I got completely lost somewhere. But on one thing you can be certain: I do not lie; I say what I believe and think.'

'Thanks,' he said, for want of anything better to say. 'I should probably go soon, but, if I may, I would like to ask one more thing.'

'And that is?'

'Earlier you were talking about the mythological and philosophical trend in religions, if I can put it like that, and about the fact that they are all linked by an understanding that we, the whole of existence, depend on something else, on an otherness which in Christianity is God. I don't know much about Buddhism, but does it have anything equivalent to God, a kind of otherness? There's Nirvana, but Nirvana is only a complete extinction, the end . . .'

The Teacher shook his head. 'That's an example of a misunderstanding of Buddhism that's distorted in its simplicity, admittedly and unfortunately a widespread example. Buddhism is a very old religion, and it has all kinds of layers, whether mythological or philosophical. But to me it's completely clear that from the outset, since Buddha himself, a totally different conception of that otherness has existed. Nirvana is not simply the end, it is that completely other reality. Or a completely different way of seeing reality. Buddhism has, from its outset, been a mystical religion.'

'How can it be mystical without a god?'

'That's a question of definition, but I've never regarded definitions as prescriptive. God is our name for what stretches out to us, reaches us from that otherness, the expression of that contact in mythological language. Buddhists were probably the first people in the world who tried to abandon mythological language fully and thus abandoned any name for the otherness. Nirvana is a negative, Greek-type, apophatic concept, much as God was to the followers of Dionysius the Areopagite in the Christian tradition. It is also negative in terms of language: it means something like "being motionless", "not happening". I could put it more poetically, more freely as "calm". Buddhism, therefore, is not so far removed from Christianity. They meet at the edges. And similarly, in Taoism there is a very sceptical school of thought in which God or gods have no place at all. As far as I know, a concept such as that of our God has never really existed in China.'

'What about paradise and everlasting life? Is that not something that makes a religion a religion?'

'Not at all. The Old Testament knows nothing about paradise or everlasting life; they come to Judaism later. And generally the visions of paradise and future everlasting life in world religions are the exception rather than the rule, although in our area, Western Eurasia, they are more widespread but generally of later origin. That much can at least be determined on the basis of what we know and what has been preserved. We know very little about the ancient religion of Crete; we don't know what type of otherness they may have believed in.'

'But what is the otherness of Buddhism? Is it the negation of all this here?'

'To a Buddhist, "all this here" would more likely be the negation of "all that there". "This here" is not real; "that there" is. Nirvana, which to our form of logic and way of thinking is inconceivable, is, in fact, more real than the sane, everyday world we regard as real. What we call "real life" exists as long as we believe in it. If we no longer believe but analyse, try to understand, that "real life" becomes a blur and we catch a glimpse of another "real life", one that's more real. And there, to my mind, lies the fundamental point of contact between Buddhism and Christianity. Some of Christ's basic ideas are that when someone believes in a different kind of identity, in someone who is both God and man, and in a different kind of existence, which he calls the Kingdom of God, then it becomes true. That person will find Christ, the godhead, within himself and he will live in the Kingdom of God where there is no death and none of the sane absurdity of this world.'

'Have I understood correctly? Buddhism proceeds from the uncertainty in the realness of this world and Christianity from a faith in the realness of another kind of world?'

'You could put it like that, yes. I believe that they would concur with that, "they" being Buddha and Christ.'

'Who never met . . .'

'How would we know that?'

Now he began to get the feeling that he simply could not bear to stay here any longer: everything – the room, the flowers under the window, the time and the space – was beginning to feel a little unreal; they were beginning to sway, as if at sea, and he, too, was swaying with them. It really was time to go; he had something to think about at home and something to read about.

But then he had one, this time final, question about the thinking and reading. 'It's really time for me to go. I've already taken up too much of your time, and it's all starting to overwhelm me. But one more thing: everything you've talked about today, it's been probably the most important and most interesting conversation I've had in my life. I've tried to read and think about these topics, Christianity and

Buddhism and everlasting life, but I have no books and no one who would have really known about it. And the few ministers I've had any contact with have never said what I wanted to hear. Not that I was expecting certain specific replies. They are just small, grey and – I don't want to say it, but I have to none the less – dull people. And now I'm here and listening to you, and it's an entirely different, vast, wonderful, colourful world. You've suddenly opened the door, and I've seen that world. And now I know I have to go there, I have to see it, touch it, learn to experience it. I have no choice. Will you help me? Guide my reading and sometimes answer my novice's questions and give me a bit of advice? If I came here once a month or every two months and between times read and worked on the things you'd recommended to me.'

It was a lengthy plea – he wasn't used to asking for things and felt that it all came out clumsily. But now he'd managed to spill out his heart, and he immediately felt easier – regardless, even, of whether the Teacher was ready to agree.

The Teacher said nothing, and he could not tell from his face what answer he was planning to give. Nor was it betrayed by the line of smoke that rose from his next cigarette – the visitor was no longer smoking – into the blue atmosphere of the room.

Then, when the silence had already dragged on for an agonizingly long time, he said, 'I was thinking about what would be most useful for you to learn. But I don't know, and perhaps you yourself don't yet have a proper idea of what you want, what you most need. But I can see that you will very probably not have any genuine peace until you yourself have identified the things that are important to you. That means that you should study philosophy and theology – I don't mean orthodox Lutheran theology, I mean the history of religion but without any intention of becoming a missionary or an apologist. This means, simply, that you will find that the answers to your big questions have already been sought for thousands of years. But the final answer that applies to everyone has not been found, so every individual has the opportunity to continue to search, whether to find their own truth or open themselves to someone else's truth and formulate it for themselves. It also requires, however, a knack with words, proficiency in languages. Language proficiency in many meanings of the phrase. You will have to read texts in several languages and several keys, mythological texts, theological and philosophical texts. In some ways they often discuss the same topics, but it is as if the same music has been arranged differently.

'As far as I understand it, you can read English and Russian and a bit of French and German. It would also be useful to have a few of the Scandinavian languages plus Spanish and Italian. And Latin and Greek, of course. And if you feel irresistibly drawn to theology then you won't be able to manage without Hebrew. And, in future, it would be useful to have a thorough knowledge of an oriental language, for example, Arabic, Sanskrit or Chinese. They open the door to a world which at first feels completely different but perhaps seems more familiar afterwards.'

'Do you have any good methods or tricks for learning languages?' he rushed to ask.

'Everyone has his own tricks, but what matters is the kind of person someone is. For example, my visual memory is better than my auditory memory. As a result I speak foreign languages poorly, and my pronunciation is terrible, but I can read and write them better. And hearing a language isn't too important when learning. There are people, though, who can never learn a language properly from a book but who grasp the spoken language very quickly. For someone with a visual memory, therefore, the most important thing is, of course, to read a lot in foreign languages, and for someone with an auditory memory it is to listen to them, on the radio maybe. What sort of memory do you have?'

He had to confess that he didn't even know.

'In that case you must investigate. Try to read a text with a dictionary and listen to the radio. Work out which is more help.'

'Do you perhaps have any introductory books on philosophy, or could you recommend where to start? And on the history of religion, too? I'll have time to read over the summer.'

'Philosophy's no problem. I believe that the library has loads of copies of Windelband – it was learnt from him in my day. Ah, you have some difficulty with German.'

He thought he could try, he might manage it.

'But it would be worth reading some history of philosophy as well. In my opinion there are some pretty good books on Greek philosophy in Russian. When you get to the Middle Ages there might well be something in Russian, too. But I think you should definitely begin reading a history of Indian philosophy right away. There's a major overview of Radhakrishnan in Russian. It's very well written in a readable style. History of religion is a bit trickier. I wouldn't like to recommend any of the books currently available. It might well be better if you read various works on completely different religions. They are mostly written with genuine interest and empathy. What we here call the history of religion was mostly penned by Lutheran theologians, and their empathy wears thin when they come to addressing the Catholic or Orthodox faiths. Traditionally these handbooks were written by missionaries, and they have retained that flavour to this day. I'll look out something on maybe the religions of India for you to supplement the Radhakrishnan. I've also got some good books on Judaism and Islam. That will probably be enough for starters. I don't know how fast a reader you are, but I believe that Radhakrishnan alone will take a couple of months if you read it carefully. But I'll get some books and articles ready, and next time you come you can have them.'

It was almost what he had hoped for. He was not a formal student of the Teacher's, but he was as good as.

There was nothing else he could ask; nor did he want to. All that remained was to thank the Teacher, the words for which came out awkwardly, as always, and stand up.

The Teacher accompanied him to the door. Ellen came out of her room into the hall for a while and said goodbye as well. At the main entrance he turned back for a moment. Standing at the door, the Teacher waved to him.

Outside it was still light, but the sun was already fairly low and all that shone from it was a display of sunrays between the trees in the park. Walking was so easy, as if wings had grown under his feet like the god Hermes. In the main street he bumped into two girls he'd definitely seen around the university. He had to smile at them – he just needed someone to smile at. The girls smiled back. It was all so summery and natural. He wondered for a moment whether to say something to them – he would even have managed to do so – but his winged feet carried him forward and would not allow him to stop.

16

The last days in Tartu rushed by. The weather was still hot; in the backyards the dustbins began to smell and big bluebottles jostled their way in through the windows. Tartu was unexpectedly more drowsy and more grubby, no longer a university city but a small, provincial town, its hinterland a great military airfield, and flowing through its centre a muddy, shallow brook alongside which lone elderly anglers patiently sat. When he was a schoolboy the Emajõgi had had many more fish. In spring its banks had been full of anglers, and there were enough for everyone to catch something. He had been there a couple of times himself and taken home a pair of bleaks and dace. But they didn't have a cat, and when the fish were put in a pan to cook they were too small and too few. Besides, he didn't like eating fish. In the end he felt sorry for the fish and wouldn't catch them any more. But something was still preying on his mind, and he remembered an occasion when, standing by the river, he had watched an old man, hunkered down in a boat, haul out a large ide. That was long ago, though, during Stalin's time when fish had had better lives than people. After this had come the land reclamations, tributaries were cleaned up and straightened, and factories discharged their waste into the river. Fish stocks diminished, and even the fishermen gradually died out.

He had never been able to imagine having to spend the summer in the town, by the half-dried-up river, in the dusty streets where the asphalt melted in the heat and stuck to the soles of your shoes. His family was in the habit of spending the summer in the country. Grandfather had come from the country to the city, had started work as a teacher and later had become a businessman. Some of their relatives had stayed in the country and summer was spent at their house. That's how it had been for his mother and her brother and sister, and that's how it had been for him. Even during the time of the Forest Brothers and the deportations.

Even now he intended to cycle to the countryside as he had done in his school-days when the country roads had been emptier and lined with plaster statues painted the colour of aluminium. The verges had also been planted with trees, mainly birches, but in a couple of places between Tartu and Võru there were apple trees that blossomed but bore no fruit. Grandfather thought planting fruit trees as an avenue the height of stupidity: if they weren't tended they would not thrive or fruit, and any baby apples that started to grow would be stolen once they were half ripe. Estonia wasn't a cultured country like Germany where many of the country roads really were lined with fruiting trees with a farmer who looked after them and harvested their crop without fearing that passers-by might consider them fair game.

To make sure he was expected he went to the Post Office to phone Rein. Rein was out, replied a bright male voice, before going on to say that they had heard about him and were expecting him. You couldn't miss the church, and the place where they lived was accessible from the church by bike in the summer; in winter they might let him have a free ride down the hill on a baking tray. The day suited them too, almost any day suited them. Everything was settled.

The bicycle had stood all winter in the cellar where they kept the firewood, and where occasionally the odd stray cat would take up residence. Now he had to retrieve it, oil the bearings, adjust the spokes and check the tyres so that there would be no nasty surprises on the eighty-kilometre journey.

Grandfather had been better over the last few days and was sleeping more peacefully, reading Conan Doyle in Russian and chatting with his visitors, who even in summer were not in short supply. The previous day an old family friend, Professor P, had been around, and he had played a couple of games of chess with him.

When he had more or less reassembled the bike Grandfather came into the hall for a chat. He had to tell him what time he was setting off and which road he would take. Grandfather had memories of his own associated with those roads: he had travelled to Tartu by horse, he remembered the names of the roadside inns and those of several Tartu shopkeepers who stocked farm supplies. Later he came to Tartu for a teachers' seminar, and on a couple of occasions had walked all the way there from home as if he were the poet Kristjan Jaak Peterson, although their rural village was much closer to the university than Riga, Peterson's point of departure.

Grandfather had one more matter to discuss. 'So you're about to go off for the summer. I have one request to make of you. Would you mind typing me a document? I've been thinking – who knows how long I've got left, better to get it ready now.'

He leant the bike against the wall – the hall was fairly narrow, but it would have been a pain to take the bike back down into the cellar; he washed his hands in the bathroom, went into the room and set the typewriter up on the table. Grandfather asked him to bring another chair and sat next to him.

'The women aren't here at the moment. I thought it would be better for us like this, as they would only start nagging and fretting. But I think that what I want to do today must be done. Type in triplicate if you can. Are you ready?'

He put some paper and carbon paper into the typewriter and was ready. Grandfather began dictating. 'In the event of the rebirth of the free Estonian State . . .'

He might have thought that Grandfather would introduce things, explain in greater detail the whys and the wherefores, but for some reason he did not consider this necessary and instead went straight to the nub of the matter.

He typed carefully, although several letters were out of line. What he was typing was a will – but no ordinary will. What Grandfather had to hand down to his children was the property that had once been his and had been confiscated from him by the current government. But in the will everything still existed and belonged to him: the nationalized house that he left to Aunt Eva, the bookshop that he left to his other aunt, shares in two factories and mining concerns that he left to his uncle who lived in Sweden. Nothing was left to him – clearly Grandfather thought there was still time for that. The divisible property took up a whole page. Grandfather, he thought, had, in fact, nothing more to give his children than the piece of paper. The property listed on it had gone, and there was no real hope of getting it back. But none the less . . . Grandfather loved to talk about how much the world had changed since he was a small boy who ran, trouserless, into the snowdrift in the yard. He had been born before cars, aeroplanes, wireless telegraphy, the atom bomb and television. He had been born in a time when the map of Europe bore no Finland, Estonia, Latvia, Lithuania, Czechoslovakia or Hungary, when at song festivals Estonians sang praise to Alexander, Kaiser by the grace of God, who was soon killed by revolutionaries and succeeded, also by grace of God, by the next Alexander, and the Russian nation felt as solid and strong as its successor did now. Who could say that before the end of the twentieth century the map of Europe would not change yet again? The maps of Asia and Africa had changed so much in twenty years as to be unrecognizable. There was hope, but perhaps his wariness would not allow it to grow too much. He, like many Estonians, had reached the conclusion that living was best if there was just enough hope. And it was bad when hope was in too great or too short a supply.

Grandfather had something else as well. He continued somewhat conspiratorially, as if he wanted to initiate him into some kind of men's secret. 'You're now a university student, moving in different circles, and you almost certainly smoke sometimes. As you know, I am no longer a smoker, but I thought I'd give you my pipe bowl and mouthpiece. You might have a need for them.'

Without asking whether he wanted them Grandfather got up, picked up the copies of his will, which he had signed in the meantime in a trembling but entirely legible hand, and shuffled into the back room to his bedside table where his few personal items were kept. He shoved the folded papers in among some old dust-wrappers, took a cloth pouch out of the drawer and undid it. There were two pipes in the pouch, one large and straight with broken porcelain edging, the other small and curved, and a single crude mouthpiece made of bone that he remembered well: Grandfather had used it and repaired the apparently worn-out mouthpiece himself with fish glue.

'Look,' he said, unscrewing the bowl of the pipe. 'You can take this pipe apart and put a tuft of cotton wool inside the bowl; it absorbs the tar and nicotine that you'd breathe in if you didn't. Same with this mouthpiece. Look, you can unscrew it and push another little piece of cotton down it – that way you'll be looking after your health.'

Grandfather's lesson was both embarrassing and touching. He'd just been thinking that Grandfather hadn't left him anything. But that wasn't true: he was leaving him something whose value could be measured not in money but in something else. His pipe, hat and stick were things that the man would not have relinquished lightly: he would take them to his grave or leave them to his son. Grandfather's son was far away in Sweden, so he was giving his pipe to him, his grandson.

He suddenly remembered something. 'Grandfather, I've just thought. I heard once that this long pipe belonged to my father.'

'Yes,' Grandfather said. 'That's right. Your father was a light smoker, like me – I hope that you won't end up a heavy smoker – and when he was taken this pipe of his was left behind. When we took refuge during the war I took this pipe from among his things. His pipe and a volume of Nekrasov – you know the one; the edition from the time of the Tsar – with all the hard signs and "yats"?'

Yes, he knew the Nekrasov, and he also knew that it was part of what was left of his father. Since he had discovered Russian poetry he had occasionally read the book, but the old-fashioned spelling was a bit confusing.

'Nekrasov is still a great poet. He has the ability to write so strikingly about Russian life and the Russian spirit that he speaks to us today, too. And no writer before him knew the Russian peasants; they moved on a grander stage. You see, although Nekrasov was a nobleman and rode in a fine coach he understood the farmer's soul and wrote about it in such a way that you read it in wonder.'

He realized that he had never talked properly about his own father to his grandfather. And he now had something to ask. 'Did you talk to my father about Russian literature, too? What did he like best? What did he read most? Nekrasov?'

'No, not Nekrasov. Of the old poets the one he rated most highly was Pushkin, but I think he read many newer and more fashionable poets, too, like Blok and others. I never understood them properly.'

'How about prose?' he enquired.

'Always Dostoyevsky but also men like Leskov and Garshin – I don't know whether they told you about them at school. He said that they had a very good style – I don't know; I can't say anything on that point. But Dostoyevsky is certainly a great writer; we were agreed on that. Have you read anything by him?'

He had. Dostoyevsky was one of the first Russian authors he had read in the original. Once he was brought out of disgrace and his works were rediscovered. He had bought *Crime and Punishment* and *The Idiot* and read them one after the other. They had such an effect that he dreamt about the side streets of Leningrad, the canals and the frozen river Neva where for some reason cows were herded. He knew they were a different kind of cow that ate snow and therefore produced very white, creamy milk. Aunt Veera actually lived in that very area, near Fontanka, where once Dostoyevsky had lived. Of course, his aunt had shown him the writer's house which, at least in the dim whiteness of the winter air, was as featureless and miserable as hundreds of other similar places. He had not read any other Dostoyevsky; he was unable to explain why exactly, perhaps so as not to tarnish his first strong, bright impressions.

'They say that Dostoyevsky is the one who has best been able to portray the Russian soul,' Grandfather went on. 'Through him Europeans learnt to understand the Russians.'

He thought that it would be interesting to know who the Russians should read in order to understand Europeans, but he didn't ask Grandfather about it. Perhaps he should ask the Teacher when he saw him before the trip.

He sat with Grandfather for a while; neither of them knew what else to say. Then Grandfather got up. 'Don't say anything to the women about the papers we wrote here. Leave that between us two men. I'm just off for a little lie-down.'

It was both embarrassing and pleasing that Grandfather had, in those words, elevated him to the ranks of men. Talking to Grandfather was always difficult; he was from such a different world, a world where life had been harsh but simple. For Grandfather and people of his age things had been much clearer and more easily articulated. Black was black, white was white, good was good and bad was bad. He thought that in the interim something strange had happened to people; as if the fruit of the tree of knowledge of good and evil had lost its influence. Everything had become confused and uncertain. If only it had meant that they would regain paradise. Yet paradise was a very long way off, and that was what they heard in Marxism lectures. Perhaps man had also been thrown out of the world to which he had been expelled from paradise. Perhaps a third era was starting, a time beyond good and evil and beyond paradise.

That was a thought he could put in his notebook. But he didn't feel like it at the moment. In the back room the bed was moving and wheezing: Grandfather was lying down for his nap. He went back into the hall to sort out his bike.

He'd had the bike for several years. He had saved the money to buy it; his aunt and mother had given him something towards it, too, and then he was able to purchase it the very spring that Stalin died and he and Mart had broken blocks of ice from the bank of the Emajõgi and sent them floating downstream.

He'd learnt to ride a bike in the countryside, at the place he was now planning to visit. He had got on the bike by the well and had ridden downhill towards the forest. At first his rides always ended with a tumble on to the grass, then he got as far as the currant bushes – ending up in one of them, of course – and then to the start of the forest path. Learning was slow, but in two weeks he had progressed so far that he could ride with his cousin right into the centre to where the school and church were and where his great-aunt had once worked as a teacher.

Next spring he had acquired his own bike. Kalle and Jüri also had bikes, and he did his first longer rides with them, to Vorbuse, Röövlimägi – Brigands' Hill – the bridge at Kärevere and Ropka. There were few cars in those days and they drove slowly so it was possible to cycle around in town without much danger. But he didn't like riding in towns; he preferred using his bike for the opportunity to escape from them. When not riding with anyone else he would sometimes cycle off alone somewhere, turn off the main road and choose a spot in the shade to sit and read. He especially liked Röövlimägi, beyond Reola: there were beautiful tall pine trees there, and there was never anyone to be seen. Grandfather often asked where he was off to, and once, when he told him he was going to Röövlimägi, Grandfather had said that when he was a small boy, maybe in the 1880s, there had actually been brigands there. They would keep a look out from the forest for horsemen coming from the direction of the town, jump out at the right moment from behind the trees and stop the traveller unable to force his tired horse to plod uphill more quickly. The men would strip the traveller, take him deeper into the forest, tie him to a tree and disappear with his horse and cart.

That's how things had been once, when horse stealing was still almost a national sport in Estonia. As parish magistrate his great-grandfather had waged war against horse thieves, and his grandmother's suitors' horses had been spirited away from the hitching post next to the house.

His horse had been readied in Minsk. It was easier to look after than a real horse: it didn't need to eat, it could be kept against the wall in the hall, and to protect it against thieves it had successfully inherited a passport and frame number that he had to go and pick up each spring from the militia station. He had learnt bicycle maintenance in the summer with the local children, along with some words of the south-Estonian Võru language they spoke there. There was nothing left to do with the bike, so all that remained was to pack his rucksack and set out early in the morning. The women packed him some sandwiches, a thermos of juice and their best wishes along with a small packet of real coffee for Meeta.

17

The biggest problem was posed by the books. He would have liked to read something in English, but the Silvet English–Estonian dictionary was too cumbersome, and there weren't any dictionaries in the countryside. That left him only the Radhakrishnan in Russian that the Teacher had recommended. He hoped to finish reading it in the country, and there was other reading matter in the barn and attic. He also planned to make a slight detour on his way, although the haymaking season wasn't yet over and he had to help his host out. In the workroom, where the men had a planing bench and decent tools, he had made some useful thing every summer, and he hoped to do the same this time, too. But without really knowing what it could be. Among the woodblocks, planes, chisels and drills the idea would come without effort. Some of the plank ends or birch logs seemed to lend themselves to being made into some specific item so clearly that he was eager to take up an axe and a knife and begin. Sometimes his instinct was incorrect or his skills were wanting, but sometimes it proved accurate. The best things he produced were utensils, spoons and ladles. The carving of figures did not go so well, figures did not jump out so easily from the piece of wood as utensils did. He had made spoons for half the family, and Grandmother even now would not forget to remind him that the alder ladle from the year before last was broken and they needed a new one.

He had got up at half past six, and as he reached the outskirts of the town on his bike there was dampness in the air and the sun was not yet burning with the day's strength. In the fields skylarks were singing. In Ülenurme a mother peewit was about to lead her young brood over the road. He stopped and let them cross the asphalt strip and disappear into the spruce hedge.

Before the crossroads in Reola a small bus full of children drove past him, doubtless on a school trip. The children waved to him from the back window; he waved back and turned off to the left. For a while he had to cycle through marshy hay fields where red warblers were singing. Then came the forest, the railway station and the ascent of Röövlimägi. The hill, which farmers' horses had used to plod up slowly, was too difficult for him and he had to get off and wheel the bike along. In fact, it was a nice change to travel like this once in a while, with the bike alongside and the backpack on the luggage holder rather than his back as he went up the hill. At the top he could put the backpack on again – it was easier to ride with it on his back as the bike didn't wobble as much – and continue on his way. Röövlimägi was of special significance in his personal geography: as a schoolboy he would come here to read; here the impact of Tartu, its field of influence, appeared to peter out and the countryside, the borderland between Tartu and Võrumaa, began. Beyond there was genuine forest by the side of the main road – nothing like the rundown, polluted forests such as the one in Tähtvere and the scrub lining the Emajõgi skirting the town.

Beyond Reola the lowlands ended and the hills, climbs and descents began that continued almost as far as Võru. The road meandered between the knolls and dips; it was the old post road, and it had not yet been straightened much. In a sign of the new times apple trees and birches had been planted alongside the ditches and the odd statue had been erected – in one spot a Pioneer with a trumpet, in another a deer with broken antlers. He had ridden past that deer a number of times, and each time he had thought about stopping and investigating whether the deer was made just of gypsum or something more substantial – perhaps it had a wire frame inside. But each time he had cycled past, and this occasion was no different.

Once his Võrumaa forebears had travelled these roads to the town market. Their journey took a full six hours and led them from inn to inn: Puskaru, Ihamaru, Karilatsi, Küka, Liiva, Rebase, Reola. Now the inns had been turned into shops you could still buy vodka, although it was no longer served inside but had to be consumed outside and around the corner. The shops drew the men in nearly as much as they had in the past, and sometimes, as evening fell, drunken singing could be heard from the scrub beside the shop.

Now, though, it was early morning. The shops were shut, and the men were about their business, whether contemplating taking the hair of the dog or something else.

He didn't need the shops; he hadn't been able to bear them since his childhood and the times of the bread and sugar queues. He took his first longer break at the halfway point in the forest on the sandy knoll after the higher rise: from here it would be exhilarating to speed downhill, the wind whistling in his ears and the white wayside posts flashing by.

The day had already reached mid-morning, as they still often say in the countryside – it used to be the farmers' time for a break and refreshment. The weather was already hot and the first white puffy clouds had risen into the sky. They didn't promise rain, at least not before evening, but by then he would in all probability be at Rein's.

Somewhere very close by a chiffchaff was singing its never-ending plish-plosh, while from further off came the sound of the chaffinch and from further away still a stock dove. Before his feet ants marched on their way. He wondered whether they ever rested or whether they were active for as long as it was warm enough for them to be able to move. Perhaps numbness from cold and anabiosis meant rest for them.

He thought how he and Malle had once discussed how wonderful it would be in late autumn to hibernate as the last leaves fell and to reawaken in spring when the hepatica are sprouting. Then you could spend the height of summer and its light nights without going to sleep. What was Malle doing now? Thinking of her troubled the peace of mind he had finally found since their last failure in bed. Their relationship had begun so beautifully, but now there was something painful and difficult in it, something from which he wanted to escape. Perhaps his trip to Võrumaa was his own way of escaping. Yet he knew that one cannot escape from oneself. Or, if one can, he didn't know how.

The road went on past forested, remote spots acknowledged by frequent sign-posts GAMEKEEPER — km. Forests, gamekeepers, former inns and, for the odd kilometre or two, open countryside where there was a farm, a cow and a couple of sheep grazing and someone tossing hay.

He made his next stop as they had done in the old days, at Tilleorg. Now he could have a wash in the brook – which bore the name Tilleoja, although it was, in fact, a stretch of the Ahja river – drink some of the water as the juice was nearly gone, and soak his legs, which were aching from the cycling. He liked Tilleorg; its scenery held some kind of mystery, something that both calmed and fascinated him. After finishing school he had gone on a short hike and had walked on his own from Valgemetsa along the Ahja River as far as Erastvere, the site of the river's source. He had camped near Tilleorg for the night. Lots of people probably had places in the countryside – landscape that held a magical attraction. The Chinese were supposed to have ancient knowledge about landscape that sought out places like this and moulded them; that was what someone – perhaps Aleks Luuberg, who was in his own way an encyclopaedia of exotic knowledge – had once talked about at the café. It would be fantastic to find a place like that and build a house there for himself, to live in a place to which you were tied by a magical bond. It reminded him of the symbolists. Baudelaire – could Baudelaire be regarded a symbolist? What importance was there in that? There was a poem, 'Correspondences', of which he remembered two lines:

> Man travels there through forests of symbols,
> That all watch him with familiar looks.

Perhaps man really is surrounded by a forest of familiar symbols. Perhaps there are correspondences like this all over the world, correspondences between one man and another, between man and place, man and tree, man and rock, man and poetry. Perhaps it is man's challenge to find his own place in this network of hidden correspondences. Perhaps life acquires thereby a more gen-uine content. Perhaps the correspondences that have been found and activated begin to chime together and produce a harmony so that things begin to observe him with a familiar eye. Hitherto, life had been full of dissonance; chaotic, toneless.

Here self-criticism returned. Once upon a time he had believed that thought, especially unarticulated thought, had its own life, and once it had started moving it did so according to some form of logic that he was barely able to comprehend let alone control. Thought moved with increasing speed like a skier down a slippery incline, dragging the thinker with it. It seemed to him that he had read enough writers and philosophers to know that some caution was needed here. The more important thing was not to allow the thought to slip away freely in that manner. Like now. Was his life chaotic and toneless like this? Why was he thinking this way here, on this slope, in summer, amid the birdsong? Why did he have to bring his cares and dissonance with him here instead of allowing all his senses to enjoy this blossoming, verdant, fragrant world? Would he have been able, on some other slope somewhere, by some other brook or lake, to be fully content and happy? No – said a cynical voice inside himself – you have been a man for a long time. First you need a woman, then you would relax and see the rest. But you won't relax until you've had a woman.

He was almost in agreement with that voice. His question in the manner of Hamlet was where to find a woman. The girls he'd been out with, escorted home and kissed, even Malle now, nothing had come of it. The other kinds, the easier, looser girls, did not appear to have any interest in him. And they did not appear to notice his interest in them – most likely he simply did not know how to get them to notice. Should he pull himself together and search for what he had hitherto been lacking, or carry on waiting for an opportunity?

That, too, was a thought that, now that it had slipped through, began to pull him along with it. He didn't like it. If he had already had positive sexual experiences would he feel better here in Tilleorg, freer? Would the magical effect of the surroundings, the sun and the birdsong, reach him more clearly? The past does not exist. What he carried with him was not something real, it was just a thought, a fantasy that was no different in some ways from other fantasies, no different from the dream in which he had slept with several women, some of whom didn't even exist. Perhaps this meant he needed to be free of his illusions more than he needed a woman. Buddhist monks had to keep at least two metres away from women and could not even look in a woman's direction. They could manage it, so why couldn't he? Yogis and others had all kinds of techniques to help them, special exercises that curbed their sexual urges or transformed them. Radhakrishnan had hardly written anything specific on the matter, but he could start with him. He would find something out about yoga somewhere later. Something that would help him find his internal balance and would help him think more about philology and philosophy than sex scenes in films and books.

The sun was already fairly high and burning hot when he set off from the valley into the open fields. There were more clouds, and he could hope for the occasional shade. The wind was also stronger and, as always, in his face, as if wanting to prove sod's law. On his longer cycle rides he had almost always had to ride into the wind. This time it wasn't as strong. Soon he had to turn off the road so the wind was side-on, unless, of course, it spitefully decided to change direction.

The new road was a gravel path that wasn't particularly pleasant for cycling. Evidently it had been dressed recently – everywhere there were stones the size of hens' eggs and larger through which he had to zigzag. He had once heard a boy in a higher year, who had previously studied to be a road-builder in technical college, say that, in fact, there should be no larger stones at all on gravel paths. This was small comfort, especially now, when fatigue was setting in and there were still twenty-odd kilometres of gravel track ahead. Cars, of course, were much rarer here than on the major road, although it was abhorrent to think of the cloud of dust they would stir up there. Thinking didn't help, though, and he had to keep pushing the pedals.

He decided to make his last stop when there were fewer than ten kilometres left. He had with him an old road map of Estonia of his great-uncle's and Rein's instructions in his head. It was easy to find the way to churches even in modern-day Estonia, even here in the undulating, forested countryside of the south-east. The churches had placed themselves like ancient giants who wished to keep a permanent eye on each other. From any one church tower he could always, or nearly always, see two others. And although this church was not particularly old – it wasn't a genuine parish church but a newer building – from its tower you could see several kilometres to where the path came out of the forest and up to the hilltop. That's how Rein had explained it.

The church tower became visible even earlier than he could have hoped. And in the same valley at the bottom of the hill there was a brook. He rode his bike along the bank of the brook just far enough away from the road. The path had clearly been trodden by fishermen – presumably the brook was home to trout. In the shade of some small firs was a stone cairn; he leant his bike and backpack against it and stretched himself out alongside the brook.

During his childhood in the country, and even before then at his grandfather's house, he had loved lying on his back to watch the clouds, loved it more than he did playing with other children, which is what his mother thought he should be doing. The other children became a kind of nightmare for him; they invaded his life unexpectedly, the personal dreamland he built around the books he had read, the clouds or the stacked hay. Mother always said that he hung around in his room too much. But he couldn't go out somewhere in the town centre; you couldn't lie down in the street or on Toome Hill and watch the clouds. The town restricted him and distressed him like a great hostile force. The countryside in summer was different. In the country you could go from a room to the outdoors and from the outdoors into a room; everything was equally homely. The forest and the bog and the lake far away, where he sometimes went walking alone, were not hostile. Occasionally they were odd, even terrifying, but in truth he had a closer and deeper kind of bond with them. The forest and the bog had no hatred. During the day they accepted him as one of their own, allowed him to move freely, and sometimes, if the midges weren't biting too much, to sit on a felled tree or stump and silently watch the long-tailed tit fly with its brood from tree to tree, the buzzard hovering over the hilltops, wondering whether to fetch food for the nestlings or wait until he was a good distance away. Once he saw a fox with a bloody bird in its mouth going over the ditch; once a group of young badgers on a sandbank playing by their set. This gave him a light, happy feeling, as if an adult were telling him something in confidence, treating him as if he were on the same level. That was how the forest had revealed itself to him; it had shown him a few of its secrets, things that perhaps could not be entrusted to just anyone.

In that place on the bank of the brook there were no secrets. It was summer-bright, simple and open like a young farm girl in a romantic Finnish summer film. At least during the day – at night something secret might thrive here; something from the night world that still concealed itself from man in a place that could only be broken into by force with the aid of artificial light.

Sleep pressed down his head. Against his will his internal monologue became more and more dreamlike as if trying to draw an ever clearer distinction between summer and winter, countryside and town, term time and vacation. But he mustn't stay here and sleep. He pulled himself up out of his fatigue on to his numb feet, rinsed his face in the brook, drank a gulp of the water from the bottle, hauled his rucksack on to his back and went back to the road.

The church tower would occasionally come into view only to be screened again by the forest and hill, but little by little it did none the less come gradually, but definitely, closer. This was good because his feet were already stiff from the journey, his bottom was aching from the hard saddle and the straps of his rucksack were weighing ever more heavily on his shoulders.

Before the church the road descended once more into a valley at whose heart there was a small, narrow lake. Obviously, because of the steep drop, there was no asphalt here, only cobbles that had probably not been repaired for a very long time; some of the cobbles had sunk, some broken. Between them, flowing water had excavated deep holes and grooves. He tried to ride down the hill choosing the most even path between the broken cobbles and the larger holes, but he soon had to give it up and walk along, wheeling the bike.

The church was on a hill. There appeared to be a churchyard a short distance further off. There was a beautiful view from it down over the lake and forests. To the other side, the south, there loomed domes in a faint blue streak, and swimming slowly above them from south-west to north-east were white clouds.

Southern Estonia sometimes felt a little too beautiful, like a colour picture in a book intended for tourists.

Yes, a path did indeed lead down from the church, and there were two white houses there. From what Rein had said, one of them had to be the doctor's surgery and the post office, and the other the place where he and their neighbours lived.

In front of a small shed next to the house a middle-aged man in shorts was chopping wood, bare-chested. He slowed down. He had been going quite fast, and the bike stopped, leaning way over to the left, leaving a visible skid mark.

'Afternoon! I wish you strength,' he said to the woodcutter.

The woodcutter chopped the birch log waiting on the block in half with an elegant movement, stood up straight and replied, 'Strength always needed. Have you got enough to spare for others then?'

Not too much but enough to spare, he said, and asked whether the pastor lived here in the house.

'Sometimes he does, when time allows,' the woodcutter replied. 'Was it your lack of book learning that brought you to the church looking for him?'

He said he'd primarily come with the intention of calling on the pastor's son, as agreed.

'Ahh, so you're the vagabond I've heard about,' said the man, stretching his hand out to him. His handshake was strong and manly. 'I'm one of the pastor's son's closest relatives. We even talked to you on the phone if I'm not mistaken. So you're —.' The man took out his handkerchief and mopped his bald pate. 'Looking at you, it would seem that the best thing you could do now is go on inside. The women are probably serving something up. Have some refreshment and then you can go for a swim in the lake if that sounds reasonable to you.'

It did indeed. As if on cue the door opened and a girl of about eight with long plaits appeared on the doorstep.

'Mirjam, is Rein in his room?' asked the man of the house. 'There's a visitor for him.'

'Rein's in the back room reading,' replied the girl. 'Shall I go and tell him?'

'Yes, you could do that. Show our visitor where he can wash his hands and ask Mum or Ester to rustle up something for him to eat.'

He put his bike by the woodshed and went with Mirjam.

The girl led him up the steps. He managed to glimpse the shelves in the hall where there were a load of paperbacks with coloured jackets in German and English. In the corner by the window was a large hibiscus.

'Here it is,' said Mirjam. 'Smells like my brother's upstairs.'

She was right. When she opened the door, they were hit by the smell of strong tobacco mixed with coffee.

'You've got a visitor,' shouted the girl.

Rein was sitting at a table reading something. There was a mass of books and papers on the table and among them a coffee cup and an ashtray from which a wisp of smoke rose towards the ceiling.

It was clear from Rein's face that he was delighted with his visitor. This was great. He had been a bit afraid that the invitation to call in some time might not, in fact, have been intended as seriously as he had taken it to be.

They went into the kitchen where Rein's mother was busy at the stove. She looked small, plump and soft. Her laughter, too, was soft and warm as she wiped her hand on her apron and extended it to the visitor.

'You must be famished. Can I get you some bread and milk as a snack before dinner, or do you think you can wait just half an hour when there'll be something more substantial?' she fussed.

He said he'd be fine to wait. Rein thought that they could have a walk to the lake in that time and have a dip. He liked the idea a lot more now than he had at first. The homely atmosphere in the house had cheered him up, and even his aching legs were not so insistent that he should lie down. Of course, the most sensible thing was to have a dip in the lake and wash the sweat and dust from the long journey from his skin.

'Ester might like to come,' suggested Rein and went to invite his sister along.

Yes, Ester would come. And Mirjam didn't want to be left behind.

The girls caught them up, large towels in hand for him and Rein.

Ester was a bit like Mirjam and Rein to look at, although at first glance you would hardly have thought them brother and sisters. She was almost Rein's height, dark blonde and slim but with the heavy, downy legs of a country girl. Yet there was something light and skittish in her gait. Her warm laugh was definitely inherited from her mother, but she also had something of her father's mischievousness. He liked her immediately, and, strangley enough, in her company he felt none of the awkwardness he usually experienced in the company of women he liked in some way.

The lake was narrow but long, the other end was hidden by a cape, but the opposite shore was clearly visible; it couldn't be much wider than the Emajõgi in Tartu. Ester said that the lake was very deep in the middle, and several people had drowned here at midsummer in recent years. There was always some drunk who wanted to swim across the lake to another bonfire but didn't arrive alive.

The swimming place was small, at one time sand had been brought here and there was still some of it around. Right next to it there was a bonfire site; lying on the ground were fish scales, a couple of beer-bottle corks and paper.

'I forgot to bring a spade again,' said Rein. 'We always need to bring one, especially after the weekend.'

They gathered up the corks and the other stuff that needed collecting and undressed. Mirjam was allowed just to splash near the bank. He went behind a bush to change his clothes. When he entered the water Rein and Ester were already some way off and moving with swift strokes to the opposite shore. It was immediately obvious that they were good swimmers. He decided he would not try to swim across the lake – it would have taken too much time – so he swam a small circuit along this shore. He liked to swim breaststroke, with a frog kick; if he did front crawl his face was always under water; it was like swimming in semi-darkness. He could swim breaststroke slowly and get closer to the water birds. He could also swim for a long time and a long distance, although not quickly. But where was he off to in a hurry anyway?

He was the first one to leave the water. Mirjam was paddling by the same reed clump and called out, 'Look at these two enormous beautiful dragonflies!'

The others had gone right across to the opposite shore and were swimming back. When he had got dried and changed his clothes Rein and Ester were already on the bank.

'Eyes towards the church, please!' shouted Ester, taking off her swimming costume. Mirjam emerged looking sulky only after Rein had ordered her out of the water. She scuttled up towards the house in her swimsuit, leaving her calico dress for the others to bring.

They dressed and left. Almost exactly half an hour had gone by. Ester was in front of him, the shape of her damp body clearly visible under her dress. Once she stood in the sun, making her thighs and a tuft of hair visible: she was wearing no knickers.

He had wondered whether the family would say grace as they did in the religious families he had sometimes stayed with. They did not. The meal began with a moment's silence together; Rein's mother put her hands together as if in prayer.

It was a proper farm meal – pork with pickled cabbage and potatoes. On the table was also a plate of sweet-smelling bread; they sometimes got some from an old lady who still baked her own.

It seemed to him that Rein's father probably got on with people very well. He would have liked to ask him something about it: he had never before met any clergymen and was genuinely uncertain as to what their daily work was, apart from holding Sunday services, officiating at burials and baptizing children. But he didn't know how to ask about it without demonstrating his complete ignorance of Church matters. Rein's father, though, started to ask him questions immediately. What was he studying? How happy was he with the course? What else was he involved in? What interests and hobbies did the people on his course have? What impression did he have of their old friend Alo? It was clear that he simply took an interest in people and never wasted any opportunity to indulge his curiosity.

'Honestly, what are you giving our guest such a grilling for? You might as well be an interrogator,' said his wife, trying to keep him in check. 'He's come a long way and he's tired. Give him a chance to catch his breath.'

'And what do you know about interrogations?' Rein's father refused to be annoyed. 'The way I see it, he's spent half the day in silence with just a bicycle and the village dogs to talk to. I merely wish to know what young people today do at university. It's interesting. And it's important for the future of the Estonian people.'

His wife thought that his own daughter could tell him just as much. Rein's father did not agree. In his view each individual lives their own life at university and sees life there from their own perspective.

After dinner they had a cup of coffee and rhubarb cake. Rhubarb from their own garden, as the lady of the house said modestly. He found the cake exceptionally good, but it might have been that his system, which had lost so many calories through cycling, took greater relish in the sweetness than usual.

They then sat in silence for a while and got up. Each of them took their own plates and cups to the kitchen, and he did so, too.

Rein's father thought that he must be shattered, but there was wood to be taken to the shed later in evening that he had chopped. He said that he was ready for that.

After the meal each went about their business – the man of the house to the office, the lady of the house and Ester to the kitchen, Mirjam outside to play with the neighbour's daughter.

They sat for a while in Rein's room and talked. Now it was his turn to ask the questions because in Tartu he had not managed to get a clear picture of the educational establishment at which Rein was studying. He couldn't say that religion was alien to him, but hitherto he had been very distant from the Church. It was an area where there was not much material in Estonian literature. As a result French *curés* and English ministers and their lives and concerns were more familiar to him than Estonian pastors, about which neither Tammsaare, Vilde, Tuglas nor Luts had anything to say.

He said as much to Rein. The same had occurred to him when he had read literature at school. In his view there was a big difference between Estonian and Nordic literature. Quite a lot had been written about pastors over there, sometimes in a really interesting way, but in Estonian novels clergymen, rare as they were, were always a little odd; there were no regular characters among them.

He was reminded of Lenin's theory, which he'd studied at university, that each people's culture embodies two cultures – the culture of the exploiter and the culture of the exploited. This had always been incomprehensible and unacceptable to him. But now it seemed that there were indeed two distinct parts to Estonian culture – the secular and the spiritual.

Things hadn't been like this at first – of the leaders of the national awakening old Jannsen was a sexton and Hurt and Eisen were pastors. Did the divergence happen at the turn of the century when left-wing politics and atheism arrived in Estonia, along with the Young Estonia group and other forms of modern art?

Rein said that Alo and his father had discussed this many times when Alo had visited – once every summer they came to visit them for a couple of days. In his father's view Alo was precisely the man who was able to unite these two halves or branches of culture. And what was more, Alo was both an intellectual with a European education and a renowned expert in Judaism, to say nothing of his knowledge of what to us were the exotic cultures of India and elsewhere. He was therefore a link between East and West, as though in defiance of Kipling's pessimistic declaration that 'East is East and West is West / and never the twain shall meet'.

He asked whether Rein needed to get on with his work. He could look at the books and take a walk by the lake. It was good that he had asked because Rein was planning to sit an exam in Church history at the beginning of the next week. Nothing difficult but tons of cramming; all the Church fathers, Church councils, the wordings and rewordings of the creed, which were difficult to remember correctly and in the right chronological order. He could look at the books if he wanted to.

Church history was a bit like Party history, he thought. Yes, his father said that the Party and its ideology didn't seem to be much more than a new pseudo-faith which in many ways aped the old faith. He agreed with this. The old faith seemed more interesting at any rate. At least at the start when he hadn't known much about it. Rein plunged into a thick book in German by Harnack. He approached the shelves.

Yes, this was another culture, names and topics unknown to him: Karl Barth, Karl Rahner, Paul Tillich, Rudolf Bultmann . . . Then, one name was familiar: Albert Schweitzer. The very same Schweitzer. He had read something about him, but here was Schweitzer's own work, *Kultur und Ethik*. There was also some fiction, Rilke's *Stundenbuch* – The Book of Hours – in an old edition from the 1920s and Hermann Hesse's *Narziß und Goldmund*.

He picked up the Rilke and leafed through it. He was almost completely unfamiliar with Rilke – he had not learnt much German, and his reading in the language was restricted at first to books of fairy-tales as they were easier to read and sentences and situations were repeated. Poetry was harder, although he had managed fairly successfully with one of his favourite poets of his schooldays, Heine. Aleks Luuberg liked to quote Rilke sometimes. Yes, these were the lines that he dimly remembered in the presentation that had inspired Aleks:

> I circle around God, around the ancient tower,
> and I spin for thousands of years;
> and I still know not: am I falcon or storm
> or another great song.

To circle around God, around the tower of old for thousands of years without knowing whether you are falcon, storm or song. It was so beautiful, satisfying. Those lines said everything; there was no need for anything more. At the same time all the stories told about God were still incomplete, unsatisfying, whether they be efforts to substantiate His existence or refute it. Perhaps one must not talk about God other than in the language of poetry. Perhaps God is part of truth that lies beyond what can be depicted in prose, beyond what can be expressed in ordinary language.

He thought that he should try to translate Rilke. He had tried before to translate a couple of things that he liked, but his efforts had seemed feeble. Perhaps the problem was precisely that he became so entwined with the lines that were close to his soul that he could not remould them into any other form, not even in a translation. Perhaps one can properly translate only what has not become part of oneself. Therefore poetry translation is not the writing of poetry, a free creative process, but a serious task, a craft that must be learnt like basket-weaving or solving differential equations.

He thought he would take a book with him and go outside to read. There was a hammock between two lindens in the garden with a couple of deckchairs alongside. There weren't many more clouds in the sky than there had been mid-morning; the possibility of rain was still, this time, just a possibility.

He took the Rilke and a small German–Estonian dictionary and went into the garden. He settled himself comfortably in a deckchair: when he raised his gaze from the book he could see the surface of the lake sparkling in the sun through the apple trees and behind it the dark forest on the hill. A bee hummed in the white clover blossoms; his ears caught the chirrupings of the first grasshoppers. Occasionally a lone midge would find its way to him, although miraculously there were surprisingly few of them for the time of year. Swallows bustled in the courtyard and the garden; the chicks they had in their nests were evidently already so big that there was only barely room to twitter. From time to time a gust of wind went wild among the trees and tried to turn the page, but it soon died away.

He managed to make out one poem with the dictionary, but he didn't have the stamina to carry on with any more. He placed the book on his knees and let his head sink back and gazed at the swifts wheeling below the clouds. Their flight reminded him of the beautiful curves in an analytical geometry textbook that he would leaf through in the library sometimes. The sky here was at once far away from and close to the dome of the hill. Was the church built in a special place, maybe the site of a shrine holy to the ancient Estonians, as had sometimes occurred? Unlikely. Originally it had just been an auxiliary church constructed probably less than a hundred years ago. But perhaps the site had, ultimately, been chosen subconsciously because it was where the heavens were nearer or more open? He realized that he was unable to think clearly any more: how can heaven be closer in one place than it is in another? Once he had thought that heaven was everywhere and that people lived there, although they usually didn't notice it. From the moon or Mars we all dwell in the heavens, people along with all the other flying, crawling and running creatures . . .

He hadn't noticed the point at which he'd dropped off, and neither could he say whether he was awoken by Ester's voice or the shadow that suddenly alighted on his face.

'Mother said that I should find out whether our visitor was starting to get cold out here under the trees, that he must be tired and that it would be better for him to come in and have a lie down on the sofa in the back room if he feels he needs a nap.'

No, he didn't particularly want to lie down on the sofa in the back room. He would prefer to take the book back to the room and go for a stroll by the lake and maybe have another dip.

'I was wondering whether perhaps you'd like to come with me. I'm going to see an old lady who bakes bread. It's a lovely walk over, about two kilometres by the lake through the forest. And on the way back we could go to the lake if you like.'

Of course he would like to.

At first they walked side by side, then, by the marshy area beside a spring and in the forest, Ester went in front. He could not take his eyes off her body, which seemed to be dancing of its own accord, as if unable to express in any other way the joy of being and the beautiful day. Perhaps in her body language there was something – a kind of primitive, implicit invitation that neither of them perceived or recognized properly. He felt her nearness bewitching him; it made him slightly giddy as if, strangely, there were nothing awkward in the enchantment of proximity, none of the disabling lust and yearning that sometimes came over him when he was in the presence of a beautiful woman. It was easy and good to be in Ester's company. Just once he caught himself wondering whether it would also be easy and good to be in bed with her, although even that thought came and went without leaving any trace of temptation in its wake.

'I don't think I've seen you around Tartu. I take it you don't frquent the university café,' he chatted.

'No, the café's a place for philologists, historians and medics. We biologists steer more towards the forest, as you know.'

'So in summer you live in the forest and in autumn you fly south with the migrating birds – fly away south, baby cranes, fly away south,' he said, echoing the words of the children's song.

'Just look at us fly. You sit there in the café and can't even hear us flying high above, calling to each other.'

No, he didn't want to be a stereotypical philologist. He heard the geese and cranes flying over sometimes in the evenings. There was something special, some-thing sacred and distressing about it. He thought that the ancient Estonians must have had rituals of some kind to bid farewell to the cranes in autumn and welcome them again in spring.

'Alo said that in North America and other places lots of the indigenous peoples believed that the birds brought the spring with them and that if the birds didn't come back then neither would the spring; winter would retain its grip.'

This was something he'd never heard before, but he liked the story; it was something he could write a poem about. He wanted to know what other inter-esting things Alo had said.

'Tell me something about . . . Alo. Have you known him since you were a child?'

Yes, Ester remembered the Teacher from her girlhood. But he hadn't spoken to her much, mainly to her father about theology. It was only when Ester was at secondary school that the Teacher started to notice she was there really. He had wanted her to do biology. Because it was more sensible: it would have been diffi-cult to get a proper job in philology and history: most people who studied those subjects became teachers, but it was unlikely they'd let her, a clergyman's child, become a teacher. They would be afraid she'd corrupt the children. Medicine and exact sciences didn't interest her much, so that left biology. Personally she had nothing against teaching; she would have got on really well with the children, especially in a smaller rural school, but she would probably have to get a job in a lab in an institution somewhere. But she might be able to go on expeditions, too.

They had reached the forest where a late chaffinch was still singing briskly. Sud-denly Ester stood still, grabbed him by the hand and whispered, 'Shhh! Wait!'

Her hand was soft and cool. Nevertheless he felt warmth flowing from it into his and billowing up to his head. They stood like this for an instant, then Ester used her other hand to point to a young fir some way off in whose branches a large bird – about the size of a thrush, he thought – was huddled. A small grey bird flew down towards it and poked something into the big bird's gaping beak, which it opened even wider by flapping its wings.

'A dunnock's feeding a cuckoo chick,' whispered Ester. 'That's a sight you don't often se.'

He remembered that Grandfather had once said that one of the rarest nature photographs was of a cuckoo pushing its own egg into a garden-warbler's nest with its beak.

The cuckoo chick's stepmother fed her nurseling, looked around and gave an alarm call. She had clearly spotted them. Then she took flight, followed by the cuckoo chick, both disappearing into a thicket.

They carried on. He felt as if the girl's hand had left a warm, radiant impression on his own.

He said to keep on talking about Alo.

'My picture of him is quite different from that of other young people. To you he's a genius, a great, inaccessible figure that people wonder at and defer to, but to me he's always been Alo. We're always talking now, and sometimes he comes with me to look at the plants and watch the birds. Once or twice I've even been able to point plants out to him that he hasn't been able to recognize. I can't regard him as a miracle man. That's probably a common fault in women: first and foremost we see another person as another person, not a genius, a hero or a miracle worker.'

'But Jesus had female disciples or whatever you want to call them,' he offered.

'I don't know who they were in relation to him, disciples or friends or even wives and lovers.'

'Might Jesus have had lovers?'

'Uncle Alo talked about it once. He thinks that that woman who sinned, the one Jesus stopped them stoning to death, was actually his wife. And then there were Martha and Mary and Mary Magdalene.'

He'd never thought about that. Jesus, who talked about love, was in love, a lover, a husband.

'Does your father agree with Alo on theological matters?' he asked. 'I've heard that he's had some misunderstandings with other clergy because of his radical views.'

'I don't think his views bother Daddy. They're such old friends, although in many ways they're very different people. Daddy's no great theoretician – he's a village pastor, as he calls himself. A country pastor with no theological or philosophical ambition. Oh, he's aware of Alo's views, but he keeps them separate from his own. They are two different worlds: to Daddy, Alo is like a radio broadcasting news of distant lands. It's interesting to hear, but it has no direct effect on us. Daddy and all of us have plenty of other things in common with him. When Alo and Ellen come here we always do something in the garden. We go on a trip, Alo draws and paints, and sometimes we go to church to play the organ.'

'Can you play the organ?'

'Only a bit. I only learnt the piano at music school, but Ellen is a proper organist. When she's here on a Sunday she plays for the service. And Alo helps my father choose a good verse of Scripture for the sermon.'

'Doesn't he give the sermon himself sometimes?'

'No, he hasn't got a licence. The authorities monitor these things quite rigorously. Neither he nor Daddy would want him to. He does, of course, ask him for advice and help, but he always prepares his own sermon himself. It's a matter of principle for him.'

There was something moving in the way Ester talked about her own father and the Teacher.

'Do you call your father Daddy?' he asked. 'And Alo Alo?'

She laughed. 'That's how it's been with us, yes. My father, Daddy I mean, came back from Siberia when I was already quite big. When he was taken away I was so small that I could hardly remember him at all. Then I came to the conclusion that as I'd missed out on calling him "Daddy" as a child I would call him that now. So that they couldn't completely take my childhood away from me. But with Alo it's just something that's stuck. he used to be "Uncle Alo" and later became just "Alo".'

'I don't remember my father, my daddy. He didn't come back. I don't know what I'd've called him – Daddy or Papa or *Papenka* like they do in Russian. Or whatever term the Russians use these days.'

'Rein said that your father was Russian. Is your Russian good?' she asked after a longer pause. They had left the forest; the path went back down to the edge of the lake.

'I know it, but I'm better at reading and writing than speaking it,' he replied. 'I wasn't able to talk to my father, and the relatives he had here in Estonia didn't stay; the ones who are left are in Russia.'

'So do you feel completely Estonian?'

'I don't know what it's like to feel Estonian, Russian or gypsy. Perhaps language is the most important thing. The language you think in . . .'

'And dream in, as Alo – Uncle Alo – says. Look that's where the old lady lives,' said Ester and pointed to a grey shingle roof visible through the tall lindens.

They got the bread from the woman, had to answer her inquisitive questions about the young man and set off back.

'She must think you're my fiancé,' laughed Ester. 'She worries about me, about my not having found a husband yet.'

'What about you? Doesn't it worry you?' he asked and realized instantly that it was not the sort of question he could easily ask in jest.

'No, there's no time to worry . . . There's plenty of time for really urgent stuff like that,' she said. Again he felt a warm surge cascading over his body. Surely he wasn't falling in love with her? What on earth would it mean? He knew that he could not be dismissive of her proximity, to say nothing of her touch. And there was something in the air between them that was drawing him towards Ester and perhaps drawing Ester towards him.

They spoke less on the way back. He felt that she wanted to walk in front of him, not beside him. A couple of times when they were side by side on a wider section of path he looked at her, and always their glances met, as if a stage director had given them instruction.

'Do you want to take the other path?' the girl asked once they were in the forest.

They turned to the left and reached a small glade where there had evidently once been a farm. In the middle of the glade were two tall lindens and an oak. Charred ruins could be seen among the lilacs in the half-bare clearing reclaimed by the forest – the remains of foundations and a chimney.

'The farm was burnt to the ground in the raids. This was an area frequented by Forest Brothers until the KGB got wind of something. Someone must have talked. The farm was surrounded when the men were inside. The farmer's wife and two men died; one escaped from the fire with injuries but died later in a farm near by. His grave is in the forest on the other side of the lake. Daddy went to give him a blessing once; that's what his relatives wanted.'

'Were there lots of Forest Brothers here?' he asked.

'Yes,' she replied. 'It was very difficult for people here; Forest Brothers on one side, Soviet security forces on the other, both making demands and threats of their own.'

'My grandfather was always against Russian rule, but he came to the conclusion that the Forest Brothers' struggle was much more of a hindrance than a help to the Estonian people.'

'Daddy thinks more or less the same. The Forest Brothers caused him worry and aggravation. But most of the people in the forest didn't go there to fight; they were trying to escape being deported and arrested.'

'Why was he taken away?'

'Ask him. Perhaps he'll tell you. Sometimes, if he's in the mood, he tells really funny stories about Siberia.'

'Was Siberia a funny place to him?'

'No, not at all, but he says he wouldn't have survived the camp if he hadn't learnt to see the funny side. Like the Jews. Daddy says that he learnt how to from the Jews. But I think he inherited his sense of humour from his father; Grandfather had been the village smart-aleck when he was young. He wrote songs about what went on the neighbourhood and –'

'Can you remember him, too?'

'I do, a little. He called me all kinds of bird names – crow chick and grouse egg and swallow chick and . . . and he was the one who read me bedtime stories at night and sang me lullabies. Grandmother always scolded him because of the songs – how can you sing songs like that to a child.'

'Songs like what?'

'Mmm, "Viiu the Bedbug Maid" and suchlike. I remember I once sang for visitors: "And there he staged all kinds of acts and dramas / And performed on the table a *fata morgana*."'

'And what did the visitors say?'

'They must have laughed, Granddad included. Grandma was embarrassed and outraged. Maybe funny men's wives have a different character and don't enjoy a joke.'

'Is it the same with your mother?'

'Perhaps, a bit.'

There was something in this that he liked very much, but it was something that he did not understand fully and found it difficult to ask about. But he felt that this was the best time to try to resolve the issue. 'There's one thing I've always wanted to ask but never been able to. It's to do with humour and . . . faith in God or, shall we say, the work of a clergyman. The image I have, although I am not alone in having it, is that religious matters are always very serious and clergymen are serious people. But Alo and your father and certain others I know are a long way from being solemn. So have I been completely wrong in my impression? Are clergymen more inclined to havebe humorous than be deadly serious?'

Ester shook her head and laughed. 'Perhaps you should ask Daddy about that, too, how he reconciles the humorous and the serious. But, as far as I understand it, for a religious person, someone who truly accepts the gospel, the majority of the things that we worry about and fall out over are not usually serious. Alo has one thesis; we have several, where he writes something on the tragi-comic earnest nonsense of this world. But most pastors do not like Daddy's humour and Alo's irony. They've informed on Daddy and tried to have him ousted from the clergy.'

'But haven't succeeded?'

'No, not so far. But who knows where it will lead.'

They had reached the garden gate. Mirjam was swinging in the hammock between the trees, and from behind the house came the sound of axe blows: the reverend was presumably chopping wood again.

'We could have gone for a dip,' he said.

'We still can. You're not leaving today,' replied Ester.

Perhaps Rein had finished with his studies. Then they could go and stack the wood and after that go to the lake.

'Make sure you both tell me when you're off. The more the merrier,' said Ester.

Together they sat around the evening table once more. Ester lit two candles, and they listened to a record of Bach's cantata 'Bleib bei Uns, denn Es Will Abend Werden' that the father had brought back from Germany, and then they each went to their own rooms.

He was given a campbed to sleep on in Rein's room, which had been aired to let the smoke out. He asked Rein what had led him to follow in his father's footsteps and study theology.

His father had rarely spoken to him at all about religious matters until, when he was about to finish school, he talked to his father about the alternatives open to him for the future, including theology. Father had said that he had no right nordesire to insist that his son should seek ordination. Rein should watch and consider – he had seen his father's work close hand and met his colleagues; he had been able to gain a picture of how things were.

Did they discuss faith?

For his father, faith was something intimate between an individual and God, something that wasn't generally discussed with others, like intimate relations between a man and a woman. And, just like a love affair, coercion, proselytising and relentless pursuit were not the way to go about faith. The most beautiful way and the best was when two people – or a person and God – simply found one other. The most genuine faith was free faith, like free love. Rein's father thought that the the Christian churches themselves were largely to blame for the onslaught from militant atheism now besieging them. Compulsory atheism was compulsory Christianity in a distorted mirror, an echo of the times when people were baptized and married without being asked their wishes and regardless of their spiritual beliefs. Atheism cleansed the Church of duplicity and terror and gave it the opportunity to start again, free of the burdens and prejudices of the past. In his view, the Church must not be a country within a country with its own feudal hierarchy, clergy and saints but a communion of people living their lives in God's love, in mutual support, because in their view that was the only life worth living.

Was that what Rein thought, too? How about the Teacher?

Yes, it was his and Rein's father's joint theological space, a place he felt he now belonged. In his view there would otherwise be no reason for studying theology and becoming a clergyman.

But did other clergy and theology students think and feel the same way?

Only a few, unfortunately. Some were in the ministry because they believed it was a way to conduct Estonian matters; some wanted to be pastors. To them, entering the service of the Church was like joining the Party was for others: the opportunity to forge a career, to develop a sense of one's importance. The current era troubled them a great deal because it had lowered the status of clergy, cast them out of the highest echelons of society. A pastor, at one time with the status of a real gentleman, a squire, government official or a military officer, was no longer deemed fit to mingle with society's chairmen, secretaries and directors. This was insulting to people aspiring to holy orders; they regarded the social elite as vulgar and vile, but when someone like a chairman or director engages with them they are immediately ready to drink to a friendship with the new masters. They hope that the Party and government will ask them to take on the difficult task of educating the new generation ...

What about Estonia? Were there really no opportunities to advance it through the Church – the only institution in today's Estonia that was fully Estonian in language and mindset.

No, here Rein's father and Alo were of a different view. They thought that Christianity and the Church should not be harnessed to the cart of nationalism. Paul clearly said that there was no longer any Greek or Jew, Scythian or barbarian; all were one in Christ. Therefore there were no longer any Estonians or any Russians or any Estonian matters or any Russian matters that should be conducted through the Church.

That viewpoint disappointed him somewhat. But wasn't nationality a standard tool of human existence, and weren't its suppression and advancement evil?

The very concept was something that the two theologian friends refused to acknowledge. In their view, nationality belonged in the past, to the times of the Old Testament where nationalities, tribes, cities and clans were always fighting among themselves and, they hoped God would assist and support them in their battles.

But didn't this nationalist nihilism play right into the hands of the large nations in power? If Estonians generally thought that there was no longer any need for nations, wouldn't Estonia ultimately end up being something like Pskov *oblast*, which had no important cultural life and gave little to the world compared with Estonia and Latvia, although its population was more or less the same?

Rein shared his views ofPskov *oblast* and Estonian culture but thought that the Church must not become a cultural establishment or a nationalist institution. That would be bad for both: a nationalist Church would no longer be a real Church, and an ecclesiastical nation would no longer be a true nation.

'Anyhow, let's go to sleep. I've got used to going to sleep early and getting up early,' said Rein, putting an end to their conversation, which was veering towards the familiar nationalist concerns.

There was something in Rein's resolute manner that he liked but found mildly disconcerting. He had not got used to giving instructions in a commanding but natural manner; he lacked the authority to get others to do things. The role of leader seemed, however, to suit Rein. He thought that he would make a good pastor or officer. The thought was a mite disconcerting: he suddenly felt as if he were again the young boy in the class to whom all the others were superior and whose views never counted for anything in any gang. But, in fact, he, too, wanted to get to sleep or, rather, to fall into a reverie before he dozed as had become his habit.

Rein was as resolute in falling asleep as he was when awake. After a couple of minutes he was already snoring gently; the visitor lay on the campbed, allowing the day to glide in front of his eyes. If it had been a normal bicycling day he would have seen in his doze the edge of the road and the telegraph poles sliding past, but now the picture of Ester emerged before his eyes. Ester on the forest path; Ester by the lake; Ester in the living-room candlelight listening to music; Ester smiling, looking straight at him, Ester's face; her hair ruffled by the wind; underneath her summer dress he could see her young breasts, her hips; once, when stood against the light he saw the area between her thighs through her dress . . . *What If This Is Love,* the title of a film he had recently seen, came to him. What was love? Must there be love in order for love to be, in order to respond to the meaning of the word and the expectations bound up with it? Might there not be something else between him and Ester, something unique and singular for which there was no word, something that came into the world when they met or would at least do so when they met again? His imagination stayed with the unique and singular; it was something so beautiful, almost as beautiful as Ester there in the evening by the lake at sunset when the lake water was very warm and the sun setting over the tops of the trees created a momentary halo that shone over her head, made her a saint. The thought that Ester, that his feeling for Ester, might be something holy was like a sacred echo of the evening, recurring in his dreaming mind. It was accompanied by a feeling of joy, a bolt of happiness he had never previously experienced in his life. Ester, sun, joy, sanctity, surprise – all melted together into something miraculously light that raised him up in the air, cast him high like a bird. So this is what it must be like to have wings, he thought, and then realized that something wonderful had happened; he had actually flown out of his own body, risen up to the ceiling from where he could watch his prone body on the campbed and Rein asleep in the other corner of the room. For a moment he hovered there but then felt a strange force seize him and carry him to the window. This is how the soul of a witch moves outside the body, he thought. Could he fly to Ester's window and look in on her? He would have liked to. The strange force had already transported him out through the window. He saw the house and windows; a light was burning in one window. It could be hers. He tried to fly towards it but realized that he could not, in fact, fly. The force that was holding him and carrying him onwards had no wings; it did not have his will or mind. It was something he did itthat force? He began to feel a fear that grew as he felt he would be carried far away from the house towards the lake, which sparkled far away in the half-dusk of the summer's night. He tried to do something, although he was completely helpless: the spirit, or whatever it was that was carrying him through the air, had no limbs, only eyes and ears. The spirit, the immortal spirit was completely helpless in the hands of the forces and powers carrying him out of his body and away. Away to where? He flew to the lake like a night bird; he wondered whether any creature, an owl or bat, saw him or whether he was seen by another spirit who, like him, was afforded no night rest by an unknown force?

When he awoke in the morning all he remembered of what had happened at the beginning of the night was that he had descended to the lake and the tepid dark water had engulfed him. Perhaps the whole thing had been a dream. If he had been able to look in through a window from somewhere he would have been able to control his vision, ascertain whether he was really travelling outside his body as a spirit; it might be called a detached spirit. What did it all mean? It was all tied in with Ester somehow, of course, but how? Did the dream or the dreamlike vision presage anything? The ascent, the flying ascent and then the descent into the dark depths. No, it couldn't, it mustn't.

He had decided that he would not stay beyond lunchtime and would continue his journey. The previous day's fluidity, which had seized him in the proximity of Ester, had almost disappeared; in the morning light the world was neutral, sharply delineated and solid. Perhaps the unknown force had played with him or both of them and, upon leaving, his spirit had still been risen in flight and had plunged into the river. Who knew. Rein was still asleep. He got dressed quietly, picked up his towel and went downstairs. There was a fire in the kitchen under the stove, although there was no one to be seen. It was better that way. He felt a stranger to himself, distant. It would have been difficult to talk to anyone. It sometimes was for him – the usual everyday phrases, 'Good morning', 'How did you sleep?', 'Lovely day today', wouldn't form on his lips.

There was a heavy dew on the grass. There was no longer any wind; the midges set about besieging him. The lake was still, a ribbon of mist still hovered over the surface of the water. In the distance a red warbler was singing and a tern floated on the surface. Two white water-lilies had already opened their flowers, and by the bathing place at the water's edge floated several dark-winged water nymphs.

The water was very much cooler than in the evening, although the lake did not have the same intimidating darkness as it had had in his night vision. He swam towards the water-lilies. When he opened his eyes under the water everything was full of shimmering light; it felt very much like daytime and real. He filled his lungs with air and swam underwater as far as he could. He was five metres short of the water-lilies before he ran out of breath.

When he got back Rein's mother and Ester were in the kitchen. Mirjam was having a wash, the father was working and Rein could be heard groping around upstairs. He went up, sorted his bedclothes out and said he thought he'd get on his way that day. He couldn't make out from what Rein said or his tone of voice whether he was sorry that his friend wasn't staying longer or not. At the breakfast table Rein's mother said that she thought that their guest should remain longer; it was lovely to have the company of young people. They welcomed young visitors, particularly in summer – Ester's fellow students, biologists and geographers, were lively people especially.

After breakfast he packed his rucksack in which he had to stow a good portion of Rein's mother's rhubarb cake. Hot, fresh coffee was poured into the water bottle – it was always good on a journey, even in hot weather, as Rein's mother said. She – he thought that it might just be something in the nature of pastor's wives – gave the impression that she always knew what someone needed better than the person himself. His grandmother was like that, too.

Ester's remark on his departure was of greater interest to him – he had to admit to himself that he hoped that she would be a bit upset. But it was difficult, although not impossible, to read anything into Ester's reaction.

'Already?' she said. 'Didn't you want to stay longer?'

He replied that he might look in on his way back to the city in a couple of weeks. If, of course, Rein was here and it was all right.

Ester remembered something. 'Oh, it's around then that Uncle Alo and Ellen are coming. We'll almost certainly be going off on a trek. Perhaps you can time your arrival so that we can all go together.'

That pleased him, of course – to be here with the Teacher and Ester for a day or maybe longer. And here, in different surroundings by the lake, in the forest.

Did Ester know where the trek would take them?

'No, not definitely. Sometimes it's somewhere around here; sometimes they go a bit further on the bus so that they can get back by evening.'

Yes, he could time his arrival so that they all went on the trek together. Provided the Teacher and Ellen didn't object.

Ester was sure they wouldn't. She had heard through Rein that the Teacher had spoken well of him. And she knew when they would be coming; he just had to remember.

They all went to the lake before he left. Rein swam across again, but Ester stayed with him. They swam around the water-lilies and did breaststroke by the edge of the reeds. A mother duck and her ducklings let them get quite close. Ester said that the birds were much less afraid of people swimming than people walking on the bank. Swimmers didn't have guns.

He shook everyone's hand in turn, thanked his host heartily, heaved his rucksack on and got on his bike. He didn't cycle very fast: the muscles in his thighs and buttocks were very sore from the previous day. But most of the journey was behind him as were the steepest hills. In front of him lay more gentle terrain.

He turned to look back once more, wondering if he would see Ester. Yes, all three of them were there, Rein, Ester and Mirjam who was waving eagerly to the departing guest.

His body soon overcame its weariness and muscular discomfort, although he felt much more absent-minded than he had the previous day. Irrespective of what he thought about, his thoughts managed, either directly or indirectly, to come back to yesterday: Ester, then the Teacher and finally Malle. What was Malle doing now? Was he now in love with two women at once? Were his and Malle's paths now separating, and was his now joining with Ester's? Did she even want him? Perhaps he and Malle would stay together, and Ester would simply become a good friend, a companion, who was good fun to be with and go trekking with? His spirit was both at peace and troubled; the future was intriguing and daunting. It would be so good to be away from the city and everything, at Meeta's, where there was still something of his vanished past.

18

The country of his childhood began a good five kilometres before his great-aunt's farm. As a matter of fact, there was a lot more than his own childhood that bound him to this land. Here a smaller path turned off into the forest from the main route – it led to the mill where his grandmother had grown up. Grandmother hadn't visited it since, although several of his great-aunts – there had once been seven of them all told – had. It was here that eight sisters had lived and from here that most of them had been married. Interesting that only one became a farmer's wife; all the others married educated men: two teachers, the others tradesmen. Ownership of the mill was passed to strangers, and only very rarely did one of them come back here. When the sisters visited Grandmother their chatter often strayed to their childhood home, and then he could hear the beautiful Võru language of the previous century tumble from their lips. They hadn't even mastered correct written Estonian: the little schooling they had received had been given in German; Grandmother's confirmation Bible was in German, as were the first verses in her miraculously preserved friendship album. It was interesting that the great-aunt whom he was now on his way to visit had been a schoolteacher for half her life, like her husband, and of course had had to use the written language, yet in her old age she returned more and more to her first mother tongue and even in letters would write '*iks*' instead of '*ikka*' for 'always' and '*hain*' instead of '*hein*' for 'hay'.

The mill marked the limit of the range of his fishing places of old, which he had sometimes visited alone, sometimes with Andres, the only son of Meeta's still living with her. He was unable to say that there had been many things in his childhood that were better than now, but on one he was certain – the rivers had been cleaner and full of fish. Even little boys like he and Andres would sometimes return home with full fish bags sufficient to feed themselves and the cat, Põnts, who knew when it was worth climbing the garden fencepost and watching for the fishermen returning home. When the boys came back he would jump down, run towards them to the mailbox by the main path and lead the way into the yard, his tail proudly in the air. If he'd been able to speak he'd definitely have whooped loudly, 'We're back from our fishing trip!' Poor Põnts and his upright tail – he had come home one April in a wretchedly dishevelled state with bloody ears, one eye swollen shut and half his tail dangling lifelessly. Meeta suspected that he'd been in a fight with the village dogs, but it was only a suspicion. Põnts' ears and eye healed beautifully, but his dangling half-tail was amputated by the vet when he came over to deliver a calf, explaining that the bone was broken and that if a human being could get about with no tail at all a cat could manage with half. And he did, or at least he never showed that he felt the loss of his missing tail end.

He now turned to go down to the mill, as he always did when he was out here. The mill was no longer operational, but the big mill structure was still there, and the last miller was living out his retirement in the small house next door. He and Andres had once visited him to get some grain ground. The errand to the mill had been an errand from a poor member of a collective farm in lean times; the barrow, which each of the boys had pushed in turn, contained a bag of barley that had to be made into a food supplement for the cow and the pig. That errand had stayed in his mind, perhaps because they'd gone all the way barefoot on the damp gravel road, perhaps because while waiting in the queue he had had time to look around the mill. Plenty of things were probably the same as they had been seventy years previously when his great-grandmother kept the mill, educated her daughters and married them off. The hitching post was probably in the place it had been when Estonia's popular heroes were still horse thieves.

The mill-dam and the bridge over the river were still there but much more dilapidated than the last time he'd visited. The dam was higher and wider than average so the mill-race was providing a decent flow. The mill's shingle roof had recently been repaired so someone was still looking after it. It would have been a shame if the proud stone building constructed from boulders had been abandoned and begun to decay. If he were rich, he thought, he would buy the mill and move there. He had recently begun to think about places where he might like to live, that he might make his home. He and Malle had once discussed it even, although they had never talked of marriage. But he was homesick for here, probably because he had had neither a home nor a room nor even a corner to call his own since the Germans had thrown his grandfather out of his house; since then they had wandered from one city apartment to another until they had stopped where they now lived. Would the mill be sold if someone wanted to buy it? He didn't know, but he wouldn't have ventured to ask as he had no money anyway. But he knew that he would, by this or some other means, find a country home for himself one day. It was one of the few things that he and his mother were agreed upon. Her years in Paris and Milan had not alienated his mother from Võru; she was not able to live in the city all summer either. And when the two of them were in the countryside, mostly here at Meeta's, they got along together better. Not that they quarrelled in the city, but there was some tension between them that they both undoubtedly felt, but neither of them ever spoke of it.

When he climbed up the bank, an elderly man was standing in front of the little house, a week's grey stubble on his sunburnt face, and he smiled at him.

'Good morning,' he said.

'Morning,' the man replied. 'Have you brought a heavy bag for the mill, young man?'

'What would I want with the mill?' he replied, feeling that his Võru language skills had gone rusty again in the city. 'It's not working anyway.'

'I can work it again if needs be,' the old man continued.

'Well, next time I'll bring a bag of barley in a buggy with me. I came here once or twice when I was a child.'

'How come? You look like a town boy to me. You haven't come all the way to the mill from town, have you?'

'No, no, I stay with my relatives in the forest every summer. That's where I've come from. And my grandmother grew up at the mill and was married from here.'

'You don't say! So you must be Fuchs Mants's grandson!'

'That's right. How did you know?'

'Oh, the Fuchs were still remembered around here when I was a young man. There were loads of sisters, and there were plenty of young men came to visit; there were four or five horses at once on the hitching post every single evening.'

'Horse thieves had a good haul,' he couldn't help but add.

'Where there are horses there are horse thieves . . . That's what times were like. Is your old grandmother still alive then? And her sisters?'

He replied that his grandmother was alive and well, as were some of her sisters. The old man wasn't satisfied with this and wanted to know who lived where, how many children they had and when the others no longer with us had passed away. Then he had to say how Meeta and her children were, where her sons who'd returned from Siberia were working, who had got married and who hadn't and, finally, what he himself did and what he was studying. When he'd given an account of everything and greetings had been passed on to Meeta and Richard he felt that, in a way, he had been accepted into his old neighbourhood as one of its own. What was it? he thought, hoisting his rucksack on to his back. Oh yes, *Rites de passage*, Arnold van Gennep's *Rites of Passage*.

Interesting how many mistakes he made when speaking his real mother tongue. He should ask his grandmother more about the Võru language, urge her to talk about the old days. It was interesting how Grandmother's language changed as soon as she began to talk about her youth. It was a beautiful, vital, colourful language, something completely different from the impoverished Germanized language she and her female friends spoke in the city. He had begun to like this language very much the first time he and his mother had been visiting their relatives in Võrumaa and he'd gone out to play with the village children. What words! At night in bed he repeated the most beautiful ones to himself: 'timahavva' for 'this year', 'peräkõrd' for 'in the end', 'hüdsi' for 'coal', 'perävankri' for 'buggy', 'latskene' for 'little child', 'sõtsed' for 'paternal aunts' . . . Yes, Mother had still had plenty of aunts and uncles. When they stayed at Aunt Marta's they went to 'visit the sõtsed'. Mother's grandfather's sister had married in her own village; her grandchildren and their children lived in the old place. It was a well-kept village with a small square at its centre, narrow streets between the tightly packed houses and ancient lindens and maples around the buildings. The village was genuinely old; there had been a settlement there since the Stone Age – the Hurt collections stated that an old, holy juniper tree was still standing on the hill by the village a hundred years previously and that people had been bringing offerings to it in secret.

The path ascended a little and descended again. Instead of pines there were firs and aspens, then marshy hay fields and in the middle of the hay fields a river, this time a murky, slow-moving, somnolent river, completely different from the torrential foaming waters farther down by the mill. The river had itself changed its course several times and was later deepened and straightened. The 'old river mean-der', as it was known here, contained beautiful bream, the fishing of which required more patience than he had as a small boy, although he had sometimes liked to come here none the less. It was different here than by the big river. He could cast his line into the water and stay there, be left to contemplate his own thoughts. By the river the line was always having to be cast back upstream – that required more attention. There were different kinds of fish in the river – chub, roach, bleak. Here in the old river there were dark perch, bream and ablet – clans-men of the bream but thinner and bonier. Põnts got them to himself if Meeta decided not to make fish soup. On the bank of the old river there was sometimes also an unusual kind of atmosphere. It was difficult to pin down, as if something happened to time and space. Was it that time moved more slowly or that it was somehow older, in an earlier time, more in the time of the independent Estonia? This place always had something of the independent Estonian era about it, the thing that his mother and Meeta remembered and talked about when they met.

Then there were the Tsarist times, of which his grandmother, her sisters and grandfather spoke, but there were no real traces of them to be found anywhere; perhaps in the odd manor house or the house on Toompea Hill in Tallinn, but there was something else there, too, that interfered with it and gave another flavour to the Tsarist era – a German spirit, a German tang. For him the Tsarist era was the time of the Russians, the Tsar, faith and the motherland, an era of two-kopek currant-cake plaits and the municipal Tsarist guards. The closest he could get to a flavour of that era was perhaps at Sergei's house, where there was an icon on the wall with an oil-lamp in front of it and on a shelf about a dozen books with yats and hard signs aplenty. There was also something of the Tsarist era in Leningrad, Nevski, the odd museum, bridge and the Neva embankment. But not at Aunt Veera's. Their old apartment had been destroyed in the war along with all its furnishings and old books. There was something left of the building itself and its surroundings, but he was unable to say whether it was from the Tsarist era or something completely different, something more distant and more profound that had no name or whose name no one knew or remembered any more.

It was strange that in Leningrad names – the names of streets, people, shops and museums – were very important; without them you could not manage. Here in the countryside things were different – here there was no need for names; here all things were very clear and in their own places even without names. Things were real, they really existed, they were really themselves. Even when they weren't in their proper place and had no proper name. Like the collective farm known as 'Partisan Lembitu's' or the little old man nicknamed Napoleon who lived at the other end of the village.

Napoleon, who went about in an old, greasy jacket and a soft old hat dating back to the era of the independent Estonia (or perhaps the Tsars), with a cigarette hand-rolled out of newspaper in the corner of his mouth, had, in fact, something in common with the real Napoleon: he had an almost perfect memory. This gift had evidently not been accompanied by any special powers or interests that would have taken him to school in the city and from there into the sciences, business or the army. He had done well at school, had completely mastered German and Russian, remembered by heart all the books he had read – except there were hardly any books other than schoolbooks – and never used paper and pencil to do arithmetic. He inherited his father's smallholding and carried it on without attracting anyone's attention or admiration. Only on the odd occasion had his exceptional powers of memory been of use. When the war broke out in 1941 people had to hand in their radios, and anyone who failed to comply faced a harsh punishment. Despite this some brave people hid their radios, a feat that was easier to achieve in rural areas especially, but there was only one tiny receiver in the village, which someone with an interest in engineering rapidly cobbled together from spares. It could be listened to using headphones, and Napoleon was given the radio. He would listen to the news, headphones on, then remove them and report what he had heard word for word.

After the water meadow the path rose again. On the hilltop stood the village shop and schoolhouse, reached from the path by an avenue of larch. Meeta's younger son, Andres, had attended school here for several years. He was the only person in the family who had no interest in further study: after his eighth year he went to the technical school and from there into the army where his skills in metalwork were of great use. During his schooldays, when fishing and woodwork had interested him more than literature, they had been good friends. They had gone fishing and cycling together, slept in the hayloft and chatted into the small hours. In their own way they complemented each other: he was from the broader world of knowledge learnt from books and home, and Andres had his craftsmanship and the reasoning of a farm boy. Sometimes he and Andres would go to the village to meet other children and, now and again, would visit the travelling cinema. After the film there would be a dance at which neither of them lingered. At home he'd grown up among women, and he would have been cosseted by his great-aunt and Meeta if it had not been for Andres; through Andres he gained an inkling of the more masculine, rougher side of country life. It was here that he gained a clearer understanding of himself and realized that he would probably never fit in with the men's world with its shows of strength and finesse, derring-do, obscenity and aggression.

Yes, it was good that he'd been with Andres in those early years. Mother, who had forced him as a child to go outside and play with other children, was now surprised when she saw the boys spending half the day in the workshop, Andres crafting something, him sitting on the ladder watching in silence from on high. In the countryside the time was divided three ways: some of it he spent with Andres, some rummaging through books and some in the forest or by the river. All were good companions – he was able to spend time quietly with all of them without playing any role, just being himself.

After the village came the forest, and beyond the forest the path descended once more to the riverside. Here there was a wooden bridge that he often visited on his childhood fishing trips. From here it was good to walk home along the road. Sometimes he would sing a couple of songs lustily that he believed he knew and which he liked – the Russian song about the cruiser the *Varyag* and the sailor Zheleznyak. He was beginning to forget the lyrics:

> You are up there, comrades, everyone in his place.
> The last parade is about to begin.

It was strange to think: the Soviet Union's military nonsense had had some sort of influence on him regardless. What would his father have thought if he were alive? Would he have laughed, grieved or raged? Perhaps the *Varyag* song had something to say to the majority of Russians, whether they were Soviet citizens or not. Yet the romance of the Red Revolution was alien to his father and his relatives. Aunt Veera had made that very plain to him.

What had once been a manor park was coming into view in the distance. The manor had burnt down long ago; all that was left were an outbuilding and sheds and the gardener's house where the former manor parlour-maid now lived with her retarded son. At the edge of the park a machinery shed, constructed when there had been a tractor station, was still standing even now. Under the trees among the brushwood and nettles were strewn rusted car chassis, machine parts, tyres and fuel cans. Behind the manor there was a still new cowshed and around it an old labourer's cottage where the new labourers now lived – people who came from goodness knows where and who would move on to goodness knows where and were the greatest source of aggravation for the village. Sometimes there were booze-ups here, sometimes sluts and brawls; here you could find snotty-nosed children with scratched faces wearing shabby tracksuits, who instead of getting a bellyful of food at home often got a bellyful of abuse, children who the women at the manor, out of the goodness of their hearts, cleaned up, fed and to whom one or two gave hand-me-downs that their own children or grandchildren had grown out of. People pointed fingers at the cottage whenever an axe next to the shed or a milk churn by the barn disappeared or anyone's washing vanished from the line.

Had manors been such unseemly places in the olden days, here in the middle of the countryside where everything otherwise had its place? How, other than through them, did anything indecorous and featureless flow into the heart of Võrumaa and everywhere else? Past impropriety at least had beauty, class, the echo of Versailles or Sanssouci, which one or two generations later reached the Baltic provinces and stayed there. Contemporary unseemliness was ghastly. Instead of white pillars there were damp, empty, rusting barrels; instead of carriages, rusting car chassis; and instead of ornamental lakes there were lakes of liquid manure. The rumour was that that you couldn't see whether there was white or rye bread on the table in the labourers' cottage there were so many flies – a thin grey layer of them coated everything.

Behind the outbuilding was the hay meadow, and beyond the hay meadow the forest began. On the left the former timber farm, now the collective timber farm; on the right the national forest – great primeval pines. There was good mushrooming in there. They always went in late summer during Mother's holidays and returned with a full basket. Mother was a passionate mushroomer, as was Grandfather. About a hundred metres from the fringe of the forest there was a small glade by the path where young birch and pine trees were already beginning to grow. Here the Russian sappers had hauled the mines and shells they found by the path and elsewhere. There had been quite a pile of munitions. A small boy who tended his grandmother's cows and sheep had sat right on top of it and had begun to pound a shell or mine with a stone to pass the time. Exactly what he did nobody knows; the explosion hurled a number of trees some distance, and this glade had been created after they'd been cleared, a memorial in its way to one small victim of a big war.

He had to turn off the path to the left. The track went on along the edge of what had been the old main trench, over it through a young spinney and directly into a courtyard. The forest was sparse, and on the path and beside it a small quantity of hay was growing. He remembered how at one time Meeta and the other collective farmers were not allocated the collective farm's hay meadows, and they mowed what little area they could – the edges of ditches, roadsides and edges of fields – to obtain fodder for the family's cow in wintertime. Andres, too, had mowed hay from the forest path here; they had brought it in a barrow, a cart, to dry around the edge of the courtyard. Forest hay was not plentiful, a couple of good armfuls only, but it was something.

At the edges of the forest they had made fresh stacks of wood and a pile of unhewn logs. This seemed like a suitable job for him: of all the country jobs chopping wood was probably the one most to his liking. Mowing, too, was something he'd learnt here with Richard's help, although he still couldn't do it as well as he needed to. He didn't really like summer haymaking: sometimes it was too hot and there were horseflies and sometimes showers. Haymaking was a somewhat anxious time, the continual rush, the drudgery and sense of urgency; there was no rest until the winter hay was made, a process that sometimes went on into September. He had understood that he wasn't a practical person. He couldn't throw himself fully into physical work; instead, he had to leave some space, some distance, so that he could observe himself and his surroundings from afar. If things rushed along, the observer in him, the little philosopher constantly tingling at his ear, became constricted, and he felt bad. Descartes' *cogito, ergo sum* fitted him and probably others of his ilk, although it had obviously not originally been intended as this kind of psychological statement. He felt that he was alive and existed when he could observe his own living and being in peace.

He rested his bike against the barn wall and for a moment watched the swifts darting in and out of the nesting-boxes. This, too, was a sign that midsummer was at hand: swifts used the nesting-boxes after their first occupants, the starlings, had moved out. Sometimes he would stay and watch them for a long time, wheeling high in the sky and whirling for their nests like black arrows, slowing down for the last twenty or so metres before darting through the opening just like any ordinary bird. How did they manage to brake so effectively? That was something he would have liked to know, but did anyone? How many people knew about nature at all? If we are aware of what we don't know, are we aware of the real extent of our knowledge?

On the porch a cat, probably the third one already since half-tail Pōnts, lay sunbathing. It looked at the newcomer out of the corner of its eye and made a purring sound, as if it recognized him as one of its own, shut its eyes again and carried on dozing.

He opened the kitchen door, which was ajar, and through it came the smell of boiled potatoes and meat and the sound of his great-aunt's voice. At the door he almost ran into Meeta who was stepping out of the pantry holding a jar of cream and a dish of eggs.

'Oh, just look. *You've finally got down here!*' she said. '*You must be hungry. We're just finishing getting dinner ready and are about to sit at the table. Richard's at home, and Paul is coming home from the city this evening. We can chat in the garden.*'

Now all that remained to do was to put his rucksack in the corner of the kitchen, say hello to his great-aunt and Richard, wash the sweat and dust of the road from his face and report how life was in the city and why he hadn't made it to the countryside sooner. He also had to take his shoes off – he had always done so in his childhood, too. People in the country lived and walked around barefoot. Shoes lived in a corner of the hall next to the boots and Wellingtons. When he went back to the city in the autumn he'd put them back on again.

19

When in the evening he climbed into the hayloft alone to sleep, there were clouds in the sky, the wind was blowing inside under the eaves and whispering in the fresh-smelling hay. The weather must be changing; it might start to rain in the night. That meant no haymaking, and he could look at the old books in the attic and barn with no pangs of conscience. His great-aunt's husband had been an interesting man. As well as being a schoolteacher he had been an organist, a choirmaster and an ardent advocate of temperance. He neither drank spirits nor smoked and spent most of his salary on books. They were subscribers to dozens of journals and had purchased most of the good literature that was published. During the time of house searches, the KGB and militias had taken away potato sacks full of the most wonderful books – they clearly hoped to sell them for a decent sum of money – but there were still piles of books and journals left behind. In the living-room there were two cupboards full of the more beautiful editions of *Looming* and *Varamu*, while the attic and the barn were simply stacked with books, some in crates, some on the floor. During his school days he had spent the greater part of his summer there, absorbed in rummaging through the piles and reading anything he chanced upon that seemed the slightest bit interesting, whether it be *Eesti Noorte Punane Rist* (Youth Branch of the Estonian Red Cross), *Ristirahva Pühapäevaleht* (Christians' Sunday Newspaper), *Kasvatus* (Education), *Eesti Kirjandus* (Estonian Literature) or *Eesti Arst* (Estonian Doctor). There was a lot of sheet music, but that was something he wouldn't know how to use – he wasn't musical, and he didn't play any instruments. Perhaps musical ability had been lost in some incomprehensible way: before he could talk he had babbled away lustily and in tune to his mother's and his aunt's songs, but when he learnt to talk he put singing aside, and as an adult he couldn't even sing 'Cruiser *Varyag*' or the wakey-wakey song of his childhood, 'Hüüavad pasunad', in tune. His mother played the piano – or would have if they'd had a piano and the space for one; his father had been very musical and had learnt the violin as a child. When he was small, his father's violin had been kept in the back room on top of a cupboard with a case and bow, but it was later sold when they needed the money. He had been told that he must not pick up the violin by himself or touch it; he could look at it and use it carefully only when a grown-up took it down from the cupboard. He plucked the violin strings, drew the bow over them, but the sound that came out sounded nothing like the violin sound that came out of loudspeakers or the music-school window. The thing that brought the music out of the buzzing, rasping strings simply had to be something magical, and his father had known the spell. Just for that he could be proud of his father. His father had also written some poems that he published in a local Russian paper for which he also sometimes wrote reviews of literature as well as theatrical and musical performances.

His father was actually a great example to him; he admired and respected him and was ready to raise his fist to anyone who called him a 'Russki' – he would sooner be labelled a Russki himself than allow his father to be. He tried to imitate his father's handwriting, asked his mother what his father's favourite books had been and read them. At primary school he had a secret dream that one day he would be a violin maestro, but the dream was soon cut short. When the singing teacher had asked him to come over to sing a scale at the piano she had said nothing, but that was the one and only time that he had been summoned thither.

There was music here in the country, too. His great-aunt's husband had left behind sheet music as well as an old harmonium and a violin. Meeta's sons had learnt the violin, although they hadn't progressed very far with it. His great-aunt played the harmonium at least every Sunday morning. She would listen to the religious service on Radio Finland and play a couple of hymns herself. She had visited Finland twice in her youth and had stayed with a minister's family, learnt some Finnish and had returned home with deep respect and reverence for the country. To his great-aunt Finland was something like Zion: Radio Finland and the Finnish Church were the ultimate authorities in her eyes. Now she was a pensioner she had more time for the Finnish language, and in the evenings she would pore over an old Finnish textbook, probably the first ever published in Estonian, and read, syllable by syllable, Juhani Aho's short stories, which stood on a shelf next to her bed with the Finnish hymnal and Bible.

His great-aunt had become older and weaker – small wonder, she was the eldest of the sisters and already over eighty years old. She was still able to manage outdoors, cut hay for the cow and weed the strawberry patch. Her conversation, though, was beginning to get more and more repetitive, and her Finland-worship was becoming faintly comical. His great-aunt had already asked him the meanings of several words and phrases; he had the feeling that she had asked the same thing the previous summer, which meant she had to be forgetting Finnish more quickly than she was learning it. The evenings were mostly taken up with his having to report to his great-aunt how everyone was, what had been built in Tartu and where, what he thought of the latest Estonian literature, choirs and choral music. His great-aunt was very much in touch with what was going on – she listened to the radio a lot and never missed a concert broadcast even though her hearing, like that of her sisters, had deteriorated in recent times.

Meeta and Richard didn't question him particularly; they talked more about their own lives and what was happening in the village and on the collective farm. Richard had managed to get work on a new farm where his mechanical knowledge would be useful; Meeta didn't go to work on the collective farm any more, instead tending her own garden and home. Now she had time for the flowers she had wanted to grow all her life: there were rambling roses all around the house, by the door there were large flowerbeds where the boys had dragged interesting-looking stones and roots. The red and the white peony shrubs were a mass of blooms – such a proud display of peonies as Meeta had rarely seen. Meeta and Richard also kept bees, and he had his own experience with them – when there were no other men in the house he had helped Meeta to bring a swarm down from the branch of an oak and guide it in the evening dusk into an empty hive. There was something pleasing and moving in the way that the bees of the swarm that had stuffed themselves with honey could be scooped up with a hand or a ladle into a box without his being stung even once. The box was then taken into the cool of the barn, and it stood there until the evening, buzzing softly. There was something about this as beautiful and solemn as there was to baking bread, to the sour-scented dough rising under the white cloth and the warm, scented loaves coming out of the oven. Now even they didn't bake bread any more; instead, it was bought from a shop. Meeta's wonderful curd cheese, though, was always on the table, and the garden provided a few strawberries.

Just as evening fell, Paul arrived from the city where he worked in a cooperative. It was a good post – he was able to borrow a car sometimes or a minibus and so managed to bring home items that you never could get in the shops. Once, one summer, he had brought a bunch of bananas for his family. It was the first time they had seen or tasted bananas, although none of them was especially enthusiastic, deeming their own strawberries much better.

As always the conversation drifted towards the camps. Although he'd heard plenty of stories about them and the prisons, the supply of material was never ending – Paul, Richard and his younger brother Kalev always had something new, and sometimes completely overwhelming, to talk about. They had discussed the basic facts: the terror of the hardcore criminals and their fights with them, uprisings in the camps, contacts with the Ukrainian resistance, the Lithuanian partisans and top intellectuals from Moscow, Leningrad or Kiev, hunger, cold, back-breaking work, guards and grasses, then the coming of a new era, the softening of the regime and, finally, liberation. His own relatives were saying exactly what Andrei Sinyavsky was writing about: women who waited at the prison camp gates, who knew that they were releasing political prisoners, Article 58 . . . They would make good husbands. There were a fair few women at Karaganda and lots at Norilski and Vorkuta. Also among those released were people for whom no one was waiting anywhere.

To him, though, the details were especially shocking. The first thing Kalev had seen on arriving at the prison camp at seventeen was a line of blind prisoners holding on to one another and shuffling forward along a pathway dug out of the two-metre deep snow. There, in the camp where Paul had been during an uprising, a large box kite had been released, and it had risen high into the air. A small box, full of leaflets, was pulled up along the kite string; its construction was such that the box opened on reaching the kite and the leaflets flew miles away over the steppe. The first task of the military units dispatched to surround the camp and ultimately subjugate it was to collect the leaflets. It's likely that some of the young soldiers read them and perhaps even gained a better understanding of the situation.

Kalev was the youngest, and as a minor was among the first convicts to be granted an amnesty. He remembered Kalev's homecoming well. It was evening, and it was starting to get dark. He was sitting on the ladder on the shed roof – he liked it there; it was good to look out into the distance and at the sky, radiating the warmth of the sunset, with clouds congregating wearily on the horizon and stopping there, almost motionless. In the encroaching twilight he saw a tall man carrying a suitcase approach from the direction of the manor and disappear into the forest. The man had presumably come on the last bus: country people do not go around the village carrying suitcases. But he didn't have the instinct of Sherlock Holmes and did not conjecture who the approaching person might be; besides, he didn't know most of the people around here at all, still less the ones who lived in the neighbouring village just beyond the forest where the stranger was obviously going.

But five minutes later, when he was just coming down from the roof – it was already getting chilly and the sunset was no longer so interesting to look at – he suddenly saw that the man with the suitcase was emerging from the forest and taking the direct path towards them. He was somewhat alarmed and stayed on the ladder. The man looked in his direction once – perhaps he saw him or heard a rattling on the roof – but he didn't stop and instead took a confident step inside over the threshold. Now he understood. It had to be Kalev. Kalev had been released. Kalev had come home.

For the whole of the following week there were strangers permanently in the kitchen. Men came and went. They didn't speak; they didn't ask much. They just sat and listened. Kalev spoke. He sat and listened, too; he was happy that he was able to be there and listen all the time. In its own way it was a series of lectures: Kalev was a good storyteller, someone who even in the camp had tried to observe everything and explain things to himself. He had an eye for detail. Like the blind people stumbling through the snow. Or the mad Georgian who would masturbate and rub his sperm into his bald head in the belief that it would protect against exposure to radiation – during the uprisings, however, his reason had unexpectedly returned. The Tallinn bus driver who thrashed any hardcore criminals who invaded the barracks with a plank from a bed as Kalevipoeg did to the evil spirits. Now he realized that Kalev needed to talk; it was his therapy. By talking he liberated himself from the past, which might otherwise have become a nightmare for him and for ever disturb his new life. Were the people who had been through Vorkuta, Karaganda, Kolyma ever released from their nightmares?

In the evening Paul and Richard had taken half a bottle of wine out of the cupboard – the family's former teetotal traditions were set aside – they had shown him how butter was smeared on bread in the camp with a spoon (the butter was from parcels sent from home) and how contact was maintained from cell to cell by knocking. Even now they remembered the prison Morse code. The wind picking up outside reminded Paul of the blizzard in Komi in which the prison convoy had to struggle to get to work – sometimes the workplace was a kilometre or two from the barracks. Getting lost in a snowstorm like that was certain death. The guards worried not about the prisoners' lives and health but about the fact that losing people would get them into a lot of trouble. Although human life was not worth much in the Gulag, the prisoners were a precious commodity, which was accounted for, handed over and accepted with pedantic accuracy.

Sleep was on its way: his thoughts were starting to take their own paths and becoming images; they were beginning to live their own dream-life. He tried to think of Malle but could not picture her face – only her silhouette. Ester, though, he remembered almost with visionary clarity as he had the night before when he flew out of himself. Now, too, he felt the strange lightness buzzing in his body as it had then, but it did not go as far as flying. The image of Ester faded gradually, leaving behind something that he might have called happiness and peace. Someone was rustling in the hay by the wall. Like when he and Andres used to sleep here, sometimes mice would run over them. Once one had got caught in his hair; he pulled the mouse free and hurled it away, but the terrified mouse had peed on his hand.

In the morning when he woke up the wind had grown weaker, but on the other hand, it was raining lightly. It had to be late, the others had to be up. Someone was moving in the hay next to him. He started in fright but then saw that it was the cat. He wasn't allowed in the house overnight, but he had found a warm spot next to a human being in the loft.

Breakfast was ready, and coffee – not, of course, the real thing – was steaming on the stove. Paul had eaten earlier; he had to be at work in the morning. He told Richard he would like to chop some wood and practise mowing. What was his hurry, wondered the others, let the rain blow over, and then Richard will be pleased to show you and help you. At first, though, no one was in a rush. Tomorrow, if the rain held off, as the weather station had promised, they had to spread the hay that had been stacked to dry outside. That's when they would need him;not before. This meant that he could devote the whole day to his books and Radhakrishnan. It was better to be in the hayloft and the outbuilding than in a room: here his great-aunt was always offering him something to eat and asking about all sorts of things.

There was an old armchair in the barn. If he took it to the window and opened the shutter he could read there and, if he put a bigger book or a board across his lap, he could write. The lid of the old churn that was standing right here next to the wall caught his eye. That would do very well as a table.

At first he made good progress with the Radhakrishnan; he read the book for an hour from the very beginning, but then he began to weary of the old philosophy centred on Vedas and scholasticism. He leafed through the latter part of the book: yoga and the Buddhists seemed more interesting, although he had promised the Teacher that he would read the whole thing through carefully. That, however, was no easy task: the names of the schools and the philosophers piled up a bit too much. His thoughts began to wander, and he felt he should probably stop. There was still something seeking a way into consciousness; it came from somewhere in the depths of his body and broke the surface. He knew that something quite well already but could not understand what aroused it, what this drive was that rapidly erased his contentment and swapped one set of mental images for another. The Upanishads, ancient books and swifts in the window were shifting; in their place came women, women he knew and women he didn't, whether he had seen them in real life at the cinema or in pictures, women he had read about in books. It was strange but disquieting to observe oneself changing into a thoroughly sexual being; as if somewhere within him a vessel of colourful liquid had exploded or opened that spread everywhere and tinged everything. It no longer went away; it remained with him and was beginning little by little to send his thoughts in one direction. He knew where it would ultimately lead: here in the country he had learnt how to satisfy himself, and things were much the same now. But he didn't like it; he felt that he was entitled to find contentment and peace in a more natural, nicer way. Why was it that for a young man like him the road to being with a woman had to be so long and difficult? Was it because he had grown up among women and had become accustomed to relating to women as you would a mother, aunts, grandmother, mother's friends but not a partner? If ever the women at home talked about anything erotic they did so disparagingly. Sexual interest and love-making were treated with similar ridicule and contempt as wiping your nose on your hand, sitting at the table without having washed your hands or calling Victor Hugo 'Victor Hyuugo'. Their tone of voice, facial expression, way of speaking while leaving something unspoken made it crystal-clear: sex was something that well-brought-up people should have nothing to do with. Doubtless his mother and aunts would not have agreed with this proposition. Surely some opinions and principles, once formulated, lost their force and authority.

Books with which to arouse himself, to say nothing of pictures, were scarce in the country; no Estonian parish-clerk-cum-schoolteacher would have anything like that at his house. But, as his frustration had gradually grown, he had found stirring material almost everywhere: in old women's magazines, the works of Tuglas and Tammsaare, the Song of Solomon in the Bible.

He had also realized that this kind of surge of lust came with inactivity and that physical exertion helped him overcome it or restrain it for a while. And that was what he wanted to do. Soon the rain had blown over, although there could be showers later. There were puddles in the yard, yet the air was entrancingly warm and humid. He decided to go for a little walk near by and maybe go to the river for a swim.

His great-aunt was having her lunchtime nap in her little room. He told Meeta he was going for a walk and left. The cement steps were already dry, and the cat was basking in the sun as it had done the previous day. The swallows were flying high, so the weather had to be improving. As he passed the white dog-rose he was aware of the faint perfume from the single late bloom, a perfume his nose was able to distinguish from the summery scents of the moist earth and grass and which in its northern gentleness was still so familiar. And soothing.

A new lid had been made for the well. There were no longer any bugs on the dog-rose clambering over it, drinking and mating. Living and loving in the roses – it was something to envy. He was thinking about the strange unease he had felt when in his childhood he had watched the insects clasped tightly to each other's flanks. Why did they excite and unsettle him? He would have liked them not to act this way; sometimes he even pulled them off each other, once even crushed them to pieces against a stone. Thinking about it now, he was ashamed. As he had delved deeper into Buddhism he had even given up fishing and, to a large extent, eating meat; but, none the less, he would like to understand why watching creatures mating awoke such strange and somewhat sadistic feelings in him. Was it envy? Or a boy's subconscious hatred of his own sexuality, which, when kindled, threw his little world into confusion, depriving him of contentment and confidence? Does a yearning for a different, asexual world, perhaps even for ancient, primeval life where there were no men or women, where reproduction was by cell division, live within us? Was the Kingdom of Heaven as proclaimed by Jesus, where there is no man or woman, where life is lived in heaven as God's angels, an expression of the same yearning in the theological language of his own time?

Just beyond the garden the forest began, and it soon became marshy. The wind carried the scent of marsh rosemary from there – at least that's what it seemed like to him. He didn't like this particular scent, yet it was perversely arresting. It was associated with an erotic summery dream; there was something difficult and even evil about it, just as there is in literature from the beginning of the century with its symbolist tang – Leonid Andreyev, Tuglas and Gailit. The scent of marsh rosemary, the lascivious lap of the great wild woman into whose clutches of white-hot passion man sinks as if into a bog . . .

The great old main ditch marked the boundary between their farm and the neighbouring one. Under the land reform seven smallholdings had been demarcated on the land that had once belonged to the manor on the edge of the forest. The Estonian Republic must have been a very unusual country in its day – a country of small farmers the like of which probably did not exist anywhere in the world. But, of course, a country like that did not have the means to stay that way: urbanization, which was enforced by foreign power with blood and violence, would have happened regardless. People no longer wanted to till the land as before and keep animals. The toil that was the farmer's lot seemed too much like serfdom to the young.

What would have become of the Estonian nation if the Russians and the Germans had not invaded and established their own new regimes? They had discussed this matter several times in the city and sometimes here when Kalev and Paul were at home. And once the Teacher had disclosed his own opinion, the opposite of the commonly held view. What was it now? 'A country of social climbers who imitated everything German, where the national language was German with Estonian words, where the rulers wanted the Germans to come and take power.' At the time the sentence had made him feel physically ill, opened cracks in his vision of the world, which he was no longer able to repair. What was it all about? Did the Teacher say what he said just to annoy Ellen, or was that what he really thought?

Here on the farm track in Võrumaa, where everything was in its place, the Teacher's words felt almost out of kilter, like the things introduced by the new regime and its reforms, the manor that the State had made into a stock farm and the rusting car chassis under the ancient lindens. A former KGB man had told him how it amazed him how well the 'grey barons' of Viljandi and their sons had adjusted to their new circumstances after the war. They hadn't joined the Forest Brothers, but the children of smallholders and farmhands from Võrumaa had, the ones who would have been regarded as 'the poor' under the new regime's system of classification.

Meeta, whose family had seen three of its men go to prison, the eldest aged fifty and the youngest seventeen, had discussed the matter a couple of times when his mother or aunt were there. Meeta even felt a tinge of blame for bringing up her children in such an Estonian way, for having the flag of blue, black and white on the table and celebrating Independence Day. But it was in the air; there was even something natural in it. It was part of life, like the Võru language and the short-haired red cows.

Men from this family did not become Forest Brothers, but they did shelter and feed them. Kalev and Paul had associated with Foresters; they, too, had their own arms and belonged to a youth organization that held secret meetings and distributed leaflets, where people were called upon to fight the Communist occupation and collected and cached weapons in cellars and attics for use in battle. There were many organizations of this type, but the KGB quickly discovered them, and their members were sent to prison camps along with Forest Brothers who had been apprehended and people who had served in the German armed forces. Kalev and Paul were also found out during the searches when a German automatic weapon and a couple of full magazine cartridges were found in the house buried in sand in the attic. That was enough to have Richard arrested as well.

The KGB knew a great deal but not everything. They failed to discover the farm's biggest and saddest secret. The secret's name was Jaan. Jaan, real name Johann W, was a young German who had deserted from his division and stayed in Estonia. Somehow he had happened to come into their area and had stumbled upon Richard and Meeta. He lived there on and off for almost a year until the situation became so dangerous that he had to leave. Jaan was not a Forest Brother. He didn't want to fight; he was not taking revenge on anyone. He wanted to live, get home and continue his unfinished study of the organ. When he had to leave he teamed up with the Forest Brothers but was soon killed. Some said that during the clash on the forest path he hadn't even attempted to escape; he had continued walking along it until a punishment-squad bullet took him down right there. It had almost been suicide. When Meeta learnt of Jaan's death she had tried to claim his dead body for burial – they had a friend in the hospital mortuary to which the bodies of Forest Brothers who had been killed were sometimes taken, as Jaan's had. But the person on the nightshift at the time was a stranger whom they couldn't trust, and the next day the corpse was taken away somewhere. The KGB clearly had their own secret locations where they buried the people they referred to as 'bandits'.

Jaan had been a good, gifted man. In the two years he had been living in hiding in Estonia he had learnt Estonian so perfectly that at first no one would have thought him German. He was originally from a small town in Pfalz and from a strict Catholic family that was also strongly anti-Nazi. His father had told him that if he joined the Hitler Youth he would break his fingers to ensure that he would never play the organ again and thereby defile the Church. He didn't join the Hitler Youth, but there was no escape from the Wehrmacht; when the opportunity arose, however, he deserted. Perhaps it would have been more proper for him to have given himself up to the Russians – he might then have had a better chance of staying alive. But who could have known that in 1944 or 1945? The Estonians alongside whom he lived still believed that a white ship would come, that the Western allies would demand or fight for the Baltic countries to be free of the Russian bear. There were horrific and gruesome stories about the Russian prison camps, where POWs were held alongside political prisoners and ordinary criminals.

Jaan was talked about many a time over dinner. While he had lived on the farm he had taught Paul and Kalev music, played the harmonium and the violin a bit and had composed several pieces himself. He had also had his own hiding-place: the little coal hole next to the cooker in the kitchen – in an emergency its boarded entrance could be covered with the same bricks as the rest of the floor. He had on a couple of occasions fled there during searches. Once the KGB had arrived so unexpectedly that Jaan had had nowhere to go. He stood in the gap between the door and the wall and waited there, quiet as a mouse. The search was hurried and cursory – most likely the Forest Brothers somewhere had pulled something off and escaped unpunished, and the KGB, wanting to demonstrate that they were not asleep on the job, searched suspects' homes without any hope of finding anything. One man lit a match in the corner by the door so he could look there, but the match went out and Jaan remained undiscovered. It was miracle, but miracles don't last long.

There, where the ditch reached the main road and was hidden for a while in a crude cement pipe, re-emerging on the other side, a pair of young oaks were growing. The first time he had been there the trees had only just been planted, and a plaster figure of a Young Pioneer stood between them holding a bugle. Now all that was left of the figure was the large chunk of stone on which it had stood, but in ten years the oaks had grown into trees. A man like him could climb to the top of them should he want to. As a child he loved climbing into the treetops and sometimes did so now. There were a couple of oaks, two large birches and a large maple tree growing in the garden. Between the branches at the top of the maple he had found a spot where he could make himself comfortable. Sometimes he would sit up there for hours reading a book. Põnts the cat had once come to the top of the tree with him and sat there for a while but then tired of it and climbed back down. If he sat there for a while and read, the birds would come very close; perhaps they didn't know how to fear a person at the top of a tree. Once a covey of chiffchaffs flew towards him, and he was able to watch them at his ease from a distance of a couple of paces.

His great-aunt had talked a bit about her father-in-law, his great-grandfather. Old Ado had been a very particular man; in his old age he would listen to no one but his son – his grandfather – who had gone to school in the city. Grandfather was a child of his time, became an atheist and socialist at a teachers' seminar, and in the end old Ado also stopped going to church. On Sunday mornings he had read the Bible a little himself and had a stroll around his own fields. No one was allowed to disturb him during that time; it was the old man's religious service. He thought that his own religious observance could be when he spent some time sitting by himself in the top of the maple and birds flew towards him. When old Ado was on his deathbed a woman said to him, 'Listen, Aadu, you're about to die. Don't you think we should send for the real pastor?'

The sick man replied, 'I don't need them here!' and turned over with difficulty so that his back was turned towards his questioner. They must have been his last words.

Neither Grandfather nor his mother had had anything to do with the Church – although his mother and father had been married there and he had been baptized by an Orthodox minister – because of his father and his family. Nor did his father have any profound interest in religious matters. He was perhaps the first member of the family to have a renewed interest in spirituality. But it was easier for him: in his grandfather's and father's youth there weren't clergy like the Teacher and Ester's father.

The bathing place was here behind the willow bushes, where there were the remains of a sloping bank from when the river was deepened at the start of the 1930s. As a boy he had fished here, too; the roach were easy to catch. The water felt quite warm. He could try swimming for a while downstream, perhaps as far as the meander in the river where the old Vaglaraua farm was, and from there dash back over the meadows. That meant he couldn't swim naked; he had to put his trunks on. This he did, and his shirt and long trousers were left on the log which someone fishing or bathing had left there. No one would take them.

He swam upstream for a bit to warm up, reached the first deep place and turned downstream. Now and then plants in the water stuck to his legs, but the current dragged them downstream and they didn't hinder him much. When he reached the first bend he was already good and warm and no longer needed to move his arms and legs vigorously; he could allow the current to carry him and just steer, sometimes staying in the centre of the river, sometimes veering more towards one bank. At the ford beyond the bend the river was slightly wider and the current slower; water-lilies grew there as did a tangle of reeds and rushes just beside the bank. At one point a mother duck's head appeared among the reeds – perhaps she was hiding her brood there. Yes, that was it. He spotted a couple of small brown balls of feathers disappearing among the plants, and heard the mother duck's warning quack. Over by the water-lilies there was the splash of a fish. The river smelt as the lake had done the previous day; the smell was a combination of mud, water-lilies, willow bushes and the sun. There was also something oppressive, even disquieting, something that clearly reminded him, painfully, of Ester, her body as it looked underwater, the inadvertent touch of her foot as they swam back from the water-lilies. The oppressiveness did not overcome him entirely, however; it did not adhere to him – his motion in the current was too gentle for that; he bobbed in the river like a fishing float so that sometimes even the birds did not regard him as a person but more like an old alder log that someone had thrown in from the bank and which was now floating downstream. Neither alder logs, twigs, dead dragonflies, leaves nor he were truly themselves; they were part of the river, the flow itself.

He would have liked to stay here, to disappear. The thought of suicide was not alien to him at all – on several occasions he had genuinely contemplated it – but the thought he had now was not really of suicide. To perish, to melt into the earth's great bloodstream is not suicide: it is not an act; it is simply acceptance of going, flowing, changing – although this was not something that he could have done here in the narrow weed-filled river of his childhood where his body would be found immediately. What a lot of worry and pain that would cause to everyone. No, that is not how someone disappears; to disappear one would have to disappear from everyone's memories, disappear with one's own past, forget and pass out of mind. Just as his distant ancestors had passed out of mind, the people who lived two hundred, three hundred, three thousand years ago. And the earlier ancestors somewhere in southern Europe who hunted reindeer and painted mammoth and bison on cave walls. And earlier ancestors still somewhere in Africa, who had just learnt to fashion blades from stone and keep fire burning. And their ancestors who were certainly not people, and their ancestors who lived in the treetops, and their ancestors who were tiny creatures that nested in bushes and crevices, and their ancestors who clambered out of the sea and on to the land . . . He wanted to return to the sea. To the sea where everything had started. Things had to come full circle.

He shut his eyes and swam a slow sidestroke, relaxing into the water, feeling that he might even doze off while swimming like this. What would happen then? Would he drown or awaken in alarm when the water went into his nose? Or would he still swim along with the current in his sleep, moving his arms and legs like a stork in a rising current of air. Do storks or eagles sleep on the wing? What about stormy petrels and other birds that can stay in the air for a very long time?

He had swum quite a distance, eyes closed, and opened them only when he happened upon a willow bush growing partly in the water at the next bend. On his left was the large bathing place, the diving spot they had frequented most often in their childhood, sometimes with the village boys. Ten years previously there was much less vegetation here, and swimming was much more pleasant than it was now. Before he could swim well he was always frightened when pondweed or water-lilies touched his legs. He would begin to flounder, and once he really had been in danger: he could not move, and he began to sink. Then he yelled, his mouth already half in the water. He cried for help to Andres, 'Shit! I can't move, come and help me!'

Andres could see that he was really in danger, waded inton the water, which was only waist deep, and stretched out his hand to him. He took Andres's hand and pressed his feet into the riverbed, gasping so much that his lungs threatened to burst. Later he wondered whether he might really have drowned only a metre away from shallow water that he couldn't have reached by himself. If he had been alone . . . No, if he'd been alone he wouldn't have swum across the river; he would have splashed about right here, close to the bank or a dozen paces downstream. Perhaps Andres had saved his life. Did that mean anything? There were only two people he could say such a thing about, although he wasn't entirely certain about either one of them. One was Andres and the other his grandfather's friend, Professor L, who treated him when he was continually ill as a child. He had been ill a great deal in his childhood and had missed more than a couple of days of school a week; he was weak and anaemic, as they said in those days. The illnesses stopped when he was eleven, and he began going to the river in the summer. Before then he had been afraid of the water, and his mother could never force him to go swimming. It might have been her own fault: when he was small she had wanted to toughen him up and had given him cold baths. The child would not allow himself to be toughened up more than twice – as soon as he saw the bathtub in the yard he would begin to struggle and shout. It was years before he overcame his fear of water. Strange that he began to go swimming with the other village children here in the cold water of the river. When he messed about with them he realized that the feeling of cold soon passed if he stayed in the water longer and kept moving about, and after that he became a regular bather and, several years later, a regular swimmer, too. In its own way this fitted in with his interest in romantic poetry. Mother or Grandfather had told him the story of how Lord Byron had swum across the Hellespont from Europe to Asia – or the other way round – and in *Looming* he had read a translation of Swinburne's poem about the meditation of a swimmer with the motto *Somno mollior unda* – the billow is softer than the dream.

While swimming, his body and mind acquired a distinctive rhythm different in nature from when he was walking, sitting or lying down. The rhythm was soothing, even soporific; it would have been good to abandon himself to it, to allow his internal flowing and billowing to merge into that of the water around him. He was no longer consciously swimming; rather, he was allowing his body to swim while he observed in wonderment how well it was managing. Rarely did he take such delight in his body as when swimming. Usually, on land, his body tormented and perturbed him with its weight, smells, needs and desires.

Here in the flow of the river, which was now faster, then slower again, there was a meeting of body and mind; they didn't torment each other. Here all was good and calm. Breathing, which had caused him the most problems in the past, happened all by itself. And it was fascinating to observe what was happening on the bank and along it from the height of the water's surface – plants, birds and the water, iridescent in the sun.

There was a large boulder here by the bank that the people who had deepened the river had not been able to remove; here it stayed, the top protruding from the water; he had sat here now and again, fishing. Birds loved spending time here – even now a wagtail was walking on the boulder and was not startled by the person swimming past it. Perhaps it lived in a woodpile or under an eave in Vaglaraua. The water had carried branches, the stems of rushes and even an empty bottle into the inlet between the boulder and the bank. There were probably a few tiny creatures there among the rubbish that had not gone unnoticed by the wagtail's sharp eye. There was a deep place alongside the boulder; the current there was fast and pulsating – his body felt it and the quivering rushes along the other bank were witness to it. He had watched them in his childhood, too – it was hard to imagine that those rhythmical movements were not made by fish or any other living creatures but simply by the flow of water. He knew now that there was nothing living in beer when it overflowed, gurgling, from the bottle. But was life itself alive? Wasn't there some kind of strange power that dwelt within him and forced him to live off it that would not allow him to be himself? Did being himself mean being dead? Perhaps life was really death and death life.

It was a strange thought – as a matter of fact, it wasn't even a thought, it was more like a door of some kind, the opening in his thoughts of the door to understanding. He swam a few more metres as if in a dream and then realized that something had happened. Everything was different, the water, his body moving forward in the water, the light in the sky and on the submerged water plants. All this was both strange and as if unlocked. He realized that he was unable to put into words what he had realized and felt.

His body, part of him, was swimming onwards confidently and contentedly without allowing him to be disturbed by the feelings of strangeness that quickly grew into something that was both happiness and gratitude. Gratitude to whom? God? Hadn't God been born out of such gratitude and happiness? Wasn't He simply the vessel into whom man could pour his overflowing joy? Perhaps his sorrow, too? The thoughts came in the form of questions, or, rather, the questions were the ripples on the surface, something that he had brought from his previous life, his previous self. They spread and faded, no longer demanding an answer – the answer was the very wonderment and joy that suddenly filled him. Something had changed, but he could not really say what. Everything was wonderfully good and beautiful and funny at the same time. Suddenly he saw that nothing in the world was to be taken seriously – people, lives, biographies, history – everything was comical, including his very self. Not even death would have changed this funny existence, so death no longer existed for him nor he for death. Death was neither a question nor an answer; it was something insignificant and simple like this little yellowed leaf floating in the current or the reed stems on the bank moving in the wind. Death existed, but it was no longer something to be remembered and feared. Death and fear of death were also funny.

He could have died, drowned right here in the river that his ancestors had once revered as sacred, plunged underwater and stayed there, but he knew that he would not do that. He wanted to live; he simply wanted to live and this will to live had nothing to do with fear of death. Life was just something beautiful and interesting. Like music or dancing, which cannot, should not, be interrupted, which must be danced, played to the end.

He breathed deeply, allowed his body to inhale deeply and then to plunge underwater among the pondweed and swim on until his ears began to sing and he hurt from lack of air. He wanted to test whether the feeling of pain was also different. It was and it wasn't. His body was as before, perhaps not so tense, but he was no longer so attached to it. He and his body were like two partners, each of whom can live separately, relinquish the other, but simply want to live together. Like husband and wife. Why would they live life separately? It wasn't important. It was a silly question.

He now allowed his body to come up to the surface and looked around, panting. Vaglaraua was behind him; soon the river turned south again. The best thing to do was to scramble out here at the bend and scamper back along the bank to his clothes. Such was his thought process, and in that process he realized that, in fact, he wasn't even thinking, or at least he wasn't thinking as much as previously. No longer did his thinking contain any doubt, endless hesitation or wavering; thought moved with the same self-evident simple confidence as his arms did when swimming or his lungs, which, when out of breath, recovered from their latest exertions.

Here, where the current was again faster and the bank stonier, was the best place to clamber out without getting his legs all muddy. The thought, though, of his scuttling over the pasture land, legs muddy to the knees, made him laugh. It would have been utterly hilarious to smear himself all over with mud and run through the village naked. But he had never been inclined to provoke and shock the bourgeoisie, let alone the village folk. It came as a surprise to him that he was already beginning to get used to the idea that almost everything he did, that his body did, seemed funny. He took his trunks off, wrung them out, put them on again and began to backtrack along the river path to his starting point.

A cloud had moved in front of the sun and there was a chill in the slight breeze. He trod more quickly and without noticing broke into a jog. Yet there was something external, superficial, about it all; neither the chill breath of wind nor the swarm of midges and horseflies pursuing him could disturb what he had already in his mind described as 'a moveable feast' after the Hemingway book he had recently read. Yes, there really was a feast within him, a something-someone was dancing, singing, playing inside him; he could almost hear the joyful rhythm of the dance that bent everything else to his will. In that rhythm he breathed, ran and even thought – yes, now he realized that thinking, too, could be a rhythmic action, that thinking was easy and good once you had found the right rhythm.

There was something strange, funny and interesting in all this. He had to take stock of himself to understand what was actually different from before. He had to think how everything had been before and how it was now. One thing was clear: thought moved differently, although the thing that moved was not really a thought; rather, it was the entirety of awareness moving all at once, the entire mind, all feelings, thoughts and memories, which for some reason – and this, too, seemed genuinely funny – would be separated into categories on that basis. Previously thought had moved with an effort, as if it were a heavy burden; now the weight had rolled away and his mind-thought had wings.

His clothes were still on the log. The run had dried his body and only his trunks were still damp, but with this warm weather it didn't matter much. He put his trousers and shirt on an alder branch and sat on the log. It was the best place to think over everything again, although the thinking process was not really thinking. Thoughts came and went, glided by like clouds in the sky above, like a great, white, billowing cloud, almost a cumulus with its promise of a thunderstorm, the shadow of which was now over him. That cloud was also part of his thinking or feeling; there was no longer any clear boundary between his own self, his thoughts and the white clouds and between the swifts overhead, below the clouds. He felt that, in fact, he was unable to think about anything; the mental picture of the notion that man places himself to think, thinks about something he wants, felt funny as did many other things. When he got up the question occurred to him for the first time how he would be, how he would relate to others in his strange mystical condition. Had he become a stranger to others, moved away from them, or, on the contrary, had he moved closer to them? He had always found it difficult to relate to others, especially strangers, and here in the country he didn't really meet anyone apart from relatives.

Now, though, his first unexpected encounter awaited him. When he went through the alder grove he saw Old Kapp walking towards him, axe in hand. Was he planning to cut some wood? Why now in the middle of summer? The birds have chicks and the trees are full of sap.

'Good afternoon,' he said when he got closer. 'Off to do some wood-cutting?'

'Afternoon, afternoon. Oh no, no forest work this time of year. I'm off to the clearing for a couple of alders for pole ends for smoking the fish. If you take them now, they're dry afore autumn sets in.'

They exchanged a few more words before he set off along the path again. Before the main road he suddenly realized with consternation that for a few moments he had lost the wonderment in whose complete power he had so recently been. What did it mean? Had it all been only a passing giddiness, a fancy, an illusion? Schizophrenics and people with certain other illnesses had periods of exceptional clarity and lightness like this, as did, so Dostoyevsky claimed, epileptics. Perhaps it was a symptom of some kind of illness?

No, it couldn't be. No, everything was completely unlike the way it had been before. Thoughts of mental illness and illusion came and went but did not affect the contentment that had grown in him. Contentment and clarity were there still, although the shape they took was constantly changing: they moved, billowed within him. Funny to think that 'contentment' and 'clarity' were two words that were used so much without knowing what they could mean.

But what was that thought about, the scare-doubt that suddenly came and went? His previous existence, his previous self? Thoughts, doubts, fears that crossed a clear blue sky like solitary, dilatory clouds. What he felt, what he was now, could simply be described as the 'This' with a capital 'T'. The others probably wouldn't understand this This. The Teacher would, undoubtedly. But perhaps it was better that he had no possibility of talking to the Teacher now; it meant he could reach a better understanding of everything perhaps. Perhaps the ecstasy full of bubbling astonishment would develop into something simpler and clearer. Develop, not fade away. In case the This had been given to him only for a while and would fade away again. That was how it had been for many mystics. Plotinus only experienced true ecstasy a couple of times in his life.

But how would he cope now at home – that is, Meeta's and Richard's? When he had talked to Old Kapp it hadn't been anything extraordinary; it had actually been simpler to communicate this time than it usually was. There was no fear, which he often felt when communicating with simple people; conversation had come automatically, and he had managed better with his Võru language. Suddenly he realized why mystics were so often also recluses, moved into seclusion, cloisters, the forest or the hills. No, it was not that the world was wicked, foul or misleading, although it was indeed those things, but that was not the main reason. The main reason was that, in being among others, in relating to others, a person has to assume a role:, he has to be the person that society has defined him as being; he has to be the 'himself' that is often very much removed from the self, the real 'self' that the mystic is striving to find. He realized that, in fact, he, too, was something completely different from the person people took him to be, from the person he took himself to be and the person he portrayed. It was so funny that it made him laugh. It was funny that they regarded him as NN and that he in like fashion portrayed himself as NN. In fact, he was someone-something else, he was ... Suddenly he knew the word that fitted here, the word by which he could define himself: freedom. Freedom was the only thing that mattered; freedom was real. Other things existed, but they were nothing in comparison. Now, though, he had to go and again be something that wasn't the real him. And yet he felt that it was no longer difficult; he was also able to be the him he could be, even though it wasn't the real him. Perhaps this ability was also part of the really-being. But that wasn't important. It was like a drama, like the entire person-being. But in knowing this it could perhaps be accepted more easily, be played more easily.

Meeta was weeding the strawberries in the garden. From the fringe of the forest came the sound of axe blows: Richard was there chopping wood. This would otherwise have been his job, if he had been here; he thought he should go to the woodpile straight away and take over with the axe from Richard. But Meeta had spotted him already. She straightened up and said, *'We waited for you but gave up.*

Go and see what there is to eat in the pantry. Have some cottage cheese and cream from the shelf under there. I made it this morning.'

His great-aunt was nowhere to be seen; perhaps she had gone to the cowshed or was sitting under the oak in the garden on her own little bench. Good. The thought of having to spend another half-hour talking to his great-aunt about Finnish and university did not appeal. Even the This would not have been able to switch off the irritation he felt when he heard the shuffling steps crossing the little room towards him. So there were at least some weaknesses of which he was not free. Including hunger. It had pounced on him as soon as Meeta had mentioned cottage cheese. And with good reason. Meeta's cottage cheese was something the like of which he had not had anywhere else: it was strained and pressed dry so that it crackled when eaten. It was always topped with fresh sweet cream; that's what they'd done in those first poverty-stricken years when he'd been here.

He put the food back in the pantry, the dishes into the big basin in the kitchen and went outside. Afternoon lassitude was already in the air. Out of the corner of his eye he saw his great-aunt coming from the cowshed, dish in hand. That was right; there was a broody hen in there and his great-aunt would take it something to eat so that it wouldn't have to leave the nest for long and risk one of the others trying to break the eggs. This was a bad habit one of the white hens had got into.

He quickened his step, although he didn't escape from his great-aunt's field of view before he was noticed. He said he'd already had some refreshments and was off to chop wood. Always make sure that the axe handle is on properly, his great-aunt managed to say. He pondered the idea that these pieces of wisdom passed on to the young were the most common mantras of mothers, aunts and great-aunts, some universal and some individual. His aunt in the city would always remind him about his scarf and handkerchief; his grandmother would offer bread and milk, his great-aunt was most worried that he would be trapped by a falling tree in the forest when it was windy or would go walking by a boggy river with marshy banks where a couple of boys who had gone there to swim had drowned. He had not previously heard his great-aunt's worry about the axe. It was something new.

'*I wish you strength,'* he said when he found Richard at the woodpile.

'*Strength is always needed,'* Richard replied and lifted the next piece of wood on to the block. It was not like him to be easily disturbed while at work.

'*Listen, Richard,'* he went on. '*I'm going to take over from here. I'd like to chop some wood, too.'*

'*Now hang on! You haven't come here to chop wood! You've still got your bookwork and paperwork to do. Leave each of us to get on with his own job. I chop the wood; you do the written stuff.'*

'*Richard, I came to the country specifically to chop wood. In winter I did so much sitting around with books and writing that I got blisters on my fingers – that kind of life makes you really unfit – so now I'm here in the countryside I'd like to do a different kind of work, and chopping wood is just the thing. When you chop a couple of cubic metres of stacked wood you feel you're a real person; otherwise, you feel like a hopeless lazybones.'*

This time there was no need to talk Richard into it. He was clearly tired or had other urgent jobs to do. In any case, he left the axe and some words of instruction with him and set off towards the woodshed. Richard's chopping area was as tidy as a watchmaker's work table: splinters in one pile, the larger bark parings in another, the resinous trees which weren't suitable for burning under the stove – they made too much soot – in individual piles. Even the bundles of alder had to be put in a separate pile – they were for the sauna.

Wood-chopping was something his grandfather had taught him. And there was not much that could actually be taught, only a few tips such as putting the wood on a chopping block with the lower (thicker) end downwards and the fact that the thick blocks are easier to chop if you start from the edges. Everything else, the real art of wood-chopping, he had to teach himself; his own body had to allow itself to learn. The first time he happened to read a summary of a book, the title of which was, he thought, *Zen in the Art of Archery*, he immediately thought that it should be possible to combine Zen with the art of wood-chopping. Indeed, it was an art; it was something that could become an art if it was approached as such and was practised with care over a long period. It was a question of attitude. For aristocratic and speculative Europeans wood-chopping, haymaking and stacking could certainly not be an art, but to the Japanese, whose imperial castles were more like old farmhouses than castles, wood-chopping could indeed be an art. Or meditation.

It was what it was (the Buddha's name *Tathagata* – one who has thus come!), but Richard's axe was very well balanced, the shaft sat pleasantly in the hand, and it was exactly the right length. This axe simply had to be allowed to chop wood. All he had to do was lift it to the right height, give the correct swing and drop it on the correct spot. The axe did everything else. And his body, the body that suddenly was not 'his own', was part of the something-someone that itself lived, moved, acted and worked strangely.

They were a mixed collection of trees, cut and then fetched by tractor from the area of national forest bordering the road that led here to the boggy lake and then went on into the marshes and forests of Peipsi and Russia. The alders were already half dried out, the pines and birches were still damp. Resin and the smell of damp wood oozed from the pines and quickly made hands tarry. The white grubs that had already mated under the bark of several logs had fallen out and were squirming on the ground. He was unable to help them; presumably they would soon be food for ants. But even ants had their enemies: here in the greyish sand at the edge of the forest he had found ant leaf traps at the bottom of which there lurked a tiny predator waiting for its next victim. An ant that chanced into the leaf would try to scuttle up the sloping edge but would slip back down, straight into the jaws of the alerted larva.

He had never been able to believe that something like this could have been thought out and constructed by some Good Heavenly Father, a loving God who listens to children's bedtime prayers and gets cross with the ones who talk nonsense or don't do what their mothers, grandmothers or great-aunts say. He could accept the idea of a superbeing who, from empty space, conjured up fields, particles and, ultimately, galaxies, who created stars and planetary systems. Such a demiurge, architect of the cosmos, could genuinely be intelligent and good, must at least want good for those whom he assigned to inhabit the house he built or found themselves living there. Imagining someone thinking up all the dragonflies and antlions and the even more revolting parasites, ichneumon wasps, roundworms, tapeworms, tsetse flies and other creatures that invaded others' bodies and set about eating them from the inside . . . No, if life like that had been created by a higher intelligence it would not be godly but devilish.

That was how he had thought once; now, though, his old way of thinking seemed strange and senseless to him. No, being was not a type of construct; it was a strange power, a flow that had its own vortices, deep pools and shallow points. It also had points where there existed something that could be called good and evil, but the good and evil points were not numerous. The flow had very dark and very light spots. Like the place in time and space in the chopping area by the edge of the forest where the logs virtually stacked themselves; it seemed to happen automatically that the axe rose and fell on to the block, chopping it in two, with the two pieces then stacking themselves with the others at the end of the pile. It was like a dance that he had never learnt but that he had now mastered for himself. Or, who knows, perhaps he had, in fact, been learning the dance unawares since his childhood. Dance and music . . . Can there be dance without music? What was the music of this dance? The soughing of the forest, the gritty song of the finches and the many cheepings of the members of the tomtit family that roamed the fringes of the forest from tree to tree?

The woodpile had risen considerably. The thought of the marsh led to the thought of the forest. The light pine glade of Vōrumaa or the dark spruce grove. Yes, he wanted to go into the forest, to see how things were there now. The axe had to be put away in the woodshed; there was no one in the yard, only the cockerel with the hens, a large red-brown cockerel whose face was the same as the one he and Paul had tried to get drunk last year. The cockerel, though, was a gentleman; he divided all the vodka-soaked crumbs among the hens and didn't eat a single one himself. But they'd had neither enough time nor vodka to get the whole flock drunk. It might be the same cockerel or a different one; perhaps even the son of the one here last year. He beckoned to it; the cockerel gave a cautionary puk-puk-puk-puk-puk and flapped its wings. Striding towards the forest he had the thought that the cockerel was probably convinced that he had shooed an adversary away from his harem. He trod on his shadow which was already markedly more elongated than it had been at midday. But the sun still had a long way to go before reaching the triangulation tower visible behind the lake where it set in midsummer. Andres and he had visited the tower once while at school; it was old, but the ladders that took you to the top still felt sturdy, and they scrambled off them on to the small platform. From up there they could see the town, Munamägi Hill and a number of lakes. The small handrails around the platform were full of carvings of names. Andres took out his pocket knife and carved his own name and the date; he didn't want to inscribe his own name, so he thought for a few moments and wrote LUDWIG VAN BEETHOVEN.

This was the glade formed by the ammunition explosion that was now being reclaimed. A short distance ahead the path forked in two. He took the left fork up the hill and through the heathy pine forest to the lake. He liked the pine forest. He had cycled along this path a couple of times, by lonely lakes and bogs, over sandy hills. There were few people here; the old villages in the forests had been left empty after the deportations and the battles between the Forest Brothers and the KGB. Former farmland was beginning to be reclaimed by the forest. But he didn't go that far this time; he went only along the sandy path and then turned left again until he reached the lake from the other direction. The other shore of the lake was similarly sandy and high; reindeer moss and heather grew there. The lake itself glittered between the pines. The sun was already slanting into evening. He wanted to see whether the forest and the countryside were different from before. They were. Everything felt larger, whiter. And more serene. It was as if forest and lake were open to him. And he to them.

Behind him he heard a familiar chattering. A squirrel scampered up a pine trunk. For a moment he felt that they had switched roles: the squirrel was standing here on the sandhill, and he was scampering on up the tree trunk. He might just as well have been the squirrel – what big difference was there between them anyway? He waved to the squirrel, said 'Bye' and started back.

There were two burial mounds in the forest with signs that said that they were archaeological monuments. He stopped in front of them. Who was buried here? Warriors from the east, from beyond Peipsi? Or local people, perhaps even a distant ancestor of his? He now realized that his own bones might just as well rest there. What difference was there between his and his ancestors'? The bones of the living and of the dead? Everything was or was almost one. He was a tiny part of the great This, a tiny part of the universe and the consoling oneness of that universe.

He arrived home just in time for the evening meal. Paul wasn't there today, and conversation at the table was firmly in the hands of his great-aunt, who soon took it back once more to her memories of Finland and finished by playing played a religious song on the old harmonium that the young people had sung at the parson's house where she had lived sixty years before. He escaped without difficulty from his great-aunt's questions this time. He felt he needed to sleep, and straight after the meal went to the hayloft. Radhakrishnan awaited him tomorrow.

Sleep came in the blink of an eye, as it had in his childhood. When he awoke he couldn't for a while work out who and where he was. There was just black emptiness, not even any feelings, neither fear nor happiness. Then came the fear, followed by understanding that he was, should be someone, should be the person they had named. It took time, though, to come to this realization, and soon there was only distress of a kind he had not experienced before. Everything faded, fell together, drew itself into dark mass where there was no longer any difference between time and space, near and far, earlier and later. There was no time, so he was unable to say afterwards how long the horror lasted. Then he managed the thought that maybe hell was like this, a timeless, everlasting torment and misery. Torment that had no point and no basis – which in itself was a torment.

Then, however, came the light. There was light. A tiny ray of the morning sun that came in through the shingle roof and restored space to him. At first there was nothing but the light, he saw nothing else, but as a start it was a source of help. The light nimbly created everything that in the meantime had faded, vanished into the black horror. The light created space, then time, then his own self, his body, thoughts, memory. Memory, where sentences, phrases emerged. 'And God said, let there be light, and there was light . . . And the life was the light of men . . . Endless light – Amitabha – Ein Sof . . .' He sat up, looked around. Yes, everything was there, in its own place, the hay, the rafters, the roof-boards, the door, the walls, everything. But the light was on everything, as if beaming with pride at its own creation, as if wondering what it was capable of doing. He no longer saw the light; tears came into his eyes, began to flow down his cheeks. He sank back down, hid his face and sobbed into his pillow. All this in one day had been too much; in one day he had been to paradise and hell, or at least to the gates of paradise and hell. He lay down, the tears flowed. In the yard the cockerel was crowing; a current of air brought the gentle smell of a summer morning to his nose. He didn't notice that he fell asleep crying.

He woke up again an hour or an hour and a half later. It was probably already mid-morning; the warmth of a summer's day just beginning could be felt in the air, and voices were coming from the direction of the house. It was time to get up; the others had obviously had breakfast already. He always felt respect for country people who rose so early, sometimes as early as four or five o'clock. He was incapable of it. He had tried but the result was simply that he would end up sitting in the library or at the table at home, dozing. Discipline of this kind gained him no time at all, so there was no sense in continuing with it. In summer when there was no school he usually got up between seven and eight. But it was much later than that now. He threw off his bedclothes, shook the hay off his shirt and trousers and pulled them on.

As he slid down the ladder from the hayloft he suddenly remembered everything that had happened the previous day. He stood by the door and looked around. Today everything was normal, so normal and ordinary that it felt strange in its ordinariness. What had really happened to him? Something with which he no longer had an obvious connection. He was once again the same person as before; it felt as if what had happened in the meantime had happened in a different time and space and to a different person. He couldn't fear it, regret it or yearn for it; it had done him no good and no ill; he could have said that everything was normal, even the giddiness after everything he had experienced. But could this normality still be simply normal? He remembered a question that he had tried to answer as a child of five or six. He had held some blue and red pieces of glass up to his face one after the other and everything, the whole world, had gone blue and then red before his eyes. He had wondered then whether, if he had glasses of a given colour – blue, for example – in front of his eyes all the time, the world would look blue or would it have no colours at all any more. Blue is only blue when there are other colours; if there's no red, green or yellow, then there's no blue either. He would have liked to do an experiment, to spend a few days wearing blue glasses or living in a room where there were blue windows and blue lightbulbs; then he would have found out. But he had never tried it, and he forgot about it. But there was another question, too, and this now seemed more important; this, too, was something he had stumbled upon in his childhood when he suffered bad earache and tears would seep unbidden from his eyes despite his attempts to hold them back. He had wondered what would happen if he had been born with earache and it had suddenly gone away; would he then feel that he was better, or would he feel ill?

Earache was probably a bit different: pain cannot be an ordinary, normal thing. The recognition of pain and pleasure is the heritage of each living creature, and they cannot change places; pain cannot be regarded as pleasure or pleasure as pain. The cessation of pain is therefore always soothing and a pleasure, even for a newborn, who can explain nothing and to whom nothing can be explained. And what he felt in the night could never in any way be pleasurable. It was horror itself, and horror cannot be anything but horror. To someone who has emerged from horror normality is magnificent; to someone who has emerged from bliss it is, on occasion, loathsome.

Now, though, he had to go. His great-aunt would undoubtedly be worrying whether he was ill or whether something had happened. It was so bright in the yard that for the first few moments he had to keep his eyes shut. A slight breeze was blowing but was unable to dispel the growing sultry heat. He would just have to go for a swim in the river today – that thought reminded him immediately of another: would something similar to the events of the previous day happen to him there? Two swifts darted into the nesting-box with a whoosh. From the outbuilding came the clucking of a hen that had evidently just laid an egg; the cockerel scratching about on the dunghill shook its wings and clucked gently, who knows whether in approval or admonition. Not a single human soul was to be seen either in the garden or the yard. Directly in front of the gate he stepped in some hen shit, which he painstakingly scrubbed off his toes on the grass. Once again the present incarnation of Pônts was drowsing on the porch but this time ignored his arrival, presumably resting from his night-time hunting expedition. At the kitchen door he almost collided with his great-aunt, who said she was just off to find out what was keeping him for so long. No, there was nothing wrong, it was just that the country work, the country air and his long swim had worn him out . . . As ever his great-aunt hurried to fetch milk-butter curd cheese from the pantry and bread from the cupboard. The coffee had been kept warm on the stove. The weight-driven clock on the kitchen wall said half past nine already. His great-aunt sat opposite him at the table, and he had to tell his stories of the town again – it seemed that his great-aunt had already forgotten part of what they'd talked about on the day he'd arrived. Then he had a thought. Could he get her to talk about her childhood and youth? Were there still people in the area who knew the old folk songs? It became apparent that his great-aunt didn't know what these songs were; he had to explain and even sing a couple of lines from the only Võrumaa song he knew, which was:

> Weeping, weeping, poor soul,
> Weeping was I in the berry garden.

No, his great-aunt didn't remember anything. This was strange. Her younger sister, his grandmother, did remember how one old woman used to sing the old songs, but the younger ones would rebuke her with 'What are you wailing through those dreadful old dirges for? It sounds like a creaky barn door opening' to get her to sing a more beautiful, more modern song. And so the country people shamefully forgot their own traditional songs. He was ashamed that this had happened, that Estonians had not cared for anything old and authentic, unlike the Georgians, who sang their old multi-part songs with pride and fervour. He asked one more thing. Did his great-aunt know her own grandfather's and grandmother's names, and maybe their parents' names, and where they had come from originally and what they did? She didn't know much about this either. Oh yes, they were from the Mulgimaa area – Halliste or Karksi – they had been mill tenants and lived somewhere in the Tartu or Võrumaa areas. His great-aunt's father, that is, his great-grandfather, had been a miller by trade and had been the tenant of a mill before they settled in this area. So there were two generations of millers among his ancestors; both Grandma and her sisters and their father had grown up among the flour dust and met lots of people – a mill was like a tavern, visited by all sorts of people and the place to overhear all kinds of gossip.

His great-aunt would not let him clear the table or wash up: she would do it herself as long as her stiff legs and hands crippled by rheumatism allowed her to. It was her way of resisting old age to the last, and that was something to be respected. He took the opportunity and left for the hayloft and Radhakrishnan. After he had opened the book and read a few lines he suddenly felt that until that moment he had acted like a robot, without thinking what he was about to do and wanted to do. In fact, he did not have a clue. It was obviously something to do with the This. The This beside which everything else seemed at once empty and distant, whether reading or writing, science or philosophy. The thoughts moved slowly and reluctantly; something was missing, whether the will to create or the will to live or a combination of the two. It was probably almost the same as what the romantic poets called 'spleen'. The book felt alien and lifeless. He closed it and looked out the window. What he could see through it was more vital and more beautiful. There was something in it that was absent from reading and writing. Perhaps a soul, the thing that makes the living alive? He had a strange and daunting thought. Perhaps he, like most other people, in fact, had no soul; perhaps everybody was living dead, zombies, robots of flesh and bone? Then the life they lived was dead life and everything they did, thought or wrote was also dead. Then he was alive only yesterday when he met the This. Perhaps the This was the same as his spirit, or the Spirit generally; perhaps everything, in fact, had the same spirit?

Did any living people exist? Jesus had probably been alive; hadn't he said to let the dead bury their dead? How about Buddha and Lao-tzu and certain others? Perhaps the point is that their words live on and can revive life within us. So, we are not really dead as long as we still have a tiny dormant or forgotten spark of life. Yesterday, perhaps, he had been alive, he had had a soul, but why did it leave so quickly and forsake him? No, the writing was giving him nothing. Better to go and chop some wood for a while or do something else outdoors. For the moment it would be better to be among the trees and the birds. He put Radhakrishnan back on the hayloft shelf and went outside.

It was hot in the chopping area. He set the chopping block in the shade of a large birch tree – it wasn't particularly cool there, but he wouldn't have been able to bear being in direct sunshine for long. Nothing good lay in store: the first gad-fly was buzzing around his head. The almost cloudless blue sky had whitened slightly as if in anticipation of a drought. Meeta and Richard should have no trouble making hay this year; he and one of their sons would help. Perhaps it would require such an effort from him that his mind would be swept clear of mystic and erotic thoughts for a while.

Today the axe did not sit so well in his hand as it had the previous day; it did not catch the heart of the wood and its impact was either too weak or too strong. There was no rhythm either in his body or his movements. He chopped the wood as if chopping windows or tableware. Over and over again, instead of chopping the log beautifully in two, the axe chopped a thinner splinter from one side and it was too difficult to chop the thick part that was left over. The work was not enough for him to escape from the emptiness that had overcome him in the hayloft. And the number of horseflies was growing all the time; in swatting them he disrupted any rhythm. He had to stop for a while. Perhaps it would be better to resume in the evening when it was cooler outside and the horseflies had gone into hiding. He lodged the axe in the chopping block and went back to the barn.

Philosophy no longer felt so absurd. He was able to read and even made some notes. The desire to read did not last long, though, and his thoughts began to wander and a gap sprang up between the words and his thoughts and interfered with his understanding. He had never understood why it was thought that man thinks in words. There were continually thoughts that were perfectly clear but difficult to articulate. And words that did not express a thought were not the origin of understanding. Thoughts and their origin were odd things: they mostly arose somewhere in the dusk, in what was called the subconscious, and gradually rose to the surface, became clearer, acquired a shape and sometimes also a name.

He felt now that one of those wordless thoughts was searching for a way out, wanted to come into the world. There was a brief moment before he began to gauge its thread. His gaze fell on a copy of *Looming*, and he immediately remembered an erotic story by Ast-Rumor that he had read in it a couple of times. It was the same issue he had used once when masturbating. One glance sufficed for the passing fancy to become a full thought, this time a daydream, the desire in which he clothed his thoughts and pictures or, rather, the desire that his thoughts and imagination used to serve their own purposes.

But yesterday he had hoped, had absolutely believed, that now, thanks to the This, he had escaped from the clutches of desire, that he was free. But that was a mistake. It was wicked and humiliating to be a weathervane to his desire (was it really *his* desire?). Women and sex didn't really interest him that much: he merely wanted them, but the wanting also contained an aspect of freeing himself of desire, finding peace and returning to more interesting things. And now, especially since things had not worked out with Malle, there was also nervousness in the desire. He knew that he had to step over the first threshold, irrespective of how and with whom. The This hadn't helped. Again he was in the clutches of the That. No, he didn't think he should free himself from sex, live the life of an ascetic. He wanted only peace.

Hitherto he had found satisfaction only by satisfying himself. This was, however, semi-satisfaction and humiliating to boot. Something he really didn't enjoy and a painful reminder of his failure to be with a woman. The idea of real sex, union with a woman, being one body, lived so strongly within him and refused to allow him to be reconciled with what he had so often done in a hidden place somewhere here in the country.

No, this time he wanted to be stronger. Perhaps there had been so much from the This that he would now be able to leave that issue of *Looming* unopened, get up, fetch his towel from the room and go to the river for a swim. It wasn't even difficult. Perhaps easier than on some previous occasions. When he trod along the edge of the ditch towards the river he was almost pleased with himself for several moments.

The satisfaction did not last long, though. As he approached the swimming place through the alder wood he suddenly noticed that someone's clothes were on the grass. He looked around, startled, and wanted to turn back the way he'd come and go swimming somewhere else, but it was already too late.

'Don't be afraid. There are no tramps around here. No thieves either; only the village people,' said a voice from the willow bushes and out stepped a young woman wearing a swimsuit that she had evidently just wrung out.

'No, I'm not afraid, I was just thinking I'd be disturbing you,' he mumbled in reply. He thought he knew her: she must be Old Kapp's daughter from the farm near by. She lived in Tallinn but always spent the summer here. He had met her a couple of times when he was a child when she had come to the village with Andres. The boys had told smutty stories about her and all the other girls that at the time had both revolted and thrilled him. Now she was suddenly here, combing her wet hair, and he was looking straight at her, an attractive woman of about thirty.

'No, you're not disturbing me. It's not that easy to disturb me anyway,' she replied. 'So, has our college boy come to visit his country cousins?'

So she knew he was a university student. No surprises there.

He could only say yes, he had come here as he had done every summer for the past ten years to help his relatives out a bit at the end of the haymaking. The woman picked up her towel and dried herself.

'It's so refreshing when educated men don't turn their noses up at country work,' she said. Now he remembered her name – it was Helge or Helgi.

'Hard work doesn't break your bones – it's just something you need after a long winter at university,' he replied.

'Yes, a healthy mind in a healthy body, as they say,' she said, looking at him directly again, this time for longer, making him feel a bit strange. Was it because of her glance or because she was talking about bodies? There was a pause in the conversation. The woman carried on drying her hair, but it looked like she wouldn't be leaving immediately.

He felt he should ask something in return, otherwise it would look funny.

'Have you come to your grandparents' to help out, too?'

'Yes indeed. A short holiday – and, of course, I'm giving them a hand, too. They're elderly, and I don't have my brother's excuse – he has so much work of his own and no time to come out here.'

He'd heard about Helgi-Helge's brother: he'd been a tramp, then had given up the drink, gone to Russia to work in construction, driven animals and gone off to Saaremaa or Hiiumaa to work as a fisherman.

He would have liked to ask how long she was staying, but he didn't know how. He didn't want her to go away, yet didn't dare say so. He was unable to work out whether she was willing to draw their meeting out further or not. This pause in the conversation was longer than the previous one. The woman put her dress on but didn't button it up.

'Right, I should probably go. I'm wasting our good college boy's time for no good reason,' she said, breaking the silence.

Was there an expectation in what she said and in the way she said it of his responding with 'Not at all; it was really nice to bump into you; there's no one to talk to here or go anywhere with'? If he'd said as much, then maybe ... But instead he said something that came from inside himself awkwardly and pointlessly, 'Don't say that ... you are not wasting my time at all ...'

The woman laughed and said, 'See you, enjoy your swim', turned and set out on the path back home.

He watched after her, his gaze on her legs and hips, the sway of which was not masked fully by her unbuttoned dress. When she had disappeared from view he felt how his heart was beating unexpectedly strongly. There was a strange feeling in his loins, too – yes, his body had reacted to this encounter in its own primitive way, but his mind had not dared to go along with it. He was cross with himself. Another opportunity wasted. Perhaps something would have come of it, perhaps Helgi-Helge wouldn't have had any objection ... He didn't know whether she was married or not, but that was no concern of his. Perhaps he was wrong, had imagined something in her glance and words that wasn't there. He was a stranger, they had nothing in common, and if he had attempted to make advances to her he might have been left looking a fool as he had on a couple of previous occasions.

Was this how to cheer himself up? In any event, contentment had gone for the moment. Now there was nothing else to do but get into the water and cool off. Perhaps a swim would bring the vanished This closer again, would help the That be freed of temptation. Meanwhile, part of his mind had gone with his body and was busy creating a mental picture of what might have happened if ... Before he got into the water he looked back. Perhaps the woman had forgotten something or was coming back anyway ...

No, there was no one on the path. The horseflies had been bothering him for a while. They were now beginning to sap all his energy, pursuing him even when he started to swim downstream. For the first instant the water felt colder than the previous day, but it was probably only because he was hotter. Strange, he thought, that what we feel isn't the actual temperature but the change in temperature.

It was pleasant in the river. The water quickly cooled his flesh and removed the images from his mind. Swimming was harder, though, than the last time. Once more he was unable to find the correct rhythm and felt he was tiring more rapidly. His arms and legs became stuck in more plants, and once, when he turned on to his back and allowed the flow to take him, he drifted headfirst into a log floating by the opposite bank. There was nothing left of the This. For a few moments his mind was simply empty and light, for which he was thankful (to whom?).

This time he didn't swim so far, climbing out even before the Vaglaraua house and loped at a gentle trot back to the swimming place. For a moment he hoped that Helgi-Helge might have come back, but there was no one there.

On the way home he glanced towards the Kapp family's yard, but there was not a soul to be seen, only a pair of white hens scratching by the gate.

In the barn he tried for a while to delve into his notebook, but nothing much came of it. The images returned, transported him to the riverbank with Helgi-Helge, in the old hay barn, allowed her to undress herself slowly and say, 'Come here!' It all ended as it had so many previous times in the hayloft. His erection was so strong that it hurt, and his ejaculation was more vigorous and long-lasting than ever. He thought that in the end it was always better to gain release from his torment like this than to waste time and energy fighting salacious images without really being able to concentrate on anything. After all, it was only letting steam out of a boiler; he realized, if he were to extend this comparison, his male anatomy was looking for a safety valve. And why not? Where there's a boiler with a strong fire underneath, the steam must always have a way out. How could the fire be extinguished or tamed for a while? He did not know. He had heard that they gave men in the army something that calmed their urges; there was supposed to be a similar substance in some cigarettes. He wasn't sure whether it was true. There were so many stories of all kinds about the army – some of them clearly nonsense. Like the military legends about the Winter War with Finland: the Mannerheim Line, bunkers with rubber roofs and courageous Finnish women warriors.

This was not true mental peace, it was more like narcosis. He still had problems with the Radhakrishnan and did not feel like reading anything else. The most sensible thing was to chop wood – it went better than it had in the morning, and he felt almost at peace with himself. He was not able to chop the wood for long as Richard and Meeta came home – they had been to the village to try to borrow a cart for the haymaking.

When he clambered into his bed in the hayloft that evening his head was spinning as if he'd been smoking. He didn't smoke in the countryside; he took no cigarettes with him and didn't want any of Richard's Belomors.

When he closed his eyes pictures started to appear before them more clearly and more vividly than during the day. He never understood properly whether he had created the pictures himself or whether they came from somewhere else and carried him off. The somewhere else could even be within himself, in his subconscious, or whatever it was called. Helgi-Helge hadn't vanished anywhere; she was coming towards him on the very same path, laughing; they embraced, her body was against his, her hand was gliding over his back. His own hand took courage from this and moved towards her buttocks, the elastic of her knickers, and was unable to overcome the temptation to pull them off . . . The picture went no further. Now he had to get out of bed and calm himself down again.

Clearly the image had gripped his lower body at least as strongly as it had his brain. Now, as he helped it in its release, the pictures also dissipated, and before his eyes there was not a woman but a landscape, a wood-cutting area and pines on the forest fringe. He was once again disappointed in himself. How could an encounter on a riverbank with a woman who was almost a stranger disrupt his contentment so much? If it had been Malle or . . . no, in fact, he'd wanted it to be Ester. And then, suddenly, came the recognition that Ester could be exactly the person he needed. Ester could help him to unite the This and the That, the upper and the lower, soul and body. Ester might be the holder of his freedom and escape. He said her name softly over and over: Ester, Ester, Ester. Ester would understand him, Ester would help him, help him become a man, help him live. It would be just as good to be in bed with Ester as it was to be wide awake with her, in the forest or in the city. Even her name, even the thought of her was comforting and cleansing, a mantra that gave him faith and hope. No, it couldn't be Malle, it had to be only Ester. He hadn't loved Malle, he didn't even know what love was, but now he was beginning to understand it. In a couple of weeks he would have to go back. He would obviously go via Rein's and Ester's; the Teacher might be there, too, and they would go out on a trip somewhere, as they had discussed. They were good thoughts. They made him feel good in himself and grew unnoticed into a dream that had nothing in common with the day's events or thoughts, with the This or the That.

When he awoke in the morning all he remembered of his dream was that it had been light, beautiful and oddly good. He couldn't remember whether Ester had been in it, although it had definitely had something to do with a girl. The thought of Ester – her name was now his mantra – had helped him and he believed in it.

20

The following weeks went by almost at a fixed pace with no surprises, almost everything repeated itself. In the morning he would get up at a certain time, eat, chop wood, go for a swim, write some poetry and read Radhakrishnan – although he was only getting through it very slowly – help bring the hay home and hoist it up to the hayloft. Paul visited frequently; once Kalev, in a hurry as usual, came, too. He stayed only from that evening to the next, although in that time he managed to weed the large strawberry patch and rockery, make hay, talk about his memories of the camps and accompany him to the bog island beyond the lake where there had once been a Forest Brothers' bunker, one that the KGB had found thanks to a traitor who had known to escape at the time of the attack and had survived. A grenade thrown down a ventilation hole killed the two unsuspecting men and one woman inside.

A few days before he left Andres also came on holiday. He arrived by car and with a lady, a divorced teacher who had clearly progressed from sharing a landing with Andres to sharing a bed with him. Richard and Meeta did not bother them with detailed questions, but Silvi – that was the pretty teacher's name – achieved a real coup with his great-aunt, who was more nosy: she had a good command of Finnish and even had some Finnish friends.

The three of them went on a day out together: Andres wanted to show Silvi the school of his childhood and some of the local beauty spots. A dozen kilometres from the farm there was a row of old mills by the river, most of them abandoned, and sandstone rocks home to caves where the old people said that people had hidden during the war. Near by there was a small lake with clear, clean water that they'd cycled to when younger. They stopped there, went for a swim and drank lemonade. It wasn't exactly fun for him to be in Andres's and Silvi's company; he felt he had been invited more out of politeness and that, in fact, they'd have preferred to be on their own and be more affectionate than they dared to be with him around. They were fairly daring none the less. It was strangely bittersweet to see how Andres's hand moved from her hips to her thighs and once slid between them. It aroused him, although it also gave him a measure of contentment. He was both jealous of the lovers and happy for them. He couldn't stop himself imagining what they did in bed at night or would have done here in the open if they had been alone. What position did they most often do it in? He, like other schoolboys, had read Van der Veld's *Marriage Technique* book. He wondered whether he would have liked to watch others have sex, whether it would have hurt him or brought him contentment? He had heard that some people only achieve real sexual pleasure as onlookers; the boys had heard talk of men with binoculars on the lookout for couples near the forest beyond the city on the Emajõgi meadow. Did he have that kind of a streak in him? Peeter Härmsoo, who was probably the only friend to whom he had expressed his sexual preoccupationss, had once said that all men are voyeurs to a greater or lesser extent.

Here he clearly remembered his failed dates with Malle; he remembered his swim with Ester and Rein. Why did his world have to be so erotic? Why did everything always have to remind him of sex, arouse him, take his peace of mind away? Sometimes he'd wondered about monks and other ascetics who fought their desires, conquered them and were contentedly engaged in prayer, theology and philosophy. But even they didn't always succeed: he remembered the unhappy story of Abélard. There probably were men who were stronger than their desires and men whose desires were stronger than they were. But he would much rather have known what the ascetics actually did, how they fasted, prayed and meditated. He would have liked to discuss it with someone. Perhaps he could with Ester? She was for ever on his mind, although the emotional outpouring that had seized him that evening was nearly forgotten, and he would no longer have dared to say that he believed so devotedly in Ester and loved her so completely. But he longed to see her, even if just to understand what his feelings towards her really were.

In fact, he should have phoned them before his arrival to find out whether and when the Teacher and Ellen were coming. But a phone call would have to be made from a post office five kilometres away where a call had to be booked and waited for. In town he could cope with this system of long-distance calling, but it would be too much bother for him to do so here. It was easier to go at the time they had more or less agreed and see whether the Teacher and Ellen were coming or not. Perhaps he would really get to go on a trip with them. He could not imagine any greater joy, and he was already sorry that his time there would come to an end. It probably had something to do with the fact that home didn't feel like home to him; home was not a place he wanted to be, and his relatives – his grandfather, grandmother, mother and aunt – were not the type of people he wanted to live with. Here in the countryside he was more at home, probably even more so at Rein's. Yet he knew that he was still only a guest and would not be able to stay there long; he would have to return to the home that was not actually a home.

Did home really exist? Perhaps it was merely an illusion, the illusion of a traveller who occasionally finds shelter, food and friendliness somewhere. Indeed, perhaps people are hospitable to travellers because they are strangers with whom there is no cause, as yet, to quarrel. There were, in fact, never any arguments in their home, but sometimes it felt that everyone was a bit cross with everyone else yet managed to control their irritation. There is no irritation at the beginning of a friendship, but gradually it emerges sooner or later. The same happens in a marriage. Are people not kinder and more attentive towards strangers than they are to their families and old friends?

Did Andres and Silvi think like this, too? Did Silvi believe that everything would work out differently with this man than it had with the previous one? Perhaps it was only a summer fling for them, a short romance in south Estonia? No, that couldn't be it, otherwise Andres would not have brought Silvi here to his parents' home. He looked at them and suddenly saw them with different eyes. He no longer saw a stirring, erotic picture that made him jealous but two people looking for support in one another. This was easy to detect in the woman: she was resting her head on the man's shoulder; the man had put his arm around her waist; he wanted to be someone who could provide support for someone else; he wanted to be a man, a solid object whom the woman could trust and on whom she could pour her tenderness. The man's face did not show how much he needed her tenderness. But he, a man who had not yet attained full manhood, knew, he understood, that between desire and longing there was no clear boundary, just as there was no clear boundary between a real man and a little boy who needs a lap on which to lay his head, needs someone in whose embrace he does not always have to be a man but can be a child longing for tenderness.

On their way back Silvi suddenly asked him whether he had a girlfriend.

'No, no one special,' he replied. What else could he say? The fact that Silvi had asked him and looked at him gave him pleasure. He felt that it had made him a small part of their desire and flirtation. He had been drawn into it in some small way, he was no longer so alone. Perhaps Silvi's feminine intuition had sensed his loneliness, noticed the sadness or envy in his gaze and was now trying to put things right.

'You're such a bright, good-looking boy. You must have your pick of all the girls,' she went on.

If there were girls aplenty, he said, it would be difficult to choose.

'You must be on the lookout for a woman who's as clever and attractive as you. But, take my word for it, don't choose a very clever woman. Choose a woman who cares for you and helps you out, someone who won't try to compete with you intellectually.'

That might well be good advice, but not for him and not right now. Right now the most important things for him were love and sex; they both meant intimacy, huge, almost mystical intimacy. An encounter with a woman had to be like an encounter with God: complete surrender, fusion, becoming one. This was what he longed for, and even if this yearning was absurd he could not live without it.

They ducked into a mill. Empty, deserted houses had always fascinated him although he couldn't explain why. In some cases it was obviously for the objects you could find inside. Here, in summer, he had often cycled to where there was an uninhabited house. He just liked old things, whether a rusty tool, an ancient newspaper, a book from the days of the Estonian Republic or an old bottle. He always took something small away with him from the d houses, as a souvenir. He found nothing valuable or useful in his visits, but the buildings always stayed in his memory. Sometimes he even dreamt about the old houses. He saw himself going from room to room, climbing into the attic, rummaging through cupboards and drawers full of knick-knacks. Upon waking he never remembered exactly what they were, remembering only the thrill and satisfaction he felt at his discoveries.

Andres and Silvi had no particular interest in the mill; they went over to the dilapidated weir that was now becoming rapids and stood hand in hand on the embankment. He went up the steps, opened the door that was hanging off its hinges and went inside. The mill house was also a place where people had lived: the living-rooms and milling areas were under the same roof. There was still furniture in the rooms: old beds, a large wardrobe, a sideboard and, strangest of all, a grand piano, its polish worn away by the rain dripping on to its lid through the damaged roof. The white sheaths had also come away from the white keys (he wondered what material they'd been made of – real elephant ivory?) leaving just pegs behind. The black keys, evidently made from black oak, were intact although twisted askew. He raised the lid: the piano strings seemed to be in one piece. Could this piano still be repaired, restored? Who were the people who in this isolated spot – a mill house where the roar and chatter of wheels was undoubtedly heard during the day – had acquired a grand piano and played it? Was there a genuinely musical person in the family? Perhaps the miller's wife had brought the piano with her as her dowry and had played it from time to time? But maybe the piano had originally been among the belongings of a baronial family who had left for Germany, and it could have been bought for a pittance. And no one in the family had particularly wanted to take a grand piano home; ity took up too much space and was very loud. An upright was better suited to a normal family home. So it might well be that a baronial grand piano was offered for nothing or next to nothing to a number of people until in the end the miller took it for himself. He had larger rooms. It would be interesting to investigate the piano's history, visit the people in the surrounding area, one or two of whom would certainly know something about it. Perhaps someone in the miller's family was still alive; perhaps they had been deported but had returned; perhaps they had moved out to the city when the mill closed. Who owned this mill? Did it belong to the collective farm? If it did, then this wreck of a piano did, too. What would become of it? Would the mill be restored one day and the piano removed, or would it collapse to leave only a ruin near the rapids. The trace of rot was visible in the mill-house joists. It would not be many years before they were rotted through and could no longer support the roof. The first thing to give would most likely be the joists that bore the greatest load, the ones that supported the larger pieces of furniture like this piano.

What was it, in fact, in these deserted houses that captivated him? Some

feeling that was both grief and a reconciliation with grief, a gentle feeling of tran-
sience that had inspired so many poets. The *sic transit* feeling.

He went into the second room. Rain had come in here, too, although the bookcase in the corner had remained dry. There were only a couple of books and a pile
of papers in the cupboard. He rummaged through them. They were mostly pattern sheets from old women's magazines; there was a school exercise book from
the days of the Republic, and there were a few letters, a poultry-farming hand-
book, a couple of elementary-school textbooks and a book of southern-Estonian
songs. He took a letter out of an envelope. It was written in pencil and began in a
rousing fashion: 'My dearest girl'. The writer invited his girl, whose name was not
given, to a temperance-society tea party. The letter bore the stamp of heraldic
lions. He picked up the letter, put it back in the envelope and stuck it into the songbook. He had once before seen a book of songs from southern Estonia and found
that it contained more beautiful and more poetic songs than its northern coun-
terpart. His ancestors had sung from a songbook like this; perhaps it even included
the infamous 'pain of hell song' that his grandfather still talked about. Its lyrics
had been 'there the devil dragged you and thrashed you from wall to wall'. The
advent of new times meant that the song about the pain of hell fell into disgrace
and was no longer either taught or sung. Most pastors nowadays didn't talk about
hell and probably didn't believe in it either; hell was left to the religious sects,
who had a closer relationship with it and its master. And hell was not even much
mentioned in church any more. Only the old Catholic priest whose sermon he
had once stayed to hear talked about the devil, about people choosing whether to
be the children of God or the slaves of the devil.

When he got back to the car Andres and Silvi were not yet there, nor were they
by the lake. He stopped, picked up the songbook, closed his eyes and placed his
finger on a page and opened at random. Under his finger he read:

> My beloved on the Cross
> My love is Jesus Christ . . .

What was this called? It must be bibliomancy – divination using books; one of
the many mancies, some of which are in fashion, some abandoned. He would have
liked to believe in methods of divination, but he was unable to. Yet they had their
own charm. Divin['/ taken in that spirit.

He went back into the mill and stood in the back room where the old wardrobe
was. It contained nothing more than a few crudely crafted hangers, clearly home-
made by someone who lived here. On the riverbank, seen through the window,
there grew a large linden tree that made the room very dark. Suddenly he realized
that it was almost completely silent in the room. The window was intact, and the
roar of the rapids sounded quiet in here, the silence undisturbed. The silence was

strange and, combined with the twilight, even disquieting. He had felt something like this in his childhood, in mid-evening when the sun was setting and the twilight was gradually beginning to fill the rooms. No, he couldn't stay here any longer, and he hurried, almost ran, through the rooms, his footsteps and the crackling of the rotten floors under his feet sounding unexpectedly alien and sinister. As a child he had sometimes fled from a room like this for fear of the twilight. Once, panic-stricken and in tears, he had gone across the stairway and corridor to the kitchen and his grandmother. The dark did not make him feel uneasy like this; the dark could also conceal, make things invisible, and invisible was something he had always dreamt of being. Invisible or minute like an elf that can go anywhere, step over national borders and travel to far-away lands on a bird's back like Nils Holgersson. Yes, he remembered the Nils Holgersson book well, and Nils meeting a real elf, who cast a spell on him and turned him into an elf. That had happened in a room where the boy was alone, perhaps also in mid-evening.

Outside it was still fully light, and the evening's approach was scarcely noticeable – strange that he felt it more clearly inside. Perhaps there was still something there in the house, something that it was better not to name, something that really menaced him. No, he didn't believe in ghosts, phantoms or spirits, and yet the uneasiness that he had felt was not consistent with natural affairs but with what he had read in Eisen's folk tales or other books of fairy-tales. Now Andres and Silvi were coming around the corner of the house, Silvi holding a couple of yellow dahlias.

They didn't talk much on the way back, perhaps through fatigue. Perhaps something had happened between Andres and Silvi: they were very quiet and no longer touched each other. He did not dare to start a conversation.

The weather stayed dry and the hay was brought in. While bringing in the last load he tried to see if he could still remember how to haul hay with a horse. In this area the hay was taken on a large wagon; its sides were like those of a standard farm wagon but very high and had long rods instead of pegs. It was easier to put hay into this kind of wagon than into a load, although you had to go carefully because it was narrower and more likely to topple over.

The woodshed was now completely full. Andres and Silvi had gone, but Paul and Kalev were both at home. It was hot and dusty up there; wisps of broken hay stuck to his skin and his hair was full of them. But this, too, had its own charm, the charm of genuine work that new-age man was rarely able to experience. They made hay for Milli, the same red, short-haired cow whose milk they drank, and her calf. When they had finished the three of them – he, Paul and Kalev – went for a swim, Kalev with a fishing-rod in hand, and by the time he and Paul had sat down, chatted and fed the midges Kalev had caught several large roach and ae chub in the deep-river pool at the edge of the alder wood. They slept in the hayloft at night among the fresh hay and talked for ages. He heard about their grandfather for the first time, his great-aunt's husband, who had been a very unusual person. He never washed with soap although he did go to the sauna and whisk himself, but usually changed only his shirt in the belief that cloth kept his skin clean. He ate eggs with their shells on and with food drank only clean well water, saying that 'water can carry great ships, so it gives great strength'.

He dreamt that he met his own lost father in a room that was similar both to a mill and a church; his father did not want to speak to him, and in the end ran up along the broken steps. He wished to follow his father but found himself in a labyrinth of stairs and ladders, climbing ever higher and was suddenly in the library where all the books were spread on scaffolding in an enormously high room. It was twilight, and not a single person was there. He was suddenly seized with terror. He tried to shout for his father, but no voice came from his throat. Then he summoned all his strength and cried out, 'Where is everyone?' Only a husky whisper of his cry remained, and then he woke up. Outside it was not yet light.

21

The morning of the day of his departure was one of fine mizzle. His great-aunt and Meeta persuaded him to stay – how could he go anywhere in the rain anyhow? – but Richard looked at the sky and said that when it was misty like this in the morning it might brighten up during the day. In any case, he packed his things, checked his wheel-bearings and pumped up the tyres. By the time he had had his breakfast the rain was easing and the sun could be distinguished more and more clearly behind the clouds. Despite his protests his great-aunt still gave him sandwiches for the journey and Meeta a small jar of honey as usual. His flask was full of Meeta's good corn coffee – a mixture of real coffee and ground grains.

'*I don't know that you'll see me again when you come next summer,*' said his great-aunt, half in Võru, as she had already on many occasions, adding, '*Be on a good lookout all the while. Those car drivers go tearing along so fast. Keep right to the edge of the road when you're on your bike.*'

They stayed to wave him off, all three of them. When he reached the road he stopped and looked back. The others had probably gone, but his great-aunt's white spotted handkerchief, the same colour as her hair, was still visible beside the lilac bush.

He rode a few kilometres along the main road and then turned into the forest, following the old road that went past two small lakes and finally came out at the larger main road. It was a more direct route to Rein's from here but a more difficult ride because in several places it was sand rather than gravel. There were also fewer cars; it would have put his great-aunt's mind at rest if he had bothered to tell her. There was an old farmstead by the forest path a short way from the main road. He remembered that the first time he had been here there was still something left of the farm buildings, but now all that could be seen were the foundations, which were becoming increasingly concealed by bushes and lush hay. On the site of the house willowherb was growing, already a bloom of mauve. Was autumn really not far off? Summer was too short. Summer was a tearing rush of flowering and growing that was over before you managed to get used to it. Yes indeed, there was something of late summer and early autumn in the air already. And there were more spiders' webs visible in the grass and bushes than when he had come this way before.

Then came the lake with a house visible beyond; there used to be more of them, but the years of the Forest Brothers, the deportations and the collective farms had left just this one behind. Of others there remained only foundations, lilac bushes and the odd ailing ancient apple tree. The path was sandy here and uphill, and he had to dismount from his bike. Flowers had emerged on the tops of the heather, another sign of autumn. Autumn had always been a more serious time for him, more of a time for work; he had written his best poems in this season, the poems he liked most. In summer some part of him was asleep or absent, his spirit was like a bird that occasionally travelled outside his body, flitted from tree to tree, flew from forest to forest. In autumn it returned and stared him in the face. It was therefore strange that the This had happened to him in the heart of summer and not in autumn. He had tried over and over to find the This again but to no avail. He tried to recall what he had thought and done when the This happened, but he couldn't remember exactly. Perhaps it was irrelevant and the This was only a mystical, dark occurrence, something that could inadvertently capture anyone's consciousness, in utter disregard of the essence of that consciousness. Perhaps the This merely came and went, plummeted through him like a meteor and vanished, burnt itself out, leaving behind the yearning that surely no earthly thing could quench. Except perhaps a woman. Except perhaps . . . Ester . . .

He had tried to meditate, sitting on a chopping-block in the woodshed and on the bedclothes in the hay fort, legs crossed. He had prayed in the evening and tried to write poetry in the day, but nothing much came of it. So, was everything old; had nothing changed? All he had gained was an understanding that something beautiful and flawless existed. Would he then spend his whole life yearning for the This? Would he become an unhappy man?

The forest bordering the path changed: on the right, over there, where the lake was, there was a wet peatland forest with low pines and birches, some of which had withered. Once there must have been a larger lake where now there were only two small waterholes, the one he had skirted by on his bike and the one that was not visible from the path. He had been here once with Andres. You had to come along a narrow forest track, which was just bogland in places. The lake could be approached from one direction only. The water was very murky, and the two perch they had caught that day were so dark that you couldn't really see the band on their flanks. It was strange to swim in the bog lake; the water near the surface was warm but cold as iron lower down.

This time he didn't go to the edge of the forest lake. He wanted to get to Rein's in good time. There was a strange, slightly thrilling and slightly hollow feeling in his stomach. He wanted to get there; he wanted to see Ester, but at the same time he was afraid of her, afraid of Rein, his mother and father. It was as if he had been split into two: a normal him plodded along the sandy forest path with his rucksack on his back, wheeling his bike, and another him hovered over the first him's head, looking down on him from afar and marvelling at how everything was as it was. The first him acted as if driven by an alien force, the second him was alarmed by this but unable to do anything about it. Sometimes he thought he would tell Ester everything, Ester was capable of understanding him, but then the thought would feel unreasonable and would scare him. After all, he didn't know her that well; it would be more sensible just to be with her, talk, meet up some time in the city. Like people do, like other people do. That was what he thought for the moment. The path was level again here, and he could ride easily. The rhythmic exertion affected his brain oddly. Images whirled in his head and allowed him no respite – the This and the That, Ester and the Teacher – it was as if in so doing they bled themselves dry, their might and acuteness spent. Although he could not control the images, nor could the images control him. He was like a robot, a machine once set in motion by a single thought proceeding from the inertia of that thought that had perhaps now already vanished and changed.

The next sandy incline before the main road was the best spot to stop and have something to eat. The coffee in the flask was still warm. The sandwich in its wrapper was warm, too, and the butter had soaked into the bread, although it tasted better here than from the table at home.

Only a memory of the rain was left; even the path was already dry and might well throw up dust soon. It was more of a nuisance on the big gravel road. There were cars there. The sky was hazy, but the sun was shining quite powerfully already. Although he hadn't been working especially hard, his shirt was damp under his rucksack.

Ahead there were no more great forests. The road snaked between hills bound for the north-west, sometimes rising, sometimes falling. He pedalled the bike up most of the rises, although once or twice he found himself out of breath and had to dismount. When he reached a crest he would stop and look back. On the horizon, beyond the forests, the blue hills of the Haanja uplands were visible.

In the other direction Rein's church was coming into view – it must be twenty kilometres away or less. Had the road been smooth he would be there in an hour, but the hills and slopes drained him of speed, and it would take him a lot longer, perhaps two hours. Once more he was split in two: on the one hand, he would have liked to arrive immediately, on the other, he was wavering and afraid. He rode on without hurrying but without pausing for long breaks; he allowed his body to take over.

The last five or six kilometres were the longest. By the side of the road were open fields. The heat was making him thirsty; under his backpack his shirt was wet with sweat and drops of perspiration were flowing down his face into his eyes. He began to count the turn of the pedals but soon became confused and just kept repeating 'nearly there, nearly there'.

Fortunately he only met two cars, but even they threw up thick dust; he felt it settling on his sweaty face, forcing itself into his eyes, nose and mouth. But once he had pushed himself up the hill the church tower loomed ahead very close. It was as if the tower or the knowledge that there was a lake there that he would soon be able to plunge into had beamed new strength into his weary limbs.

As he was coming along the now familiar path to the house the first person he saw was Rein's father, chopping wood by the woodshed.

'Right, more for the sauna on the way,' shouted Rein's father in the direction of the garden after they had exchanged greetings. 'Mum, it's probably about time to get the sauna going.'

Only now did he realize that it was Saturday evening – being in the country he had got his dates muddled; at Meeta's and Richard's he didn't even usually listen to the radio; the papers came only twice a week and in summer there was never much in them apart from plan-implementation charts for the collective farms and reports from the hay fields. Was Rein at home?

No, but he should be back in a few hours. And tomorrow Alo and Ellen were coming.

How about Ester? He felt his heart thumping in his chest as he said her name.

No, Ester was on a practical. She would arrive the following week.

He didn't know whether this information brought him sadness or relief. In reality he still didn't know what Ester meant to him. He had been expectant and fearful precisely because he didn't know how his meeting with Ester would go. Could something definite come out of all this if he couldn't see her? No, evidently not, but perhaps he should achieve some kind of certainty before he met her? For an instant (how long was that instant?) he lost all sense of time; it was restored to him by the voice of the man of the house.

'So what were you thinking about so intently, young man? I have a simple proposal for you. You put your bike in the woodshed, your bag in the kitchen and go and wash the dust from your journey off in the lake. After that Mum and Mirjam will have got something on the table. Rein is coming home today, too. And in the evening we have the sauna and sauna refreshments. And we've got space as always for overnight guests. Does that sound all right?'

He said that he accepted the proposal with thanks.

The lake water was muddier this time, but not a single bird was singing in the reeds and bushes. A lone grebe was visible some way off, but when it saw him it dived, only to reappear much further away. A duck swam into the shelter of the reeds from the bathing spot with her now quite large ducklings.

There was no one to be seen close by. The bonfire site was still there but no fire had burnt in it for some time. He took off his clothes, beat them against the trunk of a stout alder and stepped into the water. He immediately had the thought that everything around him – the lake, the water-lilies, the vegetation on the shore without birdsong, the now-grown ducklings and something else that he hadn't even noticed meant one and the same thing – time was advancing quickly and inevitably towards autumn. Oh yes, and the grasshoppers with their stronger, more passionate song. The water was strangely warm, even warmer probably than the time they had come to swim as a group.

He swam as far as the water-lilies where he and Ester had swum on the day of his departure. There were fewer blooms. The leaves were now ragged, they had been eaten by insects or slugs; some of them had begun to yellow and some had browned at the edges. This, too, was part of the same autumnal message. The thought did not leave him: everything now felt like a message, everything had meaning. It meant late summer but much more besides. It was odd how all the best insights and ideas came to him when he was swimming or setting off on a swim. It was odd how the thing that sent the messages (to whom? to what end?) reduplicated them so much, said the selfsame thing over and again. Was it expecting the message to be better understood? Yet – and he thought this as he stepped on to the shore – life itself was also an endlessly and chaotically repetitious message.

What message was he a repetition of then? Was there someone somewhere in the world who was almost the same as him, who was different from him in only some trifling minute detail? If there was indeed such a person, would he ever be able to meet him? Would it be very important to meet his double? Perhaps the other person had received a much better education and much broader experiences of life, meaning there would be much to learn from him.

When he stood upright near the bank he suddenly heard the loud voices of a number of men. A group of people, apparently quite drunk, was on its way. A harsh reminder that the Kingdom of Heaven and the water kingdom existed next to the earthly kingdom where it was Saturday evening. He swished most of the water from his body, grabbed his clothes and scurried towards the house in his swimming trunks.

None the less he was seen.

'The priest's daughter must be in season. All sorts of guys are running around here,' shouted one voice, obviously deliberately loudly so that the retreating swimmer would hear. What the other voices said he could no longer hear. He dried himself off properly by the garden and got dressed. Perhaps the devil, he thought, does exist after all and shows himself at the right moment, just when it's most unpleasant for his victim. The voices that contained everything that made him feel humiliated and powerless, that unleashed intractable disgust and loathing in him. What was it? Was it that people did not want of their own free will to be sentient creatures but became power-hungry, hedonistic half people? Power was the opportunity to treat others unjustly, and they liked it. Why? Was it because injustice had been done to them? He thought that he had never really talked to anyone about it. With his friends he talked about Baudelaire, the Soothsayers and Coudenhove-Kalergi; with the Teacher about distant lands and cultures and about God; with Malle – now he suddenly remembered Malle – about the cinema and themselves. He suddenly had the feeling that he was like a summer marsh-treader that skates along the glittering surface of the water under which there is something dark and brutal that he does not comprehend, something he fears and instinctively tries to avoid. But, occasionally, under the surface of the water something or someone appears and reminds him of the existence of the dark, underwater world where all things devour each other. What if the dark, underwater thing rises to the surface specifically to grab him and swallow him up? He didn't know whether he feared death, but the under-water darkness, those mouths, the grabbing, the tentacles – he did indeed fear those.

In the kitchen the table had already been set. The others had eaten, and only Mirjam came to keep him company – she thought that people could always squeeze in one more slice of jam and bread and drink a cup of milk. It was as easy for him to get on with Mirjam as it was with Ester, although he usually felt awk-ward when he had to talk to children. Mirjam chatted away, without waiting for a reply or asking for her views to be endorsed. She was definite that when she fin-ished school she would study medicine and work as a rural doctor. She didn't at all like being in the city, and she did not want a job that meant living all the time in the city. She had been to Uncle Alo's and Aunty Ellen's a few times; it was very nice; there were gardens all around them, apple trees and flowers. Mirjam liked the spring and autumn flowers best, especially the stocks because they had such a lovely scent. The scent of stocks always took her back to her earliest childhood memories when they lived somewhere else and had stocks growing in the flowerbed.

Rein's father came in from the yard, sat beside them for a while and asked where he'd been and what he'd seen. It emerged that he knew the area where Meeta and Richard lived; he'd even taken the odd service there when the local pastor had been away. Then he got up to go to his own room and prepare the sermon for the following day.

'Do you always read your sermon from a piece of paper or do you sometimes just extemporize?' he asked.

The question was a sensible one: Rein's father said that he had no liking at all for reading from a piece of paper and that a sermon was not a literary or rhetori-cal masterpiece; instead, it was a narrative for people, talking to people. A pastor was someone who had learnt the Scriptures (if only that were always the case!) and was able to explain them to the congregation, awaken faith and understand-ing in them. But that was something that could only be done by talking to people, not by reading out a prepared text. But because of the authorities he always kept a paper copy of his address. Pastors had had problems; they had been arrested on accusations of delivering anti-Soviet sermons, and now and then KGB officers had recorded his sermons so he had to be ready for anything. If there was a problem over a particular address it was useful to take the text out of the drawer and pro-duce evidence.

Had he had difficulties with the KGB? He was thinking of more recently, when the KGB was known as the KGB, not in Stalin's time.

'Who hasn't! Intellectuals who think with their own heads have to have dealings with the authorities whether they are this side of the Iron Curtain or not. You probably will, too, so be ready – and keep your powder dry, as the English say.'

'What should you be most on the alert for when dealing with them?'

Rein's father thought most of all that the KGB and the whole apparatus of power wasn't as strong and powerful as it appeared. A repressive apparatus of this kind was something that was the purview of weak countries; it helped them to keep going, establish an impression of strength and power. The security forces and Party bosses were afraid; their famed watchfulness was a sign of fear. A frightened person endeavours to make himself frightening to scare others. How does a cat behave when it meets a dog? Its fur bristles, it hisses, it tries to make itself look more terrible and stronger than it is. In his view Russia was exactly like a cat that bristles and hisses to display its power to the Western world. The Kremlin was deceiving and scaring many people, but its deception could not last for very long. Fear steered the actions of state leaders, but fear was renowned for being a poor counsellor.

'It looks for the moment as if Russia is gaining victory upon victory. It is displaying its power in the world and in space. Country after country is falling into Communism as if into a black hole.'

'My young friend, that is just what I mean. The bristling fur and the sinister sound of the cat. There's also the fact that when national leaders can't cope with the affairs of their own country they are tempted to undertake a little international adventure – victory in war is the best way to pacify the populace and get around them. But the Western countries have acted wisely: they have established such a strong defence system, NATO, that Moscow cannot be confident of emerging victorious from a war with the West. So it is in an absurd position: an immense war machine is ready, but it cannot use it. The Russians must have more tanks than all other countries in the world put together; the aircraft and other hardware they have goes way beyond what anyone can comprehend, and now all that iron is stationary, accumulating rust and growing obsolete. It still does not give the Russians overwhelming superiority.'

'But haven't the Russians been cannily surrounding the West from the east and the south by way of Africa, Asia and South America?'

'They are clearly trying to, but that, too, is unlikely to succeed. The Russians have indeed acquired bases and support in a number of poor African countries, in Cuba and on the Asian rim but are losing China. China has clearly turned its back on Moscow; its former everlasting friendship is no more, and I believe it is only a question of time before they finally part company or even fall out. And there's probably no need to give a great deal of thought to which is the more important ally – the great eagle of China or a handful of sparrows from the black continent. That's the way it is. Look, I've got to get on with my work, but your question was what should you bear in mind in a meeting with the KGB people?'

That was indeed what he had asked.

'When dealing with them it's always worth bearing in mind what I was saying. They are not strong but weak – I mean the system is weak. The system will not endure very long; you will live to see it fold – perhaps even I will. It does mean, though, that there's no point boasting to them, provoking them, measuring yourself against them. In any case they can flatten people like us even if just to frighten others. But that's of no use to us. We will need every individual with a head and a heart. We will have to start from scratch one day, and it will be wonderful if youngsters like you have grown up then. So my advice is look after your life and your health. But also look after your conscience. Juhan Liiv was absolutely right when he wrote that

> It is easier to lift mountains,
> it is easier to carry cliffs,
> it is easier to take care of the world,
> than to nurse a troubled conscience.

'Be civil to them, but don't accept an offer to cooperate with them. At any time they can flatter or coax you and threaten you, but don't defer. Plenty of people have come to me to make confessions and complain and my take on it is very clear: there is no way now that they can force anyone to do their dirty work. Take care not to give them any opportunity for blackmail. Don't get involved with any boys'-own things – arms, leaflets and secret organizations. Be ready for D-Day, but don't try to hasten its arrival. The day will indeed come, and it may well come sooner than you think. Study, study, study, as Lenin or some other bearded wonder of theirs said.'

Rein's father gestured to him, winked and went upstairs to his room. He stood stock still for a moment; what he had been told was probably the exact type of thing a good father would say to his son. No one had ever talked to him about anything like that, but then, he had never had a father. He had a grandfather, but Grandfather was distant, someone from another time. But his grandfather and Rein's father were probably the same type of person, intelligent and reliable, who in their time helped found the Estonian State and even now, if D-Day came, would be ready to do what was required. And there was something else: Rein's father had expressed his confidence in him, had accepted him as one of his own, as a fully fledged representative of the next generation who would have to be ready to do the same. Would he be capable of it?

Rein arrived a bit later than anticipated. His bus had been cancelled, and he had

had to catch a different one that went via the main road and then walk a good four kilometres. The sun was already sinking behind the treetops, and the sauna was ready. They took large towels with them and two bottles of homebrew that one of the local villagers had made. Rein's father didn't come with them; he was always last in the sauna. The women went in first, and the wife was always the last one to leave. She washed her husband's back and then came back into the house, leaving her husband alone for an hour to whisk himself with the birch twigs and enjoy the warmth. Rein liked the heat of the sauna, but, and on this they were agreed, he didn't enjoy lying on the benches in the steam room for extended lengths of time. Certainly the most pleasant part of a sauna was to jump directly into a lake, but it was too far to go. Rein thought it was better that the sauna was not on the lakeside – all sorts of people went there; they would probably have broken into the sauna and some of them might even have set it alight. That's what had happened in several places: the pastor's family knew a lot about life in the area and one or two things had been heard from other colleagues. The water barrel was full of cold water, and was a pleasure to splash it on after the steam room. A couple of buckets of rainwater had been positioned next to it for hair-washing – it thoroughly cleaned the hair, and the next day it would be light, as if trying to fly away.

They had washed and rinsed their hair and were off back to the steam room when there was a knock at the door. Rein's mother, obviously much agitated, shouted that someone was drowning or had drowned in the lake and they should run to fetch help. They hastily pulled their underpants on to their wet bodies and ran to the bathing place, Rein in front.

Even from a long way off the loud crying of a drunken woman and her shouts for help could be heard. The campfire was still burning; it was already dusk. By the fire there were two other men as well as the screaming woman, one of them clearly so drunk that he was incapable of anything. Tthe other, who was more sober, was trying to explain something to Rein's father who had already got there. One man was already in the lake. He was swimming close to the shore there and dived under the water for a while. He obviously knew where to look for the drowning man, but the twilight was not making his job any easier.

'Is that where he is?' called Rein.

'So we understand,' replied his father.

Rein leapt into the water and in a couple of strong strokes was at the spot where the other man was swimming in circles, panting after his dive. He, too, jumped into the lake without really knowing what he should do. Rein's father evidently noticed his perplexity and shouted to him, 'If you're a good swimmer try to dive down. Otherwise better get out of there.'

Was he a good swimmer? For a moment the burning desire to help, to rescue, to do something good, battled the fear of hampering the others in his ineptitude and self-consciousness. His hesitation was fleeting, however. He had jumped into the water and was wading towards Rein and the villager, his ears resounding with the screams of the drunken woman that he tried to ignore:

'Oh shit! . . . stupid bastards . . . oh God, if you drown him . . . Help! Help!'

'You look over there!' panted Rein to him, nodding towards the edge of the reed bed.

He took a breath and dived. Under the water it was even darker, but the bottom wasn't far down. He tried to grope around, but the first time all he could feel was roots. He went underwater a second time, again without result, then Rein shouted, 'Got him! Come here, come here.'

Rein was indeed swimming towards the shore, dragging the drowned man behind him by his hair. It was not far to swim. The three of them, including the villager who had been the first to help, carried the man's lifeless naked body to the shore. There Rein's father took over. First they had to pour out the water that the man had inhaled and start artificial respiration. He didn't know how to do this, but there appeared to be some in the assembled crowd who did. He stood there with the others feeling relief that the man had been found and brought to the shore and regret that he had not been able to do anything. As a child, and even occasionally now, he had dreamt of rescuing someone, dragging a child from a burning house or from water, defending a girl against assailants . . . Now, for the first time in his life, just such an opportunity had arisen, albeit that the drowning man had not been a nice little child but a village drunk whose inebriated roaring had earlier made him hurry away from here. And even now it had fallen to him to wade ineptly in the wrong place and then as a bystander to watch whether they could breathe some life into him or not.

The drunken woman had fallen silent. She staggered closer and watched two men pressing down on the drowned man's chest in turn. Then came the sound of a distant mechanical roar; it came closer, stopped, and some moments later a man and woman in white came running over, probably a doctor or medical attendant and a nurse. The people let them through and the men giving artificial respiration stepped aside, allowing the medics to take over the still lifeless man lying on the ground.

'He's completely naked,' said the nurse. 'Put something over his nether regions.'

Someone approached with a large sauna towel. When the nurse covered the man lying on the ground up to his waist, the drunken woman said quietly, as if more to herself than to the people there, 'Why are you covering him up? He had such a gorgeous cock . . .'

'You should've grabbed him by his cock and not let him in the lake drunk,' said someone near by.

'Let's go. There's nothing more we can do here,' said Rein. He suddenly noticed that he was almost shivering. It really was time to go back to the warmth of the sauna. But perhaps the shivering was not down to the cold. He faltered – perhaps he should stay a little longer to see whether they managed to bring the drowned man back to life or not. Which outcome did he really want? Both, he felt. Perhaps even with a slight preference for the latter. That's how it was. Some part of him would have felt satisfaction at the drunk's death. Was it because he had fled from them earlier, or simply that the man and the whole group were repellent to him? But, on the other hand, the shamelessness of the drunken woman's words went to his heart. The woman had been completely sincere; more so than he was. The lakeside scene had acquired a touch of something quite archaically tragic and Old Testament-like.

He and Rein sat on a bench in the sauna's steam-room silence. He still could not get warm, and his teeth were chattering even more than when they had been outside. Only when Rein had thrown two more ladlefuls of water on to the hot stones did he feel the heat returning to his limbs.

'Do you think he'll live?' he asked.

'Don't know,' replied Rein. 'I doubt it.'

'Do you know the people there?' he continued.

'No. I've heard a bit about them, but I don't know them. Dad will.'

'Does he have much to do with people like that? Do they come and see him now and then?'

'Pretty rarely, I should think,' said Rein. 'But they have mothers, sisters, girl-friends – and they definitely do.'

They spoke no more of the drowned man. The feeling of cold had gone and even outside it no longer felt cool after the warmth of the sauna. Far off by the lake there was no one to be seen, so the story had reached its conclusion. The first thing he asked when he entered the kitchen was whether they had been able to revive the man or not. Rein's father shook his head. Help had come too late, the man had obviously inhaled a lot of water. Who was he? Who were his parents? The usual story: father in the German Army then in the prison camps, mother slaving away on a collective farm, two sons with no supervision. One became a decent citizen and later went to the Academy of Agriculture to study agronomy, but the other had no desire to learn, wanted to earn money, did courses on tractor-driving but never worked at it properly, began drinking and was chucked out. Recently he'd undertaken casual labour hitching up tractors, assisting in work-shops, picking out stones in the field and doing whatever was required. The women had liked him – he had a child with a girl in the town – but just as he had been a poor son to his mother he was a poor father to his son. And now he was nothing to anyone any more. The mother cared deeply about him as a child, per-haps that was the cause of it. The other one, the elder brother, had to look after himself; he'd not been spoilt. When their father returned from Siberia he was strict with his sons and demanding, exactly the opposite of their mother. Perhaps this prompted defiance in the boy. He did not get on at all with his father – in fact, his father had thrown him out a couple of times but had allowed him to return when he saw the mother's grief and distress.

'One of many tragic Estonian life stories, the kind no one ever writes down, least of all the person concerned,' finished Rein's father.

'Would there be any point in writing about it?' he asked.

'I believe there would,' replied Rein's father. 'There's probably something valuable and informative in every individual's life story. The problem lies only in the fact that it is so difficult to allow another person into it, to see and understand it. People who are able to talk about themselves and their lives find it easier. Those who aren't are not understood and perhaps do not even understand themselves.'

'Do you think that people in general want to understand themselves? You men are always so intellectual,' put in Rein's mother unexpectedly.

'Yes, I really do,' said her husband firmly. 'I saw, especially when I was in the Siberian camp, that a person is stronger when he finds certainty, when he understands who he is and what he wants from life.'

'And perhaps what life wants from him?' he asked, sensing that what they were talking about concerned him more than he could have initially thought. Perhaps it was the shadow of the recent death that had made them earnest.

'People usually talk about the meaning of life, searching for the meaning of life,' replied the father. 'If you think about it it's not clear what this meaning of life actually is that people are seeking. When someone addresses that issue, and it does happen from time to time, I start with Hemingway, who quoted John Donne the theologian poet. Donne wrote that no man is an island, that we are all one together; we all reach out to each other and are involved with each other, and any man's death is to a greater or lesser extent everyone's death. Human existence is collective existence, a joint existence. But it is not easy;, it is not easy to bear one's burden by oneself, let alone those of others. And so unnoticeably, subconsciously, automatically, we try to be on our own, independent and heedless of everyone else. We think that alone is easier. But in fact it isn't. Together is easier; together it is easier to bear human existence. That was probably what Jesus had in mind when he said that where two or three were gathered together in his name he was there also. To understand this idea is to find the meaning of life or at least an important part of it.'

The pastor's conversation was verging on a sermon, but that fact did not trouble him at all for the moment. He remembered something that had once surprised him when he had thought it.

'It has occurred to me that it is not true that we are born and die alone. When a person is born he is not alone, his mother is there giving birth to him. And a dying man, as far as I know, is also very much in need of the company of someone else. It is much easier for him to die if he is not alone . . .'

'That's absolutely right, I can confirm it on the back of my work and experience,' agreed Rein's father. 'In the camps perhaps the only good thing that I managed to do in the hospital was to hold the hands of the dying and talk to them while they were capable of hearing and understanding. And I know that a dying man is much more peaceful and that it is much easier for him if he is not alone . . .'

'So does faith mean that a religious man is never alone either in life or in death?' he asked.

'Yes, it does,' replied Rein's father.

22

He slept deeply that night, but his dreams were strange, even troubled. When he woke up in the morning he could remember the last one. The Teacher and Ester were in it, of course. They, along with someone else who was a mixture of Rein and Jüri Targama, had to take a train to a place whose name for some reason or other was Windward Paris. He wanted to go with them but couldn't get his packing done; then he wanted to run to the station, but the street was full of people; then he tried to run through the old wooden houses with interconnecting doors, but the doors were old and nailed shut and he had to break them open. He knew that he would definitely be late, that he was late, but still he hurried on, now out of sheer despair and anger.

It was a relief to wake up. Through the gap in the curtains a sunbeam shone straight on to Rein's cluttered desk, and the scent of a summer morning came in through the half-open window. Everything augured well for a beautiful day, a wondrous day for him. The Teacher was coming here, and they could spend the whole day together.

Rein was still asleep. He got dressed quietly and went downstairs. His hostess was busy in the kitchen.

'You're up early,' she said. It was true, it was only just seven; usually he didn't get up so early unless he had to, and then he was sleepy and grouchy. But this time everything was different. At ten o'clock they would go to the church service; the bus from the city would arrive here after quarter to one. They would have a bite to eat and go on a short walk, perhaps even around the lake. The Teacher and Ellen were staying until Monday when they would return to the city. As would he but on his bicycle. He was a bit disappointed at this. If he had not had his bike he and the Teacher would have been able to travel together and talk. But all this might well have been too much. No one should be that lucky.

The pastor himself had drunk his coffee and was already in the church in the vestry, where the iron stove probably had to be lit even in summer to give the room warmth. Rein said his father always sat there before the service, collecting his thoughts.

They didn't talk much at the breakfast table; they ate in silence, as if they had to collect their own thoughts for the service. He wasn't particularly hungry or in much of a talking mood; it was as if something were pressing down on his chest. He would have liked to be alone for a while. So he said that he was going for a walk for a bit and left without particularly thinking where he was going. His feet and the path took him towards the church and then past it to the cemetery, a place he had not visited before. The old iron gate under the stone arch was rusty and falling down; it had clearly not been moved for years. Perhaps the newer area of the cemetery was reached from somewhere else. From the gate a cobbled path strewn with weeds led to the blessing-house – that was what his family called the little house with tiny windows. Several tiles had fallen off the blessing-house roof; someone had tried to cover the holes with sheet metal. A dove dozed in the unglazed gable window.

The graves of the squires and other members of the higher classes had once been here, but now nothing could be seen through the dense bushes but a few crooked iron crosses and moss-covered stone sculptures. He pushed the branches aside. Here behind the twisted iron railings, which had been partially prised open, he could see large, heavy gravestones, evidently for the noblemen. Moss and litter shrouded them. He approached the first one, pushed aside the fallen leaves and twigs and tried to read the writing on the stone. He wasn't particularly successful; the dead person's name was indistinct, and the only thing he could see clearly was *Hier ruhet in Gott*. Next to the stone lay an as yet unrusted tin can and a vodka bottle; in the grass he could see another bottle and something that had once been a newspaper.

There were no railings around the next gravestone; people seemed to have tried to move parts of what had been the high stone circle and had even succeeded in places. Of the three gravestones one was broken, probably by human handiwork. The writing was illegible here, too, it could be von Stackelberg, but he might have been mistaken, as Stackelberg was simply one of the few aristocratic names familiar to him. He turned back to the public road. He could have sat here and written an elegy as had once been the fashion in England. What was it now? The old professor had talked about it. Yes, it must be Thomas Gray and 'Elegy on a Country Churchyard'. Since his childhood, cemeteries had been more like gardens to him where he would go for walks with Grandfather, watch the birds and look at the flowers. They hadn't talked much about the people under the ground. When he was very small he had heard the grown-ups talking about someone who had eaten poison and died. He had understood that the dead ate poison under the ground and imagined them sitting in the dark sipping poison from old rusty tin cans. He had also seen tin cans in Tartu cemetery, either left behind by drunks or used as flower holders or candlesticks.

The burial plots of the country folk were behind the blessing-house; nearest to it were the oldest slabs from the previous century, each with its iron cross. The real old Võrumaa names – Tobreluts, Vaglaraud, Kirotaja – did they still exist, or had they been completely Estonianized? Tobreluts to Tammemägi, Vaglaraud to Varikmaa, Kirotaja to Kullamaa ...

Beyond here, the cemetery became gradually more modern. Instead of crosses there were white-stone or cement slabs on the graves – some of the more recent ones were diamond-shaped, a picture carved into them in black, sometimes a farmhouse, sometimes a torch, sometimes a cross. A black cross on white. The path was wider, and he could see broad wheel ruts – clearly someone had travelled here in a large car or a tractor. Carrying earth or a large stone slab. Or a body in its coffin. The very new graves were by the path, and one burial mound still bore withered flowers and wreaths. It was a small mound, and among the flowers there was a wooden tablet with some writing. Yes, it was a child's grave. Sirle had died at the age of four. Children's deaths were something that always affected him strongly. He realized that he had hoped it wasn't a child. Just as whenever he saw a small hump lying on the road in the distance he hoped that it wasn't a dead bird or animal. Just as when he saw Grandfather resting in bed in the room next door he hoped that he hadn't died. He would stand by the door, quietly listening out for whether Grandfather was breathing. However, sometimes at night, when Grandfather's coughing and moaning woke him up, he had wished him dead. In the morning, when he was feeling embarrassed about it, he thought that there were probably people who wished their relatives dead, plenty of them, and that he wasn't alone in his sin. But what is sin? What did that word mean to him? Something that can be felt physically, something that sticks to the flesh like mud – it is vile but, none the less, somehow fascinating. And sin was definitely bound up with a woman's body. It was hidden in the concealed places of her body, between her thighs and buttocks, even in her armpits, sometimes in her mouth and her eyes. In other respects he liked a woman's body: it was beautiful, and there was lightness in its beauty. Iit had no sin. Sin made women's bodies and even their smell heavy, at once seductive and intimidating. There was something about it that reminded him of the churchyard, or perhaps less the churchyard than the dissection room on Toome Hill and the old gardens themselves where there were more signs of death, weariness and mouldering than in the churchyard, something heavy and clammy that it was difficult to rid oneself of but which pressed the mind down towards the black earth.

Ester's body was different. It had no sin; it was light and beautiful. Probably because he had fallen in love with her. Yes, it was now fully clear to him. It was over with Malle. He would have to tell her when they saw each other in the autumn. Perhaps Malle even knew that the thing they had was not the real thing. That's why it hadn't worked out between them. It would with Ester, no question. Love solves everything. Where there's love there are no problems, there are no questions; it is bright and clear . . . Who was it who wrote that love is an eternity of itself? St Augustine? Krishnamurti?

He had made his way back to the chapel and the graves of the barons, overgrown with thickets, and stopped there. A garden-warbler was hopping in a lilac bush, calling a warning. It must have a nest or chicks here. The white tower and red roof of the church were visible further off between the trees. The thought that he had had just now came back like a bow wave, a bow wave of light. Love. What did Paul write? If I have not love . . . Love bears all things, can do all things, endures all things . . . That was it, more or less. Love was stronger than death, too. Now he felt this to be true. Where there is love there is no death, there is no sin, there is nothing that can pull you into the earth, the mire, sin and lust. That's right, love is not lust. Love is just love; it can only be love.

How had he not understood this before? It was so simple. Everything important was love, only love. Nothing else was important, death was not important. That was the purpose of redemption, not that man did not die but that death did not exist for him. Death was not important; death was completely empty, futile. Perhaps that was Jesus' message, too. The resurrection and the life, that was the same as love. If there is love then you will be resurrected from the earth, the soil, then you will rise up somewhere into the light, into another, better place and existence. How did Dante write about love at the end of *The Divine Comedy*? He had studied some Italian and with the help of French and Latin was able to understand Dante. *The Divine Comedy* was a story of love, love that starts with an accidental meeting between a man and a woman. Beatrice. What did that name mean? Blessedness? *Beata* was 'blessed', the feminine form of *beatus*. But Ester. Ester had to mean star. Now he remembered: 'The Love that moves the sun and the other stars'.

The Love which (or who?) moves the sun and the other stars. Love was the true mover which (who?) did not itself move. Love is God; God is love. Yes, Dante still lived in a pre-Copernican world. To him the sun was a star, a planet that revolved around the earth. But in love's light it was of no importance who revolved around whom, what revolved around what. Whether he revolved around Ester or Ester revolved around him . . .

Now he felt he could almost say 'God exists'. Ester had brought him to this truth. Ester, his guiding star. Sign, star, portent. The whole This began with Ester, wonder, love and resurrection. The This he felt here in the churchyard was in fact the same This he had felt while swimming in the river. Love was wonder, and wonder was love; love and wonder reveal what is called the power of God, the love of God. Beatrice. Ester.

The church bell was ringing ineffectively with a dull sound, but he felt that that, too, was a sign, an invitation. He would talk to Ester. He would ask Ester's father what he would have to know to be confirmed and enter the Lutheran Church. He would learn everything thoroughly, the catechism, the Lord's Prayer and hymns. He would become a Lutheran; he would start going to church. Perhaps he would go and study where Rein was studying, marry Ester, become a minister, a theologian. He would have to discuss the theologian part with the Teacher. He had so much to discuss with the Teacher – the This that happened to him there in the river and the other This that happened here in the old churchyard. But now he had to go; he had promised to go. Promised himself and his host and hostess.

In the church there were a dozen elderly women, two elderly gentlemen and one younger couple, presumably husband and wife. And Rein, of course. He sat in the back pew and picked up an old, shabby-looking hymn book from the desk. He had held a hymn book twice before, but each time had returned it deeply disappointed. It wasn't poetry but coarse doggerel. He had not found true religious feeling in hymns either. Reading 'A fortress firm, a refuge', he had difficulty understanding how Heine and Engels could regard it as the 'Marseillaise' of the Reformation – or should that be the Peasants' War?

The hymn book here seemed to be in southern Estonian. It was interesting to leaf through on linguistic grounds if nothing else. His eye was caught by a hymn he had not noticed before:

> Give us gentle rain, oh Lord,
> for soil that's dry as sand.

They were not the words just of a religious song but of a religious poem, so to speak. Was this also a sign – the fact that he had now found this beautiful hymn? A sign that even in the bosom of the Lutheran Church there could be a place for a person like him. But could there be any doubt on that score when the Teacher and Ester and the others were in that Church? The hymns . . . But the hymns could be retranslated, reworked – he himself could even set to work on this. Perhaps it was even his calling?

The organ began to play a new piece, more loudly. He lifted his gaze and saw that Rein's father had come in and was standing before the altar. This must be a ritual: first talk to God, then to the people. The minister is the middleman, he must make one voice audible to the other. It was not enough for the congregation, though; it produced its own voice. It was a little feeble, uncertain, some elderly ladies sang the psalms, whose numbers were given on the board on the wall, as loudly as they did wrongly. They were singing from the hymn book written in formal Estonian. He put down the volume in Tartu dialect and reached for the other one on the rack in front. He looked at the hymn and suddenly felt that his world and he were split into two worlds moving at different speeds and to different rhythms. It was strange, but it also hurt. Both worlds, both hes, had their own rhythms, each of which was incompatible with the other. He felt this incompatibility, interference, almost as physical pain. In the cemetery he had not really noticed that a rhythm had arrived together with the ecstatic brightness; now, against the background of the dragging, wavering hymn, he felt it clearly. The hymn cut into the flesh like a blunt, rusty blade. One him closed his eyes, wanted to put his hands over his ears, run away, but the other him would not let him, held fast to the rack – now he realized why there was such an expression as 'racked with pain'. Which was the real him?

The first, the real him, was like a child; yes, it was the child in him, the person he had once been and, in fact, still was but who had been unable to move in the garment he had outgrown, had for some reason or other even forgotten that he existed and who he was. But hadn't Jesus said that you had to become like a child, and didn't he say to let the dead bury their own dead? So who was he? Living or dead? Living like this, a normal everyday life was also dying, the shell of habits, beliefs and commitments that grows around a newborn child is a coffin, a sarcophagus. No, that must not happen; he had to remain a child, had to become a child again, he repeated to himself almost in panic. He did not want to be one of the dead who sometimes buried their own dead here in the churchyard. No, he didn't want that.

The hymn ended with a plaintive, polyphonic sigh. He had not actually noticed the words only subconsciously registered that they were empty and ugly. It was something similar: living power, the power born as a child was confined to clumsy verses, deadened into something that occasionally sounded like poetry but had nothing to do with it. Poetry was something that could arise in a child's mind, in the mind of one who had become a child, not the pages full of theologically correct and metrically awkward – couldn't they at least have scanned well? – stanzas.

Poetry as an innocent childlike mindset, poetry as becoming a child, the return to the original light, which always came to his mind when he tried to rewind his thoughts to his earliest memories. A light-grey flickering light in which there was nothing yet everything that would later come and had to come. Did he want to go back there?

He looked up at the church windows. There was light there, too, but it wasn't this, this was only the morning light of late summer shining through the window, light beams through the linden leaves, spiders' webs and dead insects that had died in the window, struggling towards the light. The church as a light trap, the church that catches the light within itself but from which there is no escape to the light.

Rein's father had gone into the pulpit. In his black gown and hat he looked strange and even stranger when he began his sermon. It was from Mark, about a deaf man to whom Jesus gave hearing. He thought that he should tell the story to the deaf, either to the genuinely deaf or to people who have ears but who do not hear. The preacher would probably steer his story in that direction, too.

He noticed that he was again one person; he was once more the person he had been before. Was the This he had met in the cemetery gone? Was he now once more back in his old self, his old shell? The thought startled him. Reversion after ecstasy was one of the most ghastly experiences, he was only too well aware. Where was the other him, the child who saw the light? Where was the light? No, it hadn't disappeared; it was still there, in spite of the dragging hymns and the dull sermon. The realization came suddenly along with surprise that it hadn't come before. Light is love, love is light. The thing that could cut through his shell, bring him back to what he called the light, was love. In love there are children, in love one becomes as a child. All this was part of one thing: love, God's love and the fact that we are God's children. God is love, God is light . . . . Divine and earthly love? His love for Ester? No, there cannot be two kinds of love; love is something that knows no boundaries, connects everything, makes everything one, man and woman, child and adult, brings everything into the light that has no boundaries or shadows.

He was incapable of listening to the sermon, although it seemed to have been put together well and professionally. A sermon about ears that do not hear to ears that do not hear. Or maybe they do . . . He turned his gaze to the windows through which the light came. It bore a slight resemblance to the light that had been there a short time before, and for a moment he saw the form of a woman emerge clearly in the light. A transparent, barely visible form. Who was it? The light itself? Love? Ester?

Dismayed, he sensed that the sermon was now and then evoking in him the same dissonance that the hymn had previously. When preaching, Rein's father was like a reincarnation of the stereotypical pastor who reads the explanatory-admonishing text to the people. Something that had little relation to the wonderful individual he was and even less to the word of God.

Yet now Rein's father was saying something that he would not even have hoped to hear. He was talking about the sounds of nature, the sounds of God's nature that we, the people, do not, cannot or will not hear. Yet those sounds occasionally speak to us, want us to hear them. Now he felt that today's sermon had something for him, too. For him, for the others, for everyone. Strange how the pastor's sermon could, in love's light, acquire different, deeper or higher meanings as the Koran or the Bible did to mystics.

He began gradually to get cold: the burning spirit was unable (or unwilling) to warm his body. The cold brought with it weariness – he already knew that the ecstasy sometimes ended like this. Now he only had to wait for the end of the service. The sermon wasn't long, perhaps because there was something in it for him. The hymns, though, felt long and drawn out – they were even more depressingly empty and ugly. What did God, in whose praise the hymns were conceived, feel? What did God ever *feel*? What did He need? Praise? Gratitude? Love?

Outside, the late summer day shone especially bright. The sun warmed his back pleasantly and somewhere in the churchyard a young chiffchaff was practising its song. He waited for Rein, and they walked home together. In two hours' time the bus was due and, travelling on the bus, the Teacher. The thought made him at once cheerful and anxious: he was both looking forward to and fearful of the Teacher's arrival. He feared he would not be able to say or ask the things he needed to say and ask. He feared and wanted to talk about the thing that was now most important to him – love, Ester, the This that had overwhelmed him here in the chapel garden and there swimming in the river. But he knew that the This was very difficult to talk about.

23

He went to meet the visitors with Rein. The windows in the shelter at the bus stop had been broken and the walls had those drawings and graffiti on them that appear on all bus-shelter and toilet walls. His gaze alighted on the word 'cock', and suddenly he saw the drowned man and the woman crying over his withered manhood. Perhaps someone from the group yesterday had written this word here. Why? What did it mean? He felt that he failed to understand any of the things that were so obvious to people who think and question less . . . But further pondering of his thinking and doubting was something he had no more time for: the sound of the bus could be heard in the distance, and in a few moments it came around the corner and into view. The dust cloud fell further back; a strip of tarmac ran through the village.

Yes, there they were, Ellen and the Teacher, and then . . . he felt both hot and cold. The third person to alight from the bus was Ester, carrying a faded green backpack.

The Teacher bowed as ceremonially as in the city; Ellen smiled and nodded, Ester smiled, too, a little slyly, he felt, and said, 'They brought me along, too, as porter.'

'We've got some goodies from the town in there,' added Ellen.

'Great that you could come as well,' said Ester, smiling. This time it was definitely directed towards him.

The heat and cold had become torpor; he was afraid he would be unable to open his mouth if he had to say anything. But she gave him a couple of moments more to collect himself.

'Did you know we were coming? Were you able to phone Dad?'

No, he hadn't phoned. He'd just happened to arrive at the same time as them. But Ester wasn't supposed to be here yet.

No, she wasn't, but it just so happened that the practical ended a bit early, and Alo and Ellen sweet-talked her into coming with them to help carry their bags. So she had. She had even surprised herself a bit.

No one could have been more surprised than him, but he didn't dare to say so. At least not now. First he had to collect himself.

He would have liked to carry something but there was nothing left. Ester would not have handed over the large backpack anyway, and Ellen's bag had been monopolized by Rein. He also felt incapable at first of saying anything to the visitors. So he walked behind the others, especially Ester, whose only visible features were her head of fair hair, the green backpack and her legs. He wondered intently whether he would be able to talk to Ester and what he should say, what he should tell her. Once more he had divided into more than one: one him, the boy in love, trod along the road and said not a word; another him marvelled at this and felt slightly embarrassed; a third him looked upon all this from afar without feeling any particular interest – to this him the walkers were like small insects with their own loves and fears in the middle of a landscape anticipating the autumn. Which of these three hims – he sensed that's how many there were, that there may even be more – was the real, true him?

After a snack they decided to go on a trip around the lake. The Teacher and Ellen had done the route before, not to mention Ester and Rein, but, as the Teacher had said at the table, it was not possible to see the same country scene twice: every season, every time of day, every moment it was different. Besides, he hadn't been to the other end of the lake for probably five years. The trip was a good ten or twelve kilometres – a genuine achievement for the Teacher, who had heart trouble. But perhaps he was the best judge of what he could do and what he wanted to do, and anyway Ellen would not have allowed him to embark on anything too adventurous.

At the table everything was more straightforward than he had feared. The Teacher and Ellen talked nearly non-stop to the family; they reminisced about their old university days, professors, fellow students and colleagues who had been scattered in any number of directions all around the world. All the clergy had now returned from Siberia; letters and books had arrived from those who had taken refuge in the West – some had even risked a visit to Estonia. The young people did not have much to say on this subject, but at one point Ellen noted that nowadays university could not be as interesting as in the past, and Ester said that in some areas – for example, geography and geology – it was probably more interesting because they went on lots of expeditions to places like the Kola Peninsula, the Urals and the Far East. Rein's father disclosed his fear that the university was becoming provincial; the Teacher stated that the opposite was the case. In his view, during the Republic the university had been more provincial than it was now as young people read books other than ones in German these days. He was of the view that they would come to make greater use of ties with Russia; there was more to learn from the Russians than Western Europe, at least where oriental studies were concerned.

'But there's no theology or proper philosophy,' persisted Ellen.

'What was the old Tartu theology?' said the Teacher. 'An institute to prepare men for the ministry, helping them to find a good job. Faith and theology didn't interest anyone much, only some part-time young women students who attended before they got married. Things are much better these days at our little college: the students who come are there because of a genuine faith or for a genuine humanitarian education. Sometimes it is a sheer delight to lecture them and sit on the examination board for the oral exams.'

He had never before felt so free and confident in a place that was half strange to him and among people who were half strangers. It meant that there was no need for him to remind the others of who he was, or to try to attract attention like young people do, as even he did sometimes. It was more pleasant to listen, and in so doing he could also watch Ester in peace; she, too, was listening more than she was talking. She listened very attentively. Watching her closely, you might get the impression that she listened with eyes and ears at once. Where he was concerned, he listened more with his eyes; in other words, he watched Ester and largely ignored what was being said. There was no need for anything else; it was enough to be near Ester, see her, listen to her voice. It would be bliss. It was bliss, a bliss that not even the pendulum clock ticking away on the wall could spoil when it reminded them that they really ought to get down from the table soon and go on their trip. The trip promised to become part of the bliss, and there was a long day ahead.

They took the same path as when he and Ester had gone to get the bread. The greenery was already looking tired; closer inspection revealed that all the leaves on the trees were covered in dark fungal spots and full of holes made by maggots. Once Grandfather had shown him – it must have been in Toome or maybe even in the cemetery – and explained why death was a necessary thing in nature: the old leaves fell ill and became crippled like old people and animals and had to fall to allow new, young, strong ones to grow. Grandfather was a materialist. His world was simple and clear cut and honest in its own way. It had no place for faith or mysticism. Sometimes this world felt banal and grey; everything that interested his grandfather was distant and alien to him. But now, as he remembered that long-ago walk somewhere in a park in Tartu, he suddenly felt that he had been reconciled to his grandfather and his grandfather's world. Grandfather was very honest indeed, sometimes downright foolishly honest. He had emerged alive from the ruins of his world and his home without losing his own faith in the pattern of nature and history, even though the brave new world had cast him aside, ordered him to live in poverty in the back room of a communal apartment. He should definitely, he thought, say something good, something friendly to his grandfather. Such things did not happen often in their family: affection was not expressed; love was not really shown. He was thinking of the awkward, strange feeling he had when Grandfather had once called him 'my dear' or the last time he had wet the bed and talked of his love for Grandma. Now he would probably be able to talk to Grandfather; something had opened up in him, he was no longer ashamed to talk about what he felt.

He knew he would soon talk to Ester. Perhaps he should talk to Malle first. It was over now with Malle. But he should talk it through with her. He didn't really even know what he and everything that they had had between them meant to her.

The Teacher walked in front with Ester; next to them – or behind them, where the path grew narrower – came Ellen, then, a short distance behind, he and Rein. Rein was comfortable with silence, and he was grateful for it because he wanted to be alone with his thoughts and the chance to watch Ester, her fluttering fringe, which she occasionally flicked from her face with a charming, feminine gesture, her sunburnt brown arms and the bobbing of her buttocks under her skirt. It was probably too much. For the first time he clearly felt lust for her; a desire that hitherto had been concealed below something else – it had to be love – had now broken free and was insistent. Yet the road to this point had been a long one: he had not even talked to her; the memory of his inability to do so in the spring distressed him, and he was startled by the realization that there was something within him that was stronger than he was, something capable of suddenly taking the reins from him. Yes, perhaps at any moment he would lose his self-control, do something stupid. It cowed him. He tried to look somewhere else, inhaled deeply several times and then held his breath for a short while. After several attempts he felt steadier. He was even able to wonder what had become of the This, the great certainty-light that he had last met in the cemetery and the church. Was it vanishing, too, as it had last time, leaving depression or internal chaos in its wake? He was mildly astonished to realize that he did not even understand whether there was anything left of the This or not. Fortunately they were walking fairly quickly, even the Teacher – perhaps he had caught Ester's nimbleness. Ellen seemed to be a good walker, too. The pace gradually began to tire the body and relax the mind.

Ellen now lagged behind the Teacher and Ester and joined the two boys. 'I sometimes think that youth is mildly infectious,' she said. 'Look at Alo. In the city he sometimes drags one foot in front of the other. Now he's skipping around like a young goat.'

'Isn't that the influence of youth and nature combined?' he suggested, feeling relief that he could take up a conversation.

'Probably,' agreed Ellen. 'For us, these walks in the *Grüne* – sorry, it's better that Alo doesn't hear me using Germanized words or he'd be angry – are so important. We probably couldn't carry on without them. As a young woman I failed to understand that in old age you feel how your body insists on having what it missed out on in youth. Rein and Ester are proof that playing sport has a positive effect on people. Although Alo has never done any sport he at least worked hard on the land as a boy, otherwise his illnesses would have killed him long ago. Do you do any sport?' Ellen asked, turning towards him and touching his arm.

He felt how the familiarity of her gesture suddenly made him feel as if his feet were somewhere very far away and were walking automatically along the path among the undergrowth. But his reply was almost automatic. 'Not so much sport any more, but I do cycle around southern Estonia.'

Ellen had also cycled in her youth. She even complained that Alo could not ride a bike and that had meant she'd had to stop when they got married.

In the end the undergrowth and the path brought them to a small clearing. This was the best place to get the flask of coffee out and the sandwiches. Usually they wouldn't have, but they all seemed to be aware that the Teacher was not to be allowed to overstretch himself. He was probably aware of the fact himself. There was even a small cloth in Rein's backpack, and it was spread ceremonially on a large tree stump.

'Just like the city Germans in the *Grüne*,' the Teacher acknowledged, one corner of his mouth pointing down, the other slanting up.

Ellen winked surreptitiously at him and Rein.

The sandwiches did indeed taste different here, perhaps because Ester had made them. Ester was sitting on a log nearer the lake; it was so good to be able to see her and the lake at the same time. Here around the edge of the clearing the wind was blowing, a wind they had not particularly felt in the forest and on the path. It seemed to be stronger on the lake; among the poles and roots along the bank the waves had worked themselves into a white foam in places.

'Real windy day today,' remarked Ellen.

'I've always thought that the wind had a part to play in the process that gave rise to what we describe as consciousness in man,' announced the Teacher, lighting a cigarette. 'The wind was a very enigmatic thing to man's ancestor: it can't be seen, yet it moves and moves things, you feel it on your face and in your hair; it touches you, but you can't touch it . . .'

He thought he would be only too glad to be the wind right now, gusting from the lake and ruffling Ester's hair. He would be able to feel her all over, as much as he wanted.

'But isn't the biggest catastrophe that man acquired a consciousness that he is unable to do anything intelligent with?' he pursued the conversation.

'Yes, so I've thought myself on many an occasion . . .' nodded the Teacher. 'But we still probably do not know why we were given consciousness; we haven't yet learnt to use even the smallest part of it correctly.'

'So what do you think man could achieve with consciousness?' he asked.

'Well, who can tell? There are so many opportunities. There are so many beautiful utopias that become much more possible as man's opportunities grow. Personally, I have always thought that we could transform the world into an enormous park and garden, an earthly paradise . . . By the way, have you read anything on Roger Bacon and Franciscan spirituality?'

He had to confess that he had come across Bacon's name somewhere once, but that was all.

'Bacon was, to my mind, one of the more original figures of the Middle Ages, although there were other thinkers like him. Bacon was an engineering nut, a bit like Leonardo later. He dreamt of flying machines that moved under their own power and other things. But Bacon also had his own philosophy: he believed that man had been put on this earth to work a great transformation on it and to make everything new as the prophets had foretold. Bacon also had an interest in alchemy, and this was evident in his discourse. Do you know what a catalyst is?'

He did.

'Good. I would even go so far as to say that Bacon saw man as a catalyst who had to set off a reaction here on the planet that would transform the earthly and low into the heavenly and exalted; the earth into heaven, desert into paradise. And he believed that that was why man had been given reasoning; that was why he had to build up his knowledge and skills using the classical method *scientiam et technem*. Or, as we would put it, science and technology.'

'What would your Bacon say if he could see what man has done with science and technology?' Ellen interrupted.

'I have, when in a dark mood, occasionally thought that Auschwitz and Hiroshima would sound a deathblow to Bacon's utopias. But sometimes I think perhaps not. There are always possibilities.'

'Aren't there just too many people on the earth already?' he asked.

'Do you know how many gardeners the kings and nobles of old needed for their parks and gardens?'

He couldn't even guess.

'At least a couple of hundred but sometimes more. And if planet earth were one huge garden there might be a need for even more gardeners than there are people now. Besides, you probably haven't read about experiments where field crops were grown in beds like garden vegetables? No. Small wonder. The results were shocking: one seed sprouted a mass of stems and heads and produced up to a hundred seeds. The earth is bounteous when it is cultivated with care and love. Crop cultivation, though, is a compromise between human convenience and the needs of the earth. But a price must be paid for convenience sooner or later.'

A thought came to him that he could not keep to himself. 'So is the Old Testament wrong then when it says "in the sweat of your face you shall eat bread"? Hasn't history shown this to be true?'

'Of course. And as you've brought up the subject of the Old Testament then I would infer something else. The fact that God put man here on the Earth as lord of the manor, as it were. He gave us His manor, as it were, with all its crawling, flying and running creatures and said that we should govern it. Then He left – perhaps He had other, maybe more important things to do than deal with planet Terra. Sometimes, when I can't sleep, I wonder what will happen when He comes back to call us to account for what's happened to the manor. He will open His register containing the names of all the types of animals and plants and ask what's become of the first one, the second one, the third . . . One day we will have to render account of what we have done to the mammoth, the moa, the passenger pigeon, Steller's sea cow . . . Have you read anything on ecology?'

He shook his head.

'Ecology, if we stay with the manor metaphor, is the science of housekeeping, instruction on the great system of nature where everything is linked to everything else. The science that an astute lord of the manor must know. Ecologists have recently begun to make their voices heard; they are trying to explain to the lords of the manor that their view of the world must change, that things cannot continue as they are. Man is poisoning nature and in so doing is poisoning himself. I presume you don't know what effect the DDT that we use to kill bugs and flies has on nature?'

He did not, of course.

'Right, well, I don't want to hold a lecture on it here. Ask Ester. She can tell you about it. She's more of an ecologist than I am. Isn't that right, Ester? Tell this young man about the eagle eggs . . .'

'I will, but another time. We should be off now if we ever want to get around the lake.'

Ellen backed her up. They hadn't come here to give a lecture or listen to one. He could do that in Tartu when he came around. In fact, he could go to the consistory to study – at least he would get a proper humanitarian education there.

Ellen had taken the words out of his mouth. He had said nothing. The next time they stopped he would take it upon himself and discuss it with the Teacher himself. He looked towards the Teacher and Ester and thought that they were the two people he now loved most of all. How strange and sad that he had probably never been able to tell his own mother or grandmother or grandfather that he loved them. Perhaps because they'd always been with him, perhaps because love was something that seeks to draw closer those who are further away. Something you understand from a distance.

The Teacher and Ester were sitting in the same pose; even their heads were both leaning to the left and their eyes squinting in the sun. They were unexpectedly similar, as if they were related. Were they, he wondered, thinking the very same thing at that moment? Did he and Ester think, would they think the same if . . . ?

The path led diagonally up through the clearing and now weaved along the flatter land. Ester explained that before the war the lakeside had chiefly been flat hay meadows, pasture and strips of land for crops. Now it was all covered in thickets because nothing could be done on the steep slopes with heavy machinery. Many of the farms had been abandoned. People didn't keep as many livestock so didn't need to make hay everywhere as they used to previously. And individuals weren't allowed to have their own strips of land.

'Sheep would probably be the best thing to keep here; they'd keep the slopes cropped and open up the views across to the lake,' said Ellen.

'Sheep present problems in south Estonia,' said the Teacher. 'There are lots of spring fens on the slopes and in the hollows between the hills. There are also all kinds of worms there, and they spread liver flukes to the sheep. In the old days the waterfront pastures of the west of the country were regarded as the best place for rearing sheep, but hereabouts, as far as I recall, there was always concern about various illnesses and parasites.'

Once more he could not but marvel at the Teacher's knowledge. He could not have anticipated his being able to say anything about the subject of sheep husbandry . . . He looked forward to the opportunity to talk about his own idea of perhaps going to study theology. He would have to talk to Ester about it, too, but again felt that it would be better to do so in the city. He would have to ask Ester casually whether he might occasionally visit her in town. Find an excuse or . . . but perhaps he didn't need an excuse; he would simply ask whether he could call in.

They made their next stop at the site of the old hill fort. This, too, had been overgrown by thickets, and a stranger would not have been able to distinguish it from the other hills and mounds. At one time a higher mound had clearly been dug into a hollow, and the soil banked up into an earthwork around the mound. What had been on top of the earthwork no one knew for certain. So said the Teacher when they had climbed up it, decided on a flatter spot where there were a couple of moss-covered boulders and sat down. It was definitely better to walk and sit in the shade of the trees than on the flat ground where the late summer sun still tried to extract sweat and gadflies besieged the travellers.

What era was the hill fort from, and had it been used? Once again the Teacher was the person who had to answer the young people's questions. It had presumably been built in the tenth or eleventh century and had presumably never been involved in a major battle. In fact, no one had excavated the site thoroughly, so everything was mere speculation.

'The fact that no arrows or shafts have been found doesn't mean that they weren't used here. Just like the fact that because professors of scientific atheism haven't met God does not prove that God doesn't exist.'

This was the best place to talk about the thing he had considered talking about.

'As the discussion has already moved on to God and atheism I've begun to wonder recently whether it would be the right thing to do to drop out of university and start studying theology at the consistory. So that I could find out more about it . . .'

'Of course,' put in Ellen. 'In any case you get a better education there than you do now at university. But if that's your intention . . . Alo, you could explain to our young friend in more detail and more thoroughly what the courses really are, what they do there, what they teach and what the requirements are.'

The Teacher inhaled deeply on his cigarette and looked at him directly with one eye like a large, white-headed bird.

'Our teaching options are very restricted. To use a current phrase, it's a distance-learning activity. Students attend for a week, have lectures, then go home and study for a month. There's a library, of course – in certain spheres it's actually very good and up-to-date. There are several instructors; some can be regarded as real professors, some are more like stand-ins . . . What requirements are there? You can get an idea from Rein and he can tell you how things look from the other side, so to speak. Indeed, since the consistory is an educational institution whose existence is acceptable to the authorities only to the extent that it trains pastors; all it requires of its students is that they are members of the Church and ready to enter the ministry when the need arises.'

This led nicely on to his next question. 'I can't really say right now whether I'm ready to go into the ministry, or whether it would ever be right for me . . . But the first step is to become a member of the Church. What do you need for that? Do you have to be confirmed? And is the baptism I received from an Orthodox priest regarded as a valid baptism by the Lutheran Church, too?'

'The baptism is indeed valid,' said the Teacher. 'But let Rein tell you how things are done these days. My memories of the pastorate here will probably barely be of any specific help to you.'

'I can show you the plan of one of my recent confirmation lessons,' said Rein. 'Dad should have them somewhere still.'

The conversation rolled on to how difficult it was currently for clergy to fulfil their duty, namely to proclaim the word of God. Just like Rein's father in the past, the Teacher had not agreed with what he called the recent lamentations of Käsu Hans on the difficulties brought by the loss of status and pastorates. He was of the view that the new, difficult circumstances – which were nothing compared with the things Christians had to put up with in the Roman Empire and in Japan and in Islamic countries – had opened up completely new opportunities for preaching. The pressure from the authorities might purge Christianity of the contamination it had experienced and restore something of its original spirit. And it was young people who understood that, regardless of all its weaknesses and absurdities, the Christian Church in Estonia was one of the most effective opportunities to nurture and promote culture.

He wanted to ask whether Christianity, religion, wasn't something bigger and more important than culture, whether religion was, in fact, diminished by regarding it only as part of culture alongside music, poetry and etiquette. But Ellen was already pointing out that time was marching on, and they got up. He would have liked to know what Ester thought of his intention to go and study theology, but she had been quiet and he was unable to read anything in her gaze, which he had occasionally caught.

They left, the Teacher and Ester in front again, the three others behind in a group. Once in a while they would stand next to an interesting plant; it turned out that the Teacher knew more about botany than Ester did with her unfinished education as a biologist.

'Even as a child Alo was very interested in nature, he would take a plant guide into the forests and bogs around his house. In fact, he tried to get a place to study botany but at the last minute decided theology was more useful. Anyhow, for the past twenty years we've always gone on nature trips in summer,' Ellen explained. She knew a thing or two about plants as well.

He decided that he, too, should take up walking into the countryside with a plant guide, as the Teacher had recommended. He would have to talk to Ester about it. There may be a chance of going on a trip with her . . .

They made their next stop when they reached the other tip of the lake. If they'd got there earlier they'd have seen the lake fully iridescent in the sun; now, though, the sun had sunk lower in the west and the lake was bluish-green as it always was on a late summer afternoon. The Teacher talked about water pollution, more specifically 'eutrophication', a word he was hearing for the first time.

'In layman's terms "eutrophy" means well fed or something of the sort. It's originally from the Greek,' the Teacher explained in answer to his question. 'One day you'll have to learn Greek . . . But the biological meaning is that there are so many nutrients, like phosphorus and nitrogen, in the water that the higher plants cannot consume it all. As a result, algae begin to thrive in the water and they develop and multiply rapidly. Country people called the process "water blossoming", and in spring, and sometimes in summer, too, when there is a lot of mould from the previous year's plants, if there is plenty of light, the water bloom is normal. But when there are too many algae they create an imbalance in the aquatic environment, produce too much oxygen during the day and consume it all at night, thereby making it difficult for the fish to breathe.'

'And is that what ecology is?' he asked.

'That, too. The thing that's happening in the lake is part of nature's house-keeping, one of its ways. Perhaps Ester has something to say on the subject?'

'No, nothing, only that eutrophication is more than just blooms on bodies of water in summer. Eutrophication also causes a proliferation of surface plants and the lake gets clogged up. The algae produce a lot of slime that falls to the bottom and buries some of the plants . . .'

'Do you remember, Alo, how beautiful and clear Lake Elva in Vapramäe was when we went there some time in the fifties? Now the bottom is miry and the water isn't really transparent any more.'

It would have been better if Ellen had not mentioned this. Suddenly he remembered the ill-fated erotic picnic with Malle in Vapramäe, as if someone had squeezed his insides with cold, hard fingers. He had the feeling that if anyone had been watching him at that moment they would have seen his face fall. But no one was. Ester was looking in the Teacher's direction, the Teacher was looking ahead, lips pursed – he was piqued that at last the young biologist knew more than he did about something.

They spent the last part of the trip more quietly. This was probably through fatigue, but perhaps the Teacher was really in a bad mood; in any case, he walked on his own more, bowed occasionally to examine the odd plant, now and again exchanged a few words with Ellen who was now at his side or directly behind him, and made more frequent smoking stops than before.

He walked at the back and did not feel his best. The euphoria of the morning had been replaced by weariness and occasionally even nausea. Ester, who was walking in front with Rein, and whose dancing hips and thighs he could not take his eyes off, was further away than before, and he no longer knew whether he was able or willing to tell her everything. Perhaps he should wait. The see-saw of moods, the unexpected coming and going of the This now made him slightly anxious. Perhaps it hadn't been a mystic experience but instead the symptom of some mental illness. Perhaps he should go straight to the psychiatrist's in the city. He was aware that some people had done so and had taken study leave. Perhaps that might be useful. He would be able to read and write in peace and wouldn't have to attend lectures.

Perhaps it would be right to put off talking to Ester until everything was resolved. Perhaps he should talk to Malle first; after all she was waiting for him. Everything was suddenly a huge whirl, a mess that was growing somewhere between his chest and his stomach and making him feel his burden in a physical way. Strange, the thing that was giving him the feeling was not his heart but more his liver and stomach or whatever they were. Once a doctor friend of his grandfather's had said that human beings are a mystery of our times – we know the birds of Australia and the islands of Indonesia, but we don't know where our livers, spleens and other internal organs are. People of old had undoubtedly had much better knowledge on that score. They had killed and butchered animals, and, without knowingly or consciously doing so, they had practised comparative anatomy and had understood and interpreted their emotions in the light of their anatomical knowledge.

The thought that there might be something wrong with him, that all his ecstatic experiences and depressive periods might be the symptom of some mental illness, did not give him any greater comfort. But what assessment could he make of it all with his own mind? Indeed, visit a psychiatrist? Talk to one of the medical students he knew? Not since his childhood had he discussed his more serious worries with his mother – he would not dream of doing so now. Who else? The Teacher? He had never unburdened himself of his personal worries with the Teacher; he could not guess what the Teacher might think and say. Perhaps talk to Ester after all?

Thus he was still deliberating with himself at the supper table. He didn't even really relish the taste of the food, although the fatigue from the trip had made him hungry and Rein's mother's apple cake that they ate with their tea was excellent. Similarly, he was suddenly unable to ask the Teacher something, even though now would have been a good opportunity for it. They were both here as visitors, so there was no need to feel awkward that he was wasting the Teacher's precious work time with questions. The conversation at the table was the sociable, half-polite sort that had been exchanged at dinner tables in other places he had had occasion to be. Rein's father and the Teacher talked still about the memories of their friends, as did Ellen. The young people were mainly silent, but Rein's father addressed him once, saying how good it was to see a bright young man seeking his way.

'And, as we know, seek and ye shall find,' he said.

'Just don't think that you are a somebody,' said the Teacher unexpectedly cuttingly, turning towards him. 'Seeking is a worthy thing to do, but you should consider first what you want and what you are seeking.'

Rein's father did not entirely agree. He thought that those who were truly seeking were, in fact, seeking the same thing, although they might not be aware of it themselves. It was clear that the Teacher did not agree, but he said nothing, merely pursed his lips and fell silent for a while. The Teacher and Ellen had been given Rein's father's office as a bedroom; he was in Rein's room again. Sleep came quickly, although for a few moments he felt as if he were hovering between sleep and wakefulness in a place where the sense of time and space had vanished. The morning euphoria had gone, but this time distress did not come. When he thought of Ester he felt that she was in the same space, his spaceless space. It was a good feeling to fall asleep with. In the morning he woke early, got dressed quietly, picked up his towel and walked down to the lake. Today he had to travel back to the city. If he hadn't had a bicycle he would have been able to travel with the Teacher, Ellen and Ester. But now nothing would come of it. Soon, though, he would meet them all again in the city. He would talk to the Teacher about studying theology; he would go round to Ester's, perhaps after he talked to Malle. One thing bothered him – it was the Teacher's brusque words of the night before: don't let him think he's a somebody. He had always feared that he might do something wrong that He didn't understand what he had done or said for the Teacher to say what he'd said in the way that he'd said it.

The lake could not be seen properly in the fog. The water-lilies were still half-closed, the birds were not singing. The air was chill and dank and not conducive to swimming. He did not allow the cold to deter him: the water would feel comparatively warm, and he had learnt to swim in a cold river in the south.

He didn't have his swimming trunks with him, but it was scarcely likely that anyone would come here to the foggy lake at this time in the morning. Perhaps Ester? He could not imagine whether Ester was the sort of person who would want to plunge into the water on a chilly, foggy morning. The thought of meeting Ester here – if she came she might think of going skinny-dipping with him – was daunting and mildly thrilling. But the foggy morning chill would barely allow the thrill to swell too much. His experience was that emotions were aroused more slowly in the morning than the person they belonged to, yet by night they usually grew beyond the point of appeasement. There was time before then, and a daytime bike ride would do much to calm things down. While pedalling his thoughts would go around and around, always coming back somehow to the things that were bothering him. Now he began to think about Ester, about how and when to talk to her and what about – also about why the Teacher seemed to be displeased with him. Perhaps he should ask Ester about it? Or Rein? They had known the Teacher for a long time; perhaps they would be able to explain it to him.

The water was indeed warmer than the air; the lake still had a little of the waning summer's warmth. It hadn't been so long ago that they had swum here – he, Rein and Ester. He did a circuit to the place where the water-lilies had been flowering then. The flower buds were still shut. There was a transparent dragon-fly on one leaf, presumably waiting for the fog to lift and the sun to come out.

He was about to dry himself when he heard footsteps and someone's shape began to emerge from the fog. After a moment he was already certain: it was Ester.

'Good morning,' they said almost at the same time. He had managed to pull his trousers on to his half-wet body and mumbled an apology, he hadn't thought anyone would be coming here when it was so chilly and early.

'Don't worry,' laughed Ester, 'Daddy also likes swimming in his birthday suit, and, as he always says, what's there to be embarrassed about? It's all been honestly acquired; nothing's been stolen.'

He liked the sentiment. Ester felt both so close and homely again – on yesterday's trip that feeling had receded slightly. But the only answer he was able to give at his first attempt was 'My grandfather says the same sometimes . . . Don't let me disturb you. I'll be ready in a tick and back off to the house.'

No, she wouldn't let him disturb her. They said a few more words on this and that; he asked what time their bus left and said that he was back off to the city that morning, too. And he unexpectedly said what he'd been thinking he'd be too shy to say.

'I was thinking, it . . . it would be good to see you some time and chat.'

'Definitely,' said Ester. 'You come and see me sometimes, if you like. I'm usually at home in the evenings swotting.'

'I don't want to disturb your studying, but perhaps I'll pop in some time,' he replied feeling a kind of warmth – perhaps it was just happiness – floating up from between his navel and his chest.

Ester told him her address. It was the old house where he'd said goodbye to Rein that time – he still remembered it well – and he hurried off at a jog up the hill towards the house, thinking that he could almost say 'with wings on his heels'.

Halfway up he turned to look back. The fog had thinned, and he could see her taking her dress off and stepping towards the lake. He went on without thinking anything for a few moments; only in the garden among the trees did it occur to him that he could have stayed there – Ester would hardly have shooed him away. He could have said – he felt he would have even dared to say – that he would like to look at everything of Ester's that she hadn't stolen.

He stopped. Go back now? Tell Ester that he'd come to look at her? Say that he'd lost his comb or something else? He felt he'd be unable either to lie or speak the truth. The only thing he could do was go to his room.

Ellen and the Teacher were already up, smoking on the steps. It seemed that the Teacher was in a very good humour. He asked whether he was coming with them and when he heard he wasn't he said he should come and see them. They could discuss the theology studies thing. Ellen said that he wasn't to forget them. Didn't they understand what an important person the Teacher was to him and how he had no greater dream than to be in his company and become his pupil?

He did not stay to accompany the Teacher, Ellen and Ester to the bus; he only ate breakfast with the others, packed his backpack and got on his bicycle. Rein's father and Ester came on to the steps and waved to him – he had said goodbye to the others in the room. It was windy and showers had been forecast for the afternoon, so it was important to make good time. He couldn't put it off until the next day: next week he had to be at the university and he still didn't know anything about the timetable or whether and when he was going to the collective farm. If it was straight away he would have to find everything, wash his work clothes and think about what to take with him. He also needed to be at home. And to go to the library to see what new material had arrived in the meantime.

24

At home everything was as it had been before. Grandfather was a bit better – he'd been able to go mushrooming with his friends, and his son, Uncle Viktor, had sent a long, detailed letter and some photographs of his house and car in America. The person most delighted by the letter was, of course, Grandma; the letter also mentioned that his uncle had posted a parcel containing something for each of them. A crowd of relations and friends turned up to read the letter and look at the pictures. This annoyed his mother but pleased his grandparents.

Grandfather, Grandma and Great-Aunt Leeni, who was sitting with them, asked him to explain in detail and at length how the family was keeping, how their children, cat and bees were. Grandfather did not, of course, fail to ask whether the roadside crops were doing well. The question moved him, but he was never able to reply as objectively as he would have liked: he was unable to look at the fields with the eye of a country person like Grandfather, who had never been able to become a true city-dweller. Even now Grandfather felt better when friends took him out of the city for a while, when he could be in the forest and see the meadows. He no longer had his own fields and meadows, and he very rarely went to see those at the collective farm, so his custom was simply to ask others how the crops were doing. He did not, in fact, really expect a detailed reply. He was content if he heard that they were doing well. Would he also have been content if he'd been told that they were doing poorly? It would have confirmed his belief that Communism and collective farming were incompatible with human nature. Which was there more of in Grandfather – the amateur politician awaiting the downfall of the Soviet Union or the country man to whom the fields were more important than matters of state? Probably still the country man. Grandfather, he thought, would have eventually been reconciled with the Soviets if he'd seen that they'd made the meadows flourish and increased the cows' milk yield. But that, unfortunately, was not the case, and Grandfather remained sceptical about Communism.

Nothing significant had changed in the café either, which he visited a couple of days later. Aleks Luuberg was sitting at a window table talking loudly to two young women about Yesenin's poetry. He got himself a glass of apple juice at the counter and sat for a short while with Aleks and his female admirers. Aleks was in full swing, inspired perhaps by the young ladies, perhaps by his own story; in any case he didn't allow himself to be disturbed and continued with his monologue. He couldn't bear to spend long listening to it; he'd already heard Aleks's views about Yesenin so he drank his juice, said he had to go and got up.

'This is —, one of our cleverest young poets,' said Aleks to the ladies, who now examined him with interest.

As he left he thought they might have been more interested in him than in Aleks's monologue. But now he was interested in only one woman – and that was Ester.

He was standing by the lecture timetable in a bustling crowd of young people, most of them probably freshers, still young, green and enthusiastic as he had once been. And he had been in their very place only two years earlier. What a long time ago that was – before Aleks, before Peeter, before the Teacher, before Malle, before Ester. His life, he thought, could be divided into stages according to the people he had met and with whom he'd become friends. The time before the Teacher, the time after the Teacher. University wasn't so important; what was important was the group of people it had brought him into contact with. He had had no one during his schooldays; now he suddenly had friends, he even had the Teacher, he even had . . . Did he have a girlfriend? Who was Malle now; who was Ester? It occurred to him that Malle might be here already, that he might bump into her at any moment and that he really didn't want to see her yet. It was as he thought: a notice was pinned to the board that the following week all students in the first four years would be going to collective farms for two weeks to help with the autumn work. The head of each year would talk in more detail about it after the official ceremony to herald the academic year. Anyone who was exempt from going to the collective farm for medical reasons was required to obtain the appropriate certificate and submit it to the assistant dean.

Interesting to see where they would go. It would be great if it was a nice spot. Võrumaa or Saaremaa, for example. Last year they'd been near Valga; there was nothing of interest there if you left out the small hill skirting the path where the Julius Kuperjanov Memorial had once stood. Paju Manor where he fell, killed by a bullet fired either by the enemy or one of his own men – the village people were more inclined to blame the latter because Kuperjanov had been a ruthless man – was in that very place. The boys were ordered to carry sacks of grain into the drying room – the work was so arduous that by evening they were all exhausted, and at dinnertime they fished the meat out of the soup because more meagre fare wouldn't restore their strength. He didn't usually eat meat, but now he felt that he could not manage without it. He found it amusing that on a couple of occasions they had bought tinned ham from the village shop, switched on the electric stove in their room (which was the hall in the community centre where they had been allocated mattresses on the floor to sleep) and ate it with a spoon. He tried the ham, which was not much more than pork fat, and, wonder of wonders, it tasted unexpectedly sweet. Usually he found fatty food such as this vile; a lump of fat in his gruel would almost make him gag. Now he understood why the German soldiers during the war were fond of fat and why in the past it had been a delicacy in winter for the children to have a piece of fat suspended from the ceiling on the end of a string where they could all go and have a lick. At least he had learnt that much from the autumn on that collective farm. Without that experience it would have been more difficult for him to understand the people who had had to do hard physical work with pitiable nourishment, such as our farm-labouring ancestors or front-line soldiers.

The visit to the collective farm meant that there was no need to write his timetable down: there would be no need to do so for a couple of weeks or even a month.

He went to the library the next day. There was nothing interesting on the new literature shelf, although there were new editions of the Russian magazines he usually read, *The Ancient History Bulletin* and *History of World Culture Bulletin*. At the moment, though, he was loath to stay here any longer. *The Ancient History Bulletin* was usually more interesting than the *World Culture* one, ancient times more interesting than modern ones. The more he delved into ancient texts, the more he found modern ones paled in comparison. Was it really already a couple of thousand years ago that everything important was thought and said and all that was left for us to do was to unearth it and rehash it with the odd minor change? Sometimes he thought that perhaps literature did not really interest him, that what interested him was philosophy, religion, science – human thought in general. Life interested him and literature only did to the extent that it was part of life as a whole not a separate discipline or a world apart. And so he sometimes became bored in the café when Aleks and Jüri began eagerly discussing some translation or debating who was the better poet, Alver or Under. It was easier for him to read a book on grammar or the history of a language than a lengthy, ancient novel. There were some that he had to read, some that he tried to read out of a sense of duty, but it didn't work out well. He gave up reading most of the books he started when he was halfway through: Thomas Mann's *The Magic Mountain*, Tolstoy's *Resurrection* and Dickens's *The Pickwick Papers*. He had decided therefore that at university he would focus more on linguistics than literature. In the end he read the bare minimum he needed for his exams and a number of books that he genuinely liked. The fact that he'd not read more would occasionally irritate him now, especially when some conversation that interested him greatly and to which he could have added his own comments was lumped in with examples of books of which he only had secondhand knowledge.

As a child he had been an avid reader. He had read all the children's literature he could get his hands on, from *Doctor Doolittle* to the 'Vasyok Trubachyov' series and then began to read the Stalin prize-winners, the *Estonian Encyclopaedia*, handbooks on poultry farming and anything else he could find in his great-aunt's attic. He also read with interest *The History of Western European Literature* on his mother's shelf, which she had used for her correspondence-course exams. He remembered the names of many writers, the summaries of their works and their biographies. He read the history of literature like a novel full of characters who are pleasant and interesting and characters who are unpleasant and dull. Later, when he began to read books familiar to him from the history of literature he had read in his childhood, they were nearly all a disappointment: the books were much greyer and duller than in his imagination. Literature in its entirety was greyer and duller. This led to a deep feeling of emptiness and depression: if literature gave so little to the soul what could he expect from anything else? He longed for something else but didn't know what it should be. Philosophy? Love? Faith? Yet they, too, brought similar disappointments. From the history of literature he remembered the term 'spleen': disappointment and boredom in everything, which defined the romantics. He feared that 'spleen' was also lying in wait for him, that he could find nothing genuinely thrilling or beautiful in life, that life was not really liveable for him. Nature? Yes, indeed he did feel best in the country, in the forest. His mother had understood this in her own way when she occasionally admonished him for being so jaded and losing interest in everything. But in the countryside, probably when she saw how much he perked up and how enthusiastic he was there, she had advised him to go to the Academy of Agriculture to study forestry. Then he could spend as much time in a natural environment as he wished.

What, in all honesty, had brought him to philology? Obviously not literature, rather it was languages that he had begun tackling at the end of secondary school. Languages, which were complex and interesting things, as was nature, were definitely more interesting to him than most of what had been said or written in them. Languages were like a forest, grammar was full of oddities and surprises. Just as he had, in his childhood, sat on the sofa reading an encyclopaedia, he would now sit in the library and read dictionaries. Now he went through to the reference library to see whether any new dictionaries had been published over the summer. No. The latest one was the Malagasy–Russian dictionary that he had explored in the spring. However, Malagasy was very distant from all the languages he had come across. He would have liked to learn one of the Celtic languages, but there was almost nothing in the library about them, not a single dictionary, only a couple of handbooks on mediaeval Irish and Welsh. How envious he sometimes was of his own mother and father who, in their youth, had been able to study in Europe, in Germany and France, where they had, in fact, met. They had remained good friends with several Russians and French people, and his mother had said that they would have sent him there to study, too, to the Sorbonne, which was now across borders, unreachably far away. Mother's friends sometimes wrote to her and had sent several books, Camus's *La Peste* and Baudelaire's poetry, hardbacks with red dustjackets. Baudelaire was one of the few writers in whom he had not been disappointed, whose poems had not been a poorer read than the section on the author in the history of literature. Baudelaire's poems included some that he read over and over again.

> Andromache, I think of you! This narrow stream,
> Poor, sad mirror where once shone
> The grand majesty of your widow's grief
> This false Simois springs from your tears.

What did he have to do with the heartache of Andromache? Her tears of grief that swelled the flow of the false river Simois? What did Baudelaire have to do with it? Why is it that a mythological character's suffering, which, as in this case, wanders from one work of literature to another always to great effect, is able to enchant us? And why is the real suffering of real human beings sometimes of so little interest to us? How many unfortunate widows are there in the world, widows of the wrong men, of soldiers who had fought on the wrong side, been proclaimed enemies of the people, killed in action? Like his own mother. Perhaps Andromache was just a symbol of them all, a kind of collective image? Andromache had obviously not existed, just like Don Quixote, Hamlet, Job. That was literature; the power of literature was that it made fantasy more real than reality. He considered this thought wholly unoriginal but nevertheless made a note under a particular entry in the pocket book that he always took to the library. He looked around the large reading-room for a while but didn't spot anyone he knew.

None of his friends was to be seen in the café either. Only Aleks was there, sitting at the same table as before with the same two young ladies. He was already about to turn around and go home when Aleks noticed him and called. Peeter had been looking for him, saying that it was vital for them to talk as a matter of urgency. He must have gone home.

Peeter lived in the same district as the Teacher, in lodgings at friends of his parents. A small group of them had gathered there together now and again and discussed modern literature and read poetry – apart from Peeter and himself there was Jaan, who was a history student, and two philologists from Peeter's year: the lively and chatty Riina and the tall, serious Karmen. Karmen was the only one who didn't write poetry; she was mostly interested in philosophy. Peeter had christened the gathering 'the modern salon', and they had great plans for it: to try to attend once a month, invite guests who would have to give presentations on a given theme – for example, abstract art or existentialist philosophy – and compile a handwritten almanac of the salon poems and other writings. He probably needed to talk to him about something related to the gatherings. But why so urgently?

In the garden by the house the landlady was weeding the gladioli – she had stacks of them, they were tall and multicoloured. He greeted her, wished her strength and asked whether Peeter was at home. She said that he'd arrived an hour before. He'd looked very worried; she didn't know what young people nowadays might worry about. He replied that he didn't know either and said that he'd never seen such beautiful gladioli before.

'Oh, don't!' she said. 'They're more trouble than pets. Still, they're my cross to bear, and I haven't got the heart to let them wither and die. Like as not I'll be tending to them as long as the Lord gives me strength and good health.'

Peeter really did have a worried look, a frightened expression in his eyes.

'How was your summer? Do you want to talk about it?' he asked.

'Yes, come in. There's one thing really; one thing went really badly,' Peeter replied, perhaps without hearing the first, more rhetorical part. They sat down on the old, worn leather sofa. 'You know the Under manuscript, the collection you gave me? There's a big problem with it.'

'Have you lost it or something?' He couldn't think of anything better to ask.

'No, I haven't lost it . . . I gave it to a couple of people to read and somehow the KGB got wind of it, and yesterday I was summoned there.'

At first he didn't understand. 'What have the KGB got to do with Under's poetry? It's already been published here . . .'

'They said that the collection contained a number of anti-Soviet poems and that it was a serious matter, anti-Soviet propaganda, there's a law against it and . . .'

'They accused you of anti-Soviet activities?'

'Not directly. But they advised me to tell them where I'd obtained the manuscript, and I had no option but to tell them I'd got it from you.'

He felt something he'd never felt before, and some part of him was able even to observe the feeling. Fear was accompanied by abhorrence; everything that Peeter had said, everything that was now awaiting him, contained something nauseatingly vile. He thought with lightning speed; he asked and replied, asked again, replied again. Could they send him to gaol? Send him down from university? Could he be forced into the army? What would he say when he was asked where he'd got the manuscript from? He couldn't implicate the Teacher and Ellen. They had their own problems. He'd have to think of something.

He wanted to know what Peeter's impression and perception of the KGB men was. It had been horrible, yet the person who'd interviewed him had spoken faultless Estonian and had been polite, offered a cigarette and asked how university was going. He'd talked to a law-student friend he trusted: it was merely an interrogation technique. Force and threats were not used if astute questioning could produce results. But, naturally, they had their own coercive measures that they could resort to if necessary.

Hadn't Peeter been able to fabricate something about where he'd obtained the Under from – say that he'd found it in a library or that it had been sent to him from abroad? The thought came to him out of the blue; it could be life saving – from his uncle in America or his aunt in Sweden.

'I just couldn't,' replied Peeter, his face a picture of utter dismay. 'I would have tried, of course, but my mind was a blank and . . . I was uneasy and . . . scared, too.'

The two of them sat for a few moments, unable to say anything more. He was incapable even of feeling cross with Peeter, although he would have liked to. If Peeter had been unable to come up with something then he would have to do so himself. Peeter put some coffee on. In response to his question as to whether he'd written any poems over the summer, he took a sheaf of papers out of the cupboard in the corner and read some out. There was perhaps a modicum of strain in his voice although it seemed that reading his own poems out loud, albeit to a minuscule audience, was as much to his liking as usual. It was harder for him to listen: the words slid past his ears, unable to force through the thick padding that suddenly seemed to have filled his head. He had genuinely never felt anything like this before: if this was fear it wasn't a single, uncomplicated feeling but a bundle of feelings and images that he could not unravel or distinguish one from the other. Yet the fear-bundle definitely had an effect on his entire organism. He could never have imagined that this whole thing could be so complex and yet interesting in its own complexity. Now he would have to wait for the moment when they came looking for him. Would they come to the house or would he be summoned at the university? Or at the collective farm, for which they were soon to depart? Suddenly it ran through his head that the collective farm could be his refuge from them, but the thought was not sensible: they could find out from the university where their year was and seek him out there. He had felt something akin to this before – in his childhood when he'd been up to mischief, sometimes deliberately, sometimes by accident, and he knew and feared that punishment was imminent. Then he began to wonder which aspects of misery and punishment could be described as continuity of identity – the fact that tomorrow he would always be exactly the same as today, would have the same name, inhabit the same body, think the same thoughts and feel the same feelings. This presumably also meant that he was him. Even at that stage he had realized that he didn't at all like being him. Even when he actually liked existing. He did occasionally, but at that point he had forgotten that he was him, or the fact that he was him was irrelevant.

Back then, when he'd been a child, something had also been different. Back then he knew that he'd done something wrong, had been naughty, was guilty. But now he knew that he had done nothing wrong, had through his own sheer carelessness been caught up in the wheels of the machinery of injustice. He knew that he was guilty of nothing, that he was a true innocent like many others before him. The realization even gave him some strength, and the hope, the presentiment, that nothing truly awful would happen to him, that this time they would not catch him in their net. Somehow he would struggle free.

He wondered whether there was anyone they, his family, knew whom he could turn to with the problem. No one came to mind. But then . . . Doctors, of course, doctors could at least prevent him from being sent into the army if he was sent down from university.

He remembered the story of two frogs who fell into a cream churn and were as good as drowned. The pessimist thought it was all over and drowned, but the optimist floundered about in the cream for so long that it turned into butter and thus he escaped with his life. That's what he and Peeter were like now, the two frogs. But neither of them seemed to be the pessimist. Was life not, in fact, optimistic? The truth would out under stress: even the worst grumbler and self-declared pessimist would ardently strive to save himself. Kalev had touched on it in his own prison-camp stories. An uprising among prisoners at one of the camps (it would be more accurate to describe it as a general strike) had been led by a short-sighted historian who to all appearances was the most sickly of all the intellectuals. But there were examples of the opposite, too: during the shelling his mother's cousin, who was a larger-than-life character and a big ladies' man, had his nerves shot to pieces, whereas his wife, a normally quiet woman who seemed perpetually in fear of something, was totally calm and efficient.

He felt unable to talk about anything else any more; he had to go. When he was already by the door, Peeter said, 'You must be cross that I said I'd got the Under from you. But I was in such a state that I simply couldn't make anything up and . . . you know I'm probably going to get married. In the summer I met a Latvian girl; we got on really well with each other and she might come here to Tartu to study Russian and . . .'

No, he didn't think he'd be cross with Peeter. What good would it do? And, of course, Peeter was thinking more about his Latvian girlfriend than about him. He had to prepare himself mentally for the impending, inevitable prospect.

He said some sort of congratulation to Peeter and left. It was already starting to grow dark outside. The first lights were being switched on along the road, and in the sky a single star was shining on the horizon. It could be Venus.

Where should he go? Home? He didn't like the idea much. He was afraid he'd have a dream in the night, and if he tossed and turned in bed his aunt would be sure to ask whether there was anything wrong. There was, of course, but he didn't want to be the person to broach the subject. Perhaps he could manage it so that his family would not get to hear of it. They would only start to worry needlessly. Should he go to the Teacher's – that was who he'd got the Under from – to warn him? No, when they had been together recently he had felt he shouldn't pester the Teacher this time. Particularly with something such as this, which presaged trouble. What was there for him to say? That someone was caught with something that the KGB regards as subversive and that the Teacher was mixed up in it? No, he wouldn't say where he'd got the Under from; instead he'd say it had come in the post from his uncle abroad. If he went and told the Teacher and Ellen the whole thing now they'd start to worry and would, of course, say that he shouldn't take full responsibility. But that was not what he wanted in any case. He now had the opportunity to do something good for the Teacher, and he would not let the chance pass him by.

To Ester's? Tempting. At first it seemed a good idea, but then came the doubts. He'd intended to tell her everything he felt and hoped, but if he went there now like this with his own problems . . . What did he want? Help? Ester couldn't provide help. Comfort? It would be tame, would seem too much like an excuse. No, right now he wouldn't go anywhere. He would have to cope with his worry alone. But perhaps he wasn't alone. There was the This – either it had now disappeared, vanished, or was just an illusion. The meeting with the This in the river in the summer. The meeting with God in the cemetery. Where were they now? What was it Jesus shouted on the cross? 'Eloi, Eloi, lama sabachthani?' (My God, my God, why have you forsaken me?) It was perhaps a reference to something in Psalms. But in Aramaic, his mother tongue, not Hebrew. Strange that in death Jesus quoted the Scriptures. But it was perhaps typical of the people of the time. Serious matters were always addressed with mature words, whether it be the Bible or the myths or traditional songs. Presumably our predecessors, too, found help in their folk songs in times of difficulty. What song should he sing now? The song of a person with a troubled soul?

He realized he didn't know any folk songs properly at all. Nor the Bible. He might find some comfort in the Bible. Or something comforting, something that prepared him spiritually for the ordeal. It would be interesting to know what heretics brought before the Inquisition read to prepare themselves spiritually. Mostly they were religious people, sectarians. Some were secret Jews, so perhaps they read the Torah, even the same psalm as Jesus in death. But what about the atheists, the agnostics, the non-believers? But which was he? Did he believe? No, if he were honest, he probably still did not believe. But the This. Was the This – is the This – God? If so, then he had met God, and, if he did need more faith, the knowledge that the This, He, was somewhere, that it was possible to meet it, would suffice. Why did it come and go like a gust of wind, unexpectedly? The spirit that is like the wind, it blows where it wills. If it came now it would be with him if he had to face them alone. What did it say in the Bible? Do not worry about what you say; the words will be put into your mouth. At home he would have to get out the Bible and find the reference. What it meant, more or less, was do not worry about tomorrow; today's problems are enough for one day.

What was his worry for today? Suddenly he realized that, in fact, his worry was pretty well non-existent – as was worrying about tomorrow or the day after or any day any time. Wasn't worry something that always belonged in the future? Man viewed things, whether far off or close at hand, with a worried eye and did not notice that right there, where he was, there was nothing to worry about? He had

had something of a similar thought two years previously when suddenly – thoughts like this always come suddenly – he realized that he was actually free; he could do whatever he liked. Of course, everything that he did had consequences, although they always came later, not immediately and not at the same time. But he couldn't do anything with this freedom he had unexpectedly found. He could have taken something on, changed something in his life, done good or ill, but he realized that he was also free to continue to live without changing anything, without doing anything special, allowing his life simply to trundle along the rails pre-destined for him by his and his parents' past. Besides selective freedom there is also the unchosen freedom of existence.

Now he noticed that his legs had taken him to the railway as they had that time when he had called on the Teacher and the Teacher had been busy, and he hadn't known what to do. Even then his legs had known better. He would go for a walk here through the fields just outside the town and then home.

There were already several stars in the sky. The Plough and the North Star were shining, and of the other stars he knew he could see Vega with Deneb beside it. He knew the constellation Cygnus – ancient Estonians had called it the Great Cross.

He stepped off the path and sat awhile on a pile of old sleepers. It was really warm, and there was no chill even in the breeze. He felt that he liked this place; there was something restorative and soothing about it. Nowhere else near the city did he have such a strange feeling of space. The fields, the roads, the distant forest whose dark outline was all that could be seen, the other side of the city and its lights. All this seemed smaller, emptier next to space, which spread out over everything yet was somehow particularly close at hand. As if the sky itself had reached out to the land, had gathered it up. That's how it was in some of the Polynesian and Melanesian myths: in the beginning the sky was combined with the land then a giant separated them. He realized that it was like opening a book, lifting the book cover. Was the book, the history of the world, the book of time, already done or was it still being written? Was everything proceeding in line with some great script or was the screenplay emerging with the film? Did God open an empty book and start to write our story in it, or was that story already complete, ready for us to read through, act out, live? Perhaps we are notes, stars, words in this book of God's? Notes that mean something of which they themselves are unaware and uncomprehending . . .

Being here helped him, space reached out to him, too, crept into him, gave him contentment and stamina. Perhaps enough for the coming days, but on this he was cautious: his experiences that summer, the seesaw between ecstasy and depression, did not give him confidence that the contentment and stamina would endure. And yet, the main thing was contentment; he understood that better now, as he had still been worried and tense not half an hour previously. There was definitely an advantage in this. Now he could compare two spiritual states. Now at least he knew what it meant to be content. If he had nothing else to take away from this he at least had that knowledge.

When he stood up and set off back, his eye was drawn to a strange lamppost beyond the city buildings that seemed both close at hand and far away. His first thought was that it was a UFO, but then he realized that it was only the full moon in the ascendant. He had not seen the moon rising behind the city buildings before and pondered the fact that in his experience the moon had always risen behind the forest. Within the city, among the houses where there was a lot of light, no one even noticed the moon. In the city there was no moonlight; it was subdued by streetlights. From here, though, far away, he could see them both – the city lights and the glimmering moon. He now set off towards them, feeling his shoes gradually getting wetter: the night was cool, and there was already a thick dew on the grass. But this no longer bothered him, and neither did the thought of everything that awaited him. He was content – perhaps his contentment had something to do with the This, with God, but perhaps much more with Ester. He felt more certain than ever that he loved Ester and that his love would give him exactly what he needed: strength and confidence.

In his dream he was abroad, in a city that was both Prague and Australia. He convinced himself that this time he really was abroad, that this wasn't a dream as it had been on so many previous occasions. And yet he could not shake off a feeling of distress. He had to reach the train again but was unable to move easily; the street was full of stone cairns with small people climbing on them, humming some sort of tune. Then he went inside a house thinking that this way, through the houses, which had interconnecting doors, he would make faster progress as he had in an earlier dream. And so he did, but, finally, when he opened one particular door, there was no space behind it, only a brick wall. Suddenly he realized that Ester was behind the wall and that he had to reach her, that they had to catch the train together, but now he found himself alone in a large empty room. The door through which he had just come was locked, and he could go neither forwards nor backwards. Inside the room it began to grow dark; he suddenly felt fear, the kind of fear he'd experienced as a child alone in a twilit room. He began to shout, 'Help! Help!' and felt someone's hand on his shoulder.

It was early in the morning. His aunt was standing by his bed, saying, 'Are you sure you're not ill? You were tossing and turning in your sleep, and you started screaming just now.'

'No,' he replied, numb, 'I'm not ill. I was just having a bad dream.' For a moment he was glad that he'd woken up and escaped from the nightmare, but the moment did not last. He immediately sensed that something was distressing and crushing him. It took a few more moments before he realized what it was.

His stomach felt disgustingly hollow and empty, almost sick, as it often did when something unpleasant lay ahead – like the time he'd had to go to the military commissar's office where he and others were registered and had to walk naked from one doctor to another (most doctors were women). Military instruction hadn't been so awful – even though he didn't feel good there he could handle the old colonels, and even certificates of absence were not hard to come by – but now things were more serious. Was the mild nausea fear or something else? As he dressed and washed his face he wondered whether he had ever really experienced fear. Once, when cycling down Tähtvere Hill, he'd almost been run over by a car; only a fraction of a second and a metre or so of road saved him from a disaster. Afterwards his knees were shaking and his pulse racing, but was that fear? There had no longer been anything to fear: the danger had passed. Another time he had been surrounded by a gang of Russian boys when out skiing. That time he really had felt the approaching danger, but it did not make him shake with fear; instead, it made him completely, strangely, insensible. Perhaps this was something akin to a creature in the clutches of a predator, waiving the opportunity to resist. He did not resist either; there would have been no point – there were four of them. Nothing dreadful happened. He was simply told to give them his ski poles, so he did. He felt horrible afterwards, of course, ashamed, but that wasn't fear either. Perhaps he did not even know what fear was. Or perhaps such a thing as fear, in fact, did not exist as a single specific phenomenon at all – rather, 'fear' referred to a nebulous raft of very different emotions.

This made the meeting that lay ahead even mildly interesting. Perhaps when he was before the KGB he would understand whether fear existed and what it was. There was no hope of wriggling out of it, so it would definitely be better if what had to happen happened quickly. The thing that whirled in his stomach, his gut or his liver, nauseating him, was for the most part the not knowing. Yet another question: does a person also fear something of which he is fully aware? Probably. Many people on their way to the scaffold are afraid; some, though, are not. So, if they were not aware of what precisely lay ahead, would they all be afraid?

He had no appetite but had to eat, otherwise the family would start to worry again, would ask whether he was ill, and at this moment he could not face an interrogation. He gulped his coffee down in a rush, ate a couple of pieces of bread and cheese and went out.

The meeting for their year was in a small lecture hall that had been the venue for Latin lessons the previous term. He was one of the first to arrive – a couple of quiet girls from German philology were there already – and immediately after him a crowd of students of English turned up whose number would, of course, include the talkative Juhan, the man with a large belly who had once driven a tractor and worked on a herring boat and whom everyone called John. John freed him from the need to talk, and those sitting closer to him and the students trickling in spent quarter of an hour listening to the work he'd done and the things he'd got up to during the summer. John had a motorbike on which he travelled around Estonia in his free time with a girl riding pillion. When he talked only to the boys, however, he described – if he was to be believed – how he had wild nights in haylofts or sometimes simply somewhere in the hay, with girls who accompanied him at a mere flick of his writst.

Malle was one of the last to arrive. At the door she looked around, and when she saw him she approached, smiling, which could mean only one thing: she had been looking forward to seeing him. The seats next to him were taken, but Malle managed to get a place in front and, turning towards him, still smiling, asked quietly, 'How've things been? If you've got time after, perhaps we can go for a little walk and a chat?'

This was what he had surmised and feared, yet he knew that there was no way of not talking to her. But now something else had taken the place of that fear, and it felt bigger and more serious. He felt he couldn't say the things to Malle today that he should say, that he wanted to say. But avoiding the chat was easier because of the other fear. It was enough for him simply to say that it was something to do with the KGB, and Malle, like anyone else, would put her concerns to one side and begin to worry about the same thing as him.

The assistant dean, Liisnõmm, whom they all called Old Ma Lisna, arrived and told them the location of the collective farm where they were going. Their group had to travel beyond Võru to a place whose name he had heard before. If it was where he thought it was, it wasn't far from Meeta's and Richard's. That meant he'd be able to visit them on his weekend break if, that is, they were allowed off. When they had been in the Valga district the foreman had given them a day off only once. Perhaps he'd be able to take his bike with him – then travelling away would be easier, and he could go on short rides just for fun in his free time.

Old Ma Lisna went on to explain what they should take with them: work clothes, Wellington boots, raincoats and, of course, a work ethic. The next couple of days were free so that they could get things ready for the visit to the country. Those who protested that their work clothes were at home and they'd have to go to collect them were told by the assistant dean that they were to do so immediately so that they could return in time. And in the event that anyone could not get back in time – if they lived as far away as the Saaremaa or Hiiumaa islands – then there was no problem in their catching the others up.

She had nothing more to say about the trip. At the end of the day they were all old hands and knew the ins and outs. When everyone began to get up and leave, Old Ma Lisna came up to him and said in a very serious tone, 'You have been summoned before the State Security Committee.' And she handed him a small piece of yellow paper bearing the next day's date, an office number and a time, eleven o'clock. She said no more.

He folded the paper and stood stock still in the centre of the lecture hall. His head was suddenly completely empty, devoid of any thought, any feeling. When his thoughts returned, he saw that there were only two people still in the room, he and Malle.

'What is it?' she asked, a slightly startled look in her eyes. 'You look really upset. Has something happened?'

He showed the paper to Malle. 'Let's go for a walk. It's better for talking.'

There were already some yellow leaves on the maples on Toome Hill. The end of summer had been dryish, and someone he had been at school with who was now studying biology had explained to him that trees in cities suffer stress. Perhaps that was why some of them were starting to yellow earlier, he thought.

At first they went towards the observatory. He told her what he'd heard from Peeter. Malle linked arms with him for a moment. 'Don't be afraid. Whatever they do, it's a load of rubbish. Just go and have a coffee and say you won't do it again, and everything will be fine.'

He hoped she was right, but he wasn't confident. They'd mentioned a couple of articles on anti-Soviet propaganda to Peeter; perhaps they happened to be Article 58, the very article under which Paul and the others were sentenced to the camps? But they really had done something; what they'd picked up were arms not some of Under's poetry. Strange, he'd thought that incidents like these no longer happened under Khrushchev, but it would appear that they did.

'You know, I wanted to tell you that my dad is renting a room for me this autumn, so I'm more my own boss. And we can be together more if you like. Study together, for example, and ...'

'Was it because – was it because of me you wanted the room?' he had to ask.

'Well,' Malle was hesitant. 'Perhaps I was thinking of you, too. I think of you a lot, perhaps even more than you can imagine.'

No, he couldn't tell her anything now. They walked on in silence, he looked towards her and suddenly felt he desired her. The feeling was unexpected and surprisingly strong, subsuming everything else for a moment and momentarily depriving him of his power to say anything sensible. Ester was a long way away somewhere, a shining statuette, a beautiful name, but Malle's young, warm body was here beside him, available, ready to be with him, to make him her own, and that was more important than anything else. Even the summons to the KGB headquarters, the little piece of yellow paper in his pocket. Desire robbed him of both strength and speech. He was suddenly unable to say anything, and instead he took her hand and felt how its touch both calmed and excited him.

'Have you got the room already?' he finally managed to ask. It was capitulation, something he wouldn't have expected of himself even half an hour previously. He wondered if it was a kind of enchantment, as if Malle had bewitched him, worked some charm on him, almost an alien force that drew him irresistibly towards her, forced him to do something contrary to his intentions. Perhaps Malle had indeed done something; perhaps such things were indeed possible?

'Not yet,' she replied, smiling. 'I'll be in the dorm for a couple more days. I'll be moving when we come back from the collective farm. Would you help me move?'

'Have you got a lot of stuff to move?'

'Only a couple of lorry loads,' she laughed.

His desire had reached its climax and began to subside very quickly. Before he was able to collect himself and understand what had really happened, the rush of passion had receded, leaving something painful and wet in his loins. His fear and perplexity had not disappeared, though; for the first time he had experienced desire for a woman's body as being stronger than anything else, stronger than fear and even stronger than love. Was a love that was so easily surrendered in the rush of passion, still love?

'Are you really worried?' asked Malle. 'Don't be. Everything'll work out, I'm sure. I know it will.'

'Not really, no. I don't think it's anything serious. It's just horrible.'

Malle understood this, of course. They carried on walking for a while, stood on a knoll in Vallikraavi Street where they could see the tails of aircraft standing far in the distance. Because of the aircraft foreigners were not permitted to enter Tartu, and students of English or French did not meet a single native English or French speaker during the whole of their time at university. He had once exchanged a few words with a French person in the Hermitage when the Frenchman's guide hadn't known what 'pine tree' was in French.

'When you come back from there tomorrow come and look me up. I can wait in the library for you or the café,' said Malle when they parted.

He promised to come to the library, and perhaps they would go for a walk.

To his surprise he slept well, although he woke up a couple of times and had the same dream: he had to go to the interrogation with Aleks but for some reason couldn't; his feet became stuck to the ground, and Aleks was talking all the time – something about war in the South Sea Islands – then there was the street, which they tried to go along, through the dusky corridor between them that now had many more doors. He asked Aleks what doors they were, but Aleks's place had suddenly been taken by his father who wouldn't talk to him, just looked at him sadly and shook his head.

In the morning he had to give his grandfather a report on the university and the forthcoming trip to the collective farm. As always, Grandfather told him to look and see how the prime crops were doing – they had to go and help harvest the oats and barley. It was good that at least they had been allowed to go and harvest crops rather than pick potatoes as they usually did. The wet weather meant potato picking was filthy work and often there was nowhere to dry and wash clothes. Picking potatoes, like all dirtier work, was mainly for the girls; the boys were allocated heavier but cleaner tasks, like that time in Valgamaa when they had lifted and hauled sacks of crops.

He didn't want to say anything more to anyone. It would be better to stroll around the city for a while, recite poetry in his head. Poetry was for him a substitute for prayers or mantras – it helped him if he had problems. Before facing the military board he'd sat in the café and read some verses of Alver's and Talvik's that he'd copied down. He would have taken the file with him and sat on a bench somewhere in the park to read some Under, but he didn't dare. It would be even worse if he were caught somewhere with the poems and thereby caused trouble for the Teacher. It would not solve anything. He had to break the chain and thought he knew how to do so. His relatives in Sweden had sent him lots of Estonian books and extracts from abroad, and most of them had reached their destination. Consignments were probably examined,, but there was still the hope that 100 per cent monitoring of everything did not occur in their building. In any case, he'd mentally prepared his story.

During his childhood the KGB offices had been somewhere else – on the crossroads of Riia Street. It was called the Grey House and was talked about in anxious whispers. Most of the horror stories of beatings and torture and people who never came out of there again had vanished without trace. Once – this was later, when the Grey House accommodated a regular government department – someone had confirmed to him that there had been a great meat-grinder in the cellar that had been used to break up the bodies of people who had been shot dead or died under torture and who were then buried in sacks somewhere at a secret location, probably in Tähtvere Forest. The story was hard to believe although he knew that the twentieth century had seen more grisly and even more unbelievable acts. Yet the rationalist in him wondered why they would have to grind up the dead when they could just as well be buried whole.

All that, though, was in the past. After Stalin's death and the overthrow of Beria the KGB had changed its face. Nothing much was known about it now, and when it was talked about it was without the horror that had shrouded everything associated with the Grey House. The new, smaller, more inconspicuous KGB had moved to smaller premises that he often walked past. It had been the home of some squire, and there was a long flight of steps up to the front door, a strip of lawn under the windows, which was home to a lilac bush, a tall mountain ash and a concrete tub of flowers. He had wondered who tended the flowers until one day he saw an elderly man watering them. This was the new face of the KGB during the Khrushchev thaw. He had never before even given any thought to what was behind the new, flowery face. Now – and it was bizarre but true that it was thanks to the Teacher – he was to become more closely acquainted with it.

The door of the house was ajar but stiff – perhaps that was why they didn't go to the trouble of closing it. And when it was warm there was no need to do so. Uninvited visitors rarely came here. Behind the front door was a glass door that was closed and led to a lobby with khaki-painted walls. Beyond the lobby was a dusky gallery, which plainly led to a corridor. In the corner stood a small writing-desk, and seated behind it there was a woman of indeterminate age with hair of a indeterminate colour, whose figure was not what it had been, the likes of whom he had seen sitting behind many security desks in offices both in Estonia and Russia.

He greeted her. She asked him in Russian what he wanted. He showed her the yellow paper.

'Your passport,' she demanded in an official tone.

Fortunately he had it with him. It would have been interesting to see what would have happened if he had lost it, he thought. Would that mean he would not be allowed into the office where he was expected?

The woman picked up a telephone – there were three in total on the desk – dialled a short number and announced, 'Ülo Andreyevich, a visitor for you.'

He had to wait for a moment, then out of the gloom in the corridor there appeared a shortish man.

'Aha. You are bang on time. Good,' he said and went to shake hands. 'We need to have a little chat. I hope it won't take long. Please come with me.'

The office was small and smelt of tobacco smoke. A thick net curtain covered the window – the smell of smoke, he thought, would linger in there for a long time. By one wall there was a cupboard, probably for files, on another a picture of Felix Dzerzhinski.

'I haven't introduced myself – Investigator Kask,' said the man. 'Please have a seat.' He indicated the chair by the table, sat down in his own chair behind the desk on which there was a single folder and asked, 'Are you a smoker? Can I offer you a cigarette?'

'I smoke occasionally,' he replied, took the proffered cigarette and accepted a light.

Now he could scrutinize the office owner more closely. He looked over thirty but not yet forty; his already thin hair had been combed with care. He was wearing a nondescript, greyish suit with a striped, unostentatious, reddish-brown tie, and on his face he sported something that could have been a smile. The only striking thing about him was his cigarette holder, the tip of which was in the shape of a small devil. Otherwise the man was the type he would hardly have noticed or recognized on the street. In any case, he was more of a grey State official than a fanatical Chekist or sadistic thug. He wondered whether the Gestapo were similarly grey officials, realizing that the fear that had engulfed him till now was being replaced by tedium.

'I imagine your friend told you what this is about,' said the man, interrupting his train of thought.

'Yes, he told me something about it.'

'Right, then let's get straight to the point. Your friend spoke to us very freely, and I hope that you will do the same. The main role of this office now is not to punish people for their mistakes but to explain to them that they have erred and then to consider together how to correct their error. Our role is therefore one of preventive maintenance. I mention this so that you don't think we are something we are not. Of course, it must be acknowledged that in the past our agencies were not always guided by principles of this nature, and this had many unfortunate consequences, as you know – as a result, the Party and our directorate drew serious conclusions.' He paused – not, of course, in anticipation of any response – and then continued in a more unofficial manner, 'Yes, we know that you lost your father. He was one of many who fell victim to a personality cult. I hope that he has now been rehabilitated.'

'I don't know. My mother will never talk about it,' he replied.

'I understand. It's a tragic thing. But if you should wish to know more about the matter, or simply wish to know more about your father's fate, we will naturally try to help. That, too, is part of our role. Something for you to think about.'

He nodded. His mother had brusquely said a couple of times that she knew her husband had died and had no desire to know any more. But he couldn't say that to the man behind the desk.

He had just opened the file. 'Righ. Down to business. This relates to certain texts, poems, as you obviously are already aware. Your friend said that he obtained a handwritten copy of a Marie Under collection from you and even copied it out for himself during lectures. Is that correct?'

'I don't know whether or where he copied the Under collection, but he did get a copy from me to read, yes.'

'Good. Right. It so happens that we received a report on this matter and investigated it. Our information relates to the Under collection *Sparks in the Cinders* that was published abroad in Sweden. Is that correct?'

'Yes, it is.'

'We have approached experts, people who know Estonian literature, including expatriate literature, and who know how to appraise correct ideology, and in their expert opinion this collection contains a number of anti-Soviet poems. Does that come as a surprise to you?'

'Yes, a complete surprise. Under's poems have been published and written about in Soviet Estonia before. And I had no idea that anything had been written anywhere about her anti-Soviet poems.'

'Now that surprises *me*. You have spent eleven years in Soviet schools and two years at university and you find nothing in an expatriate poet questionable, nothing that might arouse unease, nothing that does not fit in with our ideology. And you calmly give this manuscript to others; you disseminate it. Are you aware that dissemination of anti-Soviet materials can be regarded as a criminal act for which you could be held to account?'

'Yes, I am now,' was the only reply he could give.

'I can believe it. And I would also like to believe that in disseminating those poems you had no criminal intentions, that you acted without thinking. You did not realize what you were doing.'

'Yes, I have to say that I really did act without thinking,' he said. That was the wise thing to say. And to some extent it was also true.

'I am pleased to hear it. I hope that you now understand things and are ready to help us.'

This sounded both reassuring and sinister. Did they now want to recruit him, get him to spy on others? He would not walk into that trap. He would clearly have to dodge about, play the true Soviet citizen who acknowledges the error of his ways but is not ready to do everything wanted of him. Rein's father's words had proved prophetic.

'Naturally I will do my duty as a Soviet citizen.'

'Excellent. I would first like a couple of pieces of information about this manuscript. How did it come into your possession, and where is it now?'

'I received the manuscript in the post from relatives in Sweden. It was in small type on thin paper, so I copied it out.'

'So there are two copies of the Under manuscript in your possession?'

'No, now I don't even have one.'

'How so? Did they just disappear?'

This was the most difficult part of the scenario he had thought up. He had never been a good liar, yet now he had to be. He couldn't involve the Teacher in this.

'No. The first one, the typewritten manuscript that came in the post, I threw out because it was barely legible and on poor paper. And I copied it into a folder in which I have other poems. And I threw my personal manuscript away yesterday, into the stove, after I'd talked to Peeter R. I thought it would help if no one could ever have the manuscript from me again, either intentionally or by accident.'

This did not seem to best please the man, whose eyebrows creased slightly. But destruction of anti-Soviet material could not be deemed a directly anti-Soviet act.

After a momentary pause the man said, 'Yes, that would have been the correct course of action when you received the manuscript. Anti-Soviet materials must be destroyed. Or, even better, they can be passed on to us. Regardless of whether the material has already been disseminated, or whether we have received reports about it, it would in any case have been correct to pass it on to us. Otherwise it smells of – what's the expression they use nowadays – it smells of destruction of evidence. And that can cast a definite shadow over you . . . But, all right, let's suppose that the manuscript that's caused all this bother no longer exists. Its content must still be made known to us. We still need to know precisely where, from whom and when you received it and who you gave it to to read – and, unfortunately, to copy.'

The man took a sheet of paper out of the file and unscrewed the top of his fountain pen.

'So, from whom did you receive the Under collection, and what was its title?'

He told him his grandmother's cousin's name and, in response to other questions, an address that he happened to remember. And the collection's title *Sparks in the Cinders*. He had to describe the form in which the manuscript had reached them and the type of file he had copied it out into and when and how he had destroyed both copies of the collection. To whom had he given it to read? Only Peeter. And his grandmother and mother at home. He also mentioned that his family had seen the collection in the apartment but had not passed it on to anyone else. This information seemed to suffice. He wondered whether the man opposite was really taking the matter seriously or not. The KGB should be dealing with genuinely anti-State goings-on, exposure of secret organizations, interception of foreign spies, capture of the last Forest Brothers, if there still were any out there, not with poetry. But no emotions could be read in the face of the man behind the desk. He was doing what he had been given to do, clearly nothing more, nothing less. Properly but presumably not diligently. This could be a good sign.

The man offered him another cigarette, leant on the back of the chair, smiled and announced, 'I hope that our meeting has helped clarify this matter – and perhaps dispel certain prejudices and rumours still in circulation about our organization.' Then, after a brief pause, he added, 'As you can see, we have no shortage of work. There is a great deal to do. And we cannot do everything with just our own forces. To be more accurate, we cannot do everything as well as we need to. Our work specification requires extensive contacts with the people; we give explanations, like our little chat today, and the people understand. And help. We need people who share our concerns and can help us diminish them. I hope that you now understand those concerns. Am I right?'

'I hope so, too,' he replied, already imagining the direction in which the man was steering the conversation.

'Then our meeting has served its purpose to some extent. And that leads on to my other question. Are you ready to help us in our work as well?'

He had been expecting something of this kind, although it was nevertheless difficult to answer. But answer he must.

'I hope that I have already done so to some degree.'

'Yes, indeed you have – although I had in mind something on a more regular basis, say, for example, more systematic help. Meaning that we could always turn to you if there were questions or problems. You would help us to investigate matters, find out what certain people are planning and thinking. Perhaps on occasion we would ask you to become involved, talk to them and, if that proves unsuccessful, then leave the matter to us.

'There are many people who work with us, and they are a great help. They are, so to speak, our eyes and ears. And, if they help us, we can help them. For example, look for opportunities for them to study in a particular Soviet university, in a people's democracy or even elsewhere abroad. As you know, Soviet specialists work in most friendly countries in Asia, Africa and elsewhere. And you as a philologist could, for instance, spend some time working as a translator, which would be excellent language experience. We place our trust in those who trust in us, and we set certain irregularities to one side. That means that we do not interpret them as serious offences; we are not looking for a criminal offence – I hope you are familiar with the concept – instead, we regard them as misunderstandings, minor instances of thoughtlessness that will not curtail your study opportunities or career path. Otherwise, someone who has erred once may leave a blot on his copy-book, as they say. And that blot may cause problems later . . . So, what do you think of my proposal?'

He had been expecting this; he had given it some thought but without being able to come up with anything definite. Don't think about what you'll say to them; words will be put into your mouth . . . Would words come if he opened his mouth?

He did not rush to reply. He inhaled deeply on the cigarette which he was still less than halfway through. His mind was moving unexpectedly swiftly. In a few moments he managed to consider several options. If A, then B; if C, then D; if . . . Some part of him or someone within him monitored all this, monitored it dispassionately otherwise it would have alarmed or surprised him when he realized he'd started to feel some liking for the man behind the desk and his proposal. What was this? Fear or simply a feeling of human solidarity emerging at the wrong time and in the wrong place? The emotion he felt on those rare occasions when he sensed he was being trusted . . . Being trusted. Were they sly enough to exploit that trust in this way? Become their eyes and ears? To go abroad . . . perhaps in almost the same capacity . . . ? No, he couldn't. Even though he would like to – yes, admittedly he wanted to a bit; there was temptation, even liking – but he couldn't. He wasn't the person to do that kind of work, it didn't suit him . . .

Here, then, was his reply. It didn't suit. 'May I thank you for your trust in me. I wasn't expecting it, and it's obviously important to me . . .' This was the right place for a pause. 'I shall, of course, have to think your proposal over. But I can tell you one thing straight away: this kind of work requires certain qualities in people, such as discretion, the ability to keep a secret, and those qualities are sadly in short supply in me. I am a very impulsive person and inclined to open my heart and – although it doesn't happen often – under the influence of alcohol I tend to lose my self-control and afterwards I don't remember what I said or did.'

This sort of thing could be said about many other people, but he'd been unable to come up with anything better. As a matter of fact, he was more or less right about opening his heart and doing things when drunk that later were the source of bitter regret. It would have been even more true if he'd remembered everything he'd done everything that had happened to him. Someone like that was usually not suited to the secret police or secret intelligence but would definitely be suitable as a spy; the requirements for spies were probably not so stringent. Being a spy would suit almost anyone, judging by the literature he'd read. But perhaps literary spies were exaggerated, caricatures, different from the real thing. He wasn't sure. But one thing he did know; of one thing he was certain: he could not abuse the trust of people close to him, inform the secret police of things he'd been told in confidence. He could not give information on others that might bring them trouble – and he could not say where he had acquired Under's poetry.

These thoughts were interrupted by the man behind the desk who had similarly been lost in thought for a moment, perhaps considering what to say. Perhaps his argument had been correct . . .

'Yes, well, if that's how things are, then that does present problems. I think you may have some difficulty in cooperating with us. Although,' – here there was a pregnant pause – 'if it is not possible then that in itself will give rise to other sorts of problems. The university management may become interested in your conduct, and it is not impossible that they may ask questions about whether your place is at university. They may find that it would be useful for you, for example, to spend two years in the army and then return. But, of course, that is not a matter for us; it would be their decision. And, naturally, we are not interested in your leaving the university. But, if things are as you say, it may be difficult for us to give you a fully positive character reference should we be asked to do so. So questions still remain. But for the moment I have no further questions for you. Perhaps you have some questions of your own?'

'No, not for the moment,' he replied, sensing how his voice was suddenly thinner, less resonant than before. The army – that was something that really horrified him. To avoid it he would perhaps . . . no, not that. At least not right now. Right now he just wanted to leave the building; he wanted to get out into the free air.

'Good, that concludes our meeting for the time being. Very probably this won't be the last; we may well need to examine the odd detail. I have an idea the university *partorg* may wish to talk to you in the near future. And you may have some concerns that we may be able to help resolve or information that you consider important to share with us. We would obviously be pleased to receive it. In any case, I wish you a good start to the academic year and . . . certainty of mind.'

The phrase 'certainty of mind' was still resounding in his ears when he was on the street and had mechanically directed his steps towards Toome. Did the man feel any sympathy towards him? Did he want in his own strange way to tell him to stick with what he had said? It would be strange, but who knows? Reason had stopped, his head was aching and whirling with shards of memory and camouflaged quotations from recent conversations, like the words of tedious pop songs. 'Whether your place is at university, whether my place is at university, whether university's place is at university . . .' While going along Vallikraavi Street up to Toome Hill he suddenly felt sick, so sick that he had to stagger behind the nearest bush and throw up what was left of his breakfast.

With the aftertaste of vomit in his mouth he walked to Ingli Bridge and for a moment contemplated the east where, behind the trees that grew ever taller and denser, the tails of bomber aircraft could be seen. He stepped forward to the sacrificial stone and sat there on the cold stone seat on the little bridge where two linden leaves, now yellowed, lay.

What to do now? Malle was waiting in the library, but he felt he couldn't go and talk to her yet. Talk about everything that had happened with the KGB? The thought of it made him feel sick again. No, he couldn't talk about everything. Nor did he want to go home. He would definitely look a bit preoccupied; his aunt would notice, and he would have to explain that he wasn't ill but that he felt a bit sick. Then his aunt would give him a coal tablet and his grandmother wouldn't call him to supper. He didn't even want to think about food.

The Villem Reiman Monument had stood here once, fronted by a sandpit that he had occasionally been brought to play in. He remembered probably all the sandpits and monuments in the city centre from his childhood. Now there were fewer sandpits and some of the monuments had disappeared, while some had been replaced. That's what had happened to Kalevipoeg. It must have been when he was in year two at school. It was spring; they were running by the river at play-time and saw a tractor revving up to drag the stones from the statue's plinth away with wire. Kalevipoeg's crime was that he had been erected as a monument to the War of Independence and embodied its questionable spirit even after the years 1918–19 had been removed from it. It and the plinth therefore had to disappear, and some time later Kreutzwald appeared in its place. Villem Reiman, who was known to him in his childhood by name only, had also gone. In his place there was just an empty space.

Kalevipoeg was comical. He was holding a large sword, yet he himself was naked, except for something covering his willy, supposedly a hedgehog's skin. He no more understood the reason for this than he did the reason why certain naked men or women in his mother's art books had leaves in the same place. He'd also sensed that his mother didn't want to explain why; she would only say that in the old days it was the custom not to show a naked human body, and that they had to be covered by a fig leaf at least. And the art books did contain pictures where there was nothing covering the men and the women, pictures he scrutinized in private, trying to get an idea of what a woman's more secret parts were like.

As well as the Father of Song there were other new columns: Pirogov and Burdenko. They were supposed to celebrate the historical friendship of the Estonian and Russian peoples, to represent the gratitude of the university city to its big brothers among their populous neighbours who had worked here and brought prosperity and renown to the city. What thing of import Pirogov had done he was not entirely sure, but Burdenko was another story. Burdenko had cured his grandmother when she had had tuberculosis of the spine as a young woman. She had had pains in her legs and back that were treated as nerve or joint pain but to no avail. Burdenko had noticed instantly that one of her legs was more slender than the other and had also found that part of her spine was damaged. Grandmother had had to spend ten months flat on her back in plaster – there was no better treatment at the time – but she did recover and was completely cured. And the young Russian doctor – with whom they communicated in German, of course – was always talked of with the greatest respect in their family: he was the doctor who had performed a miracle.

He noticed with surprise that he had been sitting on the stone bench for a long time contemplating the memorials. It almost made him smirk and gave him confidence. Everything would, in fact, be more fun without the veiled dilemma of whether to become one of their agents or to join the army. Was one more awful than the other? He did not know, yet it was ghastly even to consider the army. The army to him – and not only in his imagination – was as awful as a prison camp. If he were sent down from university, even if only temporarily, there would be no escape from the army. If only . . . Only illness would save him, he would have to find a doctor who could help. A doctor who would perform a miracle. Like Burdenko. A neurologist. No, the only type of doctor who would do would be a psychiatrist. Perhaps one of his friends knew a sympathetic psychiatrist whom he could call upon and discuss the matter with; at least by insinuation if not directly.

But now it was time to go. Malle would be waiting in the library. No, he wouldn't give her a blow-by-blow account of his recent conversation but would talk only of the principal points. Of what the interrogator wanted to know, the proposal and the veiled threat. He did not want to discuss his and Malle's relationship – he would not even be capable of doing so. The previous day's rush of passion had shocked him, stirred a whirl of confusion in his heart. He loved Ester – no question about it. So what was the feeling that suddenly, brutally, drew him to Malle? Merely desire? Perhaps he would have desired any other pleasant woman just as much? No, that would be an exaggeration. At least today, at least now. He was unable to cope with everything at once; just put affairs of the heart to one side for now and deal with the rest first. He acknowledged that he was even grateful to the KGB man for rescuing him – at least for today but perhaps for a few days hence – from a certain difficult conversation. What was it Churchill had said? – A problem postponed is a problem solved. Love shouldn't be a problem, nor should Malle, neither should Ester. Why was everything always like this? Why was everything so difficult and complicated?

From Toome Hill the more direct route to the main building and the library would be through the back entrance, but he didn't like it. It was sometimes locked, and between the two doors there was a smell of the men's toilets. So he turned around, went down the hill, turned left and directed his steps towards the main entrance.

When he reached the corner of the main building he saw three girls in the street ahead, one of whom . . . yes, it was Ester.

The girls turned in the direction of the river. He ran after them. His feet were light and weak as if they had grown wings for an instant but had not yet learnt to fly.

'Ester!' he shouted when he was close enough.

She turned around and her face beamed in a smile. 'It's you! I thought I wouldn't see you and my other friends for a month.'

'Are you off to the collective farm?' he asked.

'Not for the time being,' she replied. 'Final years are spared – until distress calls start coming in from the country. So we'll be off in about a week probably.'

The words were coming from somewhere far away as if they weren't her own. Ester's companions were waiting a few discreet steps away. There was no opportunity to talk in greater detail for the moment. But he wanted to talk – he was suddenly certain of it.

To his surprise he had no difficulty in asking Ester whether she would be at home that evening. He would like to come round; he needed to talk.

'Of course. Please come. I'd like that,' she said and smiled.

He would have liked to tell her how her smile shone for him, warmed him, pierced his heart, but instead said, 'OK, I'll come round some time in the early evening,' thinking that he had a strange, perhaps simply foolish, face when he looked at Ester and that the other girls clearly understood it. But that was no special concern of his. Ester's smile would be enough for him for a while. At a stroke it swept away all thoughts, including the sickening memories of the KGB offices.

They said goodbye. Now the meeting with Malle would be even more difficult. He would much prefer to have gone for a walk, even by himself, but he couldn't. She was waiting, and he had promised. Everything would have been easier if he had not unexpectedly bumped into Ester.

Malle was sitting in her usual spot and smiled as she usually did, although the smile could have concealed concern. There were few people in the library, but it wasn't completely empty as he thought it might be.

'You're back. Shall we go for a walk?' she asked.

'Yes, all right.'

Even as he went down the front steps he was able to talk without disturbing those who were studying in the silence of the library. Nothing dreadful had been done to him, although the interrogator's words contained a clear threat: if he wouldn't work for them he might be sent down and then into the army.

'Oh my God, what a choice,' Malle said. 'All because of a couple of poems. Did you ask which poems they were?'

No, he hadn't, but one of them was probably the one that ended

> We will wait, we will not break our vow.
> Thus we can live more proudly and bear death more easily.

He had, in fact, known this poem from an earlier time. His grandmother had learnt it from someone and copied it down. The poem stood alongside one by

Anna Haava and one by Debora Vaarandi in her little son's, his uncle's, folder with his uncle's documents and drawings. His grandmother wrote using 'w' instead of 'v', the way she had been taught as a child.

Malle didn't remember that poem, although she had read the Under collection.

'Never mind that poem now,' she said. 'We need to think about what to do next.'

They had passed the main building and began to go up Toome Hill as if they had agreed where to go.

'I can't do anything now. I'll just have to wait and see what happens. And this won't be the end of it. I'll definitely have to see someone else. That's when things will start to become clearer.'

'No, listen. Waiting's not the only thing you can do. I think I should talk to my father at least. He's got friends in Tallinn. And here in Tartu as well. I think he'd even be able to talk to the chancellor if necessary.'

It was both moving and startling. She was thinking seriously about how to help him, and perhaps what her father said really could influence someone. But then he would be dependent on Malle. Gratitude was a liability he could never truly repay. Although she was walking beside him, she was actually far away; between them was the smiling memory of Ester, Ester whom he loved and to whom he would soon go.

'Let's wait a bit. There's probably no point mentioning it just yet,' he said.

'Well, it's up to you, but, if you think it could help, just give me the word. And I'll speak to my father anyway. There's no harm in it, is there?'

What should he say now? The direction in which Malle suddenly wanted to steer things was something that almost irritated him. He was not in any way tied to Malle's family, and neither did he want to be.

'I said let's wait. I haven't spoken to my own family about it yet; not to my mother nor the others. Perhaps there won't be any need. Why cause them unnecessary worry? Everyone has their own problems . . . And . . . have you talked about me at home?'

'Not to my mother, I don't really get on with her. I did to my father, though, when we met. Are you cross?' she asked, presumably seeing a flash of disapproval or concern in his face.

'No . . . No, but . . . I just can't think about all this at the moment. How can I put it . . . I feel ill, I feel physically ill because of it all. When I came out of there I felt sick and ended up throwing up behind a bush. Anyone looking on from a distance would have thought it was a student who was either drunk or hungover. It's great that you're concerned for me and are trying to help . . .'

'Forgive me, darling, I'm probably bothering you too much. Let's forget about talking and just walk for a bit. It will probably do just as much good for you to be with me as it will for me to be with you.'

'It always does,' he said, knowing, at least at that point, that he was not speaking the truth. The truth was Ester, not Malle, but he could not say that to Malle, especially now when she had so movingly taken it upon herself to look after him. Malle would probably make a very good wife and mother . . . if there were no Ester. But what if there wasn't? What if Ester didn't want him? No, that would be too much, he didn't want, couldn't bear to think about it. Yet he could not avoid thinking about it. Malle was beside him, waiting for something he was now not able to provide.

They had reached the grotto and bridge where he'd sat before and started off along the path up to Musumägi. He didn't like it much, but it would have been strange to turn back.

The view that years ago had revealed itself from the top of the hill was now obscured by trees. The only things clearly visible were the tower of the Catholic Church and the brick building on Kassitoome hillside. This had been undertaken by the engineer or architect who had been supposed to build Tartu railway station from brick but had instead constructed the station from wood and a proud villa for himself from government stone. When the story came out he hanged himself. It would be interesting to know whether Malle knew the story.

They stood atop Musumägi where they were alone for the time being. Malle turned towards him and, without waiting for a kiss, kissed him herself.

'Don't worry, everything will be fine . . . I love you, I won't let anything bad happen to you.' And, perhaps sensing the lack of ardour in his lips in response to hers, she looked him in the eye and asked, 'You do love me, too, don't you?'

'Yes, I do love you, too,' he replied, or rather some automaton inside him did so, an automaton incapable of anything other than repeating what it had heard. The mechanical parrot, he thought, angry with Malle who was forcing a declaration of love out of him in this way and making him lie for a second time. And angry with himself for lying. In fact, he had spent most of the day telling lies, first to the KGB interrogator and now to Malle. The stuff he'd told the KGB didn't bother him, but the lying to Malle did: he was deceiving someone who loved him, trusted him and wanted with all her heart to help him. He was deceiving someone who had perhaps decided to belong to him, become his wife. And yet she shouldn't have asked him that sort of question. She was like a child expecting the reply 'Yes, that's right'.

'Forgive me, darling, I should go soon. I'm exhausted. I'm not a good companion at the moment. Can I walk you to the dorm? Are you still there? And we've still not talked about what's going on tomorrow, where you're off to and all that,' he steered the conversation to practical matters.

They had been allocated to collective farms in different places, as expected. He felt some relief at this. Being apart in the country and doing heavy work was something that could help, could soothe. But what would come of the matter with the KGB? Yet that was not his concern. If they needed him they'd have to come looking for him at the collective farm or summon him to the city.

He kissed Malle cursorily – more as a brother than as a lover – and they walked down Musumägi. On their way to the dorm the conversation flowed easily. Malle talked about her own summer, the kittens and her trip to Vormsi; he about his visit to Rein's, without, of course, mentioning Ester. Malle asked whether he'd written any poems. Not particularly, but writing did not usually go well for him in summer. The right time for writing poetry was autumn, as it was for Pushkin, when nature and her splendour were no longer so exuberant: the birds had flown, the sun was sinking lower and the nights were long and dark. That was something Malle understood. Summer exhausted her, too; it felt like a capricious, wide-eyed dream. Autumn was more tranquil; in autumn she felt more alert, more vigorous.

'Perhaps you'll be able to come and visit me on the collective farm – it shouldn't be far away,' she said as they stood by the entrance to the dorm (exchanging not a kiss but a long, warm handshake) and said their goodbyes. 'I don't want to even think about not seeing you for a whole month . . .'

He promised to see how the time was planned and what the bus timetable looked like. He promised, in any case, to get in touch with Malle and let her know if anything important happened. There was still plenty of time before the evening, before his meeting with Ester, so he thought the most sensible thing to do was to go home and get his things ready for the trip to the country.

When he stepped into the house his mother got up from the table where she was clearly doing some translation or marking children's work. From her face he knew that something had happened. Was it Grandfather?

'Your tutor has been here . . . She said you're in big trouble. Because of some poems apparently. You've not told me anything about it . . .'

So, Mother knew. Now there was no escape from the one explanation he most wanted to avoid.

'I didn't have any idea about it myself until yesterday. Peeter was looking for me in a complete flap and said that the KGB had summoned him about the Under poems. And today I went there myself.'

His mother sighed deeply and said, 'I've always been afraid that you might get into this sort of trouble. You're so like your father in some things . . . But this tutor of yours who came here, she was very concerned, and she really wants to help you as much as she can. She said that the university and the faculty *partorg* want to have a meeting with you tomorrow.'

'But I've got to leave for the collective farm tomorrow!' he exclaimed.

'That's had to be postponed. Once all the discussions are over here you'll be able to join the others. Or some job will be found for you here in Tartu. I don't know quite what, but she said you were to go to the department or if you came home late to phone her. She wants to speak to you herself before tomorrow.'

That, too! More complications. He went into the kitchen where Grandmother had put some dinner in the oven to keep warm for him as usual – fried potatoes and cabbage. He had to eat something despite his lack of appetite. He didn't want to stay in the city. Things might be tough on the collective farm, but there was always something pleasurable in it. There would definitely be so now: physical work, the country air, the forest and fields would release him from his distress, from all this trouble that was now weighing on his shoulders. In the country, at his great-aunt's house, he had learnt that the best medicine for depression was chopping wood. Indeed, the same was true of lugging sacks of corn for threshing on the collective farm.

However, if he stayed in the city he would be able to meet Ester, go to the Teacher's and from that draw help for his troubled soul. But what was to become of him tomorrow or in a month now depended on others – the KGB, the Party, perhaps the chancellor and other important people in the university. He had been given one option that morning: become an agent, but he had not done so. It would be interesting to see if the offer still stood. He thought for a moment. If the situation went belly-up he could always . . . No, clearly he could not, he would never survive it. Juhan Liiv and Rein's father were right:

> Your conscience will consume you,
> your conscience will slay you.
> Yours will be a life in darkness, a hollow tread
> and an encumbered heart.

Grandfather was presumably having a nap in the back room; Grandmother had gone for a walk or was sitting in Werner's café with a friend her own age. That was good: at least there was no need to talk to them. Talking was difficult right now, and it appeared that there was to be no quick escape from talking and explaining. It was good that Mother at least understood and hadn't asked too much, although it was clear from her face that she was very worried about her son. Unfortunately, he thought, this was not the first and definitely would not be the last time.

He took his dishes into the kitchen and put them with the others. When Grandmother came back in the evening she would heat some water on the oil-stove and wash everything up in one go. Now he had to go to the university – Madame, as they all called her, might still be there and that would obviate the need to phone her. He had feared and hated public phone-boxes since he'd been at secondary school and had tried to phone a girl he liked, but he never got connected properly or was cut off just as the conversation had reached the point where he was about to invite her to the cinema or a concert.

Before he left, however, he had an irresistible urge to spend some time looking through Dante. It was on the shelf next to the Bible – *La Divina Commedia* in an old, shabby leather binding that his mother had bought from an antiquarian bookshop in Milan when she was studying there.

There it was: the one section that he had always read in times of distress. The fifth canto of the *Inferno*, which includes the tragic love story of Paolo and Francesca:

> Nessun maggior dolore
> Che ricordarsi del tempo felice
> Nella miseria.
> [There is no greater sadness than remembering the happy time in misery.]

Why was it that those particular lines pierced and fascinated him? Had he had a happy time that would make him ill if he remembered it? Indeed, had he ever been fully happy? He had. That time on Toome with Malle. In the country by the lake with Ester. And then there in the river when the This happened. But the This was something completely different, different from happiness and probably greater than it. But had he ever been just happy, as people sometimes are if things are going well for them, when they receive or do something good? An utterly startling thought struck him unexpectedly: perhaps he just hadn't enough patience to be happy. It was as if some urge had continually been forcing him to hurry on, urging him to take part, learn, understand. In order to be happy one had to be able to remain in the given time, in the present, leave worries for the future and put regrets to the past. That was perhaps something he had to be able to do, something he had to learn even. It was perhaps meditation or a prayer, where man was alone, in communion with the Eternal Present.

These thoughts did not fade away on the way to the university. Perhaps the This was simply a reminder, an admonition to him to turn to the present, simply to be. The state of being can be acquired only in the present – being is the same as the present – and this present had been given to him once as a titbit is given to a cat. He had been taken into being so that he could see and experience what being meant; the state of being had swept him away for a while.

Yet. Yet . . . what if now, this moment, this worrisome present were his happiest time? What if there were no happier times in the future? There was no point wondering whether now, this moment, perhaps would constitute the happiest time of his life. These were comical thoughts to think while climbing the steps towards the faculty where the next discussion, or at least the prelude to a larger discussion, awaited him. This whole thing was nonsense, absurd, something he would not have thought possible if he were not at the heart of the absurdity. The KGB, the university and the heads of the faculty – all of them dealing with a couple of poems that someone had read and copied out. In truth, he didn't even like those particular poems of Under's, they were too pathetic, too focused on 'we':

> We will stand, we will not break our vow,
> Thus we can live more proudly and bear death more easily.

What vow? What proud life? Words like this felt strange to him. They sounded proud, but how could one live proudly? Live happily, live well, yes . . . But at the moment he would have liked simply to live more peacefully, live the normal life of a Soviet university student, sit with his friends in the café, see Ester and get his things ready for the departure to the collective farm the next day.

Madame was in her office, as he had hoped, and when she saw him she acted exactly as he had feared.

'My dear child, what have you got yourself into?' she shouted, jumping out of her chair. 'What's going on? We are all so worried about you. We must consider immediately what to do. Your mother must have told you that the university *partorg*, Comrade S, has asked for a meeting with you tomorrow. Pull yourself together now. Think carefully. Ddon't do or say anything stupid. You must understand that your future is in the balance . . .'

Madame's questions were rhetorical, she did not expect a response, and it was not really possible to interrupt her in full flow even when she wasn't agitated as she was now. All he could do was listen.

The faculty *partorg* – the faculty's Communist Party representative – had sought Madame out and talked to her. He had asked about him, and she, of course, had said only good things about him because there was no reason to say anything bad. The young man was gifted, although sometimes perhaps too thinly spread, he was juggling too many things at once; he should focus on his own special area. But politically, ideologically and morally the academic staff had nothing to reproach him for. Oh yes, the *partorg* had also asked whether she, Madame, knew what his relationship was to the theologian Alo K. Rumours had reached them that he visited that person's home, was also in contact with Church people and had even discussed the possibility of studying for the priesthood in one of their seminaries.

Madame was now no longer able to continue prattling on, so she paused for a moment to ask whether he was really in contact with Alo K and about the nature of their relationship.

He said that Alo K was probably one of the most erudite philologists in Tartu and the whole of Estonia; he knew languages no one else knew, such as Indian lones, and his interest in oriental languages had been inspired by Alo K.

'Listen, my lad, I don't know this theologian. They say, certainly, that he is enormously erudite, but I wonder why he shares his knowledge only with religious society. What's a genuinely intelligent man doing there among the dog-collar brigade? He should leave that job to the old men and women and come and teach languages to the young people of the Soviet Union. But there is one thing more I have to tell you.' Madame continued in an almost theatrical tone, 'I said I don't know this theologian, but you know, my lad, Tartu is a small city and people have something to say about anyone of the slightest renown. And what I have heard about him is . . . well, you're an adult, I don't have to explain it for you to understand . . . what I mean is this, this Alo of yours . . . is apparently – how shall I put it? – a pederast, a homosexual. Unfortunately it would appear that many young boys visited him and . . .'

'But Alo K is married!' He was unable to control himself.

'Listen, my lad, I don't know for sure, but that's what they say. But where there's smoke there's fire. What do you know of life yet, especially these types of goings-on? Pederasts are often married so that outwardly, let's say, everything is normal, things don't appear to be too suspicious. And there are also some who go with women . . . But I certainly shouldn't be discussing such matters with you . . . Yes, how tragic that you have no father; sons talk to fathers about these things. Incidentally, as far as I know, your friend and teacher has no children. That is significant.'

That was right, Alo and Ellen had no children. He remembered that he'd mentioned this to someone and that that someone (it was Aleks or Rein) had said that the Teacher and Ellen had decided that times were so dismal that they would not have children. They could have if they'd wanted to. But this, too, was hearsay.

Madame had nothing more to say. He would leave for the collective farm when the important matters with the important people were decided and perhaps when the important decisions had been taken somewhere. But her impression was that the faculty *partorg* was very much against sending him down, and although he was only the faculty *partorg*, he had very good contacts on the Central Committee and perhaps even with the KGB in Tallinn. And the chancellor would hardly want to send him down. But, as usual, there were also some people who would like him to be severely punished, as a warning to others and a show of strength. And she had heard that they were also investigating the possibility of sending him to university in Moscow or Leningrad to study Indian or Indonesian languages, but she shouldn't really be telling him that because it was still up in the air, although it was her sincere hope that it would work out. So be careful, don't slip up, but don't say too much about what he thought and felt. He could do that in the future when things had moved on and his thoughts and views had matured. If he had to stay in the city for a few days or weeks he would be given a job here, probably in the library. But tomorrow the *partorg* would be expecting him.

As he left he pondered the fact that Madame could sometimes say the sensible thing, such as what she said about revealing his thoughts and opinions. It looked by all accounts as if he would be dealt with by the upper echelons of the Party within the university. But hardly for his own sake. He was a nonentity, a piece in a great game of chess for power and career. Or a horse with a bet riding on its success or failure. He did not want to be a racehorse, yet neither did he want to let down anyone who had had a flutter on him. They were definitely not the worst of people.

As he went down the steps he was troubled more by what Madame had said about the Teacher. They had ferreted out the information about himself, the Teacher and Ellen from somewhere; all that was missing was for them to discover the real origin of the Under collection. His fabrication would be blown apart and trouble would rain down on the Teacher. And then there was the pederast story. He had never been bothered about whether someone was homosexual as long as nobody bothered him. It had happened once, in Tallinn, in the company of bohemians where a man involved in the theatre who was standing beside him had stroked his thigh and even tried to kiss him. He had found it most unpleasant, although it didn't make the man utterly repugnant to him. But the Teacher . . . That would be another matter. He did not believe that the Teacher was a homosexual but could not be certain of it. And what if he was? What if some time he tried to caress him, wanted to kiss him? What would he do?

Really, what would he do? Was there something more in his passion for the Teacher than passion for an intelligent person, a genius? Didn't the fascination of genius also contain erotic fascination? Wasn't being a genius just fascination, witchcraft that dazzles others? But then genius was as much subjective as it was objective, at least in the arts. It depended on the individuality of the creator as much as it did on his actual achievements. How about in science? Wasn't Einstein also a wizard of genius who fascinated everyone? But no, he was obviously getting nowhere with this line of thinking; he must be tired, and he was unable to steer and check the flow of his thought, which was out of its usual groove and had burst itse banks. Anyway, should thoughts always be steered and kept between the banks? Perhaps the Teacher's strength, the secret of his fascination, was that he did not choose his thoughts; instead, they were given their freedom so that his own thoughts were not spoken through his own mouth by the Teacher himself – a small, ill man in a small city in a small apartment – but by many other people, big and small, living and dead, friends and strangers? The Teacher was like a choir, an orchestra that thinks, plays and speaks with several voices at once . . . And yet? He knew he wanted to be close to the Teacher, to be able to listen to him endlessly, work for him, be his secretary, servant, hired hand, anything so that he could be close to him. He yearned to see him, walk alongside him, hear a good word from the Teacher's mouth, some expression of approval and always feared he would do or say something wrong and make the Teacher cease to care about him, tire of him . . . When he was with the Teacher he tried desperately to be what he believed the Teacher would want; he wanted to be what the Teacher would want. Wasn't this love? Couldn't it be said that he had simply fallen in love with the Teacher, whether that love be homosexual or something else? Was the name for this type of love even important? Would anything come of it? Does the label on the bottle change what is inside?

The afternoon was still young, and he didn't know what to do. He would have most liked to go to Ester's, but it was probably still too early as he had promised to call around sometime in the early evening. There were still two empty hours that had to be filled somehow. He had no desire to go home or to the café – in both he would have to talk, interact, answer annoying questions. Where to walk to? He didn't really have the strength, he felt so physically and mentally tired. That left the library. A couple of hours in the library where, with luck, there would not be anyone he knew. He could look at the shelves of new books – they usually had a book he was keen to read – and if nothing else he could browse a journal or leaf through the old encyclopaedias. He had liked encyclopaedias as a child and still did.

He set off up Toome Hill but could not rid himself of the thoughts that had begun to tumble through his mind when Madame had talked about the Teacher. Yes, he could say that he loved the Teacher just as he could say that he loved Ester. Without knowing whether Ester loved him. He would be able to find that out, though. But the Teacher? Might the Teacher love him? He hadn't thought about it like that. What did it say in the Bible? Jesus had a disciple, an apostle he loved, who had leant his head against Jesus' breast at the Last Supper. It was John, Jesus' favourite disciple, the one whom a particular secret order of monks regarded as having had a homosexual relationship with Jesus.

One or two items of interest had appeared on the New Books shelf. His eye rested on a history of North Africa that had been translated from French. As always, he read a bit from the beginning and the end of the book. On the final pages before the bibliography there was an account of the slow fade of Christianity in the Maghreb. Under Byzantium there were a couple of hundred bishops in North Africa; at the beginning of the eighth century there were only forty. In the eleventh century there were still Christian congregations in the largest cities, but in the twelfth century the last Christians were forced to convert to Islam on pain of death. He wondered whether the same would happen in the Soviet Union, where the last Christians would have to declare themselves Leninist and the last churches become storehouses, museums or cinemas. No, he didn't believe it would be possible. Communism was not Islam; in his view, it was exhibiting clear signs of fatigue and Christianity had been able to live on underground. It was said that Russia had a healthy underground church with its own priesthood. But there, where the authorities closed the churche,s the congregations of Baptists, Jehovah's Witnesses and Pentecostals had immediately revived and grown, although the last two were banned in the USSR. But the forbidden fruit is the sweetest. Was that the reason why religion had started to interest him so much? No, the Teacher was a stronger influence on that point. If the Teacher were an atheist he would probably have become one as well. But could the Teacher be an atheist? Could such an intelligent person be an atheist? Hardly. And yet, here in this very library he had once read Bertrand Russell's pamphlet *Why I Am Not a Christian*. Russell was plainly an intelligent person ... But now there was something else, someone who bound him to the Church. Ester, the pastor's daughter. And the few days he'd spent there at Rein's and Ester's. Rein's father, who had been so confident in his own faith and yet such an open, humorous and sensible person.

There was nothing else worth looking at on the shelf. There was still plenty of time so he wandered into the journals and newspapers room, picked the last two editions of the Russian *Ancient History Bulletin* from the shelf and looked to see whether there was anything interesting in them. He liked this journal, perhaps because it was as far away from the reality of the Soviet Union as possible. Despite that, even when examining the Sumerians or Spartans, there was no escaping or skirting around what was called the Marxist view of history. It was rather hackneyed and sometimes artistically and deceitfully effective, but there was always something interesting in it – sometimes a brief observation about a newly discovered sarcophagus inscribed with Etruscan script or a scrap of papyrus bearing a line of verse by Sappho or Alcaeus, or something from Sumerian or Akkadian mythology. This long-since vanished world – the Sumerians, Etruscans, pre-Hellenic Crete – interested him most; the classical culture of Greece, and Ancient Rome in particular, did so much less. He could not have explained why, but that was how it was. He was interested in the things that he and others knew little about, things from the border zone between pre-history and the history that archaeologists, philologists, papyrologists and who knows who else were painstakingly investigating, deciphering, interpreting and revealing fragment by fragment.

As a child he had dreamt he would invent a time machine and travel back to the time of the ancient battle for independence with a group of submachine gunners, help Lembitu to annihilate the crusaders and unite the whole of Estonia. Now that militarism featured less in his dreams, he would have liked to escape for a while, even for a day, to some Etruscan city or Knossos to see how people lived there, to listen to the voices of the people and try to learn some of their language. Regardless of whether a time machine could exist – the students studying physics whom he sat with sometimes in the café declared it impossible to go back in time – clairvoyance seemed to be something that did, although it did not appear to be subject to any kind of control. If he were given the power of clairvoyance, or if he were to meet someone (after all, he might) with the power, he would try to find out something about the Etruscans or Crete. Perhaps the clairvoyant could help to read an Etruscan or Minoan Cretan inscription, explain something about their writers. Or, by looking at a potsherd from Crete, say what happened there on the island in the fifteenth century before our time.

Until that time he would try to progress with the help of scholars, put a broken vase together from fragments like them. Nevertheless his fancy focused more on other things, the people, their thoughts and feelings, the things that knowledge cannot clearly restore. True, some hint may trickle through to us occasionally in a poem or art. The swallows, the dolphins on the Cretan frescoes that he had admired at length, as if trying to get into the picture. Enter the picture. There was a Chinese story about that: an artist was painting a stork that came to life and flew off; he then painted a scene of wooded hills into which he finally stepped and disappeared for ever.

How wonderful it would be now to step into an old picture like that. To disappear into Crete or vanish among the Etruscans. Or into one of the Dürer etchings that had fascinated him since he was a child. To the place where the Prodigal Son fed swill abroad to the swine, remorse in his eyes, homesick for his father. There were so many places where he could go. He would even escape into a photograph of the free Estonian Republic, into the Tartu of the 1930s that one or two of his friends had talked about. A couple of boxfuls of photographs of Tartu were equally as fascinating as the Dürer pictures. They evoked peace; they spoke almost audibly of a different time, a different pace of life.

Oh, if I could only walk into a picture, let the KGB come and find me. It would be interesting to see what would happen if he stepped into an old etching here in the library; there should be an original by Dürer or another great old master. They would investigate, ascertain where he was last seen, and they would discover that it was here in the reading-room of Toome Library. Or in the Old Books section studying the scripts. What would they conclude? That he had committed suicide, fled to the forest, abroad, into the expanse of his great homeland? What a lot of time and trouble they would spend looking for him.

It was a pity that he had to be himself from birth to death, to bear his own name, carry his memories, assume responsibility for his deeds, whether justly or unjustly, as now. He felt again what he had felt so clearly when he had heard the bad news from Peeter. He had first come to this realization in his childhood when he was made to stand (he didn't remember whether justly or unjustly) in a corner and wanted so dreadfully to disappear, melt away or become someone else, something else. Was this impossibility of escaping from oneself, the compulsion to carry the burden of one's past, the parings of deeds done and left undone, was this what Christianity called sin? Then redemption was when a person escaped from himself, no longer had to be himself. He felt that he could not take this thought any further. His head was suddenly weary and full of other thoughts: Ester, the Teacher, the morning performance at the KGB offices. He had mechanically read half a page of an article on Sumerian temple records: it was more or less apparent from this that in their day the temple had acted as a kind of storehouse for the city people where, if he had understood it properly, surplus crops were kept. Yes, Marxist historians were quick to analyse the commercial function of temples, and they were probably often right. It would have been of greater interest to him to know what the worshippers in the temple – if the Sumerians ever worshipped –

actually felt, believed, hoped. He would have liked to get closer to them, be one of them for a while, think their thoughts, feel their feelings. But it wasn't possible. At least not for thetime being.

His watch moved slowly, as if spiting him. His reading was not progressing well. Over and again he noticed that he had read a couple of sentences, even while thinking about something quite different. In reality he was just waiting. He was waiting for the clock to move more quickly so that his time of departure for Ester's would come around. It was getting towards five; in another hour and a half he could go. Perhaps it would be most sensible to get up and leave now, have a long walk beyond Tähtvere, come back along the riverbank, sit on a bench somewhere and smoke a cigarette. He could easily waste half an hour like that.

He got up, put the journal back in its pigeon-hole and left, leaving behind a pensioner whom he knew by sight and a female student engrossed in the *Unesco Courier* at the large round table.

Outside the air was more autumnal than before, perhaps because the sun was sinking lower behind the treetops, perhaps because of the yellow leaves that already lay on the footpath. He had inadvertently, yet perhaps not completely so, set off on the same path he had walked along the previous day with Malle. For some reason that fact clearly came to mind, as did the desire that walking beside her had aroused in him for a moment. Was that love, too? How many faces does love have? In his eyes it now had two or three: Ester, the Teacher and perhaps also Malle. Yes, why not Malle as well? Yesterday the rush of passion had intimidated him, but now he felt that he had also suddenly become more tolerant. Of himself as well or of himself at least. No, Malle was not bad for him; the only bad thing was if she expected too much from him. He was under no obligation to stay with her, marry her, be faithful to her. Yet he could stay with her if it felt good to him, good to them both.

But what about Ester? No, if Ester cared for him then he would be lost, unable to stay with Malle. He simply couldn't. What if Ester had no feelings for him? Then he would still be lost. He was incapable, actually incapable, of imagining what he would do if Ester didn't want him. Would that bring him back to Malle? Would he use Malle as a substitute for Ester, be reconciled to her? No, there was no point thinking like this before he had been to Ester's. Before tomorrow morning. He had had more than enough for one day: the KGB, Malle, his mother and Madame, Ester. A large knot of several strands. A tangled mess. Grandfather had taught him how to disentangle snarled fishing lines. Grandfather always said there was no knot or tangle that could not be undone with skill and patience. That was undoubtedly true, provided that someone else on the other side of the tangle was not making it worse. Like now.

The aircraft tails were visible again from the hill. Sometimes, when engines at the airfield were being warmed up or tested – who knew for sure which? – there was such a noise overhead on Toome Hill that you couldn't hear your own voice. The sounds crossed straight from one side of the river valley to the other, so down by the river the noise was not so loud. How awful it must be to live beyond the city in Raadi or Aruküla where the aircraft practised low flying. Once, while cycling out of the city on the Narva road, he had seen a colossal low-flying plane. The cows grazing at the roadside had fled in fear to the other side of their field.

He'd just finished reading a book on hypnosis, telekinesis and other such things at the time. He had left his bike leaning against a post and tried to direct his thoughts to the aircraft or its pilot to suggest to the terrifying twin beast that it should crash. It did not. Instead, it gained height and soon disappeared from view. His power of thought was too weak against a great war machine. Some aircraft had crashed, though; proof enough lay among the tombstones at Raadi cemetery where ten or eleven men lay in a row, all with the same date of death. Once, when he chanced to see them, he had suddenly sensed that his wish to down an aircraft using the power of thought or other means had been stupidly puerile. The men flying in them were from his town, men whose wives or children he met every day on the street, in the shops or at the cinema. Twice – when travelling from Tartu to Moscow and Leningrad – he had chatted with such men. They were more intelligent than they were usually taken to be by the city folk, usually highly educated engineers and better versed in world affairs than the average Soviet citizen. And the average Estonian. On the other hand, their world view had peculiarities that seemed comical to him. The pilots could be critical of things the Estonians described as 'Russian', rebuking Khrushchev and admiring the productivity of the Western economies, although they were also staunch Russian patriots nevertheless. The idea that their Great Homeland in the personage of Stalin or Beria should ruthlessly punish all its foes, including nationalists of all types, was perfectly natural to them. The idea that Soviet MIGs might be downed by American fighters or French Mirages was more painful to them than the terror of the 1930s, which had affected some of their grandparents or great-grandparents so severely. He had heard stories from officers and their wives of deportations of kulaks and shootings of old Communists, of which those telling the tale did not approve. Yet, for all that, none of them condemned Stalin, at least not in his hearing. Instead they resented Khrushchev for condemning Stalin. In the eyes of these military men from Tartu, Stalin washed away all his sins by commanding the army in a victorious war – albeit that the war (mostly because of the Great Commander's own errors) had witnessed appalling losses throughout.

It was truly surprising to him that these otherwise intelligent and balanced people – and phlegmatic people were said to make the best pilots – could on one matter be so lacking in sympathy that no mutual understanding between them and his Estonian relatives and friends could be possible regarding matters Estonian. To them, the independent Republic of Estonia was a temporary misunderstanding, part of a conspiracy against the Great Homeland; what he and his family regarded as brutal occupation and annexation was for them merely the re-establishment of a historical right which the imperialists, with help from the nationalists, had trampled underfoot. The deportations and prison camps were an inevitable part of restoring this right, but even so some of them agreed that repression had gone too far at the time – but without reaching what he viewed as the natural conclusion, namely that after a year of Soviet power some Estonians welcomed the Germans as liberators because Soviet power had introduced brutality, falsehood and absurdity here. No, for them the power of the Soviets was something that was part of the Great Homeland and therefore was self-justifying.

He had often thought that these people, the patriots of the Great Homeland and Communists, were like religious people, like sectarians. He was never able to come to the same understanding with them on certain things either – things that were sacred to them, things that could not be criticized, analysed, things in which they thought they had to believe and in which non-belief was not allowed.

The meetings on trains had set him thinking more seriously about the true nature of faith and piety, the thing that united patriots, Communists and sectarians, all of whom he had come across at some time in his life. He had previously classed all of this as faith and had regarded faith as something he would give a wide berth – and would recommend as much to anyone who would listen. Yet now there were several things to think over. The Teacher and Rein's father and their relatives – Ellen, Rein's mother, Rein himself and Ester – also believed; faith was a very important aspect of their lives. Nevertheless, he would not have regarded them as religious compared with the Communists, the patriots of the Great Homeland or the sectarians who occasionally asked him with earnest faces whether he believed in God. Faith was clearly different from being religious. He could now say yes to faith, no to religion. *Cuba sí, Yanquis no* . . . Rein, Ester, the Teacher *sí*; the others *no*.

His legs had brought him to the edge of the park. In the distance two horse-riders were trotting around the grounds in the area where people had always, for long as he could remember, gone for a ride. They sometimes even held competitions that he had gone to watch with his mother. Once pedigree horses had been shown in the shows, including two stallions whose penises dangled a long way below their stomachs. The scene both startled him and aroused in him a strange feeling that he was unable at the time to regard or describe as a thrill. He wanted to ask his mother why the horses had such long willies but didn't dare. Afterwards, when he saw riding horses or pictures of beautiful horses, the strange feeling returned. Later, when he'd started noticing girls and imagining the contours of their bodies under their clothes, the experience he'd felt looking at the horses came back to him. He realized that he'd had his first sexual thrill while looking at a horse, although he couldn't explain why at that time the body of a horse affected him more strongly than the bodies of the naked or almost naked women he could see in art books and on the beach. Yet at the time art-book depictions of horses fascinated him as much as those of naked women.

He stopped among the sickly Siberian pea trees, lit a cigarette, sat down on the old crooked stone post and eyed the riders. Against his will, his thoughts turned to sexual eccentricities and perversities, as they were known. Homosexuality, which today had unexpectedly become such a problem following his meeting with Madame, a problem even in his special relationship with the Teacher. But he did not wish to dwell on that any longer. He remembered other keywords such as fetishism, sadism, voyeurism, exhibitionism and so on. A medical student planning to specialize in psychiatry had once explained that there was at least one such perversion in everyone, and that the best basis on which to describe an individual's personality was the sexual perversity to which he was inclined.

So what was his sexual perversity? At the time he had thought through the keywords, looked them up in a medical encyclopaedia but had not been able to categorize himself under any one of them. Did that mean he was abnormal, a pervert with no perverse proclivities? Or was his attachment to the Teacher homosexuality? No, perhaps the homo part was right but not the sexuality bit. He believed he knew what sexual passion, lust, was, although he could not yet say the same for sexual satisfaction. There was nothing in his feelings for the Teacher, strong as they were (and they undoubtedly were), that resembled his feelings for Ester. And Malle. Love, yes, but not sexual love. No perversity. It was very likely that the theory he had heard from the young medic didn't fit. Either that or his perversities were simply very suppressed.

But then again. Perhaps . . . the horses that he had been watching. The sleek, taut haunches of the horses that swayed to the rhythm of the trotting, the swaggering odour of sweat that so excited bees but could excite and arouse a person, too. The penis dangling below the stallion's belly . . . Yes, there was something in that. Something that could be called 'hippophilia', a form of zoophilia – love of animals. It hadn't occurred to him, but now he couldn't take it seriously. Perhaps the body shape of the horse alone was most similar to a person, reminiscent of a woman's body, the parts of a woman's body that work on a man's instincts, only more piercingly, more strongly.

It was probably more logical to think that way. He at least could not imagine sexual relations between a person and a horse, although somewhere he had heard once that at the end of her life Catherine the Great used to engage in such practices and even died of an injury caused during coitus with a stallion. Had the person who told the story or invented it ever seen a stallion and its cock? Hardly. He had, although he had not seen Catherine . . .

The feeling was coming over him that his thoughts were changing, evidently because of the day's long, trying experiences – becoming weirder, strongly reminiscent of Aleks's. Perhaps Aleks suffered with chronic fatigue and hyperexcitement syndrome, and it rather dimmed his logic and gave free rein to associative thinking. He could pursue this no further, however, as he would soon have to go to Ester's. To Ester's. That changed everything, even the thought of Ester was like a blast of fresh, cool wind to a brain reeling under stale imagery.

There was still time enough to go down the hill to the river and walk or sit there for a while. The city came to an abrupt end here by the old manor houses; at the bottom of the hill there was a glade of willow thicket, a dumping ground where they had hung out in their childhood and sometimes found interesting things like a thin gravel path alongside a deep ditch. Right here, barely a kilometre from the most stylish district of Tartu, there was a paradise for frogs, nightingales, stray cats and drunks. There was also a romantic little spot for the drunks – a little inn by the river where the formal beach ended and the wild woodland began on the bank. He and the colonel had once celebrated exam success in the inn and fraternized.

The inn was open now. There were still a couple of tables outside in the fresh air under the awning – fortunately none of his friends was there, although the riverside drinking place was popular with students. Right now, though, he didn't want to see or mix with anyone – except Ester. With that he hopped across the ditch to a drier place and walked along the narrow path that led to the river. The water here was perfectly clean; the city sewers were downstream. At the end of school he would come here with a couple of friends for a swim: it was more peaceful, with fewer people, fewer sunbathers, although occasionally they would come across lovers in the bushes. In general, though, the meadow and the riverbank were a little too wild for lovers: damp, full of nettles, meadowsweet and cabbage thistles, chest-high in places. The riverbank itself was fairly steep, peaty and crumbled into the river in places, sometimes taking the willow thickets with it which would continue to grow in the water until the spring ice tore them from the bank and carried them downstream with other litter.

The river in springtime had always fascinated him. The river as it was now, in late summer or early autumn, was an entirely different creature: shallow, lazy, featureless, filthy water. But in spring it was vigorous, broad and gushing. The ice dragged sections of pontoon bridge along, threatened to destroy the wooden bridge near the market hall, flooded the low-lying streets and gardens in Supilinn district, forcing people to use boats to travel from one building to the next; carried support structures downstream as well as bushes, boards, even vestiges of shacks or barns that it had lashed and dislodged. In spring the river was mutinous, full of the urge to destroy, scour, carry away everything that lay before it on which it focused its might. He had sympathy for the river in that state; it stirred him to mutiny, too. He dreamt that the water would carry both bridges off and flood the whole of the lower city. The river helped to awaken the mutineer, the revolutionary within him, who could not have tolerated the restraint and inertia of both water and city in summer; could not, in fact, have tolerated that city, this city, this life, this country at all. At that time he did not engage in self-analysis, much less in moral evaluation of his own rebelliousness, chief among which nestled the desire for destruction, a yearning for catastrophe, as he now had to acknowledge in hindsight. He understood this more clearly at secondary school when he went to Riia Hill to watch the main building of the Academy of Agriculture burning. He had started to observe himself by then and could not help but notice that something within him yearned for the fire to vent its rage, for the blaze to engulf the large building completely. He wasn't a pyromaniac, although a pyromaniac lived within him. After the fire he was better able to understand the spirit of true pyromaniacs. The urge within them was simply greater and stronger, so strong that it overshadowed and overpowered everything else. It was as simple as that. He couldn't guess how many of his friends, how many people carried something of a pyromaniac, a flood fanatic, a luster after disasters within themselves. But there were definitely more than you might think, more than the people concerned dared admit to themselves and others.

He stood for a while by an old bonfire site on the riverbank. It was peaty here, too, eroded by the freshet; it would probably crumble into the river next spring. Once in his childhood he had read that this was how rivers eroded one of their banks – he could no longer remember which one – and thereby gradually changed course. If that was the case here, then a hundred years ago the riverbank would have been a little way further off and courting students could have walked along the path that was no longer there; now it was the place where the muddy water lazily lapped among pondweed and water-lily leaves. The Emajõgi was not his river, even though he had grown up on its banks and had rowed along it several times, once as a boy with a neighbour and his friend for quite a distance downstream to Porijõgi. Yet there was always something alien about the river and the riverside landscape. He felt he didn't belong here, that this wasn't his proper place, unlike on the banks of the river Võhandu in Võrumaa or the banks of the Ahja. Nevertheless, the water here, torpid though it was, was water still, and the pondweed and water-lilies were the same as they were there, at home – the lost home, as he was almost ready to call it. If you could just watch the slow, southwards flowing, shallow water, forgetting the surroundings with the tins sooty from the campfire and the fish bones in them, forgetting the power lines over the river and the riverside inn, you could find company in the river, you could give something of your own worries, distress and weariness to it for it to carry away downstream.

The thought came unexpectedly, in a blink of an eye, and carried off a whole series of hurried but clear memories and fantasies. Didn't poetry have something to do with a flow? Wasn't an elegy originally a song sung by flowing water so that sorrow could be made to flow in the form of a poem, allowing the river to grasp it and carry it off to a far-away place, to the sea, which is the end and the beginning of everything? The sea as death and rebirth; the sea from which we originate and which for followers of Jung is a symbol of death. The globe's waters, tides, streams like a single great bloodstream, incorporating the ancient, languorous Emajõgi here to which he, too, was linked.

Now, suddenly, naturally yet surprisingly, his memory took him back to that summer's day in Võrumaa when while swimming downstream he had experienced something very strange and powerful that he had been able to describe only as the This. The memory returned with startling force and brought with it a desire to strip off his clothes and allow the languid tides of the Emajõgi, Mother River, *Mater Acquarum*, to carry him downstream. He was almost sure that he would find the This again, would find something that could change him and everything else infinitely. For a few moments he stood there in surprise, frightened, not knowing what to do. The call of the river, the mystic call was strong, almost irresistible, yet something within him was resisting it, trying to explain that this time the call was dangerous, the water was cold and polluted; even if he found the This while swimming towards the city or past it, he would not emerge on to the bank alive. What or who was this voice of caution, the voice of reason frolicking in his ear? Was it the everlasting wisdom of his own body, stirred by danger, trying to assert itself?

His hand, which was already undoing his jacket buttons, froze on the spot and fell back down. Now came dismay, true fear. There was nothing mystical in the desire to cast himself into the bosom of the water-mother, rather it was simply a wish to disappear, die, dissolve. This was Thanatos, Eros' twin, hitherto a stranger to him but now suddenly a friend. In a flash he understood the death wish, the desire to die, it was as strong and as irresistible as love. Truly the two concepts belonged together.

So why then did he not want to give himself to Thanatos this time? What was preventing him from going into the river, back to the primitive waters from which we originate? The wisdom of his body? If Freud was to be believed, Thanatos himself is encoded in the body; while someone within him wants to die in this river, this body, this very body wants to love. Love – the desire for someone else's body, the urge to melt into another body; Thanatos – the desire to be free of one's own body, the urge to melt into everything else, the river, the earth, the void. Yet does man really also want to perish in love, in great desire, to perish while melting into another? Are Eros and Thanatos not one and the same, different aspects of the same being, the different faces of one and the same primitive urge? Wasn't the This then one of the faces of Eros-Thanatos? He sensed that it made no difference how he worded the question and answered it; he had understood something, realized something that was previously unknown to him. In the river of late summer and early autumn he had found his lust for death, for his own death. But only for a short while; it wasn't time for that yet. Perhaps, though, the time was close; he had already been given a sign. Perhaps it was simpler than this: today's interrogation had upset him, aroused in him old fears and brought new fears to the fore. There in the office he had felt more than ever before the desire he had known in his childhood to disappear, vanish, melt away, become someone else.

Perhaps he should have recognized that his aim, his assertion of self, was liberation from self. He wanted to be someone else or even something else. Right now he could clearly see two paths towards that goal: love and death. They are like parallel lines that lead to infinity and meet somewhere there in infinity as postulated in Lobachevskian geometry. Was there another road apart from love and death that would lead to that goal? Faith? Religion? Now, thanks to the Teacher, Rein and his family, he had had close contact with faith, and it had given rise within him to the anticipation, the hope that there could be something in it. He had begun to have hope in faith, perhaps even to believe in faith. But wasn't love at stake in all this, the thing that Paul had called the greatest of these three: faith, hope and love? Wasn't faith also one of the lines that led to and met in infinity? Wasn't faith actually the same as love, perhaps viewed from a different angle, a different perspective?

Therefore he had his own trinity, but instead of hope he had death. Why, why wasn't hope in his trinity? Was it an error of little faith? Did it come from the fact that he had no faith, only faith in faith? Where, though, could he get faith from if he either had none or not enough? Sometimes people asked God for faith, but his scientifically trained mind protested at this: in order to ask God for something you had to believe in Him; therefore, he would be asking for something he already had and which he therefore no longer needed to ask for. That seemed very simple and logical. Yet nevertheless, he now realized suddenly that perhaps the nature of faith is to abdicate the simple and the logical, to throw off from on high into the bottomless depths, to put his complete trust in God. Faith is, if God is to be trusted more than anything else, knowledge, logic. How was it that he had not come to this understanding before? This was not contrary to science and logic; the one complemented the other, like Einstein's and Newton's theories of physics. Human logic, whether that of a scientist or a farmhand, was only a tiny fragment of the Creator's logic, the logic of the infinite of infinites where opposites could concur, parallels meet and the impossible be possible.

He stood on the riverbank by the bonfire site among the willow bushes and felt tears well up in his eyes and run down his cheeks. And with no thought of anything, merely a feeling of immense gratitude and overcome with surprise, he fell to his knees, put his hands together and prayed, now soundlessly, now in speech, to one whom even now he did not dare name. He knew what to ask for: faith, hope and love. And peace, peace – such an important word in the Bible. Peace. While asking for peace for his spirit he felt how much he needed it, how heavily lack of peace had weighed down on him, how oppressed and torn apart he really was and how that oppression and tearing apart had ruined his relationships with other people, had made him an ill-at-ease, scatterbrained, petulant young man who was not easy to get on with. He was at once ashamed and distressed by what he was, and the joy he sensed at the possibility of being released from it was different in nature, more peaceful, better, more understanding . . . So this was what the Bible called being reborn, becoming new. Only a moment ago he had thought again about the burden of becoming or of being himself and the possibility of being freed from self. Now he had been given that possibility. He had been given faith, if this was faith, and love, if this was love. He had been given a great deal at once and was frighteningly, effusively grateful for it.

'Father, heavenly Father, forgotten, rediscovered . . . I'm talking to You – I feel I can't not talk to You . . . I didn't know how . . . now I do . . . You weren't listening, now You are . . . forgive me for my sins, forgive me for being me, forgive me, give me some of Your peace, Your love, give me faith, hope and love, these three . . . and the greatest of these is love.'

He closed his eyes – he could see nothing clearly through his tears and felt that he was absent, absent from this place, from this moment and from this self. The prayer, if a prayer it was, flowed on by itself, with words and without them, over-flowed with repeated words, the same three: faith, hope and love. And when the prayer returned to love he saw Ester; she was standing before him, smiling. For a moment he did not understand which of them was true: the one he saw with his eyes closed or the one he saw with his eyes open, but that wasn't important for the moment. He smiled back and said, 'You – I'm on my way', and opened his eyes, no longer flowing with tears and saw the same familiar landscape of a torpid river, pondweed, water-lilies and willow bushes. The scene was as before but different, lighter, cleaner, gleaming with a secret yet strong light. He felt the light was within him, too, making him clean and light. He closed his eyes again and saw Ester once more. This time she was more ethereal, almost transparent, as if she were melting into the air. Yet on her ethereal fairy-tale mouth there was still a smile and in that smile an invitation. Ester. He loved Ester. Ester was the personification of love. Love was Ester. He looked at his watch. Time had now moved more than enough for him to be able to go and call on her.

26

By the time he reached the courtyard gate all that was left from the ecstasy of prayer was something that was both weariness and alertness. His thoughts flowed readily, although they gradually diminished in number, rather like stars in the morning sky. Absent, though – and this was a source of satisfaction – were worries and fears. For almost the first time in his life he felt free. He was free, and he was on his way to Ester's.

The gate opened with a creak as it had done that time for Rein, and again the sound of a dog barking came from the building; it could evidently hear the creaking through the window or door. Someone drew back a curtain, and he saw the face he had seen earlier in his mind's eye. Ester smiled and waved to him. When he reached the door, wondering for a moment whether he should knock or just enter, she was already there.

'It's great that you could come round,' she said. 'Come on in. Would you like a cup of tea?'

Ester went into the kitchen to put the kettle on the gas stove. He sat down on the sofa and looked around the room, in which he immediately felt comfortable. The board ceiling was low and on a slight slant, and from it there hung an old-fashioned lamp with a cloth shade; on the wall there was a painting of some exotic scenery, a couple of enlarged framed photographs, and by the wall with the faded flowered wallpaper there was a bookshelf on which stood Brehm's *Das Tierreich*. Rag carpets covered most of the floor and a large Chinese birch tree stood in one corner. On the windowsill behind the net curtain he could see the crimson blooms of a geranium.

'So this is where I live,' said Ester, re-entering the room. 'But I haven't changed things much; it's all more or less as my aunt had it, fairly bourgeois and old fashioned. Would you mind if I let Tuki in for a bit? He's not going to calm down until he's had a good sniff and wagged his tail at the visitor. He's a good little dog. He never goes for anyone. You're not scared of dogs, are you?'

They could hear the dog whimpering somewhere. No indeed, he was not afraid of dogs, and Tuki, when allowed into the room to meet the visitor, was one of the least scary dogs he had ever met. He was a tiny, slightly overfed little thing with a short coat whose ancestors obviously included dachshunds and terriers. He wagged his tail furiously, tried to lick his hand, stood on his hind legs, barked once from sheer joy, scuttled around the floor and flung himself down on the rug next to the visitor.

'You've now been accepted as a member of the pack. Dogs treat us as equals, and dogs are pack animals, just like people.'

With her biology training Ester's knowledge was obviously superior to his. He said that he didn't know much about dogs; they'd never had one. But his impression had been that people often regard dogs and cats as equals; they talk to them and describe them as their best and most faithful friends . . .

'It'd be interesting to know whether they view us in the same way, don't you think?' he asked, feeling even more at home – so much at home that his recent ecstasy seemed to be quickly evaporating to be replaced with peaceful, comfortable clarity of mind. He was at Ester's, and it was just good to be with her. It removed any reason to worry about how to tell her the real purpose of his visit.

They chatted a bit more about cats and dogs. Ester, who had grown up in the countryside, had more memories to recount than he did, of course. Then the water came to the boil so Ester made a pot of tea and returned with two cups and a dish of biscuits on a tray which she set down on the table.

This was the best moment to start the conversation. But before he was able to do so, Ester asked, 'How've things been? Are you off to the collective farm?'

'No, not tomorrow anyhow,' he had to confess.

'But isn't your group leaving tomorrow?'

'Yes, they are, but I'm stopping here.' He saw from her surprised look that he could not avoid a more lengthy explanation. 'I've got mixed up in some trouble that needs sorting out first. I don't really want to talk about it, but it'll probably come out anyhow. I had a collection by Under that I'd got from Alo. I copied it out and gave it to a friend to read. He in turn lent it out, and in the end someone went blabbing to the KGB, and now they're interrogating people, and it's finally got around to my turn. I was interrogated at their offices this morning . . . Tomorrow I have to go to the university *partorg* for coffee. So I'm staying in town for the time being.'

The surprise in Ester's eyes had been replaced by fear. 'Good heavens! So reading Under's poetry and copying it out isn't allowed? But she's already been published here, if I remember correctly.'

'She has indeed, but they found a couple of poems in the collection which some expert has apparently declared to be anti-Soviet. And now they're saying that I, along with others, have been disseminating anti-Soviet material, tantamount to anti-Soviet propaganda, and that's something they have to treat seriously.'

A hush so profound fell on the room that they could hear their own and Tuki's breathing.

'Oh my God, then Alo will be in trouble!' cried Ester.

'I hope it won't come to that,' he replied. 'They don't know that I got the Under from him.'

'So you haven't told them? If you refuse to tell them where you got the poems something really bad will happen to you.'

'I didn't refuse. I had a story ready for them, and I hope they'll believe it. And I've got the feeling that for some reason they aren't taking all this deadly seriously. They'll bring it to a formal conclusion, do what their duty requires without ferreting about too much.'

'It's so wonderful that you did that. Now Alo will definitely hold you in the highest regard . . . But if something goes wrong then what will happen?'

'I don't know, I don't believe it will. I've got the feeling that it won't go wrong, I'll come through it all somehow. We'll see. The only thing they can do is send me down and pack me off to the army for a couple of years.'

He said all this utterly dispassionately, as if none of it was anything to do with him particularly. The only thing that mattered was Ester, the fact that he was with her and that her beautiful eyes were looking at him, filled with admiration, amazement, respect and perhaps even something more. The something more was the thing that mattered most. He wanted to talk about that more than the KGB, university and the rest. And now was the best moment to do so.

'Ester, you know, I wasn't really thinking of that. I don't really care about it. I don't want you to say anything about this mess to Alo and Ellen; they've got their own worries and their knowing about the trouble the Under has caused won't change anything. Perhaps one day when all this is over they can be told. But . . . there was something else I had to tell you . . . I was so happy to be with you in the countryside, I am now as well . . . I would very much like to be more to you, perhaps for ever. To put it briefly, I've probably fallen in love with you. Ever since I met you there in the summer. And today I realized that nothing else really matters to me.'

His declaration of love came out more eloquently and more sincerely than he could have imagined. It came almost as a surprise to him and, of course, to Ester, who stared straight at him, dumbfounded. Finally she turned her head and said quietly, in a strangely soundless voice, 'The tea must be brewed by now, I'll pour it . . . Do you take sugar?'

They drank in silence, then he asked her, 'I've obviously startled you. I didn't mean to, but I couldn't not say what I've said, I just couldn't. I hope it wasn't wrong of me.'

'No, it wasn't,' said Ester rapidly. 'But you have startled me a bit. I didn't realize you . . . I thought we were just good friends.'

'And you don't want us to be anything more?' he asked.

Ester poured more tea in silence and offered him the sugar basin, sat on the sofa next to him, although slightly further away, as if avoiding any contact, and then without raising her eyes from her teacup or turning her head said, 'It's really difficult for me to give you an answer at the moment. I'm in a difficult position at the moment, and the stuff you told me just now makes it even more difficult . . . That doesn't mean that I'm not pleased about it, quite the opposite . . . I would like to say something very positive and eloquent about it . . . But right now I can't, please believe me, I really can't right now.'

He sat, unable suddenly to stir himself to say anything. There was a single germ of thought in his head: this must be what it's like to be paralysed. There was something awry with his perception of time as well – when, later, he made a great effort to stretch his arm out for the teacup he could not say whether a couple of seconds or a full minute had gone by. Yet the paralysis ceased with his arm movement, and there were words in his mouth that he couldn't say, yet couldn't leave unsaid. 'I don't understand.'

'Forgive me, I can't tell you everything now. I . . . do care for you, but . . . there's someone who's having a lot of problems at the moment, someone I have to help; there's nothing else I can do.'

Strange that it had never occurred to him that Ester might have someone else. That was called male egotism. Someone else? Someone who had a lot of problems *at the moment* . . . It must be some man, someone preventing Ester from saying she felt the same way as he did. *At the moment.* What about later?

'I really want to properly understand what you said, but I just don't. I just want . . . I just want to ask one more thing: does the *at the moment* thing, does that mean that in future . . . that I can hope? I've heard I might have to go to Moscow or Leningrad; they might offer me the chance to go there to study Indian languages . . . But how can I leave if . . . if you're still here?'

If the Moscow–Leningrad option Madame mentioned came off he would no longer be able to be with Ester. It was almost impossible to contemplate, yet . . .

She looked straight at him and gave him a smile. Bashfully, but a smile none the less. 'Do you really want so much to hope that I . . . ?'

'Yes, I do.' There was nothing else he could have said.

'I'm glad about that. Believe me. We're friends, aren't we, and we'll stay friends, whatever happens?'

The let's-stay-friends option was something he didn't want to hear, something that was too reminiscent of what – in books and films, as he had not had this kind of experience in life – spouses tell partners they are planning to desert . . . But what could he expect from Ester? What right or reason did he have to think that she should fall into his arms immediately after his unexpected declaration of love? He had told her what he felt, and now all he could do was wait. And have faith. And hope. Love may be the greatest of these, but what could love do without faith and hope?

They sat for a few moments in silence again, then Ester looked straight at him once more and said, 'But . . . You've already got a girlfriend. I don't know where I heard it from, but someone told me, someone who would know. Perhaps it was Ellen. She's always up on these things.'

The question was unexpected, but he could perhaps infer from it that she was not indifferent to him; she cared whether he had a girlfriend . . .

'I've a friend, yes, a girl friend – but nothing more. I wouldn't be able to tell her I love her.'

'Oh, I'm sure you have,' Ester teased, smiling to make sure the teasing didn't offend.

'I don't remember . . . But even if I had done, would that change anything that matters?'

'No, I don't know, I don't think so . . . No, it definitely wouldn't.' This he was pleased to hear.

'So this other thing . . . the person you were talking about . . . ?' He couldn't not ask, although he felt that he shouldn't really.

'Yes' was Ester's simple answer.

'Has . . . Has this person also said he's in love with you?'

'Please don't ask such questions. Not at the moment. Perhaps one day. But at the moment we're friends, aren't we?'

'All right, I shan't ask any more. We're friends. Can I still call round and see you from time to time?'

'Of course, any time. I'd be delighted, really delighted.'

This reply was so comforting, even reassuring, that he took Ester's hand in his. She didn't move her hand away, although she did not respond to his gesture: her hand in his was warm and limp. For a few moments he held it in his and then released it carefully. As he let it go Ester's hand suddenly suddenly came to life, squeezed his hand tightly and then drew firmly away.

Ester had simultaneously encouraged him and rejected him. Suddenly the thought went through his head that perhaps he should do what people whom he had reason to regard as older and more experienced would do: persist, take her hand again, kiss it, embrace her . . . Something he would have liked to do in the countryside but had been halted by his self-consciousness. Yet his hesitation now was not really down to self-consciousness; it was a reluctance to do anything that might appear rude, coarse like someone from a slum. Ester was not the type, couldn't be the type, who expected advances to be made. They were friends, friends by all means, and their friendship made zealous advances impossible.

Now, though, it was time to go. He could feel weariness sapping his strength, and nothing he might still say or do was quite appropriate any more. Too much for one day. For him and his love, faith and hope. And for the God whom he'd perhaps met there on the riverbank – and who had now disappeared again somewhere up above beyond the skies, leaving him alone with his feelings and weariness.

As he walked homewards he thought that this had probably been the most trying day of his life. Of his life so far, for who knew what the future would bring?

27

The *partorg*'s office was on the second floor. He gave the secretary his name and said that he had been asked to come in for a chat. The secretary went into the office, came back and said that the *partorg* had asked him to take a seat for five minutes and wait to be called in. He didn't like the idea of waiting and stewing at the door, but he had to agree. He sat down by the window looking out on to the corner of the cinema and the bookshop sign. A pigeon was drowsing on the sill outside – perhaps it was ill, perhaps just warming itself in the morning sun. He tried to breathe calmly and deeply and focus on happy memories. There weren't all that many of them. He realized suddenly that so far in his life there had been few happy things to latch on to in times of strife. What sort of life was this? What was the value of a life without happy, comforting memories? Had he ever really lived, or had he only ever made preparations for living?

Just one day ago he had thought of Ester, but now, after the previous day's meeting, the bright image of her in his memory had become more foggy and blurred. The thought of Ester made his heart beat faster but also flutter in pain. He didn't know whether she loved him. God, faith, the This – it now was strange for him to think of it all. Yesterday's ecstasy, turning to God, seemed oppressive and somehow inappropriate here by the embarrassingly white window of the Party office next to which stood a pot containing a large, slightly shrivelled Epi hybrid cactus. He wondered whether here in these offices, following Soviet protocol, they called it a 'Christmas' cactus or instead had to refer to it as a 'frost' cactus . . .

The office door opened, and the dean of his faculty emerged with the *partorg*. He stood up and said hello. The dean responded with a slight nod of the head. The *partorg* bid the dean goodbye with a handshake, walked jauntily towards him, squeezed his hand and said, 'Please come on in. We need to have a little chat.'

There was something in the office that reminded him of the KGB investigator's. Lenin was on the wall rather than Dzerzhinski, and the glass-fronted bookcase contained dozens of Lenin's works and several books with coloured bindings that bore the letters ESSR – Estonian Soviet Socialist Republic. He had only ever seen the *partorg* fleetingly before, once when he had made an impassioned speech about how US imperialists were devising an evil plot against Revolutionary Cuba and once at the university Young Communist League conference where he welcomed young Communists on behalf of the old. His job was doubtless some Marxist subject, probably teaching Party history. He was a generally inconspicuous man about whom no one really had anything to say. Perhaps that was why he had been appointed *partorg*, he thought, as they sat down opposite one another at the desk.

'There is obviously no need to explain why I have asked you to come and see me,' the *partorg* began. 'Our bodies inform us of all matters of importance affecting the university population – especially its students, of course, our future specialists. You must already have realized that it is of great importance that whoever picks up the baton, so to speak, from us is someone who undertakes to pursue what we have struggled for – to build Communism.'

He nodded politely, rebuffing the wicked phrase 'Communism, so to speak' that had popped into his head.

The man behind the desk continued, apparently in complete sincerity. 'Of course, nurturing young minds is a complex challenge; it is not, shall we say, a piece of cake. A person is a complex thing, a complex machine, and believe me, even I – and I have spent many years involved in nurturing and teaching people – even I have to acknowledge now and again that I still don't know everything, far from it, and that even I, a teacher and nurturer, have a lot to learn. As you know, Maxim Gorky called writers "engineers of the human soul". Gorky was, of course, a great, intelligent man, but now and again I think that he did a disservice to us pedagogues. Naturally, I don't mean to devalue writers, but, in any event, we, as pedagogues, also deserve the respectful title of "engineers of the human soul". I repeat, I have no wish to badmouth writers, but we should probably consider that a writer deals directly in words which are subsequently printed, bound in a book, sold in a shop and are delivered to a reader for him to read and interpret in the light of his own views. Yes, his own views, his own convictions. And now we must ask, where did this reader, this citizen, acquire his views and convictions? What do you say on that point?'

The question was unexpected but wasn't difficult to answer. 'At home, from his family, school and friends.'

'Correct,' the *partorg* went on. 'You are absolutely correct, although I would have added the media and literature. And the cinema, of course. But that's of little consequence; in general you are absolutely correct. And as you can imagine one of the items on that list is of greater concern to me as a pedagogue: school. And, naturally, university. We accept the material, so to speak, as delivered to us by homes and schools, and we have five years in which to mould it into young specialists, our future, the builders of our Communist society. Do you understand the nature of our responsibility?'

He did not know whether the question was rhetorical or otherwise, but he nodded anyway.

'That's the way things are. If a young specialist works hard he is commended, but it is rare for anyone to utter a word of thanks to us, the little engineers of human souls. But if a specialist should, so to speak, not succeed, fail to do his duty, then we are the ones immediately accused, the ones they point the finger at, the ones who are told that we haven't done our job properly. We are the ones churning out pedagogical dross, so to speak. No one asks us what the future specialist was like when he was delivered to us from home or school, the kind of person home and school had already turned him into. No, we are expected to work without rejects, to make anyone who steps through the university gates into an excellent specialist, a thoroughbred builder of Communism. They almost expect miracles of us, and when no miracle transpires, if we turn out a young specialist who is not a specialist, whose views are not those of a Soviet citizen, who is religious – oh yes, there have even been cases where some of our graduates later turned out to be religious – then we are the ones held responsible; the principal responsibility always lies with us. Now you tell me – you have a calling to be a teacher, a nurturer, you have to nurture the next generation, perhaps the university here even needs you; we can never have too many good lecturers – now you tell me what we should do, what we should say to the people pointing the finger at us and saying, "Look. Tartu State University is not up to its job; Tartu State University cannot train specialists with sufficiently high standards of qualifications or the moral stature society requires."'

The *partorg* paused, looked him in the eye and, without waiting for a reply, continued, 'Oh no, I'm not exaggerating. That's what people have said; that's what people are saying. That and more. They're saying that perhaps it's not right for there to be a university here in Tartu at all, a small city where bourgeois vestiges still abound, where there's little contact with our major centres of knowledge and Party leadership is weak. Perhaps the university should simply be moved away, to Tallinn maybe, or even Riga. The requirement of the times is for the medium of higher education for young people to be Russian, a language of which there is not sufficient mastery here in Tartu. Just look what they are saying to us, every time some misfortune, as one might call it, occurs.'

The *partorg* drew a packet of Priima out of his pocket, removed a cigarette and extended the packet towards him. 'Do you smoke?'

He took a cigarette mechanically, although he did not actually want it. The *partorg* lit both cigarettes and carried on. 'Huh, there's actually nothing commendable in smoking. I strongly urge you to give it up while you still can. Too late for me. I started during the war. I always shared tobacco with a friend until he was killed and left me his share. That's how I started, in memory of what one might call a fallen comrade. Yes, that's how it was . . . but unfortunately what we're dealing with today is a different kind of story. As I was saying, we at the university are occasionally on the receiving end of reproaches. Because of what one might call our pedagogical dross. And things have reached the point now that we are being asked, "we" being me – *partorg* – the rector and your dean and the *partorg* in your faculty, "What is happening in the university? Is what we've heard true that you're involved in duplicating and disseminating anti-Soviet material?" And what have I, the rector and others to say about it? And what should the rector do with you and the others who were caught with this anti-Soviet material?'

The man at the other side of the desk paused again, for a bit longer this time, and looked him straight in the eye through a haze of smoke. He was unable to do anything but respond in kindr.

They looked at each other in earnest for a few moments, then the *partorg* went on, 'The simplest thing, of course, would be for the rector to issue a directive. Saying that X and Y have been dishonourably sent down for activities bringing the good name of Soviet university students into disrepute. You would have to leave, at least for a while. Either to find a job or to join the Soviet Army. I think you would learn something in either one of those that you can't learn from books. You would learn what we would call scientific Communism in practice. Indeed, that's one option and, in our view, the simplest. Furthermore the "sending down", as you would term it, would not be final. In a few years you may, as a mature young man who has seen something of life, apply to be accepted back into the university. We would consider the matter in conjunction with character references from the army or workplace, and in the event that they were positive there would be no serious impediment to your returning. And no one would have any reason to say that the university administration had been soft, so to speak, on anti-Soviet activities or even promoted them. Hmm, now you tell me, is there any good reason why we should not send you down?'

Another rhetorical question he was unable to answer, not that the man across the desk was expecting him to.

The *partorg* took two deep puffs and continued, 'Of course, you have nothing positive to say in response. But I hope that at the very least you have understood the seriousness of your mistake.'

Another pause. He looked at the questioner and nodded and felt both relief and shame in so doing. At least the conversation was moving in a more specific direction and offered some hope that he would not be sent down.

The *partorg* carried on, 'Right, I believe that your nod can be interpreted as agreement. That's good. Now our conversation can move on. As I was saying, we must, whether we want to or not, take responsibility for the products, so to speak, that are setting off in life from these walls. And this is where the old proverb comes in: better be careful than have cause to sigh later. It is never too late to remember this saying, although it always unfortunately turns out that when there is reason to sigh we only then remember that we failed to be careful. Specifically, when a young specialist, a university student, has a problem, his tutors, nurturers, must ask what they know about this person. When I was informed of this problem of yours I immediately asked the *partorg* of your faculty to come to see me and talked to your year tutor. And, as I feared, it emerged that neither of them knew very much about you. The people who should have been most directly involved in nurturing and teaching you did not know what sort of person you are. I can say that this was a genuine surprise to me. As far as I knew and as they had heard, you aren't exactly a quiet goody-goody, a crammer, so to speak, but a gifted young man with interests who gets around, has many friends and a certain authority on the course. Yet they could tell me nothing more. This does not leave me with a great deal to work on when trying to ascertain who this particular "problem student" is. And that, essentially, is why I invited you here today.'

The *partorg* now adopted, he felt, more the tone of the interrogator.

'Tell me a bit about your parents, your family, where you grew up. Although we attach importance to people's background – many have had to suffer for it – it cannot be denied that the environment in which someone is brought up has an important role to play in how they turn out. So, I know that your mother is a teacher and your father was the subject of repression measures. Perhaps you can say a bit more about them.'

'What are you interested in, specifically?' he asked.

'Specifically . . . well, for example, where they were from originally, what they did in the bourgeois period, what was their view of the world, as far as you know.'

So this was what they were after. The KGB was an ordinary police force, even if its master here wanted it to be a thought police, to access his and his parents' thoughts.

His mother was the easier. He said that she had been born in Valga, the daughter of a tradesman, then was educated in Tartu, finished university there while also learning singing and piano and had visited Germany and Italy to improve herself. In Germany she met a Russian university student whose parents also lived in Estonia. They married, but his father was arrested in 1941 and died at some point during the war in a camp. His mother had had problems because of her husband. She couldn't get work in her field of training so worked as a hospital attendant and as a German teacher by Lake Peipsi. After Stalin's death (rather than use these words he referred to the 'exposure of the personality cult', just in case), she came back here to work as a teacher in a secondary school.

The thought policeman nodded, perhaps mechanically, perhaps even in approval, but he was interested in certain details. Were his grandparents, on either the Russian or Estonian side, involved in politics? Were they members of certain parties or organizations? And what was his father arrested for, and had he now been rehabilitated? He did not reply to the first question. Grandfather had, in fact, been a member of the city council but definitely not as a social democrat – that much he knew. But as to which party he had belonged he did not know. He had the impression that Grandfather had been sympathetic to Tõnisson, but he had to confess that he didn't know much about Estonian history and politics of the 1930s. They had been taught nothing about it at school. Grandfather definitely hadn't been a Fascist; he had heard him voice plenty of criticism of the Fascists and perhaps even of Päts and Laidoner. It was useful to mention this here, even in passing. This appeared to satisfy the *partorg*. Things were more complex where his Russian grandfather was concerned. He had never seen him. His grandfather died a year before his mother and father married. His grandmother died straight after the war; he was only a small boy at the time and dimly remembered her coming to visit them and talking to his mother in Russian and to him in a strange kind of Estonian. She had only kissed and cuddled him, making him feel both very happy and slightly embarrassed at the same time. His mother did not take him to his grandmother's funeral: she was buried in Tallinn, and after her death he no longer had any close Russian relatives in Estonia. There was Aunt Veera, his father's cousin in Leningrad, whom he had visited a couple of times with his mother, as they had his godmother and her Sergei. But as to why his father was arrested he did not know.

He understood that these were things his mother didn't want to discuss. They had been informed by reliable sources that his father had died. Someone had been with him in the sick-bay and remembered the night when he passed away. The man had visited them when he was released; he had been asked by his father before he died to find his wife and child. The man said that his father had been very hurt by the fact that he was imprisoned as an enemy of the people when others were fighting for their homeland. He had applied to be sent to the front line on a couple of occasions; he'd said he could act as an interpreter as he knew German and had served in the army of the Estonian Republic. He should, of course, have left those two facts out – at the time either one of them was enough for him to be named an enemy of the people. He wasn't allowed to go to the front, his homeland could defend itself without him and German prisoners were apparently to be interrogated by people with hardly any knowledge of German. He did forestry work until it broke him. He became weak from malnutrition, contracted typhus and died.

The *partorg* listened and nodded now and again. When he had finished the office filled with silence for a few moments and then the *partorg* turned his gaze upon him again and said, slightly more quietly, in a different voice, 'Yes, I understand. Your family hasn't had it easy. It's tragic that so many people who could have served the homeland at the front were unable to do so. I believe that, whatever your father's past and his background, he was a patriot in those difficult times. There were unfortunately many like him among the armed forces, the higher officer corps as you perhaps know. I have had some dealings on this subject, helped historians find information in the archives – I even felt a mild interest, so to speak, in the area. And as someone who served in the war I would venture to suggest that, going by my own experiences, the reason we suffered so many losses at the beginning of the war was that we didn't have enough capable, experienced officers.'

The *partorg* paused, offered him a cigarette, took one for himself, lit them and continued again in his more confident *partorg* voice.

'But, young man, these tragic events, these unfair human fates, must not make mourners of us. Quite the reverse, we must learn from the past and its mistakes. And, as you know, as we all know, our country has learnt from its mistakes, as has the Party – although perhaps I should not quite express it that way . . . Perhaps you don't know your history very well or do not recognize how unprecedented the denunciation of the cult of personality by the Party was, how extraordinary a document Comrade Khrushchev's speech at the Twentieth Party Congress was. You presumably are not aware that there were certain Communists who thought that the personality cult around Stalin should not be spoken of, that it would confuse people; it would create the danger of a split in the international Communist movement. Even certain non-Communists, respected Western intellectuals, took that view. But the Party, our Politburo, took this brave step; it was able to criticize what it had done in the past. Of course, I should reiterate that these mistakes, these tragic events, must not obscure the magnitude of our achievements, the fact that steps were taken in our country to found a completely new society for the very first time, to do something that had never been done before, to initiate, so to speak, the new history. It was inevitable that mistakes would be made during that process and we must be prepared to recognize and rectify them. Our Party has demonstrated as much to the world, and this gives us the confidence and courage to believe that our road is the correct one and that the future belongs to us.'

Here the *partorg* paused again and inhaled deeply on his cigarette.

'But let's put history to one side and come back to the matter that brought us here. I was talking about the future, but before the future there is the past, the past with its own shadows, so to speak. And none of us is free of such shadows; they travel with us for a long time. Oh yes, they follow you as well as me. I am a human being just like you, and, as the Ancient Romans said, to err is human. And we must think how we can rectify these errors, put them right, how to be liberated from the shadows of the past.

'I have heard that you have recently made repeated visits to a religious person, specifically the theologian —' and he gave the Teacher's surname. 'Other religious people, by the way, have spoken of your friendship, and one of them has even said that you may wish to take one of their religious knowledge courses, the type of course that prepares people for the ministry. That's what they say. Now, as you will understand, faith and the Church are hiding places from the past that are very difficult to break away from. This rumour came to my attention, and, to be frank, it made me somewhat concerned, especially in the light of this other matter. I would therefore be grateful if you would tell me whether there is any foundation to the rumour. Whether and in what regard you are associated with this theologian.'

This was something he had not anticipated. Even his visits to the Teacher were known here. For a moment he was confused and didn't know what to say, but only for a moment. Fortunately he had not directly told anyone he was planning to go there to study. He had only asked about the courses. So he could reply with a clear conscience, 'Yes, I've visited him several times, but the rumours that I'm planning to study for the ministry have been plucked out of thin air.' (He felt a strong temptation to say 'plucked out of thin air, so to speak'.) 'Doctor — is probably the only expert on Indian languages in Estonia, and I'm quite interested in them. And, of course, he's also an exceptionally erudite expert in philology and mythology in general.'

The *partorg* nodded and seemed to think for a moment. He, however, was reminded as if by a blinding light both of his experiences that summer, his recent anguish and of the ecstasy on the banks of the Emajõgi. Mixed in with all this there was repentance or, rather, fear: had he now for no reason easily denied his faith, his God, his truth? Here and now he should perhaps admit to the *partorg* that he had turned to God, discovered the truth of religion for himself? No, such an admission would be odd; it would feel absurd to him and, obviously, to his interlocutor. Was all this then a mere illusion, a passing spiritual conflagration. Was he, in fact, a manic depressive for ever seesawing between ecstasy and despair?

He had no more time to reflect on himself. The *partorg* had finished thinking and went on, 'Yes, I believe I understand. Although I'm not sure whether I can explain this to the others. It has just so happened that these two incidents have occurred at the same time and both are linked to shadows of the past, and both of them are casting shadows, so to speak, over you. Yes, I've listened to what's known about your friend; I've listened to negative things and positive things. By the by, some long-standing Communists have spoken positively of him, people he helped in his own way at the end of the bourgeois period, by the way – and this may surprise you – while delivering underground literature from the West into Estonia. And on the other hand, certain religious people, yes indeed, religious people in particular, have spoken negatively of him. I have certain old friends of my own among the guild, and, let me tell you, they are for ever at each other's throats and very keen to submit written reports on intrigue and complaints. As you presumably know, a single official in our republic deals with them and their problems, specifically the Representative of Religious Affairs in the government. And believe you me, the ministers flock to him – and he a member of the Communist Party of the USSR and an atheist – to complain about each other. I could not dream up any better atheist propaganda myself. I repeat once more, however: it is bad that these two shadows have fallen over you at the same time. Perhaps you understand that the Church is not the only place where people inform on each other. And perhaps you now understand that, in view of what you have done, or even of what has been said about you, we must respond.'

The *partorg* fell completely silent and blew something like a smoke ring into the air. He felt like responding in kind, although he thought it better not to. The *partorg* then looked at him sharply, albeit with the hint of a smile, and as he began to speak there was something in his tone of voice that made him feel relieved.

'So there are these shadows. But now allow me to improvise somewhat. A thought has struck me. How can we move forward? What do we do? But I would first like to ask you one or two things, and I ask you to respond sincerely.'

What did that mean? Had the *partorg* sensed that earlier he had been trying to reply in such a way as to leave an impression of himself as a correct and loyal Soviet citizen? Or was the request simply a rhetorical empty phrase? In any event, he could not be more sincere as the end of the interview apparently approached than he had been at the beginning. It nevertheless seemed that a new note had been struck in the interrogation – it might even become interesting.

The *partorg* continued, 'You said that you have an interest in oriental languages. Indian, if I understood correctly. Have you learnt any Indian languages? Do you plan to? And what are your motives, so to speak, for learning? Can you explain why you are learning them?'

Why? A simple little question-word but a very difficult one to answer. He had had some experience of it when he had babysat a couple of times for Aunt Aino's grandchild, little Ingrid, who was just at that age when children ask 'Why?' He remembered how seeking answers to the child's 'whys?' had been the most tiring thing. At that time, however, his fate had not depended on his answers as it did now, when he had to answer the 'why?' posed by the representative of power. But answer he must.

'Languages and linguistics have interested me ever since I was a child. Even more than literature. And at university I've tried to study some eastern languages as much as I can under the optional system here. At first it was Japanese and Arabic, later Sanskrit –'

'What do you think of the opportunities for learning those languages in our university? Can someone acquire a thorough knowledge of Arabic or an Indian language here, or is it more what you might call amateurish?' interrupted the *partorg*.

He replied that the standard was poor, although the man who taught the languages was undoubtedly very enthusiastic about his field and obviously had a thorough command of several of them.

The *partorg* nodded and then said, 'Yes, I understand. People can say what they will, but my view is that the various optional courses are more like tasters; you can't acquire a thorough grasp through them. And, as far as I know, it is important when learning a language to practise, to have the opportunity to speak, communicate. That's what I believe. But there is a problem with the communication aspect that I spoke to you about extensively, so to speak, just now. As you mentioned, you are interested in – what was it now? – Indian languages and Arabic. That's laudable because, as we know, since their liberation from the colonialists the countries concerned have become independent members of the world's family of nations. The nationalist freedom movement of the recent past brings them naturally closer to our homeland. Delegations are visiting us here, our people are travelling in delegations to India or Egypt, tourism is under development, books are being translated. The matter has, I may tell you, been discussed by the central committee of our Party and the cabinet. And they have decided that there is also a need to train people in our republic in these languages, as well as in the history, literature and other important aspects of the countries where they are spoken. In a word, they would be genuine experts in their field. We are unable to train experts of this kind here in our university, as you must realize. The only real option for the time being is to train them in the centres in Moscow and Leningrad.'

The *partorg* paused again, took a cigarette out of the packet and offered one to him. When the cigarettes were lit, he carried on, 'Perhaps you can see what I'm driving at.'

Oh yes, he certainly could – Madame had been right – but the expression he wore said all this came as a surprise to him. 'I think that if this is accepted . . . on high, so to speak . . . we would be killing two birds with one stone, so to speak. For one thing, we would be acquiring a specialist in the Indian and other local languages, someone who could prove genuinely useful to the republic, who could in future help to train others. Secondly, we would be sending you away from here, away from the various shadows, so to speak, to a centre where you will be able to live in an ideologically healthier and more progressive atmosphere, to study under experts of the highest calibre. This is what I have come up with – to be honest, it's not my idea alone. If you are ready to consider a solution on these lines, so to speak, if you are ready to pursue your education there and requalify in that area – and, of course, staunchly renounce all the various shadows of the past – then we shall proceed in this matter. So tell me what you think.'

All this was still so unexpected that at first he was unable to say a word. Thoughts were running through his head one after the other. The Teacher . . . Ester . . . Malle . . . home . . . Grandfather. He had never previously given any serious thought to going to Moscow or Leningrad to study. He had given no detailed thought to the hint dropped by Madame – he had had too many things to think about yesterday. Despite that, he could perhaps have thought about it. But wasn't the *partorg*'s offer, to the extent that it could be regarded as an offer, ultimately similar to the one made previously by the KGB man? Wasn't he expecting him to accept a similar future – although perhaps at a higher level? Instead of an informer they might make him a spy. Yet, on the other hand, it would be a shame to pass up the opportunity to go to Leningrad. If, of course, he could attend the university and not some special school where they really trained spies. But that might be possible to arrange. He might be able to express a preference. But first he should think. Think and spy out the land. Talk to someone. The Teacher. Ester. Perhaps even to Malle. But at the moment, right now, he could say nothing definite, could give no final answer. That is what he must say.

'What you've just said is completely unexpected. I hope it will not be taken amiss if I think it over before giving you an answer.'

The *partorg* nodded. 'Naturally, naturally. Important decisions merit thought. Perhaps it is clearer to you now what may happen if that simple truth does not stay at the forefront of your mind. Besides, I cannot give you any kind of firm promises at the moment. I hope that everything goes well – conversations have been had with certain people. But anyway, tell me honestly and frankly whether you are ready to come with us, the Party and its policies.'

Again something unexpected and awkward. A choice where there was, in fact, no choice. If he said 'no' it would all be over. Almost certainly. He would have to leave the university, join the army and later do some simple job somewhere. And perhaps the *partorg* was also right from his position. Perhaps the system was really evolving for the better, slowly but surely, perhaps the end result would be better than in the West . . . Such were his thoughts as he realized that he would be both incriminating and justifying himself in the same moment, and that in any event he now had to do something, say something that it would be much more satisfactory to leave unsaid. Yet leaving it unsaid was not an option. So he looked the *partorg* in the eye and uttered the words, 'Yes, I am ready.'

The *partorg* smiled. 'I have unintentionally made you a Pioneer and given you the job of Pioneer leader. The motto "Always ready" didn't exist when I was a child. My childhood was quite different, very grey and difficult. You have certainly been a Pioneer. "Always ready". Good. I shall now speak to the people on whose decision this matter depends. Just one request for you now and for the future: if you feel dissatisfied with something or irritated by something in our lives or, for example, in the newspapers, if you disagree with something that's being written, phone me. Or just come and tell the secretary that you need to talk. Then we'll talk. All right?'

He nodded. That was not difficult to do now. Perhaps he would really come some time. Perhaps.

'Right. I shall deal with the matter, and let you know as soon as something is settled. And have a think about whether you agree with my alternative, so to speak. If our plan is acceptable to you we shall set things in motion. If you have any questions or problems in this regard, just phone or, as I said, come here and tell the secretary. We may still have to have a short chat with the rector or another comrade. Right, you think things over, and I'll let you know if we need to have a further chat. And if you have anything to say or ask, please get in touch. As I said. Well, I wish you all the best. Think your life over again, decide, be self-critical –

often young people aren't – and . . . I wish you success in your work. I hope they'll find you an interesting job in the library.'

The *partorg* got up, shook his hand and guided him to the door. The air in the waiting-room was cleaner and fresher than in the office. He felt that he had a slight headache.

He stopped and stood by the post-box at the corner of the university. He honestly could not remember how he'd got here from the *partorg*'s office, and he honestly did not know where to go, where he should go and what he should do. To the café? No, at the moment he had no desire to mix with anyone he might meet there, neither Aleks nor Peeter. Although he could talk one or two things over with Peeter. It might even be important – perhaps they might interrogate Peeter again, so it would be good if they didn't tell different stories. But as far as he could remember he hadn't told Peeter the source of the Under poems, and Peeter had shuffled the burden of providing an explanation off on to him. And by now he must be on the collective farm like the others. In fact, that made everything easier: he didn't feel he would be angry with him because of it. It was just a feeling that he would muddle through, but he had no idea how. Only an idea that the idea would come. Soon, perhaps.

He should go and talk to someone. The Teacher? Ester? The Teacher would certainly have an opinion on the opportunity offered by the *partorg*. Moscow or Leningrad; Indian languages. But perhaps something completely different, some other languages? Farsi? Arabic? But was now a sensible time to go to the Teacher's? Now, when he had just been reprimanded for it? Would they be watching where he went? Did he have a tail? He didn't think so. Or should he go to Ester's first? No, not straight away. To Malle's? But Malle did not yet have her own room, and he had no desire to go to the dorm. Perhaps he would visit her on the collective farm. He was, in truth, a bit afraid of Malle, especially after their last conversation when he realized that she was truly ready to come to him and had probably been counting on it. But he simply didn't know what to do any more, where to start, what would become of him. Suddenly he realized that he even liked the not knowing, the uncertainty, that in some way his current situation was even interesting. All of a sudden it had opened up so many opportunities. If he really did go away from here it might also resolve his confused relationships with two girls. Perhaps he would find someone in Russia, someone with whom he would get along more easily. Perhaps he was, despite everything, equally as Russian as he was Estonian, perhaps more so. But when he left, that, too, would become clear. He would achieve a better understanding of who he was.

No, first he should just go for a walk. To Toome and perhaps somewhere further off after that. Beyond Tähtvere, to the Emajõgi floodplain. Among the willow bushes. From there the road went along the riverbank. Perhaps the fishermen's road. He would go to the place where yesterday, for the first time in his life, he had truly prayed. The place where prayer came to him and rose through him . . . No, he no longer dared think it rose to God. That word was so immense and awkward in its immensity. No, today was not God's day. Today's day, at least the first part of it, had no God, had no faith. And probably no love either. It was grey and insipid. And interesting for all that.

He directed his steps towards Supilinn. He would cross this to go to the river via Herne or Oa streets. He looked at the old low-rise buildings, the planks, allotments; he listened to the women's gossip in the shop doorways, the cockerels' crowing and the dogs' barking. There was something reassuring about the level nature, the banality of slum life, something vital. Yet Ester lived there. No, he wouldn't go past Ester's house. Not today. He wouldn't go to Ester's today or tomorrow or the day after. Or to the Teacher's. He would go to the Teacher's soon; let the *partorg* and other interrogators think what they like when they found out. The most proper thing to do was to go to the Teacher's when the decisions had been made at the university or higher up, when he was informed whether they were prepared to send him to Russia to study. Then he would go and talk to him and ask for his approval. And then he would go to Ester's. He couldn't separate himself from Ester; he could not be Esterless, couldn't not think about her, not dream about her. And that also meant that he couldn't go on with Malle; he could not meet her hopes and expectations.

A lone fisherman stood by the ruins of the Freedom Bridge, and in the river itself another crouched in a boat, two lines in the water, motionless, waiting.

He remembered how the bridge had been during the war when the Germans had rebuilt it. The current was swift here; the water whirled and foamed around the blocks of stone and concrete, and whirlpools carried them some distance downstream. Like worries, he thought. The worries that accompany you even when the direct cause of the worry has passed. As now? Perhaps? Only Ester, only Ester was eternal. Ester, who had someone who was very important to her. Ester, who otherwise would not be indifferent to him.

Emajõgi – *Mater Acquarum*, Mother of the Waters. It sounded so beautiful and poetic but was just a common-or-garden name of a river. It meant, quite simply, a big river into which lots of smaller rivers flow. In a similar vein, the mother tree on a ship is the keel, the trunk to which the ship's ribs are attached, and a mother ship is a ship that is home to aircraft. The Emajõgi was probably not sacred even to the ancient Estonians: sacred rivers were those that bore or bear the name Püha-jõgi, literally 'Sacred River', such as the upper reaches of the Võhandu.

Yet perhaps he could bring his own small offering to the Emajõgi and ask it for something. Cast a coin into the water and ask for . . . ask, of course, for Ester. Mainly for Ester to be able to come with him. To him. Everything else felt incidental, of lesser importance. He could perhaps cope with the rest; fate seemed to be on his side in the other things. If only . . . If only Ester would say that she was free and ... How then would he be able to go somewhere far away in Russia? How could he be far away from the girl with whom he was so much in love, when meeting her had brought experiences that were almost mystical into his life.

He stepped on to the highest point of the bank where once the path had met the bridge and flung some kopeks from his pocket into the rippling, foaming water, unable to articulate his prayer clearly. No trace of the falling coins could be seen in the swirling water. Just as there was no trace in the air from the words he spoke. It was all so strange: yesterday he was an upright, faithful Christian praying reverentially to his God; today he was a pagan bringing offerings to his ancestors' river. As had the ancestors who had prayed both to their own ancient gods and the new foreign gods in the hope that one of them would help. And, regardless of it all, it came as a surprise to him to realize that now that he had cast his own kopeks as an offering into the river he suddenly felt more at ease, he even almost believed that he would have Ester, that he would find happiness with her. He shoved his hands into his empty pockets and strode on along the riverbank.

28

There was no one much in the library in early autumn, no surprise as most students were on the collective farms and the ones in their final year who had stayed in the city were obviously in no hurry to get on with studying. So sometimes he was almost alone in the reading-room writing card index notes. Once a librarian who knew one of his friends approached him to ask whether he would mind helping to catalogue the Tibetan-language books or manuscripts. At one time he had learnt Tibetan script and as much grammar as there were books available on it. So with the help of a dictionary he worked hard to put the books in title order and then make out card indexes for them. If he really should go to Russia to study Indian languages he might take a more serious look at Tibetan. As a matter of fact, he thought that he was most interested in things that he didn't know properly, things that he didn't really understand. Hence, perhaps his current interest in theology; hence perhaps his current interest in God? Perhaps the value and purpose of God lay in the fact that He so seldom really exists and so seldom can Hhim. If someone were able to meet Him every day He wouldn't be God.

A short letter came from Malle at the collective farm. They, meaning the girls, had to weed the flax; the boys had to haul the grain sacks into the drier and the storehouse. Heavy jobs both. Some had sore hands, others sore backs, making it difficult to sleep well although everyone was very tired. The note was otherwise neutral; only at the end did it say 'Your Malle'. It moved and saddened him, she apparently regarded herself as his, yet he dreamt only of Ester. He dreamt always of Ester, but he didn't ever remember much of his dreams.

Over a week went by in this fashion, and he was already used to writing out the cards and was regarded in the library as one of the staff, especially after he had helped read the Tibetan script. Once or twice he was invited into the back room at lunchtime for coffee, and once the deputy director asked him half in jest whether he would be prepared to come and work for them after graduating; they urgently needed people with language expertise. He said nothing definite, and nothing definite was expected in his reply. In any case, it was one option he could consider in future if no other opportunities had arisen by then. The library, and why not.

Then one morning he was called to the telephone. It was the *partorg*. He and a comrade from Tallinn who wanted to speak to him would expect him in his office in one hour, so he hoped that he had thought things over.

The secretary recognized him and said that they were already waiting for him.

The comrade from Tallinn looked younger than the *partorg*; he was better groomed and more self-confident in his manner – although the *partorg*'s behaviour was not of the obsequious kind he had sometimes noticed when lowlier apparatchiks were dealing with their superiors. Perhaps his self-confidence came from his status as a war veteran; perhaps he had some kind of link to the man from Tallinn. Who knew?

'This is our problem child, so to speak,' said the *partorg*, motioning him to take a seat. 'How have things been going at the library?'

He replied that they'd been going well and that he'd almost been offered a job there.

'Indeed, indeed, they desperately need a good-looking young man like a cockerel in a flock of hens,' said the *partorg*. 'The women there are in great majority, like anywhere else. Indeed, indeed, and why not? But first let's have a little chat about longer-term plans. Comrade — has come to Tartu on a couple of matters, and we thought we'd take the opportunity to talk to him about you. Have you thought about the plan, so to speak, that I talked to you about last time?'

He nodded. 'Yes, of course.'

'And have you decided anything?'

He said that he would decide when he knew the specific details, but that studying languages, including Indian languages, in Moscow or Leningrad would interest him greatly.

'And do you think it could also be in our interests to send you there to study?' enquired the stranger from Tallinn. He could not tell from his face whether the question was intended seriously or more in jest.

'I'm afraid I wouldn't venture to decide with any confidence what your interests are,' he replied.

'Look,' said the man from Tallinn, now in a tone he clearly considered jocular. 'There is no equivalent in Estonian of our wonderful Russian saying "мы с вами" – we are with you. Our young friend – I hope I do not regret referring to you in such terms – immediately drew a line between us and you. No, that was not how I was thinking, I was not thinking that you should worry about our narrow, specific interests, the interests of State and Party officials, although I do not deny that perhaps such interests do exist. I meant "we" in the broader sense. We Estonians, the people who live in the republic, who want business to prosper, want us to progress, want there to be fewer problems and misunderstandings, want us to be more united in our views and better aware of all kinds of inevitabilities. Positive inevitabilities, I would say, because it would take someone very ill intentioned not to see how much our lives have improved over the last ten years. And not to acknowledge the contribution made to the improvement in our lives by our Party. In conjunction, of course, with those we describe as non-Party people, people of goodwill who do not regard the past, raking through it and opening up old wounds and arguments (plenty of us have such wounds, including me) as the most important thing but who instead attach greatest importance to progress. Despite everything, we are living in very special times, great times, and those times are inviting us to take part, whether we are members of the Party or not. This is how it is.'

'Arnold, we have lost an excellent agitator in you, but I don't think our young friend really needs an account of our achievements. He can read about them in the newspaper if he so wishes and listen to the Voice of America – there have been worries over there recently that we may ultimately overtake them, in space and on earth. Perhaps we should get down to business. You had one or two specific details to mention in reference to this matter.'

'Indeed, let's get down to business. What I said just now was by way of a preamble. As I said, as anyone with a pair of eyes can see for themselves, our lives are progressing successfully, and that means that our contacts are expanding. This affects our republic, too. We, too, have specialists working in friendly countries in Asia and Africa; we, too, have scientists and cultural workers whose ties with colleagues there are growing, and travel to these places is increasing all the time. Hence the specific need for people with language skills who can help our republic to achieve a better share in these ever-increasing exchanges. We, too, want to be one of the progressive, leading, Union Republics – finger on the pulse, in step with the times. We want to be small but clever. Am I right?'

He nodded with the *partorg*, whose face had for a moment borne something like a smirk. The man from Tallinn paused briefly, looked directly at him and carried on. 'I think you understand what my point is. My point is – if you would allow me to put it this way – you. We have discussed your case with certain comrades, including the *partorg* of your university, as you know, and have reached the conclusion that your error is serious but not so serious that it should interrupt your university education. We accept that you genuinely regret your foolish actions, and we have confidence in you. We therefore hope that you will respond to our confidence with confidence of your own, and you will never again be the conduit for the dissemination of any, shall we say, unfortunate materials, whether they be in the form of poetry or prose, and that your interest in oriental languages will not take you into the bosom of the Church. We have also concluded that it would be appropriate for you to continue your education in one of the prestigious universities in our country and that afterwards you should return to our republic as a specialist in the languages of India or another friendly country. There is no doubt that your knowledge will be useful. The ministry has been on the line to Leningrad University, and they have in principle agreed to accept you there as a student. You will have the necessary references. Provided, of course, that you agree to go there. As far as I understand it, you would have to start the first year in a new specialist area, and the exams you have taken here will be transferred to your study record. We've unavoidably arranged your future, arranged a potential life plan for you. Now all that remains is for us to ask you if you want to go to Leningrad. It could be in your interest as much as ours and, as the *partorg* presumably explained, in the university's interest, too. I hope all this is clear to you.'

'It is,' he said. 'Do I have to give my answer straight away?'

'I understand that it might be difficult to answer here and now. But there's not much time. Let's say by the day after tomorrow. Lunchtime the day after tomorrow. I hope that that will give you enough time to think it through. If you reach your decision sooner, let us know sooner. You can phone the *partorg* here, isn't that right?' He turned towards his colleague.

The *partorg* nodded. 'Indeed, and if I'm not here tell the secretary. Or phone if it's more convenient. You presumably have my number.'

He said it was easier for him to come here in person than to phone.

'Fine,' said the *partorg*. 'That's all we've got to say, or do you have something more to say to our young man?' he asked the man from Tallinn.

'No, I have nothing to add for the moment. I've said what I had to say. I hope that this won't be our last meeting and that we will have opportunities to meet in future in more cordial circumstances – although I hope that this meeting has not left an unpleasant impression upon you.'

He didn't know whether he should have answered this. But clearly no reply was expected. Both men showed him to the door and shook his hand. Was this the sign of confidence, agreement, or a customary gesture on the part of apparatchiks? He wasn't going to ponder the point at present. He had two days. To think and decide. But first he had to go and talk to Ester. And the Teacher; iirst and foremost the Teacher. Both despite and because of the fact that his relations with the Teacher had been noticed and he had been reprimanded for them.

29

There was the same smell in the corridor beyond the Teacher's door as there had been that first time in the spring. Why do people remember smells so well yet tend to forget other things, names for instance?

The door was opened by Ellen, as was her habit, and she smiled in recognition, almost in friendship. The smile might also have been somewhat apologetic because she said, 'Alo is dealing with a very urgent piece of work at the moment. He doesn't have much time. If you want to discuss something at length, you should perhaps come back in a few days.'

It was awkward. Usually he would have apologized without question and said he would come back another time, but now he had to say that he didn't want to take up Alo's time for long but that he had an important, urgent matter that he absolutely had to talk to him about.

'Just a sec. I'll go and ask him if he's got a moment,' replied Ellen.

The smell familiar from previous visits contained something of the building's own smell mixed with tobacco smoke and something else he couldn't place. Flowers? Books?

His thoughts on smells were interrupted by Ellen.

'Please sit yourself down. Alo will be here soon. Do help yourself to the cigarettes on the table.'

He did so. Ellen left to get on with her own work – from the sounds he could hear she had gone to the kitchen. A bluebottle buzzed in the window behind the Chinese birch; from the yard came the distant sounds of children playing in the neighbour's garden or the street. On the bookshelves stood the spines of the books he remembered from before. Frazer's *The Golden Bough*, travel writings and the 'Atlantis' series. He lit a cigarette and scrutinized the shelves. He could perhaps have stood up to see what was behind their bewitching title pages, but he did not dare. Perhaps it would be taken amiss. Perhaps if Ellen had said he could look at the books until Alo came. Look at the books . . . That, literally, was what he was doing: he was sitting in an armchair looking at the books standing on the shelves. There was something about them and the whole atmosphere of the room that clearly belonged to another time, another world. And there was something about that other world that was both homely and strange. It reminded him a bit of his own home: Grandfather and Grandmother and their life with their friends from the days of the free Estonian Republic, their stories. Perhaps even their smell. It was strange that the Teacher had been so sarcastic and critical of the free Estonian days in their conversations. Yet he was a product of them. Had he been

287

unable to move on from them somehow? This was a heretical thought, and as if in rebuke he heard the familiar dragging steps in the corridor and the rattling cough.

The Teacher looked a little tired and there were two furrows in his brow, although his glance and voice appeared friendly. After the customary bow and handshake they sat down. The Teacher lit a cigarette and said, 'Ellen said that you had something significant to discuss.'

'Indeed, there's one thing . . . I have to say yes or no to an important question no later than the day after tomorrow, and I feel I need to talk to you before I reply.'

The Teacher raised his eyebrows. 'Hmmmm, sounds interesting already. What question can there be that someone like me can be of assistance in answering?'

He could not mention the Under. Hhe had to say something less specific.

'Well, it so happens that I'm in trouble at the university. Because of some books published abroad that I was sent by relatives. And I've been reprimanded for coming . . . because I've visited you here. They more or less interrogated me, although not formally – the KGB and the *partorg*. They threatened to send me down, throw me out, meaning I would have to join the army. But then they suggested I should go to Moscow or Leningrad to study oriental languages, more specifically Indian languages. That way the university would be free of me, and I would be taken away from unfortunate influences here – that was more or less the gist of it. They've found somewhere – they mentioned Leningrad University – willing to accept me. So I thought I would ask you whether . . . you perhaps know how these languages, especially Indian languages, are taught there and what the standard's like and whether you might know any of the lecturers there?'

The furrows in the Teacher's brow deepened; he squinted at his questioner – a gesture he did not know whether to interpret as good or bad – inhaled deeply on his cigarette and fell silent for a few moments. Then he said, 'I do and I don't. Difficult to say. I've met some of the people, got some contacts. But is that important here? As I understand it you need to escape my bad influence. So perhaps people I might recommend are not the best ones to help you.'

This quasi-accusation was unexpected, so much so that at first he did not know how to respond. None the less, a long draw on his cigarette helped him collect his thoughts and expunge the unwarranted accusation from his mind.

'No, that's not how it was meant . . . I mean, they might have thought it, but I didn't . . . I just think . . . I realize it's not possible to learn much at university here in the area that I really would like to study . . . and as it's offered in Leningrad and presumably Moscow it would make sense to go and try it. If I come out with language skills and a diploma I can do something or other with it here. Not necessarily the things they might expect.'

'And what might *they* expect?' asked the Teacher, somewhat sarcastically, although he felt that there was less of a barb in his voice

'I didn't really understand. They said that our republic needs oriental-language experts, too, that relationships with progressive countries are developing and –'

'Well, yes, it's beginning to dawn even on the Estonians that there are people in what they term the "oriental countries" with whom it is useful to, as they say, "develop relations". Well, then. Quite a few sensible people have found work for themselves in similar fashion in Russia, perhaps it will work for you, too. With your education complete you'll have no reason to come back. You have a good command of Russian, if I remember right?'

'Russian isn't a problem for me, I learnt it at home in part. But . . .' He felt that it was now or never, he would have to come out with the real problem. 'I have another . . . problem. It's what's stopping me from giving them a definite yes.'

The Teacher looked at him directly and, he felt, with a measure of curiosity and a measure of arrogance. 'I wonder how they lived in the old days when people didn't have so many problems. They had difficulties, they had impediments, they had worries. Now it's always problems, problems, problems. Have the times changed or just the language?'

Was the Teacher asking himself or him? But it was still down to him to answer, or rather disclose the full extent of his problem, or whatever it was. 'I know I should go, that I can get a really thorough grounding in these languages in Leningrad. I thought I might like to learn some more Tibetan and . . . but it's difficult for me to leave Estonia at the moment.'

'Is it difficult to leave your homeland and your family then?' asked Ellen, who had come in from the kitchen, presumably to hear the important thing he had to ask Alo.

'That, too,' he continued. And then, almost against his will, forcing the words through his lips, he added, 'And I've probably fallen in love and can't imagine how I can leave now and . . .'

'Hmmm.' The Teacher's eyebrows rose. 'Probably fallen in love? What does the "probably" mean here? Perhaps you haven't fallen in love, perhaps the emotion you are feeling is something else?'

'Alo, why are you making fun of him? Look how hard it is for him. He's come to ask your advice.'

'I am not the best counsel on matters of the heart, and neither are you, Ellen. You never got to be a real pastor's wife. In my experience, they, at least in their own minds, are the biggest experts in this sphere.'

'Stop it, Alo,' said Ellen. 'You know very well that becoming a pastor's wife has never been a particular ambition of mine. But' – and she turned now towards the questioner – 'Leningrad isn't so far away that you won't be able to meet up with your girlfriend if you've really fallen in love. You can come here sometimes, and she can visit you now and again. You can walk by the Neva, go to the museums – and in the meantime you can write to each other. You will miss each other. Temporary separation keeps love young and fresh. And puts it to the test. If your feelings aren't strong and sure, they'll disappear while you're away; you'll find someone else and . . .'

'At the moment I can't imagine finding someone else. I'm very attached to her. Very. Since the summer when we . . . But you know her. I've fallen in love with Ester, only I don't know whether she cares for me. She's as good as said that she can't be with me at the moment, that she's got someone she can't leave . . . And apart from that she's a few years older than me.'

As he said this he looked at Ellen, whose face wore a benevolent, motherly smile. Although it didn't pass him by that the Teacher flinched, and when he turned towards him he saw that his expression had changed drastically.

'You know, if you've come here to discuss affairs of the heart then you're in the wrong place. If Ellen, whether she regards herself as appropriate material for a pastor's wife or not, wishes to play matchmaker for you or give you advice, then fine. But I do not get involved in the love affairs of young boys. I am going back to my work, and I wish you success with the oriental languages. But please do not come here again with bits of nothing. If the authorities of the Estonian SSR need experts in Indian languages they should make the arrangements for an appropriate place of learning and teachers for you. Let them send you to a diplomatic school – they produce good linguists. Linguists they need to translate and interpret for their requirements. And, yes, you will find pretty young ladies there with whom you can talk of love in Hindi or Tamil, who know as little of the subject as kids like you, who don't even know what they're looking for in life or what they want from it. Goodbye. I'm going back to work.'

He got up, bowed slightly, a scornful and bitter expression suddenly on his face, and left. They could hear him shutting the door of his study behind him.

He and Ellen looked at each other. It was clear that the Teacher's outburst had been unexpected for Ellen as well. After a moment she collected herself and said, sounding a bit embarrassed and apologetic, 'Please don't be cross with Alo. He's recently been out of sorts. He's got a lot of work, often the kind he would prefer not to take on. And he always gets grumpy if he doesn't have work in his own field, Semitic languages or those of southern India. He could teach them, but, you see, there's no place for him with the authorities. But don't worry so much about affairs of the heart. The fact that Ester's older than you doesn't matter. I've known her since she was a child, and I believe you'd make a lovely couple. But I really can't help you on this. Perhaps this thing of hers will blow over and you will find each other. For some reason I believe that she's not totally indifferent to you. And that's one thing I always notice, even though I'm not a pastor's wife. So be brave, pull yourself together, and if you really want to go to Leningrad, then go. Take your love with you and look after it. May God watch over you.'

He thanked her and got up. He had nothing more to do here today. Now he had to go to Ester's. He could not make his decision without talking to Ester.

30

As he reached Ester's door he suddenly realized he had no memory of how he had got there, which roads he had walked down or what he had been thinking. Occasionally before he'd felt he was moving and acting as if in a dream, yet now a period of several minutes of his life had passed as if in dreamless sleep, leaving no trace. It dismayed him and made him falter for a moment. Could such a gap in his consciousness or memory recur? What if it were to happen when he was at Ester's? As far as he could see, he had managed to get here despite it all; part of his brain had been working properly, had guided him to her. But what about the future? What if he were to say something without knowing or remembering what? Yet what could he ever say to Ester in his dreams that he couldn't say in reality? Anyway, everything had been said. Except the thing he wanted to say today. The thing that happened at the Teacher's. With the Teacher. And the fact that he had to make a decision that also hinged on Ester. He made to knock when the door opened and Ester stepped towards him.

'Did you see me from the window or something?' he asked.

'No, I just have to go out for a while. My great-aunt's got heart trouble. I'm getting her some Validol from the chemist's. Go in and wait if you like. I'll be back in about half an hour.'

Yes, of course, he'd be happy to wait. Perhaps it was better that way. He could compose himself, even perhaps calm down. Ester's smile was so friendly, he would even have liked to believe it was something more than just friendly. It helped, calmed him down. Or should he go with Ester? He wondered about it for a moment but then felt he'd rather sit there in the little room and wait. In half an hour he might have calmed down a bit and be able to talk. He wanted to talk, but the thing he wanted to talk about was not an appropriate topic to discuss in the street. Ester went out; he stepped into the room.

It was really tranquil here, relaxingly so; the singular suburban tranquillity that spoke of another time, something of the days of the free Estonia or even the Tsar. Lace cloths, a gum tree, old furniture and the smell of an old building that was also from a different era. The smell reminiscent of the Teacher's apartment, although more banal, more slum-like. Yet there was something of Ester there, too: there was the faint smell of perfume, face cream or new books and clothes. Or the smell of a chemical with which she came into contact in her practical assignments. Or the sheer smell of Ester herself that he almost remembered. From the summer when they went to fetch the bread and had a swim: the smell she had then was certainly hers alone.

He looked around. On the desk there was a small pile of books, topped by *Lehrbuch der Pflanzenphysiologie*. Underneath, it looked like there was something flimsy, hand-bound, perhaps coursework or . . . perhaps a manuscript by the Teacher. The temptation to look was too great, and he could not resist. He lifted up the plant physiology book. Yes, it could be, it *was* something by the Teacher. Cloth spine, the rest of the binding from a strange material, whitish with faint stripes. Then it dawned on him: it must be birch bark. He'd heard from someone, probably Rein, that the Teacher was a master bookbinder and sometimes bound his own manuscripts in birch bark.

There was no title on the cover, only on the title page in handwritten callig–raphy KURUNTOKAI, and below it, in smaller letters, *To Ester*.

He leafed through the book. It contained poems, and a foreword before the poems stated that this was his attempt to translate a small selection of classical Tamil love poems from the anthology *Kuruntokai*. The translations were born during the confusion of the war years for his own delight and consolation. The foreword also explained the peculiarities, conventions and metres of classical Tamil poetry. The pictures of scenes from nature and daytime were supposed to say what the text itself did not say directly; namely, whether there was any hope for the lover or not.

He did not care to delve into the foreword and allowed his gaze to stray over the poems themselves. They seemed interesting and beautiful, never mind the conventions and metres that the Teacher declared himself neither able nor willing to render.

> When passion ends, oh man from the hills
> where after heavy rains
> the song of the waterfalls is heard in the caves
> does love too end
> like passion?

The second poem was about mountain rivers as well.

> Where the white flows from the hilltops
> roar through the caves,
> there the elder of the mountain village
> has a younger daughter, with long arms, soft as water.
> Perhaps she might quench the flame of my desire.

The poems felt quite alike, they melted into a similar kind of flow, into the roar of the mountain river in a system of caves. A folded sheet of paper had been inserted between the last pages. He couldn't resist casting his eye over it and recognized the Teacher's handwriting.

For a moment he hesitated, paper in hand. It was obviously a letter, perhaps from the Teacher. So he shouldn't read it. But it might be a poem, a new translation ... He'd only have a quick peek, if it was a letter he wouldn't read it ... Only ten minutes had gone by. It would still be twenty minutes before Ester returned. He looked towards the door, listening. Everything was quiet as before, there was no sound, even from the room next door; presumably both the old lady and Tuki were asleep. THe unfolded the paper.

Dismay was late in coming, only when he had read the first few sentences and realized what it was ...

'My dear, only girl,' the Teacher began. 'I have suddenly realized that I cannot last even two days without you. Everything is different, emptier, greyer, sometimes downright loathsome.'

There was something even more awful in the final part of the letter. The Teacher was writing about him, disparagingly:

> I simply cannot accept that that young boy can tell you in such terms that he thinks that you, like all other lovely girls, should fall into his arms because of his beautiful Slavic eyes and slightly higher than average language abilities. I think he should first find out what he really wants. What does he have to offer you or anyone else apart from trivial discussions of art and poetry? Discussions I heard forty years ago. As far as I am concerned this youth, representing new poetry and a new generation, further corroborates something that I am increasingly experiencing, namely that the new is actually the totally forgotten old. You said that he has thought about studying 'oriental' languages in Russia ... This pains me for several reasons: I have admitted to you how much it aggrieves me to live here like this, on the sidelines, with no opportunity to work with the thing closest to my heart, the thing I could do most effectively. Without the opportunity to teach, to nurture my successors. And, when someone with the potential to fill that role appears, the scrawny hand of the authorities immediately grabs him by the throat and takes him away from me. But in my heart – if I may be so bold as to confess to you – I am also pleased. He is going. You are staying. You are staying here close to me, and that, to me, is ultimately the most important thing.

What he felt now was something he had probably never felt before. It was akin to paralysis. The inability to move, the inability to think, even feel. The whirling turbidity of his mind spat out the word 'shock'. Half of him wanted to throw the letter away; the other half could not stop reading. The other side of the sheet bore two poems, poems to Ester, of course:

The great Andromeda, queen of heaven,
keeps watch over us in the east, high above the horizon.

In her glow, in your light breath
fades all that has goaded or oppressed the mind.

Everything fades, everything disperses into sleep, into the blue heavens
When we wake, when once again we must go,

my mind is bright, reconciled with day and night
as if encircled by your loosened girdle

as if sanctified by the warm touch of your fingers
and brightened by the caressing of your lips.

He was no longer capable of reading the second poem properly. The stupor
was past;, he was being seized by panic. Hurriedly, recklessly, he shoved the letter
into the poetry book bound in birch bark, thrust the book on to the desk and fled
from the building. Outside he broke into a run, the only thought in his head was
to get further away from here before Ester came back from the chemist's and saw
him. He ran in the other direction, towards the edge of the city, and stopped only
when he reached the road he had once taken through the bushes to the river's
edge. He stopped there for a while and walked with a slower step through the tall,
faded grass towards the river.

His head was in chaos, but that chaos embodied one clear thought that cut him
to the heart like a knife: the someone else was the Teacher. *He* was the person Ester
couldn't leave. That was why the Teacher had been so enraged when he'd talked
about Ester earlier. And Ellen, Ellen presumably knew nothing; otherwise she
would have behaved differently.

Had he put the little book and the letter back in such a way that Ester wouldn't
realize he'd looked at them? He couldn't remember properly, but in any case it
didn't matter. It would be even better if Ester did realize, then the reason for his
unexpected disappearance would be obvious to her. Running away through shock,
astonishment, love, which had suddenly assumed another visage, become jealousy,
despair. Unthinkingl,y he had fled here to the place where once he had found God,
faith, as well as death, a longing for death. Which of them was it now? Had he come
looking for death, for peace in the shallow autumn river among the faded water-
lilies, or was he hoping for another encounter with the This, which that time for one
eternal moment had revealed itself to him? He needed the intimacy of the This now
probably more than he had then, but something was telling him that it was a vain
hope. He remembered a couple of lines by Raimond Kolk in the Võru language:

God doesn't come when we hopeHe will
God comes when it's His will.

When it was His will. When He wants to. But why? Why did He tease us so? Why did God behave with even less regard, in an even more arbitrary fashion, than a beloved woman sometimes did? Did He like to play with us, too, make us yearn for Him, despair, only for Him then to vanish into the unknown, the emptiness of space, where there was no place for anything human? Was God really such a capricious creature or . . . or was he merely an illusion of our own making, a delusion, a phantom born of longing who vanishes as soon as we have become accustomed to His being close by, begun to believe in Him?

He felt with certainty that at the moment Ester was very much more important, love was more important than faith, and disappointment in love a more difficult experience than God's vanishing into the void. Perhaps God was merely the product of his unsatisfied love, desire for love, ultimately simply his desire for sex, some kind of *Anderssein* of love, being other. Perhaps people who had found love had no further need for God? That much he could gather from the Teacher's poems: he wrote about love, about meeting Ester, as if he were writing about some mystical experience, *unio mystica*.

On that occasion he had stood in this very spot and knelt down, praying to the God he had once found and had now lost once again. Even the river was almost the same, perhaps a little more weary, more autumnal, than a few days previously. But he was different, more crushed, more weary, more autumnal.

He stepped up to the peat riverbank and stood looking at the water. Indeed, Heraclitus, or whoever it was, was right: you cannot step into the same river twice. You cannot stand by the same river twice. What is a river? Water flowing from Lake Võrtsjärv into Lake Peipsi. The water which was still in the lake that time must have got as far as here by now, and the water that was here must have already reached Lake Peipsi. If he wanted to, he could even work out how fast the water flowed from there to here and from here to Lake Peipsi. So what is Lake Peipsi? What is Lake Võrtsjärv? Water or banks, the bed, the landscape around the lake as a whole? Lakes are not significantly different from rivers, lakes also flow, although more slowly. The water of Lake Võrtsjärv flows gradually into Lake Peipsi and evaporates into the air. Ultimately, the landscape also changes: the water-lilies wilt, the willow leaves yellow and fall, in spring new leaves and new shoots appear, new bushes spring up. The land itself changes, the continents shift, the river bursts its banks, the land emerges; the Hanseatic waterway that once linked Pärnu to Tartu had now gone. Everything flows. Perhaps he did, too, his thoughts, his feelings, his body. Probably also his faith and love and his God. Although we believe, we want to believe, that God and love do not flow. We have a desire for something eternal, yet even that desire flows.

Where did those thoughts of Heraclitus suddenly jump into his head from? Was it that, in running away from Ester's, he also managed to escape from his own former thoughts, his shock and despair? His thoughts, his despair had perhaps stayed behind in the small room of that suburban building, in the yard in front of it. But they were hardly staying there, abandoning him. Rather, this strange philosophical mood was normal following a shock and would soon pass. He could already feel the beginnings of misery in his chest, an almost physical pain. Ester and the Teacher, Ester and Alo. Perhaps they would marry, stay together until the Teacher died. Perhaps the Teacher wouldn't live very long, then Ester would be a widow, free. Then he would have a chance. But would he be able to wait that long? Would Ester still want him? Especially after she understood why he'd run away, realized that he had read the Teacher's letter, read someone else's letter and learnt everything. But perhaps Ester wouldn't marry the Teacher. Then he would have less time to wait. Could he manage it? He would have liked to believe that he could, but realized he was by no means certain. Something had changed, drained away, perhaps been smashed. The same feeling was telling him that he was a young man, that he wanted a woman. He wanted sex; he wanted tenderness; he wanted someone to be with, to sleep with, wake up with, travel with, go to concerts with. But now, unexpectedly, he wanted a woman's body, he wanted what he had not yet achieved, what he had not managed to have with Malle.

Indeed, he had fallen in love with two people, and now it appeared that he had lost them both, that in the near future he would not have the chance to be with either of them. He had to carry on living without love, although he would definitely find someone else in time. At the moment, though, he didn't want to think about it. At the moment only Ester was in his heart. And the Teacher. Even though the Teacher had mocked him and Ester loved the Teacher.

He had to carry on living ... Or did he? Was this not the time to ask genuinely the question Hamlet posed himself, to ask 'to be or not to be'?

He took a step towards the river. But no, this time there was nothing pleasurable in it. There had been the previous time. Perhaps that meant there was indeed a water sprite in the river as they believed in the past. It reminded him of the pull that had for a moment overcome his fear of death – or was it simply the thirst for life? There was something about it that was similar to the pull of women. Sometimes love was stronger than death; sometimes perhaps not. At the moment there was neither; there was a strange kind of peace, like resignation, not caring about anything – yet not quite. The basis for that peace was also finality, the will to live. And he'd cleared something up. He had to go to Leningrad. He had to tear himself away from the tangled web here. He had to study languages. He had to find a girlfriend for himself; he simply had to have what most people his age had had; sex, tenderness, caressing lips – as the Teacher had said in his poem to Ester. He might even have to find someone for just one time, for just one night. Hitherto, this was something he had not done; now perhaps he would. If he could cope with the KGB and Party officials, he could cope with a girl. There would always be someone ready to yield to him, open herself to him, allow him between her thighs. While thinking about it he felt a mild quiver pervade his body, reach his lower abdomen, which had waited too long for the chance to prove itself. Now he would not allow the opportunity to pass him by if one came. Perhaps it would come if he was ready.

On the western side of the park a thick, dark cloud had covered the sinking sun, promising rain. He set off, quickening his step once on the path. The cloud rose quickly; it would be better to reach home before the rain fell.

Now everything was more or less clear. The Teacher and Ester. He would no longer call on them. Tomorrow morning he would go and say 'yes' to the *partorg*. Then there would probably be some paperwork to deal with. He would have to think about what to take with him, what to tell his family. Perhaps they would be sorry when he went, but it would definitely be easier for him. It would be interesting to see whether he got a place in a dorm or if at least at first he would have to live at his aunt's. His aunt would always let him sleep there for a while. Her room in the communal apartment wasn't large, but there was a fold-up bed for visitors to use there. And the neighbours weren't the complaining kind; they wouldn't cause problems. If things were finalized in the morning he would immediately write to his aunt; she had no telephone.

But what about his fellow students? Malle? Malle, who was waiting for him, who might be willing to marry him. No, he couldn't do that, at least not for the moment. He was neither able nor willing. Ester had not vanished. She was still in his heart, although now like a smarting, aching wound. Perhaps he would take control and travel to the collective farm they were staying at, say goodbye, talk to Malle so that everything would be clear. That was one option. Or write a letter. That would be easier.

31

'The way things stand now, I have to go to Leningrad University,' he said as he sat at the dinner table with his family

He had entertained no hope of avoiding an explanation, although it was more straightforward than he had feared. His mother immediately pointed out that every cloud had a silver lining: there was no way he could obtain a thorough grounding in oriental languages in Tartu, and if this was a way for him to get out of the trouble he was in then it was wonderful. His aunt and more distant relations would definitely help, and with his good command of Russian he would quickly make friends. And elsewhere in the world it had always been the custom for students to spend some time at another university. As his father had done in his time.

'But what about afterwards?' asked Grandfather, to whom the essentials had been delivered by shouting loudly into his ear. 'Will you come back to Estonia or will you stay there?'

This was something he could not answer. The deal with the *partorg* and the man from Tallinn had been that he would become the specialist his own republic needed. But perhaps there was work there, too, and maybe he would be wanted there once he'd finished university. And the wishes of the people in Leningrad presumably took precedence over those of the people of Tallinn or Tartu University. For the moment he had the feeling he'd want to go away from here, disappear, at least spend a few years far away. Then perhaps he'd see.

'Then perhaps we'll see,' agreed his mother. 'Who knows what the situation will be like by the time you finish there.'

Neither he nor anyone else could argue with that. Besides, Leningrad wasn't so far away: if he had the money and the time he could visit his homeland at least once a month. And occasionally bring Aunt Veera back with him; it would be wonderful to see her more often. Hear the news from the big city and Russia and . . .

Grandfather began relating his own memories of St Petersburg. He'd been there a couple of times in the Tsarist era and once in the Soviet time, on business and finally out of curiosity, to see what had become of the Hermitage. The Bolsheviks had sold a load of pictures from there. He should go and find out how things were now: impressionists and other more modern artists had not been exhibited there for a long time; perhaps some of their art was still there.

He promised, of course. But he knew for a fact that there was some newer

French art on display in the Hermitage: he'd been there recently while a student and spent a good hour in the company of Picasso, Matisse and Gauguin. That was something you could still do now. And go to the theatre and concerts. There were definitely a lot more famous soloists performing in Leningrad than in Estonia. And their own greats, the Oistrakhs and the Gilels and others, would certainly perform there more regularly.

Grandfather was in full swing and carried on talking for a long time about his memories of St Petersburg. Some were interesting, like the stories of the Ingrian Finns who dragged firewood into the yards, the washerwomen who rinsed their washing in ice-holes in the Neva and the Estonian craftsmen, the more prosperous among whom had set themselves up on Nevski and looked and behaved 'like proper gentlemen'.

Finally Grandfather began to tire. He, too, was dreadfully tired. The words he had heard were ringing in his head as if in an empty church bell, but they made no sense. He was incapable of either thinking or speaking. It was time for bed.

Mother remained seated at the table, marking exercise books; his aunt was busy in the kitchen. Grandfather and Grandmother were getting ready for bed in the room next door. He put the night-lamp at the head of the bed and took the file containing the Under collection out of the cupboard. The very one that had started all this trouble. Unlikely that poetry could have such an effect in the free Western world. How strange it was to live in a country where poetry and poets were feared, admired, persecuted, oppressed and exalted. What a long, glorious, tragic string of them there was: Pushkin, Lermontov, later Gumilyov, Mandelstam, Akhmatova, Estonia's Heiti Talvik. Gumilyov and Mandelstam were nowhere to be found in libraries; he had obtained their poetry from Russian philologists and copied it out. Talvik's was in old copies of *Looming* in the countryside. He'd copied this into his file from the magazines:

> No, no longer will anyone
> tend the delicate rose tree.
> Over the castle, over the almshouse
> there looms the ashen shadow of death . . .

In fact, in his own way the Teacher belonged there, too – his thoughts slid unintentionally to him. He was feared as well but clearly also respected a little. There was no great distance between fear and respect and vice versa. The things his grandfather had been saying earlier were proof enough. Perhaps he would become someone who would be feared – the KGB did not deal with just anyone, only with those people considered to be a threat and who were also perhaps revered. The men in power regarded him nevertheless as a significant individual; they had called him in for interrogation and talked to him for several hours.

Was it not so that Under and the Teacher had somewhat paradoxically provided him with the opportunity to progress in the Soviet system, to have a career? He had been noticed, he had been dealt with; something was expected of him. Perhaps that he should become a loyal servant of the Party, a small cog in the system? He had been able to say 'no' to the KGB's offer of cooperation; perhaps he would also be able to say 'no' on critical occasions in the future. He would, in any event, obtain language skills in Leningrad, and that should be the key that would open certain doors. If they needed linguists, they would not be able to set him doing anything that was totally unacceptable to him. They would have to allow him some freedom, some autonomy, as they did to scientists, even to writers. The freest people were those who dealt in areas where the authorities' needs were greatest: physicists, chemists, mathematicians. They were able to debate things that writers were not allowed to write about or that journalists had to ignore. Perhaps he was making a mistake in going to study philology. Philologists were not held in any special regard; the authority of physical scientists was greater. But perhaps oriental specialists had privileges that were denied to others. Their numbers were few, and now, with Moscow busily flirting with India and other Asian countries, there was a genuine need for them. So there were opportunities.

He couldn't read much any more. His thoughts filled his head and took his mind away from poems. He looked for the Under poems that had been classified as anti-Soviet. Poems that, in fact, had appeared earlier, handwritten copies of which were circulated among his grandmother's friends. Perhaps they spoke more to people of yesteryear than they did to him:

> Our tribe entire has crumbled,
> the shadow of death broods over our kin.
>
> We all live past ourselves:
> the alien power cannot feed our body and soul.

No, it wasn't really his type of poetry. It was the past, and it was perhaps beautiful to someone moved to mourn its disappearance. But it wasn't *his* past. His past began with pictures of war, shelters, fleeing to relatives in the countryside, Russian aircraft flying low shooting people working in the fields, aircraft upon whose approach children were ordered to run into the old barn where the thick timber walls were thought to provide some protection from bullets. His past was the ruins of Tartu where they'd played hide-and-seek and found all sorts of interesting things: handfuls of ampoules that had melted in fire, a crooked machine-gun barrel, the remains of burnt books ... And the two lines that came to his mind so often now:

We will wait, we will not break our vow
Thus we can live more proudly and face death more easily.

Beautifully said. He had not given a single promise and neither had he broken any. Except the Pioneer's promise, which no one took seriously anyway, not even the Pioneer leaders. He didn't know if he would want to live proudly. As for dying – that was another matter. He had been close to death on a couple of occasions. But . . . Perhaps he had died, was a living corpse that moved and thought, in whose brain there were thoughts, associations, but from which life itself had departed. Flown away, flowed into the autumn river among the leaves of the fading water-lilies. That was physical and intellectual death. He had no Ester; he was leaving his home here, his homeland; he had unintentionally made an agreement with a brutal foreign power. Wasn't that the same as breaking a promise, albeit that he had in fact never knowingly made one? Yet he had nevertheless been true to him-self, which was in its own way a promise. When he went to say 'yes' tomorrow, would he at that point stop being true to himself? Would he have sold his soul to the devil, as they used to say – and believe – in days gone by?

He put out the light.

32

The *partorg* saw him immediately. The conversation did not last long. He had to obtain the necessary papers from the records department on the Monday.

'Look, we've put our trust in you now. I hope that you, too, will put your trust in us,' he said and shook the young man's hand. This time the *partorg*'s manner and conversation seemed distant. Perhaps the matter was closed for him, perhaps he already had new 'worries'. But this no longer mattered. He had now given his 'yes'; the next steps would happen largely without him: papers, travel to Leningrad, formalities and probably interviews at the university there. They would get in touch with Leningrad again, at which point it would become clear when he had to be there. Until then he would continue to work in the library. There was no point in his going to the collective farm for such a brief period of time; he might have to travel to Leningrad soon, and perhaps they would need to meet again before then.

The weather was still beautiful. Summer was reluctant to go; it took no notice of the yellow leaves that had appeared on the Toome Hill linden trees and the asters that would soon stop flowering in the little square where the memorial to Gustavus Adolphus had stood, a site now occupied by a concrete tub of autumn flowers, a tub about which a Russian visitor had remarked, 'Interesting, it used to be Gustav Vasa standing there, but now there's only a vase.'

He still remembered the king's image well: he'd walked past here many times with Grandfather, who, of course, had talked to him about Gustavus Adolphus, his deeds and how he met his death on the day after he had signed the charter establishing the university. History and natural history were Grandfather's great interests. They probably helped him to live through hard times and reconcile himself to the fact that he had lost all his possessions and most of the essence of his life, which had been business. Yet he could learn from history how the same thing had happened to many people, much more catastrophically. There was some solace perhaps in that. At least up to a point.

There were even fewer people in the café than usual: the collective farms had played their part in this. He ordered a cup of coffee and a roll and sat at the table where Aleks and his circle usually hung out. A lone pigeon crouched on the metal sheet below the window outside. Occasionally the sun would appear among the white, perfectly summery clouds and cast a cross-shaped shadow from the window frame on to the table. Ester had said she didn't frequent the café; he hoped she wouldn't come here today either – he hoped they wouldn't meet at all, at least not before he went to Leningrad. And a cross was something he didn't want to see now – it reminded him of something he no longer wanted to be reminded of. *Nessun maggior dolore . . .* How could it be rendered in Estonian? 'No pain greater than remembering . . .'; 'Is there a greater pain than remembering . . .'? Actually, he didn't need to translate Dante. He could write a poem on the same theme himself. The Dante could even serve as an epigraph.

He took the little notebook he always carried around with him out of his pocket; it already contained a half-finished poem – fragments of poetry, as he called them – and thumbed through it. No, today he had no inspiration; the old lines of poetry felt stodgy and contrived. And there was nothing on which he could draw for new ones. He felt a bit like the pigeon crouched down on the metal sheet. It would be interesting to know whether pigeons could be in love. Unhappily in love, rejected, pine for another pigeon, who in its turn had someone else . . . Or was unrequited love the sole privilege of the human race? Fine privilege that was. Like a cross we all have to bear, all human beings, some more than others. Like a colony of ants and a large twig. What if one refused, said he didn't want to any more, and that was that? Could a human being refuse his own burdens, heartache, and carry on being a human being? He felt it could perhaps be the germ for a poem.

The poem, however, did not germinate because through the door he heard a familiar deep voice say 'Hello'. It was Peeter; he wasn't at the collective farm. He was quick to explain the reason why.

'I've, er, got high blood pressure, apparently. The doctor told me to rest and take some tablets,' he said when he'd sat down with his coffee and a sort of cream-filled cake known as a Moscow bun. 'In the meantime I've been to Tallinn, to the doctor's and . . . Listen, I really hoped to see you here. Tell me what's been happening with all this mess. By the way, I've got some visitors from Latvia this evening, my fiancée and a girlfriend of hers, and you could come, too, if you like. We'll get some wine and . . .'

He had nothing against the idea. But first he had to explain to Peeter what had happened in his absence, about his meetings with the KGB, the *partorg*, about Leningrad. He didn't tell Peeter about Ester, there was no need to talk to anyone about her.

Peeter listened and then said, 'You know, my dad was on the home front in the war. At first in the building and technical unit, but then they needed people in his line in Moscow, at the ministry or something. He knows some people from those days. I spoke to him, too; he's a reasonable man, he knows that this whole thing is absurd. Probably some guy trying to earn some points. Dad promised to talk to a couple of his friends. He's got friends from his time at the front all over the place in the government and even the KGB. Anyhow, when I left he said he hoped the thing wouldn't go completely mad; they'd as good as promised him something. He didn't explain exactly, but I think that they'd listen to him. I've talked to him about politics sometimes: we're both Communists but, as you know, more along the lines they have in Yugoslavia. I think things are really good there. He's been there and told me what he saw. There are other people in the Party who think on the same lines, too. Sooner or later we'll have to take the Yugo route. From what I can see it's the best version. But carry on.'

When he got to the bit about the man from Tallinn Peeter again had something to say, 'I think I know who that is. I've seen him at a function. As far as I know, he's one of the more sensible ones. Perhaps what Dad said got as far as him. That'd be good . . . You know, I'm really embarrassed I dragged you into all this mess. I should have come up with a story like that myself. It would have been easier for me: my dad's name would have helped. But perhaps it'll help you as well.'

He told Peeter not to worry; perhaps it was better that things had panned out the way they had. Perhaps it was better that he was off to Leningrad now. And he couldn't help but say that he also had a bit of girl trouble.

'Yeah, that's important. It's always best if you've got a reliable girl who you can always get it from when you need it. Going without does a young guy's head in. It's good if you love her, too, but it's all right for a while if you don't. I've been lucky, you see, there's love and more. Just a completely different feeling. No way I want to sleep by myself any more.'

He felt how much it hurt him. It could have been envy or something else. 'What do your parents think?' he asked.

'Oh, nothing really. My mother was a bit surprised when I turned up with Laima. I'd phoned in advance, of course, but even so. My dad just smirked, said they got married just as young. And what can you do? He thinks getting married's much like jumping into unknown waters – sometimes it works out, sometimes it doesn't – but he doesn't think it's better to be afraid than have regrets. And that's that.'

'What language do you speak with Laima?' the philologist in him had to enquire.

'You know, she speaks a bit of Estonian – badly, though. Her grandmother was from Estonia and always spoke to her in Estonian; her mother speaks it, too, apparently. She'll probably learn it here.'

They drank up their coffee, had a cigarette. He heard Peeter's lengthy discussion on Eliot's 'The Waste Land', which he had read in English over the summer, and made ready to go. Peeter said he had a bottle of Georgian dry wine and cheese; he promised to bring another one with him. But now it was time to go to the library. He also had to tell the women there that he might soon be off to Leningrad. To say goodbye. The library had sometimes been more of a home to him than the two rooms in which they lived. After all, the only things he had there were an old sofa on which he slept and an old writing desk.

At the library he was offered coffee and cake; it had been someone's birthday.

They'd heard that he'd been in trouble, hoped that things would go well for him in Leningrad, told him he could always come back here and wasn't to forget them.

When he left in the afternoon the wind had got up and a dense line of cloud had appeared in the western sky. There was a mild dampness in the air, which could augur more rain. He decided to go home. Grandmother would doubtless be waiting with dinner, then before long he'd be able to set off for Peeter's.

He told his mother he was going to Peeter's to celebrate his engagement, or whatever it was called, and by the way, he added, almost unintentionally, he didn't know what time he'd be back. He might stay out really late.

When he arrived at Peeter's, a bottle of wine in his bag, the day was falling into evening; the clouds already covered half the sky. Both the Latvian girls were very different in appearance. Laima was a brunette and verging on the lean, whereas Aija – that's how she introduced herself – was blonde and more inclined to plumpness. They were united in their cheerful, slightly playful smiles with which they had also infected Peeter – perhaps they had been inspired by the open bottle of wine which was already half empty. For starters he had to drain a glass: the girls said that otherwise he might be too serious an influence and might not be able to tap into the spirit of the group. The wine obviously helped in this as did the girls' jabbering, which even Peeter could not keep pace with very well. As Aija didn't know any Estonian and Laima's knowledge of it was rather poor, they spoke Russian although Laima announced that in future she would definitely not be speaking Russian at home with her husband. Aija declared that language wasn't important; the main thing was what someone had to say. Peeter could not, of course, help discussing Eliot's poetry – recently it had become his party trick, with Rilke as a support act. They couldn't quote either of them in Russian. Laima had a smattering of English, Aija of German, but that didn't help much, although he hastily tried to render a couple of lines by Rilke into Russian.

'I like poets,' laughed Aija. 'Only I probably wouldn't want one for a husband. I would as a lover, though.'

Laima thought there were definitely differences between one poet and the next. And she hoped that Peeter wasn't too much of a poet – he was more of a man.

'And foreign men are always more interesting,' decided Aija. 'You'll definitely stay in Estonia, become an Estonian, while Riga is becoming more Russian by the day. Soon we won't hear Latvian in the street any more.'

'You said yourself just now that it isn't important what language you speak, only what you say.'

'Well, yes, only the important thing's not only what you say, the person saying it's important, too. I definitely wouldn't marry a Russian.'

'Well, why don't you find yourself an Estonian,' responded Peeter. 'You see my friend here, he's a free man. I can recommend him.'

'Aija's just said she doesn't want a poet,' said Laima.

'I'm not a real poet,' he was quick to reply, aware that the wine was beginning to loosen his tongue. 'I just want to be a philologist.'

Aija thought philologists not particularly interesting people; all they did was sit with their noses in books. She would like a geographer or geologist; they travelled to all sorts of exciting places.

Peeter said that his friend wasn't going to be an office philologist but an oriental specialist and would definitely be going to India.

'Then please invite me there some time, I desperately want to see India. I've sometimes dreamt I was walking by the Ganges,' said Aija.

He promised he'd definitely invite her to India after he arrived there. But first he had to go to Leningrad to study.

'Why Leningrad?' asked Aija. 'Much better to come to Riga and learn, say Latvian! You can learn Latvian and find a Latvian wife. We're better than either Estonians or Russians.'

'Actually, I'm half Russian myself,' he found himself saying. 'My father was from there. St Petersburg. He fled to Estonia from the Revolution.'

Aija thought it proved his father was a true Russian if he hadn't wanted to live under the Bolsheviks. They had plenty of Russians like that in Riga: true Russians. But they hadn't done very well. He remembered that at home they had some Russian books published in Riga during the free Latvian Republic. Aija said that there were several Russian publishers, newspapers and magazines there; it was an important centre for expatriate culture, as far as she knew.

He had to give a brief account of what had happened to his father. Aija shook her head. Peeter opened the other bottle. He felt the need for a cigarette. Smoking wasn't allowed indoors; he had to go outside into the garden. Aija said she'd have a cigarette, too; Laima said that she and Peeter had decided to give up. They were going to live healthily.

It was really dark outside. No stars were visible; the sky must already have been completely covered in thick cloud. As he lit Aija's cigarette, their heads touched. She leant against him. He felt the warmth of her hips and put his arm around her waist. It was no great distance from there to a kiss. And she didn't seem to have anything against it.

The kiss was brief but highly charged, although the girl said teasingly, 'I thought you'd come out for a smoke.'

'I'm mixing pleasure with danger,' he replied.

'Hmm, so which one do you regard as the pleasure and which as the danger?' teased Aija again.

'You can work that out for yourself.'

They finished their cigarettes and kissed again. He felt her tongue between his lips and at the same time a warm rush of passion in his lower abdomen.

'I don't think I'll be wanting to go home very soon today,' he said as they went back indoors, hand in hand.

'Absolutely no rush at all,' was Aija's reply.

Peeter and Laima were sitting on the sofa, their arms around each other. They sat next to them and he put his arm around Aija's back and on to her hip; she stroked it now and again. The second bottle was getting on for half empty; he felt both excitement and tiredness. The conversation flowed freely; they talked a muddle of politics, poetry and increasingly of love and sex.

'I see you've already become good friends,' joshed Laima to him and Aija.

'To international friendship!' he said, raising his glass and kissing Aija.

'I want some of that!' shouted Laima. She got what she wanted. Peeter made use of the opportunity to give her a resounding smacker of a kiss.

When the bottle was empty he and Aija went outside for another cigarette and kiss, but this time it was longer and more passionate. In the yard the first drops of rain were falling. One more reason to stay, although not the main one.

'Are you staying the night here?' he asked.

'Yes, Peeter said he's got another room for visitors.'

'So I can stay, too,' he said.

'Of course you can,' said Aija.

Now that the wine was finished Peeter and Laima had no desire to stay up any longer. They clearly wanted to dissolve into each other's arms. With object efficiency and some humour Peeter showed him and Aija the other room, which was entered from the porch.

'Goodnight,' said Laima in Estonian when they'd washed and were setting off. 'No need to wish you sweet dreams.' And added something in Latvian for Aija's benefit, to which Aija stuck out her tongue.

The room was small; it must have once been the servant's room. There was barely space for two in the bed. They stood in the middle of the room and kissed long and passionately. He slid his hand under the girl's dress and up to her buttocks.

'Hang on. I'll take my clothes off. I'll just turn the light off,' said Aija.

'No, don't, I want to see you,' he said.

'You must like naked girls best.'

'I've not seen enough of them. Perhaps that's why,' he said, as Aija undressed. Her pubic hair was much darker than the hair on her head.

'Come on then,' she said, stretching out on the bed. No need to ask twice. The light was still on. Everything went amazingly easily, the girl's hands fondling and helping his erect manhood go where it was supposed to. He wasn't able to keep moving inside her body for long, his orgasm happened quickly and was so powerful that for a while everything vanished from view, there was just an feeling of indescribable happiness and relief, a warm darkness rushed through him and through it he heard the girl's rapid breathing and whispered words of Latvian that he had no need to understand; everything was clear as it was.

He rolled over next to the girl; they lay in silence, tightly holding one another's hands. Then Aija said, 'You must be thinking that I'm an easy kind of girl.'

'I'm not thinking anything. I'm just so incredibly happy to be with you. I'm . . . so very, very grateful.'

'You must have been with plenty of girls . . . You're so good-looking and passionate.'

'Not plenty. You're the first . . .'

'What? I don't believe it. You're just trying to flatter me.'

'Word of honour, no flattery at all. I've never really . . . properly been with anyone. You really are the first.'

'Oh my God. Estonian women really are thick. A guy like you and they don't want to go with you . . . Outrageous . . . Hey, you've made me all wet. I'll just wipe myself down.'

Aija wiped between her legs with a towel then, grinning, pulled part of the towel over his limp penis, climbed on top of him, ruffled his hair and pressed her mouth on his. They kissed for a long time then rested side by side, and it wasn't long before he felt he wanted more. The girl was ready; she opened herself to him, allowed him in, and this time it all lasted longer and he was able to feel more, to feel himself moving inside her moist, warm, body, hear her soft moaning. They came at the same time when Aija's internal muscles contracted strongly around his penis.

'I would never have believed it would be so good,' he said, lying between the girl's thighs when it was all finished and they were breathing peacefully once more.

'You're amazing,' said Aija. 'It's a real shame you've got to go away. Some Russian woman will get her hands on you in Leningrad. Be careful. Russian women are dangerous. But promise me you'll come and visit me some time in Riga. I really like you; I'll remember you. And I'm not with anyone at the moment . . . and the relationships I've had weren't serious.'

He promised. Promising wasn't difficult.

They caressed and talked some more and then, all at once, fell asleep in each other's arms.

When he woke up he couldn't make out where he was at first but then came the realization and a rush of happiness. Aija was still asleep. He looked at her; asleep like this she looked somewhat childlike, and he realized he liked her but she was still a stranger. He hadn't fallen in love; perhaps he couldn't fall in love with this girl from Riga. But he was happy anyway, overflowingly happy. And grateful to Aija for his initiation. And for the fact that the image of Ester had withdrawn for a while from his mind's eye, grown dim. That of Malle even more so.

Aija woke up, too, and put her arms around his neck. 'You're fantastic. I don't know what'll happen if I really fall in love with you. And you're going away.'

The thought moved him, but was also slightly intimidating.

'I'll come and visit you in Riga,' he said, although he wasn't sure whether the promise would, in fact, be just a promise. 'Leningrad's not that much further from Riga than Tartu is.'

'Do come. I'll be waiting,' said Aija, threw herself on top of him and pressed her mouth to his. The rush of desire came surprisingly quickly and forcefully. The girl took him inside herself, sat up and rocked until the inevitable happened again, this time more slowly and less violently. He was able to look at Aija and even think that she wasn't really very beautiful, although she was definitely cute, captivating in her curvaceousness and her large, half-open moist mouth for both kissing and smiling.

They got up, caressed each other again. The girl wiped between her thighs before getting dressed. Outside the sun shone between the clouds now and again. The rain must have passed over. The apple tree under the window had red apples aplenty and several yellowed leaves.

Peeter and Laima were up but still drowsy. Peeter was yawning. Conversation was not particularly forthcoming. They drank coffee in silence, then he said he should go. He had a job waiting, and he had to go home first. Peeter and the girls had to leave soon for Tallinn.

'You won't forget me, will you?' said Aija, as she took him to the front door. 'And come whenever you can.'

'How could I forget you!' he said. He was quite certain he would not. And he could perhaps go to Riga – he'd been invited. And what they'd done they could do again, and it would be just as good.

'Here's my address and telephone number. Please write. I'll be waiting. For a letter and for you,' said Aija, holding the piece of paper out to him.

'I'll definitely write when I get to Leningrad,' he replied.

They kissed again, then he left. When he looked back from the garden fence he saw Aija in the doorway, waving. He blew her a kiss and set off.

There were puddles of rain in the street, he jumped over them, feeling the fantastic power and confidence in his body. Something had changed, he'd gained something that he'd so ardently waited for, yet the reality was even more beautiful and powerful than he could have anticipated. It was as if he was a different person. Could he now say, 'I feel like a man', he wondered, turning on to the park path? It was a wonderful feeling, as wonderful, perhaps even more wonderful, than meeting the This in the summer in the river and on a couple of occasions afterwards. Yet similar, too. So was mysticism, knowledge of God, nothing more than sexual sublimation, as he'd read? Wasn't faith the same as love? Sex could be fantastic fun, never mind whether there was love involved or not – but for how long? It had been great to spend the night with Aija, but to live with her, spend the days together? No, he wasn't sure that that was what he wanted. There had to be someone somewhere that he could live with. Ester, near and far. Yes, Ester would probably do. Malle? No, probably not Malle. He had to write to Malle. Write and tell her he was leaving and didn't know whether he would come back. Somewhere there might perhaps be someone else, someone for him. And someone for Malle. But he would always have wonderful memories of Aija, memories that would stay with him until the end of his life.

33

The last days in Tartu sped by. He obtained the papers from the records office; Leningrad had sent word that he was expected the following week when students not beginning their final year were back from the collective farms (so there was no escape from that trial for the Petersburg lot either). He went shopping with his mother; they bought a couple of shirts, a set of underwear, socks and handkerchiefs. His mother examined his suit and ironed it, his first real suit, made by the tailor Õigus from the material they had received in a parcel from his uncle. As for personal belongings, he didn't have many more than the ones he usually took with him on his travels to the countryside in the summer. He only had a couple of dictionaries to shove into the trunk, which his father had bought in Paris. He was also taking his father's long pipe and a pack of pipe tobacco.

Usually he travelled to Leningrad via Tapa where he had a two-hour wait for a train from Tallinn. But this time his mother thought he could spend a night in Tallinn with relatives who she'd stayed over with occasionally, and then catch the train to Leningrad from there. Uncle Elmar had promised to buy a ticket in advance.

He wrote two letters, to Malle and Aija. It was harder to write to Malle. He was unable to tell her that on one level his leaving Tartu was the end of his life thus far, including probably his relationship with her. He thought about it for a long time and wrote that the last few months had been very difficult for him; going to Leningrad was a solution, clearly the only reasonable solution, and when he had settled in there he would be able to think more clearly about what to do next, but at the moment his thoughts were in complete disarray. He also said he thought warmly of her and would always have a place for her in his heart. This was perhaps an exaggeration, but he couldn't say anything else; he neither wanted, nor perhaps was able, to add that it was over between them. Nor was he sure of it himself. Just as he was not entirely sure whether he would visit Aija in Riga. Yet the night he'd spent with Aija had been probably at least as important to him as the days he'd spent with Malle. The thought of that night, the girl's open body, the kisses and Latvian words she had whispered to him came flooding over him like a warm wave of strange happiness tinged with a trickle of unease. So was this love? Sheer sexual pleasure? Happiness at becoming a man, at his long-overdue initiation, although perhaps that was the very reason why it had been so profound and all-encompassing? At least he had for once found a woman with whom he had as much fun, and he really had, as she had had with him. At first he could not oeither did he want to. It was fairer probably to leave his feelings to themselves, allow them to flow unchecked and blossom without forcing them into any kind of conceptual framework. What would he feel if the word 'love' did not exist, if there were no names for feelings, which would be the case if a feeling existed without a name, was just itself and no name had to be chosen for it? Indeed, in a sense love was not unquestionably love, just as Aija was not unquestionably Aija – her parents might have given her a different name. Sex was definitely an important aspect of love, but who knows, who can confidently say, how important? Perhaps it's different for different people. To some sex is very important; to others it isn't. How was it for him? He realized he didn't know yet. Perhaps he would do one day. It was a good thing that he had to go. Go away from home, away from Malle. It was probably a good thing that his meeting with Aija had been so brief that he would have time to think everything over, calm down, far away from all this. What if he were again overwhelmed by the huge yearning, lust for Aija (Malle? Ester?), that would make life and study as difficult as it had been at times? But he could not examine that point either.

He didn't write to Ester. He had neither the capacity nor the will to do so. Perhaps they'd meet one day. Perhaps he'd meet the Teacher again. But for the time being that was not possible.

Their farewells did not take long. His mother hugged him (for perhaps the first time in his adult life), his grandfather squeezed his hand with his own good hand and wondered whether they would meet again, told him to be a man and to study hard and pass on his best wishes to the Nevski Prospect. And not to go falling in love with any Russian girls straight away – they were much prettier and more highly spirited and dangerous than the girls in Estonia. (Funnily enough, dangerous was exactly how Aija had described them.) His aunt and grandmother made him promise to write. They also sent their best wishes to Aunt Veera, of course.

There was more of a chill in the weather; the air had a genuine autumnal feel and there were fallen leaves aplenty in the streets. A couple of times he saw a triangle of birds in the sky, flying south. Probably cranes. Cranes flying south augured bad weather. There was still time before the geese went. It would be interesting to see whether cranes, geese or swans flew over Leningrad sometimes – or was it too big and intimidating a city for them?

34

There was no one there yet as he settled himself into his compartment. He quietly hoped that he would have it to himself or at least that any fellow passengers wouldn't be talkative. He had no desire to talk to anyone. He wanted to be left alone, to think. And perhaps sleep. To sleep off everything that had happened, everything that he was now travelling away from.

Before the train began to move another man and a woman came into the compartment carrying large bundles. Fortunately they had no particular wish to strike up a conversation with him; they exchanged a few words between themselves and soon left, perhaps for the restaurant car.

Just beyond Kehra he could already feel his eyes closing and the pictures in his mind becoming ever more dreamlike. He took his shoes off, lay down on the upper bunk, put his jacket under his head and dozed off almost instantly.

When he woke up the train was just departing from Narva. It crossed the river and what is now (and indeed had previously been) the border. Estonia was behind him and he unexpectedly felt tears fill his eyes. He was travelling away from his home, his home town, his homeland. His homeland had, at least thus far, always been Estonia. And he was sorry to leave. Sorry about the university, Malle, Peeter, Aleks, Ester, the Teacher. The old man who had fallen in love with a young university student and had been so strangely jealous of him ... He would definitely get in touch with the Teacher when he came back, though. And with Ester. If. *Kui. Jos.* Sorry about his family. Would he see Grandfather again? He had never really talked to Grandfather at length, hadn't asked him many of the things he might know and remember. He had not encouraged him to talk even about his own parents and grandfather. His grandfather had been so close to him in his childhood; had Grandfather's grandfather been close to him, too? It would be important to find out and perhaps even write down Grandfather's life story – at the moment he knew only the scraps that Grandfather himself had talked about: being jailed in 1905, going into hiding from the Reds in 1918, buying a bookshop in the town centre, a couple of years as a teacher and then how he had to resign after teaching Darwin and showing pictures of apes. No, when he went home he would encourage Grandfather to tell it all, talk about his childhood, his first memories. Grandfather's hearing was poor, but he was quite able to talk. He liked to reminisce, as all old people do.

One day, when he had grandchildren of his own, he might then be able to read them his own grandfather's memories, and tell them his own, and thereby re-establish the cross-generational bonds that had been broken in recent centuries.

Wars and violence had torn so many places apart. He suddenly felt he had to do it, for himself, his future children and grandchildren. Do it before it was too late. Encourage his grandfather, grandmother, mother, aunt to talk. And Aunt Veera in Leningrad. Writing poetry could wait, and he didn't have to spend so much time in cafés, but their memories must not be allowed to disappear. And nor must his own. He had to start keeping a diary, immediately, as soon as he had settled in Leningrad, so that any of his successors (there would presumably be some) would have the chance to read about him. He had to write down everything as it was, without embarrassment, without embellishment, because there can be beauty only in truth, not in falsehood. He had already had to lie too much and probably would be unable to avoid doing so again in the future. But everything in his diary had to be just as it was, as he saw it, and he had to try to make an honest assessment. Only a diary of this kind was worth keeping, only memories of this sort worth writing down.

No, he wasn't going away. He wasn't leaving his past, his home, his family behind. Perhaps, in order to understand them, to enjoy a closer relationship with them, he needed to be apart from them for a while. As a young poet he had seen in the café a couple of times had put it:

> He who moves closer, moves further away,
> he who moves forward to look does not see.

Or you could have it the other way round:

> He who moves farther away, moves closer,
> he who looks from afar, sees.

The thought was a revelation, a conciliatory revelation after everything that had happened in the previous month. Particularly what was awaiting him in Leningrad. He had suddenly thrown off a burden and found something that could almost be considered the meaning of life, although he always found that expression slightly foolish. Nevertheless, he had something he had to achieve. That fact made his mind lighter and freer. Perhaps it was because of his meeting Aija, the meeting that gave him what he had waited and yearned for for so long. Perhaps because he was now travelling away, perhaps far away from all the harsh experiences, spiritual woes, depressions and ecstasies. For how long? Was something new and more awful awaiting him? Very possibly. That wasn't important for the moment. The important thing was that he felt he was finding his own way, even though he didn't exactly know where it would take him. The feeling made him both clear in his mind and sleepy. He closed his eyes. Before he fell asleep he remembered once more the words of Lao-tzu: 'A journey of a thousand miles begins with a single step.' It couldn't be any other way.

Notes

Ast, Karl (1886–1971) – Estonian politician and writer, pen-name Rumor

Chernyi, Sasha – pen-name of Alexander Glickberg (1880–1932), Russian poet, essayist and prose writer

Coudenhove-Kalergi, Count Richard Nikolaus von (1894–1972) – Austrian politician and philosopher, founder of the first popular movement for a united Europe, Pan-Europa

Kolk, Raimond (1924–1992) – Estonian poet who lived and published in Sweden

Koort, Jaan (1883–1935) – Estonian sculptor

Liiv, Juhan (1864–1913) – Estonian poet and author, a pioneer of Estonian prose realism

Looming – Estonian literary magazine founded in 1923 and still published today

Mogri Märt – a rich and arrogant farmer; a character created by the Estonian writer and playwright August Kitzberg (1855–1927), who wrote under the name Tiibuse Jaak

Old Kapp – a villager

Pskov *oblast* – the Russian *oblast* (administrative district) bordering Estonia

Sang, August (1914–1969) – Estonian poet and translator

Soothsayers (Arbujad) – a group of young Estonian poets during the 1930s that included August Sang, Heiti Talvik, Betti Alver, Bernard Kangro among others

Talvik, Heiti (1904–1947) – Estonian poet

Varamu – Estonian literary monthly, published for a short period in the late 1930s

Vasyok Trubachyov – hero of a popular series of youth-oriented books by Valentina Oseeva published in the Soviet Union during the 1950s

Veski, Johannes Voldemar (1873–1968) – Estonian linguist